*USA Today* bestselling autho~~r~~
Texas with her very own hero-worthy husband, three
beautiful children, a spunky golden retriever/standard
poodle mix and too many books in her to-read pile. In
her downtime, she plays video games and spends much
of her time on or around a basketball court. She loves
interacting with readers and is grateful for their
support. You can reach her at barbhan.com

**Lena Diaz** was born in Kentucky and has also lived in
California, Louisiana and Florida, where she now resides
with her husband and two children. Before becoming a
romantic suspense author, she was a computer programmer.
A Romance Writers of America Golden Heart® Award
finalist, she has also won the prestigious Daphne du
Maurier Award for Excellence in Mystery/Suspense. To
get the latest news about Lena, please visit her website,
lenadiaz.com

# ESCAPE: BIG BEND CANYON

## BARB HAN

# HUNTING THE CROSSBOW KILLER

## LENA DIAZ

MILLS & BOON

First Published in Great Britain 2025
by Mills & Boon, an imprint of HarperCollins*Publishers* Ltd
1 London Bridge Street, London, SE1 9GF

www.harpercollins.co.uk

HarperCollins*Publishers*
Macken House, 39/40 Mayor Street Upper,
Dublin 1, D01 C9W8, Ireland

*Escape: Big Bend Canyon* © 2025 Barb Han
*Hunting the Crossbow Killer* © 2025 Lena Diaz

ISBN: 978-0-263-39706-2

0425

# ESCAPE: BIG BEND CANYON

## BARB HAN

All my love to Brandon, Jacob and Tori, my three greatest loves. I'm proud of each and every one of you!

To Babe, my hero, for being my best friend, my greatest love and my place to call home. I love you with everything that I am.

## Chapter One

*"Mayday, Mayday, Mayday."*

Those were the last words US marshal Julie "Jules" Remington remembered hearing as the prison transport chopper
spun out of control before slamming into the hard earth.

The Huey II that Jules and her partner, Toby Ward, had
officially hitched a ride on while it was on its way to Lack-
land Air Force Base near San Antonio suffered a cata-
strophic tail-rotor failure. Their job had been to transport
one of the most dangerous and elusive criminals of her ten-
ure and deliver him in one piece to the Dominguez State
Prison.

The assignment shouldn't have turned this way.

Forcing her eyes open, Jules pushed through the heavy
fog wrapping long tentacles around her brain, squeezing.
The scene was a blur. The chopper she'd been thrown from
was smashed on its side as though it had been stomped
on first, the result of a child's temper tantrum. She'd been
thrown twenty feet from the chopper and, miraculously,
was still alive.

The Chisos Mountains seemed to rise from the dry desert like sentinels off in the distance. The landscape beneath
her was nothing more than scrub, rocks and dry dirt. She
squinted, spit dust out of her mouth as rolling, dark storm

clouds formed an ominous canopy overhead. Lightning split the sky in half.

And then she saw him.

Captain Crawford, the pilot, was strapped in his seat, gaze fixed, head split open. Still. His skin paled from all the blood pooling to his side after his heart had stopped beating. Eyes open, his lips parted like he was in the middle of a sentence that he would never finish. Had he been calling for help? Announcing the chopper was about to crash?

*Mayday, Mayday, Mayday.*

Hadn't she heard him thump the control panel and complain about static coming over the comms system?

Jules tried to lift her head up. Movement caused blinding pain. She had to push through, find the other two people who were, at present, unaccounted for.

Where was Toby? Panic caused a crushing weight on her chest. Breathing hurt.

Frantic at this point, Jules pulled on all her willpower to focus, to see. She scanned the area. Her gaze locked on to a male figure another twenty feet away, slowly stirring. *Toby!* The fact he was moving, albeit slowly, was a good sign!

Her heart practically sang. Her next immediate thought? Where was Theodore Symes, aka Theodore the Terrible or Theodore Crimes?

This bastard had eluded capture for eleven years. He was truly evil: a known rapist and murderer who "charmed" his way into a victim's life by pretending to be weakened or injured. A surveillance camera once showed him using crutches to disarm one of his victims at a gas station. The man always knew to keep his face off camera. Symes was smart.

Once captured, he'd proudly led investigators to twenty-six grave sites. He'd provided clues to what happened in at least a dozen more cases, all while smiling, clearly pleased with himself like this was a twisted game of hide-and-seek. His rampage had lasted eleven years and spanned five Southwestern states from Texas to California.

But where was he now?

A visual sweep of the area showed no other bodies in the vicinity. Had he been thrown from the chopper too? Was he behind one of the boulders? Had he managed to escape harm, roll away and disappear before anyone else broke consciousness?

To her left, the flat landscape gave her a decent view everywhere except where the chopper blocked her vision. Her last memory of flying over Big Bend National Park near the Texas-Mexico border meant they were far away from any towns.

Toby groaned. "Jules?"

"I'm here," she managed to say, though her throat felt like sandpaper and moving felt like she'd been dipped in molasses. Her hand instinctively reached for the spot on the side of her head with the most pain. Wet, tacky fingers lowered in front of her eyes. Blood.

"The captain," Toby said, grief in his tone. On his side, he managed to reposition so the two of them could look directly at each other.

"I know," she said. Her heart sank. She knew firsthand how devastating news of any kind of crash could be after the accident last month that left her beloved grandparents in a coma, let alone one that took someone's life. Captain Crawford wore a gold band on his ring finger. Someone had lost a husband and didn't know it yet. A father too? Jules's heart ached.

"Symes?" Toby asked.

She shot a look that Toby understood without words.

Right now, she had to shove all other thoughts aside to focus on locating Symes.

Movement shot lightning bolts of pain through her abdomen. A quick body scan revealed no obvious broken bones. Although, her left knee was already swelling. Since she was lying on her left side, she assumed this was the main area of impact.

Memories were blurred about what had specifically happened after *Mayday*.

"How badly are you hurt?" she asked Toby.

"I'm feeling like a punching bag," he shot back. He was talking. His sentences made sense, and he wasn't slurring his words. She'd take that as a good sign cognitive function hadn't been impaired. "How about you?"

"I'm still kicking," she said with a half-hearted smile. The sandpaper feeling in her throat made sense when she realized she'd eaten a mouthful of dust upon impact. "Symes is gone. I can't see him anywhere."

"I noticed," he said, his voice raspy. "That son of a bitch better be in worse shape is all I can say."

"A dead man can't serve time for his crimes, Toby. Symes needs to face justice for all the lives he took and the carnage he left behind."

"No argument there," Toby admitted.

Talking was draining a lot of energy. Energy she didn't have to give. Was he dead? Had he been thrown from the chopper? Was he alive?

Toby got quiet. Jules knew why. Rapists hit him harder than most criminals. She'd been afraid he might not be able to be objective when it came to Symes. So far, though, Toby had gritted his teeth, kept quiet and done the job. There was a story behind his reaction, though. One that three years of being best friends and colleagues hadn't revealed.

Asking around felt like a betrayal, so she didn't. Toby

would reveal the reason in time when he was ready. Jules respected his wishes.

"Can you get up?" she asked.

"My arm is probably broken," he said, wincing in pain with movement. At six feet one inch of solid muscle, Toby was considered slightly above average in height for a Texan and far stronger. A broken arm while stranded out here wasn't good.

"How badly does it hurt?" she asked.

"It's not great, but I'll live," Toby responded. Leave it to Toby to downplay a serious injury. Right now, as difficult as it might be, she had to focus on trying to get help and finding Symes.

Clouds thickened overhead. They'd been trying to beat the storm across the desert. Lightning shot sideways across an otherwise dark sky, illuminating the scene.

Help. They needed an EMT.

Jules reached for her cell, cursed when she realized it wasn't inside the pocket of her blazer. Where could it…?

She saw it not more than five feet from her current position, shattered. The brand-new cell didn't have all the protections put in place yet, like a case and screen protector. The damn thing wouldn't do any good now.

"Do you have your cell on you?" she asked as she forced herself to sit up.

"You're bleeding," Toby said, his voice filled with concern.

"It's a scratch." From this vantage point, she could see more of the perimeter of the crash. Still no sign of Symes, dead or alive.

"That's affirmative on the cell," Toby said after he fished inside his pocket and retrieved it, then held it up.

Was Symes lying on the other side of the chopper? Waking up? Assessing his injuries too?

Symes was equal in height to Toby but no match for his

muscled frame. Symes could best be described as tall with a runner's build. He had sandy-blond hair and blue eyes, along with a small scar on his chin and two others on his left cheek. *From his victims?*

The man was human garbage with blue eyes.

People always said you could tell a lot about a person from their eyes. Jules wasn't so sure she bought into that. She'd looked into the magnetic eyes of many pathological liars during her career, and thought she would probably have allowed them to carry her groceries to her car at the market if they'd asked. Working for the Marshals Service, her radar was always on. She stayed on high alert. The average person didn't live life with their guard up.

The most successful, most devious criminals gave away nothing in their eyes.

Toby might be the same height, but that was where the similarities with Symes ended. Toby's hair was almost jet-black. His cut was military short, revealing a face of hard angles. He had that whole strong-jaw bit nailed.

His eyes were the most golden shade of brown she'd ever seen, let alone stared into. Being attracted to her best friend was more than inconvenient. It was downright painful, considering there was no chance the two would ever be more than friends.

Jules watched as Toby moved his phone around in the air. No bars?

At least they'd survived the crash. She forced her thoughts away from the pilot. Compartmentalizing her emotions kept her focus sharp. They would hit once the case was over with the force of a brick wall.

In thinking about the onslaught to come, she'd never felt more alone.

"I'VE GOT NOTHING out here," Toby said as pain riddled his body. The year he'd played varsity football in high school under Friday night lights couldn't hold a candle to this agony.

"Could be the weather," Jules pointed out as she slowly inched toward him. Relief slammed into him with the force of a tsunami that she was alive. The image—which had been nothing more than a flash of Jules lying on her side with her gaze fixed—seared into his brain, shocking him awake.

He couldn't lose his best friend.

"What about you?" he asked. Sitting up required heroic effort. The scratch on her forehead was more like a gash. "You're bleeding more than you realize."

"A few of my brains may have fallen out, but I'll be okay," she said, cracking a smile. It was just like Jules to attempt to lighten the mood when she was bleeding from her head.

"If your IQ drops, you'll finally be down in my range," he shot back. Smiling hurt. Laughing hurt. But it was necessary to break the tension so they could think clearly.

"You're the smartest guy I know," she countered as she got close enough for him to assess the damage.

"Exactly," he stated with a smirk. "Operative word being *guy*. Women have always been smarter. It's about time you stopped being sexist and claimed superiority."

Jules's laugh was freakin' music. Her face was beauty. She had the doe-eyed, heart-shaped-lips thing down pat. Those full breasts and just the right amount of curves in her hips made her perfect on a physical level. Jules was also intelligent, funny and completely unaware of her effect on the opposite sex. If she wasn't his coworker and best friend, he would have asked her out on day one. A woman like her would have shot him down, but he would have taken a chance.

Someone like Jules deserved to know how attractive she was. The words *total package* came to mind. But it wouldn't sound right coming from the guy who was securely in the friend zone.

Right now, she had decided to add playing nursemaid to her list of talents.

"I'm good," he said as he looked into concerned eyes. "I know you want to take off and find Symes. Go ahead. Don't let that bastard get away."

Rapists were the lowest of all scum. Bottom dwellers, opportunistic feeders. He clenched his back teeth so hard they might crack as a memory stomped through his thoughts. He forced it back into the shadows before the darkness consumed him.

"I'm not leaving you," Jules protested.

"I'd rather die than let this son of a bitch get away," he stated.

"He could be dead," she pointed out.

"Either way, I need confirmation." He gave her puppy eyes that she swore were irresistible. "Please. For me."

Jules issued a sharp sigh but nodded.

"When you get back, we take care of the gash on the side of your head. Deal?"

"No, sir," she argued. "Your arm takes priority. Then we'll deal with my scrape."

Arguing with a stubborn person was a waste of time, so he said, "Okay."

Jules moved a little faster now but favored her left leg. It didn't look like she was in much pain. But knowing her, she probably refused to think about it. The headache from hitting her head would take hold later. Mild shock might be masking the pain for the time being.

Later?

Toby assessed their situation. At this point, they were potentially stranded with no food, water or shelter, aside from the chopper that currently housed the pilot, rest his soul.

Comms were nada. Reaching the outside world might not be possible. Dark gray rolling clouds filled the sky, making one o'clock in the afternoon feel more like midnight. Jules was injured. He was worse off. And, at present, they didn't have a visual on Symes.

That could change at any moment. Jules would surely spot the man on the other side of the chopper if he was there. They'd crashed on a plateau. Symes might have been shot down the hill on the opposite side. Death was an easy out. The man deserved hard time in a maximum-security prison, and the families of his victims needed justice to be served.

At the very least, Symes would have minor injuries. On the other hand, he might be dead. Jules had been right about one thing, though. This bastard deserved to pay for his crimes with a life behind bars. The thought of him escaping—as minuscule as the chance might be—sent fire raging through Toby's veins. Retribution should be served on bastards like Symes.

Jules came around to the chopper. She stopped, holding herself upright with a steady hand on the Huey. The look on her face lit a fire in the pit of his stomach. He waited to hear the words he feared were about to come out of her mouth.

"I can't find him anywhere," she said, wincing in pain as she put weight on her left leg.

"He couldn't have gone far." Toby released a grunt as he forced himself to stand. Two steps later, his legs gave out and he was back on the ground. He landed hard, butt-down on the unforgiving earth. And maybe cracked his tailbone in the process.

As if the day couldn't get any worse but Mother Nature decided to prove otherwise, big splotches of rain pounded his forehead.

Toby released a string of curses that would've made his grandmother threaten to wash his mouth out with a bar of soap if she was still living.

Hell would freeze over before he would sit here while Symes was out there escaping. "Eleven years."

"I know," Jules soothed.

"At least three dozen women, probably more," he continued, the all-consuming rage threatening to boil over as those horrific memories surfaced and an old feeling of helplessness engulfed him.

"It's awful," she said, studying him. "Worse than awful. The man is pure evil."

"We have to go after him," Toby stated matter-of-factly.

"Why don't we stay close to the chopper in case he comes back or help arrives?" she asked. Her brain had shifted into logic-mode while his was fueled by anger from the deep reaches of his soul. Considering his injuries, her suggestion was most likely the right move. The weather was changing fast.

Still. He couldn't let it go.

"What if a family is camping nearby?" he asked. It wasn't impossible. Although early November wasn't the busiest time of the year for the national park, a family or couple could be taking advantage of the lull in activity.

Jules chewed on the inside of her cheek, holding back the words she wanted to speak.

"What?" he asked, able to read her like a book.

She studied him. "Let's think this through before acting irrationally."

"I've never been clearer on what needs to happen," he countered, feeling himself get riled up and hearing the frustration in his own tone.

"You sure about that?" Jules asked, cocking her head to one side.

Toby clamped his mouth shut before he said something he might regret or closed hers with a kiss.

Where the hell did that thought come from?

## Chapter Two

"It's not safe to venture too far away from the chopper," Jules pointed out to Toby, treading lightly as she considered the look in his eyes. He was frustrated and angry...and something else she couldn't quite put her finger on. Rapists had always been a touchy topic for him. The thought of Symes getting away was eating him from the inside out. Understandable. Jules felt the same.

But they needed to be practical.

"Even if he did manage to crawl away with only a few scrapes, which I doubt, he won't make it far," she said. "He's in handcuffs, which will severely limit his ability to hunt for food or attack someone." She glanced up at the sky. "Plus, the weather is turning on him too."

Toby wouldn't make eye contact—a bad sign.

"We can request a search team once the storm dies down," she reasoned. "How far can he go with no food or supplies?"

Toby managed to stand up and stay on his feet on the second attempt. He moved near her, holding on to the Huey's body. There was so much pain in those honey-brown eyes of his, her heart ached.

"I promise we won't let this bastard slip away again," she said, but they both knew she was trying to infuse hope into the situation.

"We need to find him, Jules."

"I know," she agreed.

"We're responsible for this mess," Toby said as his face lost color.

"You're in too much pain to stand up, let alone go after Symes, so…"

Before she could finish her sentence, Toby swayed, and then his eyes fluttered.

He was about to lose consciousness.

Jules's quick reflexes kept her best friend's head from smacking the chopper or the ground or both. Holding Toby by his underarms as he faced her didn't last. Soon, they were both on the ground, with him on top of her.

"Hey," she said, searching his face for any signs of life. The pain must have been what took him down, because he appeared to be breathing well enough. A person could only take so much before passing out. Or maybe he struck his head on impact and would be in and out of consciousness for a while?

Rain was coming down in buckets by this point. They were both soaked, which didn't make Toby weigh any less.

Jules wriggled out from underneath him, then rolled him onto his side. Tucking him underneath the chopper as much as possible, she forced herself to stand up and check for anything she could use to make a temporary shelter.

Toby wasn't going anywhere. She'd moved him as much as she could without throwing her back out or risking injuring herself further. The knee wasn't improving. At this point, she could walk on it. How long would that last? Running would prove a challenge without a healthy dose of adrenaline to boost her.

Two fingers on Toby's wrist indicated a strong pulse.

Now it was a waiting game to see when he would open his eyes again.

In the meantime, she needed to secure the area. Symes might come back, figuring they would go looking for him or be dead. It was only conjecture, but she assumed he'd survived the crash, assessed the situation and bolted before either of them had opened their eyes. It was a wonder he'd let them live.

Unless he'd figured nature would do the trick for him, keeping his hands clean from murdering federal officers. Or Jules had stirred before Symes could finish the job the crash had started.

The man had survival skills. He'd bragged about spending weeks off the grid in Montana while law enforcement stayed a step behind. He would use anything and everything in his environment to his advantage. Jules's weapon was still strapped to her. The imprint of the shoulder holster would no doubt linger for hours, if not days.

What would Symes take from the chopper?

What was there to steal?

He would want food, but there was none. They'd had no scheduled stops. He'd been fed breakfast before takeoff. It wasn't like he would have packed a sack lunch. There were no snacks on board that Jules had been aware of.

Food and water would be his immediate need. Actually, water would be a priority. Dehydration would kill him faster than starvation.

Toby was right, though. This predator would hunt for signs of campers. He would have no qualms about murdering a family if it meant staying alive. A felon like Symes had no conscience whatsoever. Again, she wondered why he hadn't slammed a boulder into her or Toby's head or taken their weapons.

Maybe he couldn't risk either waking up?

At Symes's most base level, he was a coward, slinking off without a fair fight.

Refocusing on what she could use, she performed a mental inventory. Her cell was broken. Toby had no coverage. There was no way to study a map of the park to find the nearest water source without either phone.

Rain. Duh.

Jules realized Symes would most likely find a way to capture rainwater, which was a good idea for her too. Rescue should be soon, she hoped. But she had to prepare for the worst, meaning they might have to find a way to survive and get themselves to safety.

Bringing up her fingers to massage her temples as her head pounded, she searched the cockpit and located a thermal mug that had coffee remnants inside. She brought it out into the rain and rinsed the mouthpiece as best as she could, unscrewing the lid before swishing rain around to clean out the coffee. In her backpack, she had an alcohol wipe. She retrieved it and wiped down the rim where the pilot's lips had been.

This thermos looked to be about sixteen ounces. After setting it up on a rock to collect water on its own, she searched for anything else that might prove useful.

The headache pounding, moving in tempo with her pulse, felt like a drummer beating a drum inside her skull. Pushing through the pain, wishing she had thought to pack ibuprofen, she searched for another container to fill. It dawned on her that she'd brought a backpack with a few items. Mostly, it held her keys and wallet, along with the current book she was reading. But she recalled there was a bottle of water in there too and a spare for Toby because he always bummed a drink of hers instead of carrying one for himself.

*Progress.*

If Symes wasn't dead, would he have stolen one of their service weapons?

Biting her lip to keep from cursing from pain as she reached down for her backup weapon, she knew. The SIG Sauer was missing. The pain shooting down her leg kept her from noticing the weight difference on her ankle. Otherwise, she would have realized the SIG was gone sooner.

That meant Symes had enough cognitive function to think about stealing a weapon for protection. It occurred to her that he'd probably slipped the handcuff key off her or Toby while they were unconscious. He'd worked quickly.

Symes was out there somewhere on the hunt for shelter if he hadn't already found it. They were lucky he hadn't killed them. Had she interrupted him by stirring, like she'd originally thought? Based on the time when she'd checked her watch, she wasn't out for long. He might not have been either. Had he been unconscious at all?

At the very least, he had a head start. She couldn't be certain he hadn't located her phone and smashed it against a rock. At this point, anything was possible. Toby's was still intact. Symes hadn't tried anything there.

She moved to Toby and checked for his backup weapon. It was still there. Based on what she knew so far, Symes had enough presence of mind to check her for a weapon and steal her SIG.

Was that why she'd stirred when she had? Had she felt someone touching her? The thought gave her the creeps. Even more considering Symes's criminal background. An involuntary shiver rocked her. He would do a lot more than that if he had the opportunity, and she knew it.

There wasn't anything else she could use inside the Huey to cover Toby, so she took off her jacket and placed it on his torso, not that it did a whole lot of good. A cold front moved in with the rain, causing her to shiver again. She rubbed her arms. The blue button-down blouse provided very little shield from the winds that had picked up.

Could she get Toby into the back of the chopper, out of the rain?

Movement in the distance caught her eye as a figure moved toward her. The person or animal wasn't much more than a blot on the landscape at this point.

Jules drew her weapon and spread out her feet, standing guard in front of Toby. Hell would freeze over before she would allow anything to happen to him.

Where was that bastard Symes?

TOBY BLINKED. The image of Jules standing in front of him with her weapon drawn and aimed shot a jolt of adrenaline through his system. The stress hormone gave him enough oomph to sit up, but he didn't want to surprise Jules, so he coughed and then asked, "What is it? What's happening?"

"Not sure yet," Jules responded. The tension in her voice said she was strung tight and ready to snap. "It's a dot moving toward us."

He squinted in the direction her weapon pointed as he drew his own Glock. For a split second, he forgot about the wrist injury in addition to the potentially broken arm. The swelling was worse. The injury might hold him back, but he could still aim and shoot with his left hand. Getting his Glock out of the holster caused brain-splitting, headache-inducing pain like he'd never experienced.

"You're making yourself too big of a target," he pointed out. "You need to get lower."

"I will when this person gets close enough to shoot at

us," she said. "I squat down right now, and he disappears from my view."

"How do you know he'll shoot?" he asked.

"Symes got my backup weapon." The admission was followed by a sharp sigh.

"Could have been a lot worse," he pointed out. Every law enforcement agent or officer had the nightmare of being shot with their own weapon at one time or another during their careers. Jules had explained hers in detail after a beer at dinner one night. Wouldn't happen as long as he had air in his lungs. "I don't see anything."

"Exactly," she said.

Right. He was too low.

"Are you sure the dot is human?" he asked.

"No idea," she admitted. "But I'm not willing to take any chances."

Fair point. Jules was one of the best marshals he'd ever worked with. She didn't think so, but then, she was too hard on herself. "Could be debris blowing around down there."

"Are you willing to take that chance?" she asked.

"If my legs worked like they're supposed to, I'd circle around and try to catch the bastard unaware from behind," he said. It would take some of the burden off Jules while ensuring the perp was back in custody.

"Stay put," she suggested. "You'll do more good here than trying to run off half-cocked while you're hurt."

Those words couldn't be denied. He'd end up a liability, possibly putting Jules in more danger. Frustration nailed him at not being more help. He grabbed hold of a door handle on the chopper and pulled up to standing. He leaned his back against the metal. It wouldn't be long before critters and vultures came for Captain Crawford. The thought of being picked apart by scavengers sent a mental image

Toby wouldn't soon forget. It was a fate the good pilot didn't deserve.

Jules swore. "Whatever it is decided to change direction."

The spot hung a right. Was he trying to come up behind them? The land on the other side of the chopper was relatively flat. "This area doesn't get a whole lot of rain."

"How do you know that? What are you, *Farmer's Almanac*?" Jules quipped.

"My dad took me and Lila camping here a few times when we were kids," he stated. "Weird facts like that stick in my head."

"I didn't know you guys camped as kids, let alone came here," she said, diligently watching the dot that was becoming smaller by the second. All she knew about Lila was that she'd died five years ago. Toby didn't talk about his sister.

"Can't tell you everything about my past," he said with a laugh—a laugh that hurt like hell. His ribs ached, no doubt having taken a blow during the crash when he landed on the ground. A flash of the chopper spinning out of control stamped his brain.

There was a lot that he kept to himself about his past despite telling Jules almost everything else about him. He'd been tempted. It was a little too easy to talk to her. They'd closed down a bar one night, and he'd damn near told her everything. He'd stopped himself when he realized he couldn't stand her looking at him like the failure he was after letting his sister down.

Not Jules.

She still looked at him like he was a good human being, a protector. Someone who was capable of doing anything he set his mind to.

Hell, a hero.

Shame shrouded him like the dark, heavy clouds wrapped

the hilltop in the distance. That night in the bar, he'd stopped himself in time. It was the reason he didn't casually go out for a beer with her anymore.

He'd gotten a little too comfortable with Jules.

"Whatever it was, it's gone now," Jules said, breaking into his heavy thoughts. She holstered her weapon and turned to face him. "Now, we need to take care of your injuries before you lose consciousness on me again."

He opened his mouth to argue, but she stopped him with a hand in the air. Their gazes locked. For a split second, he felt a familiar jolt. The electricity and warmth that followed touched the depths of him.

It was the reason he joked with her instead of taking a serious tone. He had to keep their interactions lighthearted.

Fortunately for him, they didn't work together often.

It made life easier when she didn't stand so close that he could reach out and touch her. Or smell her unique scent—a mix of citrus and jasmine—when the wind blew in his direction.

Toby cleared his throat to ease some of the dryness. "I feel like I ate a pound of dirt."

"I've been collecting water," Jules said. "We should probably drink some so I can collect more. If what you said is true about the rain, it could stop any minute, and we won't get a refill anytime soon."

Toby tilted his head back and opened his mouth to catch a few raindrops as Jules retrieved a thermal mug.

"Here, take as much as you need," she said to him.

"When was the last time you drank water?" he asked, figuring, as always, Jules was taking care of someone else instead of herself.

"I was waiting for it to fill up more," she said before catching his gaze. "Since we might be here for a while, do you mind telling me why criminals like Symes get to you so much?"

It was just like Jules to cut to the chase when she was curious about a topic. This subject had been off-limits to her and everyone else.

Could he open those old wounds?

## Chapter Three

Rain battered down. Winds kicked up. Without communication to the outside world, Jules had no idea how long the storm would last. Or when help would arrive, if ever.

"Let's hop inside the back of the chopper and get out of this storm system," Toby said, instead of answering her question outright. Changing the subject was classic Toby.

Jules hesitated before climbing inside. For one, there was a dead man inside. As much as she didn't want to leave Captain Crawford alone until help arrived, being in close proximity to someone once they'd passed sent creepy-crawlies up her spine. But staying outside in the elements left them vulnerable. With winds whipping around, debris could slam into one of them or both. They might not see it coming until the last minute, making it nearly impossible to get out of the way. Then there was the age-old wisdom advising against standing next to a window in a severe thunderstorm. The chopper had windows—pressurized, thank goodness—and the small cabin would ensure she sat next to one.

Was it safe?

"Visibility is next to nothing," she pointed out as she climbed inside and settled in the back on the floorboard. She faced the back so she wouldn't have to look at Captain

Crawford. "We won't know if Symes is coming back until he's right up on us now."

Jules extended a hand to help Toby up. He took it and, with serious effort, made it inside and out of the pounding rain. The chopper offered a temporary shelter at best, and she noticed he was nursing his right arm.

Did she dare pin all her hopes on being rescued?

"We should sit back-to-back," Toby offered.

Jules complied. "Keep your arm above your heart to help with swelling."

The reality of his wrist being broken and not just angry meant the swelling wasn't likely to go down.

No phone to call for medical help. No way to reach her supervisor. No way to contact her family. *Family.* The fact her grandparents were lying in hospital beds fighting for their lives while she was out here hit full force. She had to push those unproductive thoughts aside.

The knot tightened in her chest. Would Symes circle back to the only known shelter in the area like a scavenger waiting for its prey to die so it could pick at the carcass without risking injury? Were they sitting ducks?

Toby grunted.

"We need to take a look at that broken arm," Jules reminded him. "There must be an emergency kit in here somewhere."

"Small, private aircraft aren't required by law to keep supplies," Toby pointed out. "I've been on some that didn't carry a Band-Aid. And turns out, it's my wrist, not my arm. Not as bad as I initially thought."

"It's broken, Toby. Let's hope Captain Crawford erred on the safety side of the equation."

Jules climbed around on all fours toward the very back. She felt around in the darkness. Then she remembered Toby's phone. There might not be bars, but it could still come in handy. "Toss me your cell."

He did.

She caught it and flicked on the flashlight app.

The battery was low, 29 percent. They would need to conserve until an emergency crew could locate them.

She spotted a white case with the telltale red cross on it. "Found it."

The ten-inch-by-twelve-inch box had aspirin, ibuprofen and an assortment of Band-Aids. The real score was the self-adhesive wrap. She could create a basic sling with it for Toby's arm, which might help keep him from using it.

"Take your jacket off," Jules said to Toby.

He smirked. "Whatever you say, gorgeous."

Jules cracked a smile despite herself. The man always knew how to make her laugh and lighten the darkest circumstances. Except when rapists were mentioned. He never joked when the subject came up, and he still wouldn't talk about why.

With a grunt, he managed to shrug out of his blazer. In a jacket and jeans, he was devastatingly handsome. Jules had no idea why the man wasn't out every weekend with a new person. The women at the office lined up to speak to him. Every time he entered the room, their fingers curled into their hair, voices raised several pitches higher and smiles widened in a show of teeth named, rightfully so, The Teeth Show.

And yet he preferred to stay home on Friday nights and hang out with friends most weekends. When he did go on a date, he never discussed the details with her. So, she kept her dating life secret as well. *Dating life?* That was a generous term for the occasional dinner out when she forced herself to swipe on a dating app and received a match. Since her career took up most of her time and she preferred silence to sitting across the table from a stranger forcing conversation over a meal, she did very little swiping. Plus, she'd rather spend Saturday night watching a movie with friends, if she felt like going out at all.

"I can't sit here and do nothing," Toby said while she worked on his wrist.

She didn't stop, didn't respond.

Toby brought his good hand up and closed his fingers around the small of her wrist. Her gaze met his—bad idea this close—and he used those used-to-getting-what-he-wanted eyes on her.

"Hey, no, it's not going to work," Jules protested. "We don't know which way he went, and we have no cell service out here. Not to mention your phone has very little battery left. Twenty-nine percent, Toby."

It was classic Toby for his phone to be near dead. He'd borrowed hers enough times when his died. She should have known.

Toby didn't budge.

"We'll never find him out here," she continued, realizing she'd already lost the battle. "Fine, then. How do you expect to locate Symes?"

"Easy," Toby remarked. "All we have to do is wait out the rain. It'll be cold and he'll be wet, so he'll figure out how to start a fire."

"He has no supplies," she pointed out. "And everything is wet. How the hell do you expect him to start a fire?"

"This man has evaded capture for eleven years, Jules. He will figure out how to stay alive under all conditions."

True enough, Symes was believed to have spent time in the mountains in Colorado during winter with no known shelter, as well as Montana. This guy had a few tricks up his sleeve. He was smart. He knew how to thrive under harsh conditions.

Facing a lifetime sentence if recaptured, he had nothing to lose. The combination was dangerous, and the reason US marshals were shot at more than any other agency.

Toby winced as she wrapped his hand and arm against his body to keep them secure and from moving. "He might have been in this area before multiple times. He could know the lay of the land. Eleven years of hiding with every agency hunting him is no small accomplishment."

Toby made more good points there.

"Okay, fine," she conceded. "We go after him once the storm lets up."

They couldn't exactly stay inside the chopper forever. The harsh truth was help might not be on its way. They might be stuck here for days before anyone actually located them in the vastness of this national park, if at all.

Symes could realistically come after them.

She sat back on her heels, assessing her work. "Try not to move it, okay?"

"I'll do my best," he responded.

"Rest is probably out of the question." She figured Symes could be working his way back to them right now.

Toby wiggled his eyebrows at her, trying to pull a laugh out of her.

When it didn't work, he turned on those serious honey-browns. "You know we can't sit around and wait for him to come for us. There will be clues as to which direction he went. My guess is that he didn't go very far. He'll circle back at some point just to see if we're alive, unless…"

It was almost as though Toby couldn't say the words.

"Unless he finds a family or a couple, kills them, and then steals their vehicle," she said after a sharp exhalation.

Toby was right about one thing. They couldn't let Symes roam around by himself. He was a danger to others, and she couldn't stand idly by while he took another life or lives.

They were going to have to go out there and find him.

"ARM'S GOOD AND the rain has slowed." Toby couldn't stand sitting around while Symes was free. "We should get going after we clean and bandage your injury."

"Hold on there a minute, sir." Jules's serious voice wasn't something to mess around with. Toby had learned the hard way. "I have medicine that will help with the pain, so don't give me the your-body-is-a-temple speech, because we're not attending to me or leaving unless you take an ibuprofen. Deal?"

Toby knew when he'd lost an argument before it started. He held out his hand, palm up.

Jules was a miracle worker. She produced two pills and more water before dropping her gaze. "What do we do with him?" She motioned toward Captain Crawford.

"I'm sorry, Jules. There's nothing that can be done with the supplies we have right now." It was awful. Toby didn't want to abandon the pilot either. There was no way to revive him. Sticking around to hold vigil while a rapist-murderer was on the loose wouldn't bring the man back. A tough decision had to be made to save the living, no matter how awful a position that was to be in.

Toby hung his head. "It's the worst."

"Should we move him?" she asked. "He looks uncomfortable."

"It's not a good idea," he said.

"What about leaving something behind so people know to look for us if someone happens across the site?" she asked.

"First of all, we need to take a look at the gash on your

forehead," he said, turning the tables. "You get to be the patient now."

The slight pout to full lips said she wasn't thrilled about being on the other side of the proverbial stethoscope.

"You're going to have to help me out," he said. "Can you open the antiseptic wipes?"

Jules picked up the packet and then ripped it open before handing over the contents. He managed to separate the two sheets of cleaner, using one to clean his hands and the other to wipe away dirt and grime on and around the cut.

A sense of urgency was building to finish up and get out there. Symes could be miles away by now, or he might have collapsed just outside of view.

Either way, Toby wanted the bastard back in handcuffs. He'd physically sit on top of Symes until help arrived, if he had to.

Once the rain cleared, Toby would also watch for buzzards. They would signal if Symes was out there dead.

"Antibiotic ointment next," he said after picking through the supplies. "Open, please."

Jules did without argument. He suspected she was just as eager to figure out what had happened to Symes as he was. Jules had always been more cautious, though. She did a better job of balancing out risk.

After opening the small tube of ointment, she dabbed some of it on his finger, then winced as he touched her forehead. He couldn't risk infection, especially if they had to survive out here for a few days.

Leaving the relative safety of the chopper was a calculated risk. Soon enough, Crawford's body would begin to deteriorate and attract critters starved for a meal. Out here, it would be survival of the fittest. The promise of fresh meat would tempt predators within range.

The thought gave Toby the willies. Once he was gone from this earth, he didn't want to know what happened to his body. With the risk in his job, he always assumed he'd go out on duty. Some felon along the way would end up using him for target practice so they could escape and would nail him with a lucky shot.

Despite safety protocol, there were inherent risks associated with this job. Risks that he took seriously but also didn't want to focus on too hard. He'd learned a long time ago the secret to living as long as he had was to keep making plans for the future. His included a cold beer, his couch and a football game.

"All right," he said. "Grab supplies and put them in your backpack. We can leave the first aid kit open with stuff we don't need so people know someone rummaged through it."

Jules took in a deep breath, like she always did before she jumped into something that scared her.

"I'm right here," he reassured her. "I'll be alongside you the whole way. We'll find the son of a bitch."

"Did something happen to you when you were younger?" she asked as they exited the chopper.

Standing up made his head spin. "Not me personally. No. But someone I was responsible for."

"That's the reason, isn't it?"

She deserved to know that he wouldn't stop until either Symes was back in custody or Toby was dead.

"Yes," he said, staring out as the rain dissipated. Visibility was still low.

"Was he caught?" she asked.

It might be the circumstances or the fact he might never get another chance to tell Jules or anyone else what had happened that suddenly had him wanting to get it off his chest.

He paused to get a grip on the anger that always flooded him when he thought about what had happened.

"What did I tell you about how my sister died?" he asked, avoiding answering her question.

"Accident," she said as they started down the hill. Going this way made the most sense because the opposite side was too flat. It would be too easy to be seen for long distances. Symes would take the hilly route with lots of large rocks to hide behind in case bullets started flying. He'd head toward the mountains.

"I lied," he admitted.

"Why?" The hurt in her voice cut to the quick.

"Because I don't tell anyone what really happened," he countered, but it was a weak excuse to give his best friend.

"Didn't realize I was *anyone* to you, Toby."

"Lila was raped by someone who taunted me for becoming a US marshal," he continued, hoping she could understand once she heard the whole truth.

"Oh, no," Jules said, her tone so soft it wrapped around him, comforting him. "I'm so sorry."

He didn't deserve it.

"Be sorry for Lila," he countered, armor up. "Not me."

"I'm sorry for both of you," Jules said with more of that warmth in her tone.

"I'm the reason she's dead." Moisture gathered in his eyes, which he quickly sniffed away. He coughed to cover the frog in his throat.

"That's impossible."

"I told her to fight back if she ever found herself being compromised," he managed to get out. The memory crashed around him, shattering him. "She wasn't the type to stand up for herself. Lila was always putting everyone else above herself. If anything ever happened, I was afraid she'd freeze up, so I told her to fight like hell. She had to have been so damn scared." He stopped for a few seconds to collect his thoughts and stop the emotions threatening to bombard him. "But she put up a valiant fight."

"That was good advice, Toby."

"Once the bastard raped her, he murdered her." His voice cracked. *Pull it together, man.* "It should have been me."

"Did they catch the son of a bitch?" Jules asked in measured calmness.

"Lila managed to scratch his face up," he said, shaking his head. "She lived long enough to identify a tattoo on the perp's neck of the outline of a dark-haired woman's face and neck embracing the head and torso of a skeleton just below her. The FBI decided it was a sick reference to his many faceless victims embracing their deaths." He'd checked the necks of every single rapist he'd ever gone after.

Jules got quiet. Too quiet.

"What is it? What's going on?"

"How certain are you about those details?" she asked.

"She could barely speak," he said. "It was the best the cop on the scene could make out."

"What if the tattoo wasn't on his neck but was on his forearm?" she asked. "And it wasn't a skeleton but was the grim reaper instead?"

Toby had a bad feeling about where this might be going. "Why do you ask?"

"Symes."

## Chapter Four

Could Symes have been the one to rape and murder Toby's sister? Icy fingers gripped Jules at the thought of the perp they'd been transporting being the one to cause such heartache and pain to Toby and his family.

"Does that moth—"

"It might not be the same person," Jules countered. "We can't be certain of anything right now."

Toby ground his back teeth so hard she heard them over the driving rain. He sat there, silent, for a long moment.

"Tell me more about what happened," Jules gently urged.

"Why?" Toby bit out. His tone was the equivalent of sharp knives stabbing her in the chest. Toby was the only person on the planet who could affect her in that way. He could turn on the charm one minute and light her on fire in the next without flexing a muscle. Then there was the side that could hurt her with words as sharp as daggers.

Did he realize the effect he had on her?

Jules decided he didn't because Toby wasn't the kind of person who would treat her emotions like a kid's toy. She'd never felt so vulnerable with any other human being, so there was definitely something special about the man, because no one else got under her skin. For the first two years of their friendship, she'd chalked it up to being best friends and caring too much about what he thought of her. Last year, she'd realized there was more to it but refused to fully admit how deep her feelings ran even to herself. Because what good would it do to go there when it wouldn't be reciprocated?

Besides, Toby always kept part of himself closed off to everyone, out of bounds. In three years, she'd never been able to break through. Despite sharing what he had just now, he'd already closed up.

"Because we're friends, Toby," she said out of frustration. "Isn't that a good enough reason?"

"It won't bring her back," he countered, holding on to every bit of hurt and anger as though time couldn't heal every wound.

"No," she agreed, softening her tone as she realized just how much pain he was in and how much he blamed himself for something outside of his control. *But it might just bring* you *back.* That part of Toby that he kept to himself also kept the rest of the world at arm's length. Their friendship could only go so deep before the wall came up between them again.

Not that Jules was much better.

"Talk to me, Toby," she pressed, glancing back at the captain. Life was short. Careers like theirs could cut the timeline in half. Symes could be sneaking up on them right now, and they wouldn't be the wiser. "We're here, together, and it might just be our—"

"We'll get out of this mess alive," Toby said, cutting her off, not accepting any other possibility.

"I know," she said, half-heartedly. It was probably her grandparents' situation that had her realizing how quickly life could change or be lost. In a snap, the people she loved most could be gone forever.

"They'll be okay too," Toby said as though reading her thoughts. It was a good thing he couldn't read all of them, or she would be busted. Her attraction was something she kept at bay, but then, women who were attracted to Toby formed a long line. He had to know she thought he was sex on a stick, even though his ego remained remarkably in check.

"What if they don't pull through?" she asked, going with the shift in conversation as they waited out the storm.

"We'll deal with it as a team," he reassured her. "Just like the way you helped me when I lost my grandmother." He'd been raised by grandparents too, which was one of many things they had in common. His grandmother had been his last living relative.

The way he put it made it sound like she was less alone, but she *was* alone. At the end of the day, she went home to an empty town house. Toby did the same, but he liked it that way. Said he could think better when he was by himself. There were times when she wondered how true his statement was, despite his commitment to the words as he spoke them. He overcommitted as if he was trying to convince himself the line was true.

Jules got it. She hyped herself up for a workout at the gym using the same tactic. *Speak it if you want to believe it* was the philosophy.

A crack of lightning caused her to tense, bringing her current reality front and center in her thoughts.

Toby was severely injured. As much as he wanted to go after Symes, how long could Toby last? How far would he be able to go in his current condition?

He was iron-man tough, but everyone had limits. Injuries could only be set aside for so long. Adrenaline had a limited life. And then what?

They could end up lost with no shelter, food or water.

On the flip side, they might find a family or individual camping before Symes did. They could potentially receive assistance, medical care and a way to communicate with the outside world. Stay here and Symes could retrace his steps to them. Because another possibility was that he might be just as injured as the two of them. He might not have found anything useful out there. He could have no other choice but to return. Killing them may not have been on his agenda at first, but much like Texas weather, that could change.

Examining all sides of a situation helped with important decisions.

"How long do you think it's safe to sit here?" she asked, also realizing they were the equivalent of sitting ducks in this downpour.

"Before we move on, you can talk to me about your grandparents anytime, Jules," Toby said with the kind of compassion that tightened the knot in her stomach. She didn't want to need him. "You know that, right?"

"Nothing to discuss," Jules stated, realizing she'd just pulled the same trick of shutting down that was classic Toby. Was it another reason they got along so well? They were kindred spirits?

It was also another strong reason they should never date. Losing Toby—most relationships ended, especially when it came to Jules's love life—would destroy her. Keeping him in the friend zone was the only way to go the distance. Because she couldn't imagine her life without him in it.

"I know," he said with a wince as he moved to turn toward her.

"Give me the truth, Toby," she started. "On a scale of one to ten, how's the pain?"

"A three," he said with a smile that was so good at disarming her. Ever since the revelation about Symes possibly being the one who'd killed Lila, there was an unfamiliar tone to his voice, even when he attempted to be lighthearted. At least he was talking now. Silence was much worse.

"This isn't golf," she countered.

"Okay, seriously," he said. "On a scale of one to ten, I'm looking at about a twenty." He quickly added, "But we both know I've dealt with worse."

"Than a chopper crash?" she shot back. "I doubt it."

The rain lashed against the glass. Winds kicked up. A loud thud sent her pulse racing and her adrenaline soaring.

Locking gazes with Toby was always a mistake this close, but Jules did it anyway.

"Stay here," he said. "I'll go check it out."

"Over my dead body you're going alone." Those words had a haunting ring to them, Jules realized a little too late. She could only pray they weren't foreshadowing what was to come.

TOBY SHOVED ASIDE a moment of doubt as he palmed his weapon in his left hand. Since his right one was temporarily trashed, he'd have to make do with his less dominant side. They were tall on risk and short on options, not to mention the fact Symes might be getting away.

"Let's do this," he said to Jules before rolling over and kicking the door open. At least both of his legs worked. That was a plus.

As he watched Jules climb out of the chopper, he noticed she favored her left leg.

"Everything all right?" he asked, motioning toward the knee.

She pulled up her slacks to reveal a swollen knee. "Damn. It's the size of a melon. How did I miss that?" She took a couple of tentative steps, wincing as she attempted to put pressure on her left side. "That's not good." A moment of panic crossed her features before she regained composure and then grabbed a couple of pills from the emergency kit. "Looks like you're not the only one in need of ibuprofen."

"Hand me your backpack," he said to her after she swallowed the medicine.

Jules placed the emergency kit inside before handing the bag over. Toby shouldered the pack on his left side without setting down his weapon, which was a miracle. Maneuvering around hurt like hell, but he was mobile. He'd survive. Once they located Symes—because Toby had no plans to stop searching until the bastard was back in cuffs—he could think about getting proper medical attention.

From the corner of his eye, he noticed a piece of metal. He walked over to check it out. "This is where Symes dumped his handcuffs."

Jules joined him. "Dammit." With effort, she bent down and felt around on the ground. Came up with a key. "Looks like he managed to strip my ankle gun and the key." She shivered. "Thinking about the creep's hands on me at all gives me the willies."

It sent white-hot fire licking through Toby's veins. Losing his sister to a rapist had messed with his head for years and would for the rest of his life. He couldn't fathom Jules in a similar fate. Grinding his back teeth to the point they might crack, Toby managed to say, "Let's go find this human piece of garbage. It's time to take out the trash."

"Agreed."

"Symes might not be far, so keep on the lookout," Toby warned. The man had to have sustained some injuries during the crash, which might have slowed him down. Clearly, it didn't stop him, though.

The rain continued to batter them, hurling big splotches

down on the earth. Despite the ibuprofen, movement shot pain rocketing through Toby's body.

Nothing would stop him from hunting down Symes.

"It's anyone's guess which way he took off," Jules said. "We might as well head this way." She motioned down the hill to a ravine.

"Good idea," he confirmed. "It's easier to head downhill than up or across since the terrain in this area is rocky."

"Visibility is low," she pointed out. "We'll want to keep close to each other."

The easiest way to attack them at this point would be to divide and conquer, so Jules was thinking down the right path. "Will do."

Since walking—or any movement, for that matter—wasn't going to get any easier, Toby sucked in a breath and headed down. The path was crooked and rocky, so Symes could be waiting behind a boulder to strike. Even with a weapon at the ready, Toby was at a disadvantage with his right arm being held against his body. It made keeping balance a challenge. Shooting left-handed was going to be interesting if the need arose.

Toby would cross that bridge when he came to it. For now, it was all he could do not to bite it as he navigated the rocky hill.

Water would be somewhere below, which wasn't a concern given the current weather conditions. Hikers and families would make a campsite near a stream. The thought of an unsuspecting family being tortured or killed got Toby's legs moving faster.

Symes was a twisted bastard. The thought Toby might be close to catching the man who'd haunted his nightmares for years sent more adrenaline thumping through him, giving him a much-needed boost.

Jules wasn't far behind. He wanted—no, needed—to keep her close. The easy explanation was that he was concerned for another law enforcement officer's safety. That was the easy way out. Jules had been a lifeline during his grandmother's Alzheimer's diagnosis. Jules had stayed by his side while he had to make decisions no grandson wanted to have to make on his beloved family member's behalf. And Jules had been the only reason he'd made it through the storm of emotions that flooded him as he watched his grandmother's casket be lowered into the ground.

So, it was far more than friendship between them. Jules was the closest thing to family he had left in this world. She meant the world to him.

Toby's foot slipped. Instinct had him trying to use his dominant hand, which landed him hard on his backside.

Sliding, he leaned back and went with the flow. It was all he could do without ditching his gun. So, he didn't fight against the fall.

By the time he stopped, Jules was so far up the hill that he could no longer hear her. Lightning streaked across the gray sky, but the flash gave him a visual on Jules. She was coming down as fast as her legs could go as pebbles came down in a landslide.

"Are you okay?" she shouted. Making noise was a mistake, despite the ceiling of rain and the insulation it provided. Otherwise, her voice would have carried for miles in this area. He should know. Lila had tested the waters by standing on the largest boulder she could find and shouting at the top of her lungs. She'd been ten years old the last time they camped here with their father.

First, Toby had lost his mother. Then he'd lost his father. His sister was the third to go but the most difficult to take. His mother had succumbed to recurring breast cancer. His

father had died of a broken heart, according to Toby's grandmother, but that had taken another five years and a back injury that ended with his father being addicted to painkillers.
Alcohol and pain medication were the worst kind of bed-
fellows. His sister had died a tragic death, leaving the once
family of four down to a lone person standing.

Then he lost his grandmother too. Alzheimer's claimed
her memories, which was a whole different type of slow,
drawn-out death, despite only lasting a year after the official diagnosis. Her memory had been slipping long before
that, and she'd become confused.

Jules had stayed in the spare bedroom at his grandmother's house during the last couple of months. And now he
wanted to return the favor by helping her with her grandparents' situation if she'd let him.

A pebble slammed against the crown of his head, causing him to quickly sit up. Pain reminded him that he was
alive, so he normally took it in stride. But the pebble felt
like it had cracked his skull.

As Jules neared, her gaze focused on a spot below his.
Determination replaced panic.

"What do you see?" he asked. Had they just found
their felon?

## Chapter Five

Something moved. Jules couldn't see clearly enough to determine if it was animal or human. But something had shifted position, moving behind a boulder and out of view.

A tingle raced up her spine. It was the kind of sensation that sparked every time she got close to her mark. A shot of adrenaline caused her senses to heighten, becoming razor-sharp. Her head stopped hurting, and she no longer felt the pain in her swollen knee. Good signs? Probably not.

In fact, she knew they weren't, but the temporary relief was welcome anyway. A brief reprieve was better than none.

Hunkering down to make herself as small a target as possible, she slipped next to a boulder in case the person or thing below was Symes. Any manner of wild animal could be out here. Between black bears, bobcats and mountain lions, there were plenty of predators that could take advantage of her weakened condition. The great equalizer was her service weapon. Toby could defend himself as well.

Was it a mistake to leave the chopper, where they could barricade themselves inside? It would have provided enough shelter to keep them safe from wildlife.

Considering most of Big Bend was a desert, the rain coming down was unusual for this climate. Did that mean it would stop soon?

Almost the second she had the thought, Mother Nature complied. At least they were getting a break there. The sky was still dark and moody, but visibility increased enough to see something behind the boulder. Hiding? Waiting? Biding its time?

Jules moved past Toby, who sat very still. They made brief eye contact. Enough to communicate she needed to move very slowly and carefully, and he had her back. If she had to be lost in a desert with anyone, she would want it to be Toby. Words weren't necessary in a tense situation with him, unlike with other marshals she'd worked with, where ground rules had to be set early on before anything went down. She and Toby could anticipate each other's moves with one look. Being in sync had never been a problem.

A rock caused Jules to slip. Her bad knee buckled. She caught herself in time to avoid biting it, but pebbles tumbled down the narrow path. Whatever waited would know someone was coming now.

Sucking in a breath, Jules righted herself and then pressed her back against the boulder. Methodically, she made her way down to the spot where someone or something had been a few moments before.

Whatever had been there was gone now.

Frustration bit at her as Toby joined her. She shook her head. He frowned, clamping his mouth shut. Without a word, he took the lead and kept moving forward. As the adrenaline boost wore off, Jules felt every bit of the pain in her knee. Her head pounded like a two-year-old with a new drum set. Those ibuprofen pills weren't nearly enough to tackle this pain. If they could keep some of the inflammation down in her knee, she'd be happy.

Half an hour later, they'd made it down to a ravine.

Toby sat down on a nearby rock. He set down his weapon

and retrieved a bottle of water out of the backpack, offering it to her first.

Jules took the bottle, twisted off the cap and held it above her lips as she drank the cool liquid. Her clothes stuck to her like a wet swimsuit. Clumps of hair clung to her face. She was a drowned rat at this point.

After handing the bottle back to Toby, she scanned the area once more. The rain washed away any tracks the culprit might have otherwise left, leaving the question of animal or human unanswered.

"This area only gets about ten inches of rain per year," Toby pointed out. "Didn't realize all ten inches came at the same time."

"I think the weatherperson can tick that box," she quipped before cracking a small smile. A break in tension was much needed. There was no one better at cracking through the most serious situations and infusing humor. It was a survival mechanism that worked to bring down heightened emotions so you could think clearly again. Putting yourself in a calmer state helped you return to problem-solving mode, which spawned the best ideas.

"You sure about that?" he asked with one of those devastating smiles that was all Toby. It might not reach his eyes, but that didn't lessen the impact. Toby smiles had a way of releasing dozens of butterflies in her chest while her stomach simultaneously performed a national-champion-level gymnastics routine.

Jules took a hard look at the sky. "I don't know, man. Maybe we need a little more." She stuck her tongue out. "I'd like to catch a few more drops, if you know what I mean."

Catching Symes had been the find of the year—hell, the decade. Which made losing him all that much harder to swallow. People would say it wasn't their fault. But he'd been in their custody. People would say the chopper crash was an accident. But it had been their responsibility to bring him in. People would say she should give herself a break. But she wouldn't sleep at night until this bastard was caught. If he managed to escape and live, he would pick right back up where he'd left off, raping and killing innocent women. Their blood would be on Jules's hands. How was she supposed to let herself off the hook for that?

"We'll catch him," Toby reassured her.

"How did you know what I was thinking?" she asked, surprised at how easy it seemed to be for him to figure out what was on her mind. Toby clued in to everything but her attraction.

"You get a tiny wrinkle on your forehead when you're deep in thought and being hard on yourself," he explained. "And small brackets around your mouth."

"I do?"

"Yes," he confirmed. "It's not hard to figure out the topic considering our circumstances, the fact we think alike when it comes to work, and the reality that I'm over here beating myself up for the same reason."

*He got away.*

"All good points," she said, realizing she did know he would be thinking along the same lines.

"The captain's death isn't your fault either," he added.

"What makes you think I blame myself?" she asked.

"Because I'm doing the same thing." He looked up to the sky. "I have no idea what happens to us when we…"

He let his sentence hang in the air.

"But I sure hope my family is back together, laughing," he said in a rare emotional moment. "I hope they're at peace."

"What about you, Toby?" she asked.

"Some people don't deserve to be let off the hook," he said, his voice almost a whisper.

"I've messed up plenty in my life and line of work," she said, not ready to accept his answer. For the first time—and maybe it was the circumstances—she wanted to push for a better response. "Do I deserve to be forgiven?"

"Of course you do," he said, like it was common knowledge.

"You sure about that?" she pressed.

"One hundred percent," he said as the arch in his brow shot up sky-high. "Why would you even question it?"

"Because I can't forgive myself for not being bedside for my grandparents right now," she said.

"You will be once we locate Symes," he pointed out. A flash of hatred crossed behind his eyes at the mention of the man's name. "Not being there isn't your fault. The accident certainly wasn't your fault. You and your siblings have worked out a plan to have coverage 24/7. You get updates on your cell as well as phone calls." He issued a thoughtful pause. "Plus, there's nothing you can do at the hospital except sit and worry. Focusing on your job keeps your mind occupied until they wake up."

"Keep talking like that and I'll think you've given this situation a lot of thought," she teased. Though, his reassurances meant the world to her.

"I think about every situation that involves you," he said with a hint of vulnerability in his voice. Before Jules could respond, he added, "You're my best friend, kiddo."

Leave it to Toby to make certain she didn't confuse friendship with anything more. He'd always been clear about his intentions and how he felt about her.

Friendship was good, though. It would last. And she

needed him more than ever while facing the situation with her grandparents.

"Speaking of Symes," she said, clearing her throat. "What's our next move?" She added the word *buddy* in her mind as a reminder. It was good to keep herself in check when it came to how she viewed Toby, because it was all too easy to cross a line and convince herself that he wanted more.

TOBY LEANED AGAINST the boulder, forcing his thoughts away from the pain in his wrist. *Doesn't hurt. I'm good. I'm good. I'm good.* Repeating the mantra had gotten him past a few tough sports injuries in his youth. Could it work now?

At this point, he'd try anything to ease the pain that a couple of ibuprofens couldn't make a dent in.

The image of Lila forced its way front and center. First, her innocent smile. She'd been protected all her life. Toby had deemed himself her guardian after their father sank into a dark hole following his wife's death.

Lila had been dubbed their miracle child since Toby's mother had had a hard pregnancy with him and wasn't supposed to be able to have more children. Apparently, she'd been warned it would be too dangerous for her body to go through it a second time. And that was the rub. His mother had survived pregnancy and childbirth only to be taken by breast cancer before her miracle child entered kindergarten.

A newly minted teenager by that point, Toby would have been rebellious as hell if his baby sister hadn't grounded him. Their grandmother was aging. Their father was gone, for all intents and purposes. Caring for Lila had fallen to Toby. The reality was that he didn't mind. She had given him purpose that was otherwise lacking in his turned-up-side-down world.

It had been impossible to turn his back on those inno-cent brown eyes as she stood at the kitchen door waiting for their mother to return home from the hospital, completely unaware of what he already knew. Their beautiful, loving mother wasn't coming home.

Becoming Lila's caretaker had given him purpose, marching orders. Look what he'd done to return the favor.

"Hey," Jules said, cutting into his heavy thoughts—thoughts he'd been able to hold at bay in recent years. The possibility—however remote it might be—that Symes was responsible for Lila's murder brought back all those haunt-ing memories.

It was time justice was served. For Lila. Toby owed her that much.

"Where did you go just now?" Jules asked as Toby re-focused, looking at her instead of the sky that seemed to go on forever.

He didn't respond. What could he say? That if they found Symes, he couldn't be certain he wouldn't mete out his own form of justice, born from a need that had been simmering for more years than he cared to count.

Jules studied him. "You all right?"

Normally, she was good at reading his emotions too. But this hatred ran deep. She didn't know this side of Toby. He'd kept his darkness away from her because Jules had been the only peek of light in his life. He wanted to hang on to it. Let her keep believing he was a great person who always did the right thing.

But when he came face-to-face with Symes again, Toby couldn't be held responsible for his actions. Not when the image of his little sister's life being choked out of her after being brutalized haunted him.

"I will be," Toby finally answered after a pause.

## Chapter Six

Jules got the impression the sentence was left unfinished. She'd seen him go quiet before. It seemed like a good time to give him space. He'd go dark on her for a couple of hours— sometimes a day, if they were off work—and then he would resurface like nothing had happened. "Right now, though, we need to get on the move."

Jules decided not to keep prodding. He would talk when he was ready.

"Let's go find a water source," he said. "Water is the ultimate life-giving source, but it takes lives too. It only takes seconds to drown."

Jules took note of the change in Toby's tone and decided to ask him about it later.

Symes most likely beat them to the punch. He had a head start, which gave him an advantage. A lingering thought as to why he didn't kill them when he had the chance sat heavily in the back of her thoughts.

She would let it marinate. See if any plausible reason stood out other than the simple explanation that said he plainly thought they would die either way. Killing them was unnecessary when nature would take care of it. The easy answer was usually the right one, so she settled on that for now and ignored the niggling feeling there could be something else to it.

Heading farther down was a slow, methodical process.

How had Symes made the trek? A bigger question followed. Were they even on the right track?

Toby's reasoning made sense. Symes would want to find water. He must have left the crash site in a hurry, because he'd walked away from her backpack and medical supplies. A weapon would have been a priority. He'd managed to steal her SIG. Why not fire a few shots before taking off?

Because a wild animal scared him off.

Or had Jules stirred?

Jules had never seen an emptiness in Toby's stare like the one she'd just witnessed, like he'd been filled with a sudden darkness. Should she have told him Symes might be the person who'd killed his sister?

In hindsight, it might not have been the best idea. Especially since she couldn't be certain one way or the other without proof.

Every step caused her head to pound a little harder. Much more and the pain would be blinding. Had Symes counted on that?

"Where did you say the tattoo was, and what did it look like?" Toby asked when he finally stopped to take a drink of water and lean back on a rock.

"I think the first question we need to ask is how reliable the investigators on the scene of your sister's…" She couldn't bring herself to say the words out loud that would certainly gut Toby. "You know what I mean?"

"Yes," he confirmed.

"Thanks for not making me say the words."

He nodded his understanding.

"Symes has the outline of a dark-haired woman's face

and neck embracing the head and torso of the grim reaper on his forearm," she supplied.

"The Bureau decided it was a sick reference to his many faceless victims embracing their deaths." Toby hung his head. "I've checked the necks of every single rapist I've gone after ever since." He shook his head as he avoided her gaze. "Lila managed to scratch his face up too. Symes has scars, but I assumed they were from other victims."

"Which could still be true," she said. "The tattoos are similar, but there's no concrete proof they are the same person." She studied him for a long moment, realized a losing battle when she entered one. "Do you need to be pulled from this case?"

"No."

"You seem to be losing all sense of objectivity, Toby."

"I won't deny there's a lot of truth to that statement," he agreed. "You can turn me in, write me up or do whatever you need to do to cover your backside. But I'm not leaving." He made a dramatic show of waving his hands in the air. "And, in case you haven't noticed, we're stuck in this together, whether we want to be or not."

"What the hell, Toby?" She couldn't hold back her anger. "Is that what you think? All I'm interested in is covering my butt?"

He issued a sharp sigh.

"Because we go back, and before today, we went deep. If that's changed, you should have given me a heads-up. Because I'm in this with you up to my eyeballs, and I need to know what I'm getting into." She huffed out a breath. "And, in case you didn't know this, I'm trying to cover *your* butt, not mine. You could lose your job over something like this."

He didn't speak, just stared out in the distance as though his gaze could magically cut through the low clouds.

"Not to mention your life if you go after him half-cocked, not thinking straight and while you're seriously injured," she continued, trying to break through. It was like trying to punch a fist through a six-inch-thick steel wall. The subject of his sister was sensitive. Her heart went out to Toby for his loss. The tragic manner in which his sister had died was unforgivable. But he couldn't take it out on someone who may or may not be responsible. It was their job to deliver the perp in one piece so he could stand trial. Everyone deserved a fair trial, even Symes, as much as she hated the fact. Was the justice system perfect? No. Of course not. But it was all they had at the moment. Usually, it worked.

"You don't have to worry about me." Toby's words came out like he was talking to someone he couldn't stand to be in the same room with, which made her realize he was in serious trouble. This case could take him down if he wasn't careful. And then what?

Toby would have nothing left. Not to mention the fact he wasn't the kind of person who abused his position.

"You're my best friend, Toby. Don't let this guy get inside your head," she pleaded.

"He's not," Toby replied, but the reassuring words were hollow. "I wouldn't let a scumbag like Symes force me to do anything I didn't want to, Jules. You should know me better than that by now. But I won't back down from him either. I'll do whatever it takes to ensure the bastard is punished for what he did to all his victims, as well as my sister, if it turns out he's the one."

There was so much anger and hurt in his demeanor, his words and his expression that Jules barely recognized him.

She tried to put herself in his position. What if this sick son of a bitch had killed her cousins Crystal or Abilene? Would she be able to objectively do her job?

The answer came instantly. No. Absolutely not. Especially if she'd seen images from the crime scene. They would burn into her skull, and she would see nothing but fire if she was in the same room with the man who'd snuffed out their lives after torturing them.

Being out here, there wasn't a whole helluva lot she could do about having Toby replaced. Normally, she would make the call on his behalf, because she wouldn't have the presence of mind to be able to pull herself off the case either. She, of all people, knew how Toby thought. They were similar in that way.

"I wouldn't be objective," she admitted, hoping Toby could be honest with himself as well.

"That's your problem," he replied in a tone that said the conversation was over. This wasn't the time to put up an argument or try to get him to see reason. All she could do was nod. When and if the time came, she would work hard to ensure Toby didn't do anything that could come back on him later. She would have to step up her game in order to protect her friend.

Blinded by his anger, he couldn't see the potential damage he could do to his career, let alone the rest of his life, if he didn't handle the situation properly.

Jules resolved not to allow any harm to come to Toby or his reputation. She couldn't lose him too.

TOBY DIDN'T NEED PITY, and he didn't need a guardian. He needed revenge for Lila. The urge to find Symes took over. He had to be here somewhere. The man had to be injured. Life couldn't be so cruel as to allow him to have survived the crash unscathed while taking the life of a decent person, the pilot. "Let's move."

Haunting memories looped through his mind for the next

couple of hours. Along the way, Toby periodically checked for bars. No such luck finding cell coverage out here. It had been too long since the last time he'd visited the national park for him to recall any specifics, like where a ranger station might be. By the time they reached a water source, hunger crept in. If he felt the pangs, Jules must be starving. The term *hangry* applied to his best friend when she was forced to skip a meal.

He couldn't look back at Jules if he wanted to keep his focus, but he heard her as she fell into step behind him. She hadn't spoken since he'd been a jerk toward her earlier. He wished he could go back to being the carefree version of himself that she was used to, but something snapped in his mind when he realized Symes could be the man he'd been searching for over the last five years. Raping and murdering the sister of a US marshal might have been a pinnacle in the bastard's career. The theory had been dismissed by the FBI profiler on the case.

Disgust nearly overwhelmed Toby. What kind of monster would hurt someone as kind and innocent as Lila?

His baby sister was one of the most decent people he'd ever known, along with Jules. Having kind hearts was where the similarities between the two ended.

Toby located a good spot near the water's edge. If they didn't make it out of the desert soon, temperatures would drop. Their clothes were soaked. They would freeze. He needed to figure out a way to start a fire now that the rain had stopped.

Glancing around, he was reminded that everything was wet. Under normal conditions, there was enough material to use for tinder everywhere. Toby always carried a lighter and flint, an old habit from becoming a Boy Scout after his father flaked out on him. His grandmother had signed him up—much to his rebellion—to give him male role models, or so she'd explained.

Toby eventually agreed when he realized he needed to be there for Lila. Having practical survival skills couldn't hurt, and he'd feared that his sick grandmother would be taken from them too soon. Becoming a Scout not only gave him the skills to survive, but it had put him on a straight and narrow path to college for a criminal justice degree and then a career in law enforcement.

Texas had been in a drought, so park rangers would be watching for any signs of smoke, which could play to their advantage. No doubt, there would be a ban on all fire in the park despite the recent rain, which rolled downhill because the ground was too dry and cracked to accept it. Finding a ranger out here could save their lives since they would have better communication devices.

The state needed to be alerted to Symes's escape from custody. If Toby and Jules couldn't recapture Symes, the world needed to be on the lookout.

"They'll be sending out search parties for us by this point," Jules said, breaking the silence that sat between them like pregnant rain clouds.

Toby was thankful she finally spoke up. Could she forgive him for being a jerk? "There's a lot of ground to cover out here."

"True," she concurred. "But it's something."

Darkness blanketed the sky. Toby's eyes had long since adjusted, but it was impossible to see very far. There were no streetlights out here. No roads. In reality, search parties might not pick up until first light.

"My family will receive word and be very worried," Jules pointed out. "They already have enough going on with our grandparents."

She was lucky. No one would miss him.

"Of course your family will be concerned about you," Toby said, mustering as reassuring a voice as he was able. "They love you, Jules." He wanted to add that he loved her too, as a friend. "I'm not going to let anything happen to you." It was a promise both knew he might not be able to keep. "Though, I have a feeling you're the one who will be keeping me alive."

Normally, Jules cracked a smile when he made a statement like that, along with a *damn right* type of remark. This time, she barely nodded when he risked a glance at her.

Jules being mad at him was a rare occurrence. One he disliked with every fiber of his being.

This time, he feared she might never forgive him.

"I'll check over here for more tinder," she said, walking away as she followed the winding riverbed.

Being lost out here meant she had no ability to contact her family or receive updates about her grandparents. Toby didn't mind losing communication with the outside world as much since it wasn't like anyone would stay up all night to wait for word as to whether he was okay or not.

*Jules would*, an annoying voice in the back of his mind reminded him.

Toby ignored it as he gathered underbrush; the tops were wet but not all of it. He cursed his luck at the timing of the rain. Then again, he could chalk it up to the dark cloud that seemed to follow him around. Even as a teen while working as a lifeguard at the local public pool, a kid had drowned under his watch. Would Jules be safer with another partner on this assignment?

More of that familiar shame cloaked Toby, tightening like a straitjacket around his chest and arms, making it hard to breathe.

Steady wind created a constant white noise in the background, making it impossible to hear where Jules had gone. Toby kept a visual of her in his peripheral. Not only did they have to watch for Symes, but there were other vicious animals that could attack. In the grand scheme of nature, being human could put them at a disadvantage.

Toby had promised to keep Jules safe. He would give his own life in a heartbeat if it meant saving hers.

"Hey," she shouted, her voice echoing. "Toby. Come here. Quick."

A noise like footsteps running sounded to his left.

Was Toby the only one who heard?

## Chapter Seven

One look at the stress on Toby's face as he came barreling toward her made Jules realize she'd just scared the hell out of him.

She put both hands up, palms out, in the surrender position. "I didn't mean to freak you out, Toby. I'm good."

Toby halted with the same force as a charging bull in front of a butcher knife instead of a red cape. "It's fine." He panted like he'd just sprinted across a football field. "I just thought that something—"

"I know and I'm sorry," she said, cutting him off before he went down the rabbit hole of imagining something bad happening to either one of them. Being out here as night fell while a killer was on the loose was bad enough. Being here alone was the only thing that could make the situation worse.

His gaze shifted to a spot behind her. It was the reason she'd called him over.

"I haven't checked inside the camper, but it doesn't appear that anyone has been here in a while," she stated, turning around to the green-and-white-striped abandoned camper van. "Looks like someone parked here and then left it."

Toby walked the perimeter of the vehicle, giving it a wide berth. He leaned in. "There's no smell, which is a good sign." He circled the camper before returning to a spot next to her. "Have you checked the doors to see if they're unlocked?"

"No," Jules admitted, pulling her weapon from her shoulder holster just in case. "But I thought it might make a decent base camp for tonight. Keep us out of the elements and provide safety against wild animals." She couldn't say the same for Symes if he found them. The man was unpredictable. She also realized they might have gone in the wrong direction in their search, because a survivalist like him wouldn't waste an opportunity for free shelter. Would he?

Barely to Toby's right side, she kept her weapon trained on the door as they moved a couple of steps toward it.

Toby reached for the handle with his left hand, turned it and then opened the door. There was no stench of abandoned food or, worse yet, bodies. That was a good sign. Toby stuck his head inside. "Can't see a thing in here."

"Hold on," Jules said, reaching inside his pocket for his phone. She flipped on the flashlight app and moved so close to Toby their arms touched. Under different circumstances, she might notice the trill of electricity shooting up her arm like stray voltage from the point of contact.

Extending her arm until her hand was deep inside the camper, she slowly panned left to right.

"Looks like someone might have left this here for stranded hikers," Toby reasoned. "It's not in bad shape. There's no food, of course. Bears would rip the door off if they got hungry enough. There's a stack of blankets on top of the bed that's pulled out."

A dark thought struck that Symes might be familiar with this area and, therefore, know about this spot. Anything was possible.

"It seems safe to go inside, and it will keep us from the elements and wildlife," Toby reasoned.

"Will it make us sitting ducks, much like the chopper?" Jules asked. It was impossible not to think about Captain Crawford at the mention of his aircraft. Her chest squeezed.

Toby shrugged. "I hope not." He stepped inside the camper. "Our other option includes using these blankets to pitch a makeshift tent. It won't necessarily keep predators away, but we could insulate ourselves against the elements."

"Seems smarter, though, doesn't it?" she continued. "In case Symes finds this camper. He might expect us to be inside."

"We'd have the element of surprise in our favor," Toby reasoned. "But that won't stop wild hogs from attacking."

Jules sighed. "Or a few others, I'm sure." She stopped to think about it. "Maybe it's best to stay inside the camper tonight and then head out at first light." Searching for Symes in Big Bend National Park was the equivalent of finding a needle in a haystack. Not attempting to find him wasn't an option despite being battered and bruised from the crash. It occurred to Jules the gash on her forehead might not have come from the accident. Symes might have left Toby for dead and smashed her head with a rock.

Would he go back and check? Would he wander far from the relative safety of the chopper?

"Part of me thinks Symes might have slithered away from the chopper far enough to wait us out. Based on our injuries, he might not have expected us to live," she said.

"I thought the same thing, Jules."

"Should we go back? See if he circled around to check on us?" she asked. "We aren't too far away." They would have to climb up rather than make their way down, which could prove a challenge with her knee and Toby's general condition.

"At first light," he said after a thoughtful pause. "We should rest."

Jules had a feeling her pain would only increase.

"Elevating your knee above your heart should help with some of the swelling," he continued as he took a step inside the camper and then offered assistance with his left hand.

As Jules reached out to him, the crack of a bullet echoed through the air. A ping in the camper sounded two inches from her ear.

She immediately dropped to the ground as Toby dived on top of her, covering her with his six-foot-one-inch frame. An instant later, she drew her weapon and aimed at the source of the gunfire.

They were out in the open, exposed. Toby had just risked his life by covering her when he should have slipped inside the camper.

"I don't have a shot," she whispered.

"He's on the move," Toby said. "I can feel it."

"It has to be him," she responded. "Who else would shoot at us without identifying themselves?"

"Toss your weapon toward us," Toby ordered after identifying them as US marshals.

A haunting laugh echoed over them and across the river behind them.

"We need to get around the camper," Jules said. They needed to put some metal between them and Symes. And Symes was the only possibility out here in the middle of nowhere.

"You go first," Toby said as his body tensed, no doubt in pain. With his right hand taped to his body, crushed underneath his heft, the man had to be in excruciating pain. "I'll cover you."

"I got this, Toby," she argued back. He needed more time, and she intended to make sure he got it. Under normal circumstances, she wouldn't hesitate to go first, but she couldn't leave him. His injuries would slow him down.

Another shot fired.

There were only fifteen rounds in her SIG. Two down. Which left thirteen to go. *Too many in the hands of pure evil.*

Symes had thirteen more chances to end one or both of their lives.

Her first thought was that she couldn't lose Toby. Her second was that she couldn't die without seeing her family one more time.

Since she had a finite amount of ammunition, she refused to waste a single bullet. But Symes had given away his location for a few seconds.

"Go," she urged Toby.

With a grunt, he managed to army crawl to safety. He immediately drew his weapon and aimed. "Now you."

Jules sucked in a breath, said a quick prayer she'd learned a bazillion years ago and then crawled toward Toby. Movement made her feel like her head might explode from pain. Her knee pulsed and throbbed to the point she could feel every beat of her heart in it.

Bullet number three fired, hitting its target...*her.*

TOBY RELEASED A string of curses as he fired his weapon to back off Symes. The shot from his left hand got off too late. His reflexes weren't nearly as quick. Now Jules paid the price.

At least he bought her enough time to make it to him. Immediately, he tucked her behind him. There was no time to assess the damage for himself.

"How bad is it?" he whispered, desperate, as he scanned

the darkness for any sign of Symes. They had an escape route, but it was risky.

"I'll live," Jules promised. Could she keep her word?

Toby couldn't lose her. Period.

"We can make a run for the river," he said. "But we have to decide now."

"The river is raging," she pointed out. "I can hear it from here."

They were about twenty-five feet away. "I know, but it'll carry us away from Symes."

Jules hesitated for a moment.

"You're shot and we need to assess the injury, possibly even dress the wound," he said. "I wouldn't normally run in a situation like this, but we can't catch him if he kills us."

"Okay, good point" was all Jules said before she tugged at his good arm.

In a split second, they made a run for it, diving into the chilly water after Toby managed to secure his weapon. With one good arm, he would wear out easily in the frigid water. The cold splash was enough to shock Toby awake.

Temps at night could hover around freezing this time of year, but taking a water route was their best option to escape and regroup.

Toby used his good arm to sluice through the water, keeping as close to Jules as humanly possible.

"My knee already feels better," she said, her voice trembling with cold. "I can already say that much."

"We shouldn't stay in long," he said. Fighting the current to swim to shore was a whole different issue. One they were about to face if they wanted to stay remotely close to Symes.

Toby listened for a splash to indicate Symes had followed them. Instead, he heard an evil laugh that made his skin crawl.

And then it happened. *Splash.*

Never in Toby's thoughts did he imagine Symes would be determined enough to follow them into the water. Symes was roughly twenty seconds behind them, which meant he might be able to catch up to them when they exited the river. The cold water numbed their bodies, which helped with their injuries but would slow their movements.

They needed to find an exit before they froze to death.

"Toby," Jules said with a tone that sent his blood pressure sailing.

"What is it?" he asked. "Are you all right?"

"The blood," she said as he managed to get to her. How on earth he pulled it off with one good arm was anyone's guess. He could thank his Scout survival training that included swimming fully clothed under various conditions. Otherwise, he would be a goner and no help to Jules.

Blood pulsed from the base of her neck on her right side. Her lips were blue, another bad sign. He needed to get her to safety and deal with the wound immediately, if not sooner.

"Stay with me," Toby said to Jules as he slid in behind her. Body to body, she leaned into him. "Put pressure on the wound, Jules."

He could see her eyelids flutter. If she lost consciousness, it was all over. The thought of losing her was a knife stab in the center of his chest.

"I can't lose you, Jules," he whispered. "Keep fighting for my sake. Okay? I wouldn't survive it."

If he had to die on this assignment, he would want it to be with her. If she went, he wanted to go with her. Period.

"Talk to me," he whispered, needing to lock Symes up for the rest of his life before cashing in his chips. "And keep talking."

"Do you remember the first time we met?" she asked, her voice trembling with cold.

Toby would never be able to erase the image of Jules on her first day at the Marshals Service. She walked into the conference room, and his heart thumped double time inside his chest. He'd been certain she would realize his instant attraction to her, but she didn't. In fact, she walked directly toward the seat next to him and introduced herself. The first thing he noticed were her legs. They seemed to go on forever. Up close, though, it was her blue eyes with thick black lashes that smacked him in the chest. Her blond hair with wheat-colored highlights framed a near-perfect Blake Lively look-alike face, complete with a mole under her right eye close to her nose. With her looks, he'd expected a diva, not the down-to-earth, belly-laughing beauty who must have never looked at herself in a mirror. "Remind me."

"You think it was the conference room on my first day at work, but we actually stood in line together a couple of times at Dark Roast Coffee in Austin two months before I ever walked into that room," she said with a smile in her voice. He didn't need to see her face to know when she smiled. He could hear it through the lightness in her tone.

"No way," he countered. "I would have remembered you."

"It was early in the morning, and I had on sunglasses and a baseball cap," she quipped with more enthusiasm in her voice now. "Plus, I was behind you, and you never once looked back." More of that smile came through.

"Doesn't sound like me, even though I do frequent Dark Roast when I'm in the capital," he stated, trying to reach back into his brain for the possibility they'd been in the same room before without him realizing it. There was no way he wouldn't have seen Jules. She was far too beautiful not to notice. "But no way."

"You were deep in what had to be intellectual conversation with a brunette," she said, sounding smug. "I mean, she wouldn't leave your lips alone."

"Do you mean Clingy Carin?" he asked with a laugh that made his ribs hurt. The ever-present danger twenty seconds behind them could be closing in, but Toby couldn't think about that right now.

His focus had to go toward keeping Jules alive and getting them out of this river. The current carried them downstream at an increasing pace. The rush of water sounded ahead, which meant one thing. Waterfall.

Toby couldn't let Jules know about the dangers. *Keep her talking. Figure out a plan.*

*Think.*

## Chapter Eight

Jules was cold. Her teeth chattered. Heavy, wet clothes made lifting her arms to swim even more challenging. Her legs weren't in much better shape. The struggle to stay afloat was real. She had no idea how Toby was pulling it off with one good arm. The man was a force.

Fighting the overwhelming sense of exhaustion, Jules realized she needed to help get them to shore if they were to survive.

She let the Clingy Carin comment go. They could finish this conversation later. It had been a much-needed distraction, but she had to face the fact that if they didn't get out of the water soon, they were going over a waterfall.

Symes was somewhere close behind them too. She didn't risk a backward glance. She was focused on figuring out a way out of this current.

"See the branch coming up?" Toby asked.

"Yes," she said, shivering.

"I want you to grab it," he said. "I'll help push you out of the water. Then I want you to get on solid land."

"You'll be right behind me?"

"Yes," he reassured her as the branch came within reach. "Go."

Jules grabbed hold as she was hoisted out of the water.

She grabbed on for dear life and then immediately searched for Toby. His head had gone under the water.

She frantically searched the surface of the water for him. Nothing. She scanned the area for air bubbles. *Where are you?*

With one hand on her neck to put pressure on her wound and stem the bleeding, she managed to shimmy onto shore like he'd instructed. Knowing Toby, he had a plan. Toby *always* had a plan. It was only a matter of time before his head would surface and he'd pull himself out of the water a little downstream.

*Toby, where'd you go?*

Jules made it to shore and could kiss the soil, except Toby was still out there, and she still hadn't seen him. Maybe he'd popped his head up for air and she'd missed it while she was shimmying to shore.

Symes was out here too. She searched the shoreline first and then upstream for him. There was no sign of him either. It didn't mean he wouldn't come floating down in another second or two or running down the shore with gun blazing. At last count, he had a maximum of twelve rounds left. Enough to kill Jules and Toby.

Heart pounding, Jules frantically searched for Toby. He meant far too much to her to lose him in this manner.

With a curse, she waded ankle deep into the river. The current was strong, and she feared he might have been swept over the waterfall by this point.

Moving toward the rushing sound, she hopped on her good leg so she could get there faster. Wet clothes hung on her like fifty-pound weights, but nothing would stop her from finding Toby.

She focused her gaze on the water, skimming the surface. Movement on the opposite shore caught her eye. Symes?

No. Not Symes. Toby. He was lying flat on his back. The waterfall was less than ten feet away. Was he alive?

Panic squeezed her chest as she calculated the odds of being able to successfully swim across the current to get to him. She clamped her mouth shut to stop herself from calling out to him. If Symes was in the area, she didn't want to give away their position.

Then again, she would be drawing him to her, not Toby. That might just be a good thing.

Before she could decide, Toby sat up. Even from this distance, she could see his chest heaving for air, but he was alive and that was all that mattered.

He was searching the opposite shoreline, no doubt looking for her.

She waved her free hand in the air to get his attention, resisting the urge to scream his name to tell him that she was safe.

The second he saw her and waved back, relief flooded her. He was alive. She was alive.

The moment of happiness was cut short by the sound of footsteps coming from behind. A quick glance back didn't reveal the threat.

The noise stopped. Was something back there, waiting, biding its time to attack?

Getting to Toby was her first priority as she drew her weapon. Downstream where they were, the river curved and thinned. She signaled for Toby to hike back toward the direction they came. It would be safer to cross at the shortest point in between them.

Toby got the message and signaled he would move upstream. With effort, he managed to stand up. She realized he'd torn the bandage securing his right arm to his body. Was that how he'd managed to keep from drowning?

Now his hand dangled from his broken wrist.

Dizziness set in, but she refused to give in to the urge to lie down and go to sleep. Do that and she might never wake up again.

The footsteps didn't follow. Was that a good or bad sign?

Either way, Jules had to push forward and get to Toby. Could they circle back to the camper to rest? At this point, her body was working off pure adrenaline and probably a shock from the cold. Temperatures had dropped, and she needed to get out of these wet clothes or risk freezing to death. As it was, her teeth chattered. She was certain her lips had turned several shades of blue and purple like when she'd refused to get out of the public pool on a warm day in October. The sun might have been out, but the water had been freezing. She and her brothers, along with their cousins, would beg to stay in the pool until long after the sun went down, and they were close to hypothermia.

They'd eventually been bribed out of the water with the promise of hot cocoa with marshmallows when they got home. Gran Lacy could make a warm drink sound like an adventure.

Jules should be there with her grandma. *Even more reason to keep breathing, kiddo.*

Her thoughts shifted to her father, who'd died far too young. She remembered him as a good man. Her mother had already ditched the family after Dalton was born. Now thirty-two years old, she was the middle child. Her brother Camden was thirty-five years old and the oldest on both sides of the family. Jules was closest in age to her cousin Crystal, who was a year older. Her cousin Duke was thirty years old. Cousin Abilene and brother Dalton were the babies of the family at twenty-eight years old.

Six grandchildren raised by saints, if anyone asked Jules.

Jules had no idea where her mother ended up. She didn't care either. Toby had once asked if she was the least bit curious about the woman who gave birth to her. She'd told him no and meant it. Jules didn't know and didn't care. Or, at least, she'd convinced herself it was true. Every once in a while, though, a question popped into her thoughts. Mostly around birthdays and Christmas. She wondered if her mother ever thought about her. If so, why didn't she reach out and try to communicate? Jules wasn't big on social media like so many of her peers, but she had an account. Couldn't her mother look her up? Send a message? Why hadn't she?

Grandpa Lor, short for Lorenzo, waited until Jules turned thirteen before asking if she wanted more information about her mother. He reassured her in the most loving way that her curiosity would be normal and wasn't any sort of betrayal to those who'd raised her.

Jules had decided to give the subject an evening of thought. She'd tossed and turned over the decision of whether to find out more about her mother. The most burning question, of course, being, why did the woman turn her back on her children?

After a long night with little sleep, Jules decided her mother didn't deserve that much attention. Anyone who decided to raise a child and then abandon them wasn't the kind of person Jules wanted to get to know.

Plus, she had a great childhood on her grandparents' paint-horse ranch. Who got to grow up knowing how much they were loved with siblings and cousins who were like sisters and a brother to Jules? During her teenage years, she witnessed families breaking up, causing trauma to her school friends. She saw them being used as weapons in divorces and hating the fact they would have to spend holidays split up.

Despite the circumstances, Jules never felt ignored or unloved. So, no, she had no reason to find her mother. As far as Jules was concerned, she'd buried the woman years ago. Why resurrect the dead?

Not to mention the simple fact her mother hadn't once sent a birthday card or tried to connect. So, really, why bother losing sleep over someone who didn't want you?

Glancing across the river at Toby, seeing him push forward so they could reconnect, kept her walking when she wanted to fall down. The brain was interesting because it was throwing all kinds of reasons at her to sit down and rest. But she knew that meant she would likely never get back up.

Since she couldn't fathom walking all the way to the spot where the river swerved, she focused on taking one step. Then another. And then one more.

The bend wasn't too far upstream. The threat that had been behind her must have decided she wasn't a good enough meal to attack. Unless it still hunted her, biding its time, waiting.

And then Toby's legs buckled. He landed face-first on the opposite shore.

Forget the bend—Jules had to cross now.

TOBY'S LEGS GAVE OUT, and he bit the dust, so to speak. Forcing himself up on his knees and good hand, he managed to sit back on his heels.

Splashing sounds from the opposite shore sent his pulse racing. What was Jules doing?

Before he could tell her that he was fine, she was in the water and swimming toward him. Thankfully, she'd stemmed the bleeding in her neck. By the time she reached shore, he had to help her out of the water.

One look at her told him exactly where they needed to go. The camper.

With every last ounce of strength Toby had, he helped Jules to the camper. Symes had followed them and, with any luck, gone over the waterfall. Toby didn't want the man to die, because that was too easy an out. He did, however, wish him more pain and a lifetime behind bars.

All Toby had to do was recall crime scene pictures from Lila's murder to find enough anger to fuel his steps back to the camper. "Hang in there, okay?"

"I'm good," Jules promised, forcing every forward step.

They were in the same boat, both depleted by the time they stood two feet in front of the camper's door. The need to find shelter and get out of these wet clothes before they both ended up with hypothermia outweighed the risk of Symes waiting inside. He couldn't be in better shape than the two of them. Would he have made it back first?

Or did he meet his death in the water?

The only positive thing about the second option was that Jules would be safe from the bastard.

With a tentative step forward, Toby gripped the door handle. Much like ripping off a Band-Aid, he swung the door open quickly.

Toby didn't realize he was holding his breath until he sighed in relief. The camper was empty. He helped Jules, who insisted she could manage on her own, inside. If Toby had the energy, he would crack a smile. It was just like Jules to want to stand on her own two feet. Her strength was one of many traits he admired about her. But it was those rare moments of vulnerability that caused him to love her. *As a friend*, he felt the need to remind himself.

"We need to get those clothes off you," he said to her as she leaned against the pullout bed that was probably a dining table and chairs during the daytime. Whoever last left this place realized it would most likely be used to bed down for the night, thus the folded blankets.

Toby dipped his shoulder, letting the backpack drop onto the small kitchenette counter. "What do you need first?"

"Wrap...wrist." Jules was barely hanging on. Her teeth were chattering. Those cold, wet clothes had to come off. *Now.*

"We need to undress you, Jules."

"'Bout time," she said, clearly half-delirious at this point. Normally, he would laugh at a crack like that, but under the circumstances, he was concerned. She wasn't thinking straight.

He locked the door behind them, not sure what good it might do. This place wasn't exactly Fort Knox. A half-decent rock could break a window, and it wouldn't take much strength to force the door open. But it was all they had, so it needed to be enough.

Toby placed his gun on the Formica counter and then placed Jules's next to his. He helped her out of her shoulder holster and then her blouse, forcing his gaze from her full breasts, moving behind her to remove any temptation to stare at her silky skin as her chest rose and fell. He'd unsnapped plenty of bras in his time, so this one shouldn't be a problem. Except he had to use his left hand, which trembled. He'd use the excuse of being cold because it was partly true. But the instant flood of heat and flush of unwelcome arousal kept him honest.

Jules was perfect in every way. From those intense blue eyes to hair that looked like a sun-kissed wheat field. She had curves in all the right places. He was a leg man, and hers didn't disappoint. Though, her full breasts drew his gaze more than once, he was embarrassed to admit.

What could he say? In a physical sense, Jules was like staring at perfection. Add her sense of humor, down-to-earth qualities and the fact she had no idea how beautiful she was, and she was almost too good to be true. Like back in high school when the prettiest, most popular girl took an interest in you.

Toby had been too shy to speak to anyone back then. Too shy or too wounded. It didn't matter. The result was the same. He kept to himself, took care of his baby sister and helped his grandmother as best he could once he got his head on straight.

He wouldn't exactly call himself a Goody Two-Shoes back then. But as a kid who had a lot of responsibility on his plate, he kept his rebellious streak in check. Playing football in high school had made him a champion, given him a college scholarship and a future. Without it, he wouldn't have been able to afford the University of Texas at Austin. He wouldn't have a degree in criminal justice, and he sure as hell wouldn't have a career in law enforcement. He'd been good enough to make the team, but a hotshot quarterback from Kerrville started all four years. Riding the bench had been a blow to his ego back then, but now he realized it had also given him time to study and get a degree.

That all being said, the fact Jules had walked straight over to him on the first day he remembered meeting her in the conference room and sat down was still a miracle. Them being best friends was implausible. Toby didn't open up to people. He preferred to keep to himself.

Jules was the difference. She broke down walls by smiling at you. She made you feel like you were a freakin' god just because she chose the chair next to you to sit down in.

Add her intellect into the mix, and he still couldn't understand why she'd picked him to be her friend.

So, the shaky hand with snapping her bra probably had more to do with a jolt of nerves rather than cold. Cold didn't help matters, though.

He also realized that he needed to keep her talking once he could clear the frog in his throat as her bra hit the floor. "I'm still not sure you're remembering our first meeting right." He would know if she'd been in the same room with him before. Any room.

"I am," she said, her words slurred as he helped her slip out of her slacks. A blue blouse and black slacks had no right looking as sexy as they did on her. They looked even better as piles on the floor.

Hooking her thumb onto her lace-and-silk light pink panties, she took those off next. Need welled up, forming a squall inside Toby's chest.

He couldn't find a blanket to wrap her in fast enough to stop the bomb from detonating inside his chest. He'd be lying if he didn't admit to having the occasional thought of what sex between the two of them would be like. His comebacks had always been immediate. It would blow his mind.

Wrong. That wouldn't even come close. It would wreck him for another woman, body and soul.

And then he would have to face a day when he couldn't have her in his life at all.

# Chapter Nine

Jules battled to keep her eyes open. On some level, she understood that if she let them close, they might never open again. Her first thought should probably be how much that would break her family, especially while they dealt with the other crisis. The timing couldn't be worse.

But they weren't the first people who popped into her mind.

Her first thought was Toby. How much he needed her to get through this in case Symes turned out to be the perp behind his sister's brutal murder. How alone he would be without his best friend. How much she couldn't stand the thought of being without him too.

Forget how much her body ached with need when he was this close. Not even her current pain level could completely quash the desire welling inside her.

It also gave her a renewed sense of purpose, so she leaned into it.

After wrapping her in a blanket, Toby attended to her neck wound. The man was beyond amazing, considering he had to use his left hand, ripping open packages with his teeth as he worked quickly and quietly.

"Talk to me, Jules. Tell me about that day."

"You don't think I saw you, but how would I know about

Clingy Carin if I didn't?" she managed to say as her body slowly warmed. Fighting sleep took up the rest of her energy. Talking was easier when her jaw wasn't frozen. The camper might not be much, but it would get them through the night as long as Symes didn't come back for them. His return was a very real possibility that had to be considered.

"Fair point," he admitted as he stripped off his clothes.

Jules immediately cast her gaze down to the pile of clothes on the floor and refocused her attention. She'd been a second too late to avoid seeing a backside so hard she could crack an egg on it. That same backside was also perfectly formed. Those were probably things she shouldn't notice about her best friend. But she couldn't help it. Call it accidental visual contact. Her gaze had been sliding down.

"When I walked into the conference room on my first day, I recognized you immediately," she continued, forcing the words as she opened and closed her mouth a couple of times. She felt like the Tin Man from *The Wizard of Oz*. Too bad there wasn't some kind of magical oil that could get her working again.

If they lived through the night, which was the only possibility she would allow herself to consider, she wanted a large cup of tea and a warm bath.

The naked image of Toby stamped her thoughts. Despite it causing her to use extra energy she couldn't afford to spare, she smiled.

"What's that for?" he managed to ask through a grunt after wrapping himself in a blanket with her help.

"Nothing," she said, clamping her mouth shut. "But you ordered black drip that day and the other time I saw you too."

"You remember my drink?" he asked, moving beside her after draping their garments on counters and chairs to aid in drying, where he took a seat and leaned in. For a split second, it felt sensual, but she realized he was sitting this close for body heat and not because he couldn't stand to be apart any longer.

"Only because it's the same as mine," she said. "And no one goes to a fancy coffee shop to order black coffee when there are caramel macchiatos on the menu, or so it seems."

His laugh was a low rumble from his chest. "I'd say we should lie down, but we can't afford to nod off."

"We have to stay close if we want to keep warm," she said. "Here. Move over here if you can."

Toby did as requested, which had him sitting up and leaning against a wall. This way, they could watch the windows. She managed to scoot in between his thighs, so her back was against his chest. He wrapped an arm around her.

"How's your wrist?"

"Never better," he quipped sarcastically in a tone Toby had mastered.

Feeling his body against hers, along with the rise and fall of his chest, wrapped her in warmth.

Then he whispered, "Being here with you like this is more important than any wrist pain."

He said the words so low that she almost didn't hear them. Except she did. And now she wouldn't be able to erase them from her mind.

They also instantly shifted the mood to the most intimate moment of her life. How could that be? They hadn't held hands, let alone kissed. And yet her body responded like they'd just made out, hot and heavy.

Since being this close to Toby sent heat through her body—which she desperately needed—she didn't move away. She would have under any other circumstance because those words coupled with his arm around her broke down her walls, walls that had been erected out of survival instincts because she couldn't lose her best friend to pursue romance.

Keeping him at arm's length caused its own kind of pain, but it was manageable. Neither discussed their dating life with the other, which kept it neat.

She relaxed, fully exhaling for the first time since this whole ordeal began at the crash. The urge to sleep crept over her like a slow fog inching across the Golden Gate Bridge.

Involuntarily, her eyelids came down.

"Hey, hey, hey." The urgency in Toby's voice cut through, causing her to tense up. "Stay awake. Okay?"

"I'm good," she said, hearing the weakness in her own voice. The momentary boost of energy she got after finding shelter and finally warming up faded. Now her body begged for sleep. He was right, though. She had to stay awake.

Could she?

"I REMEMBER THE first time I saw you," Toby said to Jules. "Every gaze in the room flew to you when you came in."

She shook her head. "Not true."

"Then you weren't in the same conference room I was," he countered, ignoring his own mind-numbing pain. Telling himself that he was fine got him through a whole helluva lot of hard practice sessions in football. He might not have started as QB, but that didn't mean he didn't fully participate in practices. Those sacks racked up in practices and scrimmages. He'd gone in for the starter several times to finish games and receive some time on the clock.

"I was too," Jules said, her words slurring again.

Not a good sign. He needed to keep her awake and talking. At least he'd been able to clean up her wounds and stem the bleeding. Foreheads and necks were bleeders. She'd lost more blood than he was comfortable with, especially since they had no idea how long it would take to be rescued.

No matter how much he hated Symes, Toby wouldn't risk going after the bastard again while Jules was so badly injured. He didn't care about himself, but hurting her to satisfy his revenge was a line he couldn't cross.

Period.

"Did you see Mathers's jaw hit the mahogany table then?" he continued, using the distraction to ease some of his anger at letting Symes get away.

"No," she responded. Her voice had a sleepy quality that shouldn't be sexy. "He hates me."

"Because he can't have you," he pointed out. It was endearing that Jules had no idea every single man with eyes wished they could ask her out.

"Not true," she said, then clarified, "He can't. But that's it."

"Then you explain why every guy stands up when you walk into a room," he said.

"Gentlemen?"

Toby barked out a laugh on that one. "Are you truly that oblivious?"

"What kind of narcissist would I be if I thought every man wanted me when I walked into a room?" she asked.

It was a reasonable question, even if she was off base in her analysis. "Yeah, I get your point there."

"Plus, *you* never wanted me," she said.

Was she delirious?

"That's a lie," he said before he could reel the words in. They needed further explanation. "But I settled on being your best friend so I wouldn't lose you."

"Why do you think you would lose me?" Her breathing slowed, which concerned the hell out of him.

"I'd manage to mess it up between us somehow," he admitted. This wasn't a conversation he'd thought he would ever have with Jules. Not in a million years. Though, to be fair, the words might not have been spoken out loud, but that didn't mean they didn't hang in the air. There were little comments between both of them where he'd picked up hints.

"Why?"

"Because we both know that I'm awful at long-term commitment," he explained. Was he admitting too much? No, he reasoned. Because she wouldn't remember this conversation once she was fully conscious again. This was a rare moment where he could let his guard down and tell her how he really felt.

Well, maybe not admit the full monty. But she deserved to know how much he cared about her. So much so that he wouldn't risk blowing what they had for what might be the best sex of his life.

*What if you could go the distance?*

Toby quashed the thought. He would royally mess up a relationship with Jules. Besides, she was too good for him anyway. If he didn't push her away, she would still end up hurt. It was the dark cloud that always hovered right above his head. Eventually, everyone he loved would die or be killed. This wasn't a bout of self-pity. It was a reality that he'd learned to accept. And he couldn't bring that curse down on Jules.

"What if it would be different between us?" Jules must not realize what she was saying. She didn't want a relationship with him. She'd been clear about their friendship too.

"I'm sure it would," he finally said after a thoughtful pause. "And that's what scares the hell out of me."

"Toby," Jules started before heaving a sigh that scared him. For a split second, he thought it might be her last.

"Yes, sweetheart," he responded when he realized her pulse was still going strong for the circumstances.

"If I told you that I love you, would that change your mind?" Jules asked with the most vulnerable tone, a tone that brought out all his protective instincts.

As much as he should probably warn her away from a guy like him, he didn't have it inside him to say those words while she was in his arms. Even soaked with river water, her hair had a hint of jasmine scent. Jasmine was his favorite.

"It might," he admitted in a moment of weakness.

"Good," she said. "Remind me never to say those words to you again."

The knife took a second to pull out of the center of his chest. She was right, though. They didn't need to cross that line into real feelings for each other, no matter how strongly his brain put up an argument it would be the best relationship of his life. It also said that they deserved to know the kind of real love, real passion, that would shatter all their walls.

But he couldn't allow himself to go there.

Because losing her would leave him shattered too. And he had no idea how he would ever be able to pick up the pieces again.

"You won't," he whispered. "There's no need to remind you." Once this ordeal was over, she wouldn't likely remember saying any of this. It was weakness talking plus some primal biological urge to bond with someone when circumstances became life and death. So he didn't need to repeat anything said in this camper.

*Shame.* A growing part of him wanted to throw logic out the window and go for it with Jules. Now that she'd given him an inkling that she might be interested in doing the same thing, his attraction increased tenfold.

Having her in his arms felt like the most perfect thing in the world. Loving her was the easy part. It was as natural as breathing. It was the thought of losing her—and he would—that sucked the air out of the room.

Toby needed to focus on something more productive or risk falling in too deep with his emotions when it came to Jules. There was a point of no return, and he was stepping dangerously close to the line.

He'd been so deep in his own thoughts that he realized Jules had drifted off. Should he let her rest? She was peaceful.

After checking her pulse, he decided it was strong enough to risk letting her get a little sleep.

Plus, he didn't want to move her while her body was against his and the world righted itself for a few moments, moments that would go by in a flash. Once they regained some strength, they could figure out their next move. Even Toby was realistic enough to acknowledge they couldn't continue the search for Symes. At this point, their survival had to come first.

Toby couldn't be certain how long he'd been asleep after he drifted off, but his eyes blinked open the second he heard movement outside the camper.

Instinctively, he sat straight up and scanned his surroundings. Jules didn't move. Not a good sign.

He gently shifted out from underneath her. The threat had to be dealt with first. He quickly dressed and tossed Jules's now-dry garments on the bed.

Grabbing his weapon from the countertop where he'd left it last night, he palmed it in his left hand. Not having use of his right hand made everything ten times harder.

Moving to the slatted window without making a sound, he searched for a spot where he could take a look at what was outside without the predator realizing it. Make no mistake about it—Symes was every bit as much an apex predator as a mountain lion. If he'd figured out they'd circled back, he planned on hunting them down as prey.

*Guess what, jerk wad—no dice.* Hell would freeze over before Toby allowed this monster to take another life on his watch.

A deep well of anger swirled low in the pit of his stomach as he looked for the right place to check outside. He refused to give himself away before he was ready. The element of surprise could mean the difference between life and death.

It was quiet. Too quiet out there.

Toby didn't help keep Jules alive last night to let this ordeal end with Symes winning. Could he exit out a window and get the drop on Symes?

Or was he overreacting to a wild boar or deer in search of a morning meal, none the wiser anyone was inside the camper?

An animal would have moved by now. Unless it had killed its prey and was already eating.

Out here, you were either predator or prey. Nature didn't discriminate and it didn't play favorites. Law of survival of the fittest ruled.

Measuring his breath so he didn't make an unnecessary noise, Toby leaned toward the slats of the mini blinds on the door. He might be able to get a peek outside through the small hole where the string wound through to lift the blinds.

Taking in a slow breath and then exhaling just as slowly to calm his racing pulse, Toby found a peephole.

Someone moved.

He couldn't get a good look at the person before they shifted out of view. All he'd seen was a dark-colored shirt. Navy blue or black.

What had Symes been wearing yesterday?

If memory served, he'd been in a prison-orange jumpsuit. Would he have gone back to the chopper to change clothes with Crawford after jumping into the river? Symes would have needed dry clothes to survive the night or risk freezing to death. He hadn't come back to the camper.

Did he believe they would head to the chopper for safety? Or possibly to remove the captain's clothes and use them for their own survival purposes? It sickened Toby to think someone would be capable of such a thing, but he dealt with real scumbags, who raped and pillaged any chance they got. They used any excuse that served them to become the felons they were. Rough childhood? Check. Toby knew a thing or two about being dealt a bad hand. He knew how neglect felt before his grandmother stepped in. And he knew what it was like to lose those he loved.

Didn't make him a criminal.

Or did it?

Hadn't he considered taking Symes down by any means after finding out he might be the bastard who'd killed Lila?

Toby shoved the uncomfortable realization aside. If push came to shove, Toby would do the right thing despite the line being blurred in this case. This was a one-off and didn't define his career.

Besides, there was another piece of information that he hadn't shared with anyone. The perp who'd killed his sister mailed Toby an artifact every year on the anniversary of her murder, taunting him. Even a tame animal came out fighting when injured or cornered.

Before he could get too far down that road, something with the force of a battering ram slammed against the door.

The second hit came before Toby could react.

Jules sucked in a breath, sat up. A look of shock stamped her features. "Toby?"

Afraid couldn't be the way he remembered her.

# Chapter Ten

Jules dressed and then scrambled for her 9 mm, which was sitting on top of the counter in between the small metal sink and a two-burner stovetop. "Is he here?"

The third smack into the camper door sent the gun flying across the small space. It slammed against the wall and then tumbled onto the ground.

Standing at the doorway, much to her relief, was a SWAT team.

Jules immediately identified herself and put her hands in the air.

"A ranger passed by this camper at 6:00 a.m. after another located the chopper," a SWAT officer who'd identified himself as Landry Thomas said. His face creased with concern as Jules stumbled backward before tripping on the bed. Getting up too fast had been a mistake.

"Help is here," Landry said to them.

Toby sat down as relief seemed to buckle his knees.

They were safe. Help had arrived.

"What about Symes?" Toby immediately asked.

Landry shrugged. "I'm sorry. He hasn't been apprehended as of yet. Rest assured we have a lot of manpower on this one. No one wants this monster to roam around free."

Those were the last words Jules remembered hearing before she blacked out.

WAKING UP TO the sounds of beeping machines and no sign of Toby caused Jules to sit up and spam the nurse's call button.

A short, squat nurse in scrubs with a kind face and spiky hair came running into the room. "Everything all right in here?"

"I'm, um… No," Jules said, still disoriented and woozy. She recognized the feeling of pain medication because she'd been in scrapes before that landed her in the hospital. Nothing to this degree but enough to have to take the occasional pill. "I'm fine. I think." She glanced around, blinking to bring water to her dry eyes. "My partner is—"

"In the next room," the nurse said as she moved to Jules's side.

"How is he? How's Toby?"

"I'm Pamela, by the way. And right now, I'm more concerned with how you're doing." She went about checking dials and reading monitors.

Jules didn't like the nurse evading the question about Toby. Her pulse kicked up a few notches, as evidenced by the beeping machine beside her bed. She threw covers off and reached for her IV, ready to yank it out.

"Hold on there," Pamela soothed. "HIPAA laws prevent me from discussing another patient's condition with non-family members." The nurse shot a warning look at Jules. "However, if I could say anything, I would reassure you that your partner is still under sedation but came through surgery fine. His wrist has been set."

"Surgery?" Oh, no. How badly had Toby been injured? What did that mean?

"If you promise not to rip out your IV, I'll grab a wheel-chair and take you for a 'walk' so you can see for yourself." Pamela stood there like a mother who'd just scolded a two-year-old for throwing a temper tantrum.

"I'll wait right here," Jules said.

"Good," Pamela fired back. She seemed spunky and came across as someone you didn't want to have angry at you. "We can talk about how you're doing on our stroll."

"Deal," Jules said. She would have promised anything to be able to see how Toby was doing with her own eyes.

Pamela disappeared, returning not two minutes later with a wheelchair. "We'll have to untangle you from a couple of monitors, but the IV comes with us. I can hook it here." She pointed to a metal bar coming up from the back of the wheelchair. Jules didn't care how the nurse got her on the move. All she cared about was seeing Toby and knowing he would pull through.

For a split second, she thought about Symes.

"Do you know if an escaped rapist has been recovered?" she asked the nurse, figuring the recapture would make national news.

Pamela frowned as she shook her head. "I'm afraid not. Your boss has been stopping by, asking the nursing staff to take the best possible care of both of you. I got nosy and asked around, found out why you are here. You and your partner are lucky to be alive, from what I've heard."

"Stories like these get blown out of proportion," Jules said.

"Your family has been calling on the hour too," Pamela said. "The attention you've gotten in here made us wonder if you were some kind of celebrity." Pamela paused. "Turns out, you two are actual heroes, not just overhyped Hollywood types."

As much as Jules appreciated the sentiment, all she could think about right now was making sure Toby was alive and going to be fine.

"Why was my partner in surgery?" Jules asked, then added, "Hypothetically."

"It would have been from shrapnel from a door splintering off and spearing him below the rib cage on his right side," Pamela whispered as she helped Jules into the chair.

After a couple of minutes of tinkering that felt like hours, they were on the move.

Jules's heart pounded the inside of her chest as she was wheeled out of her room and into the next. The blinds were drawn. The curtains closed. More of those annoying beeps sounded. Except there was an element of comfort to them in Toby's room because it meant his heart was beating just fine.

"Push me closer so I can see him?" Jules asked. The nurse had stopped after taking two steps inside the room. She needed to see him first. Then she would call her family to let them know she was awake and fine.

Pamela complied. "I'll leave you two alone for a few minutes."

"Thank you," Jules said as she waited for the nurse to exit before wheeling herself to Toby's bed. His was closest to the window, where it was darkest.

Seeing him calmed her pulse a few notches. Knowing he would be okay helped. Being here with him was nothing short of a miracle.

Jules drew a blank on how they'd ended up in the hospital. The last thing she remembered was Landry telling her Symes hadn't been recaptured.

She reached over to touch Toby's hand through the metal bars of his hospital bed, where he was flat on his back. The familiar jolt of electricity at the point of contact provided comfort. Did it mean he was still vibrant? Alive? That she was? That their connection was as strong as ever?

Resisting the urge to pull her hand away, she entwined their fingers and rested her head on the cold metal.

"Time's up," the nurse said, returning after several minutes passed without a hint of movement from Toby other than the beeping machines reassuring her that his heart was still beating.

"Mind if I stay a little while longer?" Jules asked.

"You should get back to—"

"Please," Jules cut in. "My partner means the world to me, and I want to be here when he opens his eyes in case he's disoriented."

"That might be a while," Pamela said softly.

"Any chance I can have my room changed to the spare bed in this room?" Jules continued, figuring you didn't get what you didn't ask for. Besides, all anyone could ever tell you was no, and then you'd be right back where you started. No harm done.

"I'll see if that can be arranged, but I can't make any promises," Pamela said in a moment of compassion as she walked out.

"Thank you," Jules said from the bottom of her heart. She couldn't imagine being taken away from Toby while he was heavily sedated. They'd already lost Symes, who could be targeting his next victim by now, for all she knew. If she wasn't so woozy and tired, frustration would nail her. At this point, she didn't have the energy.

*We aren't the only ones who want him to be caught.*

There were multiple agencies with feet on the ground and eyes in the sky tracking Symes. Good news could come any minute.

*Eleven years.*

The reminder he'd evaded arrest for eleven years slammed into her as if she'd run full force into a brick wall. At least now, law enforcement had a general idea of his location. Besides, he might have died in the river after jumping in to follow them. He could have gone over the edge of the waterfall. His body might not show up for days or weeks.

*He might already be dead.*

If not, Toby wouldn't be able to let the case go. Especially not after the realization Symes could have been his sister's killer.

Jules battled the urge to close her eyes again. She wanted to be wide-awake when Toby opened his.

Minutes ticked by. Before she knew it, an hour had slipped past.

Pamela returned, knocking softly at the door before entering, as though the room was sacred space. It was to Jules.

"You should probably go back to your room to eat," Pamela urged in a quiet, almost reverent tone.

Jules lifted her head long enough to shake it.

"I thought that might be your stance," Pamela said. She stepped into the hallway for a few seconds before returning with a tray of food. "Let's get you set up." Pamela grabbed the tray table from the next bed after setting the food on top.

This time, Jules nodded. She wasn't hungry. Nor could she think about eating while Toby was still in this condition. Pain medication always affected her stomach too, so there was that. But arguing with a determined-looking Pamela would be counterproductive.

"I'll check on you in a few minutes, okay?" Pamela's question was rhetorical. The nurse was coming back. The fact she cared about her patients came through in her tone. "There's water in the white jug with a straw, but I can bring you a Coke or juice if you'd rather."

"Water's good." Jules studied the nurse for a few seconds. "Thank you, Pamela."

Those words netted a genuine smile from an otherwise concerned face. "You're welcome." She started toward the door and then stopped a few steps short. "I know you're worried about your partner, and it's obvious to anyone paying attention you have a special bond. I can't help thinking that he would want you to eat something."

Jules cracked a melancholy smile. "He would get on my backside if I didn't at least try."

"So you will?" Pamela pressed. "For him?"

"Yes," Jules said, picking up the burger that didn't look half bad. "For him."

"Good" was all Pamela said before exiting the room.

Before Jules could get the burger to her mouth, Toby cleared his throat.

"You gonna share that burger?" he asked. His voice was the closest to heaven she'd ever been.

"Do you want a bite?" she asked, smiling a genuine smile this time.

"Water first," he croaked with an attempt to smile back. He winced instead.

"Take it easy there, Ward. Can't have you busting another rib," Jules joked.

Toby gave her a look. He was famous for being able to communicate paragraphs with one of his signature glances.

Rather than try to get up, Jules just gave Toby her water jug. The thing was gigantic, and she was sure an IV had already given her plenty of fluids. He could take down the entire jug.

After taking a sip, his expression turned serious. He wanted to know about Symes.

Jules shook her head. She didn't have the heart to say the

words out loud. Symes escaping would haunt her until the man was recaptured without any additional lives lost. Anything less and she would never be able to forgive herself.

Toby's gaze intensified as he stared at the closed mini blinds behind her. A muscle in his jaw ticked. "Have you spoken to Mack?" Herbert Mackenzie was their supervisor.

"No," she admitted, offering her burger.

"I was joking before," Toby said. "You eat it."

Jules took a bite and then chewed. "I was waiting for you to wake up before I contacted Mack. Didn't want to leave your side."

"How long have I been out?" Toby asked.

"I woke up a few hours ago," she said. "I'd have to ask the nurse to be certain, but you were in surgery, and I was next door at least twenty-four hours."

Toby searched around the nightstand next to him, along with the tray table. "Have you seen my phone?"

"No," she admitted. "Haven't thought about either of our phones, to be honest. My biggest concern was making sure you woke up."

He reached for her hand and then squeezed before finding the button that made his bed move to sitting. Any movement caused him to wince. Then he took inventory of his physical condition. "I look like I've been through hell."

"We both have," she said, mustering an empty smile before taking another bite. Now that he was awake, her stomach decided it could take down some food. "Do you want a french fry?"

"Do you think they just call them 'fries' in France?" Toby quipped, some of his usual easygoing sense of humor returning.

"Oh, Mr. Funny, coming back with the witty comments already?" she teased, trying to lighten the intense mood.

"Gotta do my part to keep you on your toes, Remington," he fired right back. At least they were going through the motions, pretending that both of their lives hadn't just been devastated. "How did your family take the news?"

"Haven't talked to them yet," she admitted. "All I could think of was my partner."

"I'm honored," Toby quipped with a dramatic gesture, that all-too-familiar wall coming up between them. He picked up a couple of fries and popped them in his mouth.

"Good. You should be," Jules shot back. Their usual lighthearted banter felt hollow now. Those conversations had lifted their spirits during rough times but couldn't make a dent now.

"How are you doing, Jules?" He caught her gaze and held it. A moment of vulnerability crossed his features. "Be honest."

"I feel like I've been in a car crash with no seat belt," she said. "Not to mention the prisoner I was sitting on got away, now able to maim, rape and murder, while I'm trying to choke down a burger in a hospital while my best friend comes out of surgery. So, yeah, pretty crappy."

"Yeah, I figured." Leave it to Toby to see through her fake smile. He frowned. "Same here. What are we going to do about it?"

## Chapter Eleven

Jules was already shaking her head before Toby finished his sentence.

"What do you mean, 'What are we going to do about it?'" Jules asked, looking incredulous as she studied him. "You're going to heal, and we're going to let our colleagues catch this bastard."

For a hot second, Toby debated telling her that hell would freeze over before he stayed in a hospital bed while Symes roamed free. What good would it do? Jules would worry. She would try to keep a better eye on him so he didn't slip out and go off half-cocked after Symes.

"We're on medical leave from work," Jules continued with a heavy dose of shock mixed with anger in her voice. Because she knew him well enough to know that he wouldn't be able to let this go. "We're both going to take a step back, Toby. Because our jobs would be on the line. And we wouldn't just be insubordinate if we attempted to arrest Symes on our own, and, heaven forbid, he ended up dead. We'd be under investigation. The possible link to your sister's murder would come up, and then we would be on the wrong side of the courtroom, needing a defense attorney. Is that what you want?"

"No, of course not," he admitted. Jules made good points.

"And if that doesn't convince you of what a bad idea going after Symes unauthorized would be, how about the fact that neither one of us is operating at half speed, let alone full speed," she pointed out. "That's not exactly operating on a level playing field, is it?"

All the logic in the world wouldn't stop him from wanting to be the one to catch Symes and ensure justice was served. As stubborn as Toby could be, he'd never been unprofessional or reckless. He took wearing a badge seriously and understood the responsibility that came along with the job.

Could he step away?

One glance at the bandage just below his ribs, the soft cast on his right wrist and the rest of his injuries said he needed to listen to his friend and trust the system to work. If, once he was healed enough to go back to work, Symes was still at large, Toby could put in a request to be assigned to apprehend the bastard.

He heaved a sigh that hurt like hell as he exhaled. Were his ribs cracked too?

"You're right, Jules."

She blinked a couple of times, clearly stunned at his about-face. "Hold on. Say that again."

He shot her a look. "You heard me."

"Did I, though?" she asked with a smug look on her face.

"You're right," he conceded. "You made a helluva lot of sense just now." He grabbed another fry, chewed and swallowed it, along with his pride. "The best course of action is to heal and follow protocol."

"I'm glad you see it that way, Toby," she said, all signs of smugness gone now. "Because I honestly didn't think I'd get through to you."

"You have my word," he confirmed.

*You're the only one who could, Jules.*

"Am I that stubborn?" he asked, grabbing a few more fries. "Do bulls have horns?"

Logic said he had to walk away from the case. Could he keep his emotions in check enough to follow through with his promise?

"ARE YOU SURE they should be releasing you from the hospital so soon?" Jules's question brought a smile to Toby's face.

She'd insisted the nurse move all her belongings to the bed next to Toby so they could share a room.

"*You're* being released," he countered.

"I didn't have surgery twelve hours ago," she said with a cocked eyebrow.

He motioned toward the machine loudly beeping his heartbeats. "No one gets rest inside a hospital. They've done everything they can do for me, and I'm out of the woods. There's no point in keeping me here, running up the bill."

Jules bit down on her bottom lip—a lip he shouldn't find mesmerizing considering their friendship status.

"I guess that makes sense," she reasoned. "Then it's settled."

"What is?" he asked.

"You're coming home with me," she stated.

"I hate to point out the obvious, but you're not in much better shape," he said on a chuckle that hurt like hell. It felt like a baseball bat had been taken to his ribs.

Jules clamped her mouth shut. Whatever snappy comeback she had died on her tongue. "At least we'll be able to keep each other company."

Toby nodded. Part of him needed Jules to know why he hated Lila's murderer from the deep recesses of his soul. "He mails me mementos every year on the anniversary of her murder."

Jules's expression softened. "What kind of animal would do that?"

"The theory about Lila being a feather in this bastard's cap developed after I called in the FBI to handle the evidence," he explained.

"I'm so sorry, Toby," she said with so much compassion that he wanted to reach out and take her in his arms, forget the past. He wished he could do just that...forget. But Symes, if he was the perp after all, refused to let Toby move on.

"He taunts you," she said. "Which is all the more reason not to play into his hands."

"Sounds logical," he admitted. "Would you be able to walk away?"

"I can't begin to know what I would do if I was in your shoes. Honestly. I can't imagine a worse hell. I just wish you'd told me all this before."

"Why?" he asked. "What would that have done?"

"You wouldn't have had to go through it alone," she said. "I could have supported you better." She shook her head. "I could have been a better friend."

"Impossible," he shot back. "You've always been a great friend." Why did the word *friend* sound so hollow now?

Did Toby really want to know the answer to that question?

He decided the topic was better left alone.

Before he could ask about her family now that they were on the subject, Herbert Mackenzie—aka Mack or Sherbert, depending on their mood—walked in.

"You haven't returned my calls," Herbert said to Toby after a perfunctory greeting to Jules. Their supervisor pulled up a chair in between their beds. Being in a hospital gown while meeting with his boss was just about the most awkward thing Toby had experienced to date. Thankfully, he wasn't standing up with his backside to the door when Mack walked in, or they both would have a reason to be embarrassed.

"No, sir," Toby said.

"There a reason you decided not to check in with me?" Mack asked.

"No, sir," Toby repeated.

"Good," Mack said. "Because I've been worried about two of the best marshals my district has ever seen."

"We're being released," Toby said.

Mack's gaze shifted to Jules for confirmation. She nodded.

"Sounds like good news," Mack said. He was middle-aged with a potbelly and a comb-over. But the man was tough as nails when he needed to be and could outrun half the sprinters Toby had ever met. You'd never find a better person to have your back. "You look like hell, though. Is releasing you a good idea?" A small bit of humor creeped out of their normally stern-faced supervisor.

"That's what I said," Jules piped in.

"You two planning to team up on me all night?" Toby quipped.

"We can't," Jules shot back. "You're being released, remember?"

Mack chuckled as he leaned forward, clasping his hands. A couple of seconds passed before his expression morphed back to its usual state: serious.

"I could have lost both of you," he said with a heavy voice.

"We made it," Jules reassured him.

"Comms didn't go out on the flight by accident," Mack informed them. "I'm not sure how we got lucky and the two of you survived, but I don't intend to let anything like this ever happen again."

"You couldn't have known the chopper would go down," Jules said.

"The site is still being investigated, but foul play is suspected," Mack told them. Toby caught on the second Mack said comms had been tinkered with.

Jules muttered the same curse Toby was thinking.

"Was someone on the inside involved?" Toby asked. "Captain Crawford?" As much as he wanted to respect the deceased, it was a fair question.

Mack shrugged. "The only thing I know for certain is that I won't rest until I have answers."

Having someone cover Symes's tracks from the inside could be how he'd escaped capture for eleven years. No one said it outright, but the others had to be thinking it at this point.

"You'll keep us informed," Toby said.

Mack nodded. "Here's the thing. You two were aboard, so someone will be coming to speak to you too."

"As in, we were part of this?" Toby said.

"Someone in the Bureau noticed Symes had a tattoo similar to the one in your sister's case," Mack stated.

"And this person thinks I would risk the lives of two innocent people to kill Symes when I could just slit his throat instead?" Toby didn't hide his disgust.

"Accountability," Mack said. "That's the theory being bantered around." He held a hand up. "It's unbelievable, but we need to take all theories under consideration. Becoming defensive will only make our office look like we have something to hide."

"We don't," Toby felt the need to confirm, even though

nothing in Mack's body language or expression said he needed the reassurance.

"Goes without saying," Mack said.

"Does this mean the agency investigating believes that I'm somehow involved?" Jules asked.

"Guilty by association?" Toby added. He could see how an investigator who didn't know either of them from Adam might draw a conclusion that Jules would do anything to help Toby without taking into account her character. Because if the investigator knew her personally, they would realize she would never willingly break the law. She would argue and fight until her last breath to stop him from doing something that could hurt him in the long run or end his career. And then she would walk away.

"I've given my statement endorsing your innocence, covering all bases," Mack stated. "It's no secret the two of you are close friends."

"Which means people will suspect me too," Jules said, coming to the same conclusion.

The realization that Toby could in no way, shape or form go after Symes without implicating Jules struck like a sledgehammer to the center of his chest. His actions would reflect on her. He'd come to the understanding that he couldn't go after Symes earlier. The point was being hammered home with this conversation. The new development that his actions would be under a microscope slammed into him.

Being treated like a criminal didn't sit well.

"Jules's name shouldn't be associated with mine," he said. "Period." Causing his best friend to come under scrutiny when she was innocent made his good hand fist.

"You know how these things go," Mack said, sounding just as defeated. "We have to let this run its course."

Toby did know. The fact frustrated him to no end when Symes was the one out there raping and murdering.

"He's been taunting you for years, Toby," Mack said, taking his tone down to a more personal level. "You've cooperated. Turned over evidence. But anyone who puts themselves in your position doesn't come up on the good side of the law if they get a chance to avenge their sister's murder. It's as simple as that."

Toby understood more than he wanted to admit. Learning Symes could possibly be connected to his sister caused him to see red.

"If I'm completely honest, I could have crossed a line in the heat of the moment if I'd been given the chance," he said to his boss. "Jules wouldn't have allowed it. She talked me off the ledge and tried to force me to see reason when I was blinded by revenge." Even more reason she shouldn't have to come under scrutiny. Because he also realized investigators could nitpick someone's career to death. Possibly even find a small infraction that would be brought to light, examined and possibly used against Jules at a later date.

"You would have done the same for me," Jules said.

"Since the two of you are under investigation, you won't be able to work any assignments together for a while," Mack said, bringing the conversation back on track.

"Understandable," Jules said.

"Still isn't fair," Toby added.

"Maybe not," Mack said. "But I have every intention of protecting you both to the best of my ability. If that means you aren't in the office on the same days, so be it."

"What about our personal time?" Jules asked.

The question hit Toby hard, even though he understood her need to separate herself from him.

"You can do whatever you want on your own time," Mack

stated. "I have no jurisdiction there." He paused, then issued a sharp sigh. "Neither of you deserve the scrutiny you're about to be under. That's what I wanted to come down here and tell you personally. But I have to follow protocol and allow the investigation."

"Okay," she said.

Mack turned to Jules. "Your leave begins as soon as you're cleared from medical. I don't want you coming back to work until your grandparents are better."

Toby didn't know how he would get through any of this without Jules. But he was a cement block tied around her neck. He couldn't let himself drag her to the ocean floor along with himself, no matter how much it hurt to do any of this without her.

# Chapter Twelve

Mack explained that he had someone waiting outside to take them home before excusing himself and ambling out of the hospital room. As he exited, a flurry of activity began as part of the patient release process. Jules gave her electronic signature several times before being cleared to get dressed. She slipped into dirty clothes, wishing she had something clean to wear.

While Toby dressed—with help that he grumbled about— Jules provided an update to her family in their group chat. She was too tired to explain everything but reassured everyone that she was okay and that she was cleared to head home.

There'd been no change with her grandparents, so not a lot of updates there. Jules would head home, get a night or two of rest and then pack up to head back to Mesa Point so she could take her turn watching over their beloved grandparents.

Toby hadn't said two words to her since Mack left. She was beginning to worry that he planned to shut her out.

"Ready?" she asked her friend, figuring they could talk through whatever caused him to close up on her during the long car ride to her house.

"I'll figure out my own ride," he said, dismissing her with his tone.

"Hold on a minute," Jules said. "What's that all about?"

"You're better off without me," he said, almost so low she didn't hear him.

"Get your stuff and let's go," she said with the voice she used when there was no room for argument.

Nurses arrived with wheelchairs when tension was about to bubble over.

"We're here to spring you out of jail," one of the nurses said with a little more cheer than the situation called for. Talk about not being able to read the room.

Toby mumbled something that Jules couldn't quite pick up and didn't dare ask about. He didn't put up an argument. She'd learned when to be quiet when it came to her friend.

Once they were out of the hospital and safely tucked inside the back of an SUV with blacked-out windows, she spoke to the driver. "We're going to my town house." She rattled off the address.

Toby started to protest, so she reached over and touched his forearm. He clamped his mouth closed, settled low in the seat and closed his eyes.

"Does this mean we aren't talking anymore?" she asked.

"You're better off without me," he repeated.

"Is that really what you think, Toby? Because that hurts."

"I'm hurting you, Jules. Being my friend is bad for you and your career." He didn't look at her. Instead, he turned to face the window.

"Your friendship is one of the best things that ever happened to me," she said, trying to keep her emotions in check. "Plus, we'll get through this investigation because neither one of us did anything wrong. It's absurd anyone would think we would intentionally damage the chopper, if for no other reason than the fact we care about each other."

Toby didn't speak, which was a good sign this time.

"Besides, what kind of person would I be if I ducked out on you now?" she asked.

"A smart one," he said quietly.

"If the situation were reversed, would you be able to turn your back on me?"

"Not the same thing, Jules."

"Really?" she asked. "Because it looks the same to me."

"You have every reason to live, Jules. You have a family who would miss you if you were gone," he pointed out. "I have nothing. No one."

"What are you talking about?" she asked. "You have me."

"I'm jeopardizing you," he stated. "If you were smart, you'd cut bait and run."

"Let's say, for argument's sake, that I'm not smart," she countered. "What happens then? Are you going to shut me out?"

Toby was quiet for a long moment. Then came, "You know I can't do that."

"Then don't do it now," she said. "Talk to me. Lean on me. Let me help."

"What if it drags you down?"

"Then I'll deal with that," she said. She had no intention of allowing him to go through this ordeal alone. "You don't deserve any of this either. Surely you see that."

He nodded without a whole lot of enthusiasm.

"Let's get to my house and try to rest," she said. "If you're not with me, I'll worry about you. So we might as well stick together at this point."

"Wrong conclusions could be drawn if we're noticed together," he said.

"Do you think I care about what other people think?" She didn't.

"Maybe you should, Jules. We're talking criminal charges if this thing goes south," he said.

"You're not a criminal, Toby," she said. "You don't deserve to be treated like one."

"Knowing that I'm under investigation makes me want to find him, Jules."

"I had the same thought," she said. "Part of me wants to do something to prove our innocence and right the situation again. If we hadn't lost him, we wouldn't be in this predicament."

"No, we wouldn't."

"But we have to trust the justice system will work for us too," she said. "If we don't, our badges do us no good."

"Damn," he said. "I hate when you're right."

"What did you say?" she teased, thankful that she'd been able to break through his walls even just a little. Was it enough?

Time would tell.

TOBY WASN'T SURE how long he'd been asleep by the time the SUV pulled up in front of Jules's town house. The first ray of sunlight peeked across the landscape. Jules lived in a cul-de-sac in a small community northwest of San Antonio as her primary address. However, she traveled most of the time for her job, same as him, so she was barely home long enough to enjoy her two-story town house.

"Hey," he said quietly to the sleeping beauty next to him.

Jules sat up with a start. Sucked in a breath as her gaze darted around. Her being on edge was no doubt the result of what they'd been through in the last forty-eight hours, give or take. The effects could last days or weeks.

"You're fine," he reassured her. He knew better than to touch her until she got her bearings, or he might end up with an elbow jab to the face.

"Toby?" she asked, but the question was rhetorical. He hated how small and vulnerable her voice sounded.

"Right here, Jules," he soothed. "I'm here."

"I fell asleep," she stated as she figured out where she was and how she got here.

"We're home," he said. "Let's get out and get you to bed."

"Nice try, Toby," she quipped. Her sense of humor returning was a good sign.

The driver parked as close to her front door as possible. He exited the vehicle and helped her out first, shouldering her backpack before leading her to the front door. Toby could walk to the door on his own. He didn't need anyone's help.

He exited the vehicle, wanting to be the one who helped Jules inside.

He'd slept most of the ride, waking on and off. He did some of his best thinking in the in between sleep and awake state while he powered down and recharged his battery.

The investigation made sense from an outsider's point of view. If he could set aside the fact he was involved and knew he was innocent, it made sense for an agency to question the motivation of everyone involved. Captain Crawford had died. The man didn't deserve his fate. So, yeah, Toby could set aside his own personal frustration at being treated like a criminal when he thought about a spouse losing a partner or a child losing a father.

Toby wasn't upset about the investigation as much as the reality Symes had bested him. The man had gotten away. Why the hell would karma be on a murderer's side?

That was one of many questions that would most likely

never be answered in his lifetime, despite his fundamental belief that the good guys almost always won.

Following Jules and the driver inside, Toby realized he'd been in his own world, forgetting to ask the driver his name. He rectified the situation immediately by putting out his hand and introducing himself to the six-foot-two-inch driver, who looked like he could start for the Dallas Cowboys on the defensive line.

"Rick Dane," the driver said, taking the offering and returning a firm shake. "It's an honor to be your driver today, sir."

"Call me Toby," he instructed, offering to take the backpack.

Rick shook his head. "Sorry, si... Toby. The boss gave explicit instructions for me to take care of any bags. This is all you have between the two of you."

"I got it now," Jules stated.

Rick made a motion to set it onto the table in the hallway instead. "Okay?"

"Of course," Jules said, ever the diplomat.

"Is there anything else either of you need before I leave?" Rick asked.

"No, thank you," Jules stated. "We have phone apps for food delivery. I put in an order that should be delivered sometime in the next hour on the way home and tacos too."

Toby gave her a look. "When did that happen?"

"While you were asleep," she said before turning back to Rick. "We have everything we need. Thank you for getting us home safely."

"You're welcome," Rick said. Toby was happy the man didn't say *my pleasure*, as so many had started saying. He liked a simple *you're welcome* because he knew that—most of the time, at least—no employee making fifteen dollars an hour or less was all that pleased serving fast food, no matter how good the nuggets might be. *You're welcome* was more honest, if anyone asked him.

After walking Rick to the door to personally thank him, Toby turned to Jules. "How are you doing really?"

"Honestly?" she asked. "All I want is a shower and clean clothes."

"Go do it," he said. "I'll handle deliveries."

"Are you sure?" she asked. "You must want the same things."

"We'll go in turns in case food shows up," he said.

"Here, take my phone," she offered. "I'll unlock the screen so you don't have to worry about a password."

He cocked an eyebrow, unsure if he wanted any personal messages popping up while it was in his charge. "You sure about that?"

"Don't be weird," she said, holding it out on the flat of her palm. "Take it."

Toby did, noticing the familiar jolt of electricity that came with making skin-to-skin contact with Jules.

"And don't read my personal texts," she stated with a whole lot of attitude.

"Wouldn't dream of it," he said with dramatic flair. "I'll just be on the couch."

"Um, hold on," she said, running upstairs and down in a matter of a few seconds. "You left these clothes after we got caught in the mud hiking and had to strip down."

"Hey, I used my spare joggers that I always keep in the back of my vehicle," he argued.

"Shame," she said with another one of those smiles that caused a knot to form inside his chest. "But these will come in handy after you shower." He noticed the clothes were folded on top of a beach towel.

"Use the towel so you don't get all that gunk from your clothes on my new couch," she said.

"Got it, Sarge," he quipped. He would salute if his right hand wasn't in a sling and his left full of her cell, along with the pile she'd just placed on top. "And thanks for washing my clothes." He managed to drop the bundle onto the couch without it spilling over. Next, he pulled out the beach towel and draped it over the cream fabric. "Happy now?"

"You know I am," she said before heading back upstairs.

Jules's two-level town house had a sitting area almost immediately after you walked in the door. The L-shaped sofa was new and looked like something he could really sink into. A flat-screen TV had been mounted over the fireplace. He should know how difficult it had been to install considering he'd done it himself. Even looking at it now, his chest puffed out at the good job he'd done. Bonus? He'd shaved off installation costs for Jules.

The all-white kitchen had a farm sink and stainless-steel appliances. The white marble island had a couple of bar chairs tucked into one side.

In the next hour and a half, the fridge was full, and they were both showered and in clean clothes.

"Are you hungry?" Jules asked as he joined her at the kitchen table.

"Some," he admitted. He refused to take more medication than absolutely necessary, and the pain kept his appetite at bay.

"Breakfast tacos should be arriving any minute," Jules said. "From that little place you love."

"In that case, I'm starving," he said.

A notification on her app dinged. She checked the screen. "He's pulling up right now."

"I got this." Toby met the driver on the front porch. Jules had an end unit in the big cul-de-sac that came complete with her own garage. The place had the feel of a small European village with iron gates and cobblestoned streets.

He greeted the driver, took the bags and inhaled the scent of bacon and eggs wrapped in a tortilla. Chopped red onions and cilantro made his mouth water. As it turned out, he was hungry for the right meal. Jules knew him better than anyone.

Back inside, he locked the door behind him before joining her at the table, where she'd set two places. The food was gone in a matter of minutes. He polished off a glass of water, thought about coffee, then decided against it. Despite sleeping for most of the ride down, he was bone-tired and suspected Jules was too.

"I should probably go to bed, but my mind won't stop spinning," she said after he helped clear the table and load the dishwasher. "I'm afraid I'll have another nightmare."

"What about TV?" he offered, motioning toward the couch. "We could put on a movie."

She nodded and then located the remote to close the blinds. The things were a miracle because they could block out almost all sunlight with a push of a button.

"Sit on my good side," he said, sinking into the sofa. His shoes were off, so he put his feet up on the marble coffee table.

After tapping the screen of the remote a few more times, the TV came to life and a menu loaded.

"What are you in the mood for?" she asked.

"Definitely not a comedy," he said on a chuckle and was reminded just what a bad idea that was. His wound wouldn't let him forget that any movement greater than breathing would be punished.

"Got it," she quipped. "*Old Yeller* it is."

"Why not put on *Hachi* as a double feature?" he shot back.

"Only if we can watch *Marley & Me* after," she continued.

"Great," he said. "Did you think to bring a box of tissues with you?"

Jules laughed and it was about the best sound he'd ever heard. "Okay, how about a documentary on quarterbacks from a couple seasons ago."

"You know I won't put up an argument," he agreed. "Is that what you want to watch?"

"I don't mind," she said. "Besides, it'll be a good distraction." She put the remote down after setting the volume at a reasonable level and then curled into the crook of his left arm before reaching for the blanket she kept on the sofa and covering them both with it. She rested her head close to his. "I can hear your heartbeat. Good to know it's still beating strong."

He could hear it too. It was Jules. She made his pulse race. He was just normally better at hiding the fact.

Within a matter of minutes, her steady, even breathing told him that she'd fallen asleep. So he relaxed too. Before he knew it, he was out.

A thud coming from upstairs shocked Toby awake. He blinked to clear some of the burn from his eyes. His lids felt like sandpaper.

A board creaked underneath someone's weight.

Someone was inside the house.

# Chapter Thirteen

Jules felt the muscles in Toby's body tense, causing her internal alarms to sound off. She opened her eyes as he shifted away from her. Cold filled the space in between them as she searched his gaze.

He brought up his left index finger to touch his lips. She nodded, acknowledging his request for her to be quiet.

It was dark downstairs save for the light from the TV. The volume was turned down, but it was still set high enough to hear what was going on. One of the quarterbacks was complaining about how tough his job was mentally as he whined about the physical toll. After being in a chopper crash, she could sympathize with the aches and pains. Yet she wouldn't choose to go down that route every week as a career path. Being in football must be like experiencing a car crash on a weekly basis.

No wonder those athletes got paid the big bucks and most were forced to retire in their twenties or early thirties. The body could only take so much. This might be what they did for a living, but it was no way to live. Not for her, anyway.

Those random thoughts were her brain's way of distracting her from her fears based on the look on Toby's face. Something had set him off.

He located his weapon and then handed hers to her. More evidence something was about to go down.

She flipped off the TV with the remote, plunging them into darkness. One of the requirements when she'd put money down on the new-build town house was the ability to make it appear like nighttime at any given point in time in the home. Jules sometimes had to catch up on sleep after a case and needed darkness to be able to pull it off.

The blackout blinds were coming in handy now as she took the lead, heading toward the stairs.

A board creaked, causing her pulse to skyrocket. Someone was inside her home.

Footsteps followed a pattern of someone sprinting across the room. Did the intruder realize they were waiting?

"Stay here," Toby whispered as he stepped in front of her. He was doing his best to protect her, but that didn't fly.

"This is my home, Toby," she whispered back. "My home."

He moved aside without so much as a word so she could pass by. Toby, of all people, would understand the need to protect his own domain.

Pointing out that she was in a better position to nail a target considering she had the use of her right hand would only add insult to injury.

By the time she reached the top of the staircase, it was eerily quiet on the second level of her home. She knew every creaky board in her house, so she walked across the landing like she was in a game of hopscotch.

Stealthily, she moved to the guest room, where she'd heard the noises coming from. The lights were out upstairs too, but the sun came through the opened windows. Toby followed closely behind, keeping enough distance to be able to watch her steps and shadow her movements.

Weapon at the ready, leading the way, she entered her guest bedroom. Toby stepped in behind her, flipping on the light. With his back to hers in case the perp came up from behind, they moved through the room.

Jules checked inside the closet first, then underneath the bed. She moved to the window, which was ajar. "He either came in this way or used it to escape."

Having an intruder inside her home felt like the worst kind of violation. She closed and locked the window, for all the good it did because she never left town without making certain her house was like a vault.

Moving into her office next door, they performed the same routine. Then the primary bedroom was checked, followed by the bathroom. Once the home was clear, they checked the windows, searching for any signs of someone running away.

They saw no signs of anyone.

"It's all good in here," she said, sitting down on the edge of her bed. She noticed that her underwear drawer was slightly open. Again, that wasn't her doing.

She pushed up to standing and then cut across the room.

"What is it, Jules?"

"Bastard stole my underwear," she said with an involuntary shiver.

WHITE-HOT RAGE burned Toby from the inside out. "So, this sicko can come after us, but we aren't supposed to go after him?"

"If it's him, he's taunting us," Jules said, always practical. He had no idea how she pulled off staying calm in a situation like this. "Think about it. Taking a US marshal down with him would be a pretty good high for a lowlife like Symes.

He wants you to make a mistake and come after him so he can flip the script, sending you to jail."

"He couldn't have known I was here, Jules." Toby shook his head. "He was coming for you."

"I caught him staring at you a couple of times during transport," she admitted. "Didn't think too much of it at the time. But there was an intensity that was enough to catch my attention."

"Why didn't you say something?"

"For one, I had no idea about your sister or that he could possibly have been the one responsible," she said, throwing her hands up. "You don't think I would have withheld information like that from you, do you? If I'd known there could be a connection to you?"

He shook his head. "Of course not."

"You didn't trust me enough to tell me about what happened to Lila or what's been going on since," Jules said.

"Trust had nothing to do with it," he countered. There was no way in hell he would allow her to believe that he didn't have full confidence in her. "I'm the one who's broken, Jules. I'm the one who brings devastation down onto everyone I care about."

Jules reclaimed her seat next to him on his left side and then set her weapon on the nightstand before taking his and doing the same. A mix of pity and sadness morphed her features.

"Don't feel sorry for me, Jules. That's the worst thing you could do. That look. The one on your face right now is half the reason I never spoke up about what happened. I didn't want you to look at me that way."

She turned to face him, bringing her hand up to his face. Her touch wasn't much more than a feather but sent rockets of desire firing through him.

As she moved closer, her gaze dropped to his lips. Toby's pulse kicked up several notches as heat flew south. Temptation to lean into her, into *his* Jules, was the strongest pull he'd ever experienced. Magnet to steel.

A rational voice in the back of his mind said he should stop this while he was able. Was he able, though? Because he'd never experienced anything that was anywhere near this powerful. He could only imagine what a kiss would be like if his body hummed with need being this close to her. Her fresh, clean, flowery scent overtook his senses. All he could think was…*more*. He wanted—no, needed—more. He needed to be close to Jules. He needed to breathe her in to remind himself that he was still alive. That life was still worth going through the motions for. Right now, he needed to feel her lips moving against his.

Toby leaned in, closing the distance between them as he pressed a tentative kiss to those sweet lips of hers. Would she pull back? Reject him?

He had no idea how this was going to go, except that the sound of her racing heart matched his. Those tender lips of hers were the sweetest taste. And nothing inside him could stop now that they'd touched.

A deep groan surfaced as he felt her tongue slick across his bottom lip. Desire like he'd never known filled him, tempted him to keep going when logic said their friendship could be on the line if they continued.

Friendship? His brain argued he'd never looked at Jules as a friend or he would have been able to handle hearing about her dating life.

Did she feel the same way about him?

Or was this pity?

The last thought gave him enough willpower to pull

back. He rested his forehead on hers as both tried to catch their breath.

"Was that a mistake?" he asked, searching for a sign she wanted this to happen because her feelings ran deep and wasn't just trying to comfort him out of pity.

"Not on my end," she said before putting more space between them. "But it can't happen again."

Toby had to clear the frog in his throat before he could speak. "Right."

"I can't lose you, Toby."

Even Jules seemed to realize he would mess it up between them, ruining any chance they could go back to being friends when he did the inevitable.

"Agreed" was all he could say.

She turned away from him and then picked up her 9 mm. "We need to call this in."

"I know," he said. "Let's get our supervisor on the phone."

"Think he'll be surprised you're at my house?" she asked.

Would that make Jules look bad? Because he didn't care about himself. "I doubt it. Mack is sharp. He knows we're close. I imagine that he would expect us to be together after what we've been through. And then there's the fact we can both use the company."

"True," she said.

"Plus, the investigator on the case needs to know we're being targeted by this creep," he continued as the being-in-love-with-his-best-friend fog lifted.

"I'll go downstairs and grab my phone." She started to get up, but he reached for her hand.

"Hey," he said. "Being with you, making love to you, would be the most incredible experience of my life." Saying the words out loud was easier than he'd expected it to be. "No one compares to you, Jules."

Her eyes twinkled with something that looked a whole lot like need, which wasn't making it any easier to step out of this moment. They had to, though. She was too important to risk losing her.

"We both know that's not an option," he continued. "And the real rub is that no one will *ever* compare to you."

She cocked her head to one side, deciding if she agreed. "And you still think it's a good idea to stay platonic?"

"It's not a choice, Jules."

She sat there for a long moment before tucking a stray piece of hair behind her ear. "Okay, then. Let's never talk about this again."

*Damn.*

Knowing she was spot-on didn't ease the sudden ache in his chest or the feeling of loss threatening to consume him like an out-of-control wildfire. At this point, he would welcome the burn because it would remind him that he was still alive.

Shutting down all feelings for Jules other than friendship meant numbing himself.

So be it.

"Let's head downstairs together," he said, standing up. Without those larger doses of pain medication, Toby felt everything. He noticed the dull ache in his right wrist. He knew when it broke there wasn't much they could do to repair the injury. Reduction, the doctor explained before surgery on his side to remove shrapnel, meant the doctor repositioned the bones to allow them to heal correctly. Then immobilization using a soft-sided cast prevented movement after realignment. All fancy terms for saying the doc straightened him out and now nature needed to do the work.

Not using his right wrist for anywhere from six to twelve weeks meant riding a desk when he was cleared to go back to work. Considering the investigation underway, he would most likely have to attend some type of mental health evaluation too. *Yippee-ki-yay.*

Toby could think of dozens of better ways to spend his time off from the job other than nursing a broken wrist and all the other injuries he'd acquired. Normally, those thoughts might include a leggy blonde. Not this time. And maybe not for a while. It wouldn't be fair to the other person when his heart wasn't into dating.

Then what?

Shoving those thoughts aside, Toby headed downstairs with Jules not far behind. She flipped on lights as they moved.

"I knew I should have replaced the windows here," Jules said once they reached the kitchen. "I did with the ground floor but naively assumed no one would go to the trouble of coming in through the second story."

"Most people don't even get that far," he said.

"We know better, Toby," she said. "I have no excuse."

"Except no one believes anything like this will happen to them," he pointed out, not ready to let her blame herself for something this perp did. "You did more than most by replacing them downstairs. Plus, you have an alarm for when you're away."

"We should have armed it," she said.

"Hell, I don't even lock my door half the time," he said. It was true. He lived on the outskirts of town, where no one was a stranger.

"The whole town where you live knows one another," she said. "Everyone watches out for each other."

Who watched out for Jules?

## Chapter Fourteen

Once again, Symes had outsmarted Jules. He'd taken the key to his handcuffs off her, as well as her backup weapon. Now he'd broken into her house while she was home and stole a pair of underpants.

What the hell?

Rather than chew on that or beat herself up further, she set those thoughts aside long enough to make the call to her supervisor.

"I'll have someone staked outside your property to watch out in case he returns," Mack said after the circumstances were explained. Then came, "Do you think it would be best to head to Mesa Point now?"

"I can't leave Toby to fend for himself," she countered. "Not in his current condition."

"You're right," Mack conceded. "Can you take him with you? It might be a good idea for him to get some fresh country air. It can be good for healing."

"Neither of us are in any condition to make a drive," she said as the wheels in the back of her mind started churning. "As soon as we are, though, it's not a half-bad idea."

"I can send a car," Mack said. "Whatever you need. Just let me know, and I'll make it happen. You deserve protection."

"Much appreciated, sir," she said, thinking it might not

be a bad idea to stay at the family paint ranch. "I'll discuss the idea with Toby and let you know what we decide."

A thought struck. Would she be bringing danger to her family's doorstep?

Then again, all six Remington grandkids had gone into the US Marshals Service. Would they be more protected in Mesa Point?

"That's all I'm asking," Mack stated, exacerbated. After perfunctory goodbyes, Jules ended the call and locked gazes with Toby. He was already shaking his head.

"You go," he said. "I'll head to my place."

Did he think Symes would leave her alone if they were apart?

"And then what?" she asked.

"You'll be with family, and I'll take care of myself while I heal," he said, point-blank.

"Why not come with me?"

"Because that would be like me admitting defeat," Toby said on a sharp sigh. "Allowing Symes to control where I go, when I go, is essentially handing over the reins. I can't do it."

"Then let me come home with you," she said. "I'll head to Mesa Point after."

"Do you really want to stay away from your family for days or weeks while I heal?" he countered.

"I don't want to be away from my siblings, cousins and grandparents, but you are just as much a part of my family to me as they are," she said.

"You have that determined look in your eyes, Jules. Don't dig your heels in on this subject. I'm not worth it."

"You are to me," she said.

"That's not helping." He put a hand up to stop her from continuing down that path. Then he moved into the kitchen and started making coffee.

"I'll take a cup," she said, figuring there was no use fighting Toby once he'd made a decision. She sat at her kitchen island, seething at the fact Symes got away with something so personal of hers.

Taking underwear was a sign. He was telling them that he could break in and take whatever he wanted. The jerk must have come out of the crash in better shape than either one of them.

Had he followed them? Was he stalking her?

Or was Toby right? Was Symes using her to taunt Toby?

Was he still out there somewhere? Lurking?

*Eleven years.*

Who could evade law enforcement for eleven years while actively raping and murdering? Most who got away didn't continue their activities. They disappeared, fleeing the US once they realized every law enforcement agency was looking for them. They reasoned it was only a matter of time before they were captured if they stayed in the US.

"We need to check into Symes's file," she finally said to Toby. When she looked up, she realized he was studying her while the second cup of coffee brewed. She had one of those pod machines that did all the work and was easy to load. Everything in Jules's life was built for ease, since she gave 110 percent of her energy to work. "How much do you know about him?"

"Not more than you," he said. "I didn't make the connection that he could be the one responsible for Lila's murder until you told me about the tattoo, so I had no reason to dig deeper into his file." Toby shook his head. "Absolutely not."

She pulled her best innocent-me act. "What?"

"First of all, you're supposed to be healing, not logging on to your work files," he pointed out. "Second, there's a digital trail that could point the finger right back at you as the person helping me in this ridiculous chopper crash theory."

"But—"

"No," he warned. "Your computer activity will be watched and so will mine. No one keeps hard copies anymore. Everything is digital."

"There has to be news stories about him by now," she countered. "He's been big news ever since his arrest a week ago."

"True," Toby said as the machine spit and sputtered behind him, mimicking coffee-shop sounds. The stainless steel and sleek black model was meant to give her an experience, not just a cup of black coffee. It also made lattes, but she was more of a straight black coffee person. It helped her think more clearly. Right now, she could use a gallon.

"We need to learn everything we can about Symes," she said as her brain cells started firing again.

"Not from one of your devices," he shot back as he handed over the first mug, then waited for his to finish brewing.

"Because?"

"It will implicate you in helping me," he said.

"The man broke into my home, Toby. We reported it to Mack. I have every right to know who just violated my privacy and stole my underwear."

Toby didn't have a counterargument there.

"Plus, if we use someone else's device, it'll make us look guilty," she continued. "I deserve to know who I'm really dealing with in case he returns." The thought caused her to shiver involuntarily. She couldn't go there mentally with what the man may intend to do with her undergarment. That just creeped her out further. "And if this creep decides killing me is the ultimate snub to you, I want to know every possible weakness the man has."

It didn't take long for Toby to agree there. She was right. No one could argue.

"What do you want to do?" he asked, joining her at the marble island with his fresh brew.

"Let's do a search," she said, grabbing the nearby laptop. "You're right about not logging in to work. We can do some investigative work right here. No need to access those files when we have the internet."

"All right," Toby said after taking a sip of coffee. "Let's see what comes up."

The term *less is more* didn't apply to information on a serial rapist and kidnapper. There wasn't much more than a few basic details of Symes's arrest. He'd been caught leaving a crime scene, too late for the victim, with the cello string he'd strangled her with, along with a shoebox full of souvenirs from the crime.

"He keeps souvenirs," Toby said after reading the same passage. "We already knew that about Lila's killer, but this is more evidence linking Symes to my sister's death."

"How did he stay in the South and Southwest without ever being captured?" she asked. "His murders go back eleven years, and that's just the ones we know about. We don't know how many victims there were." *Hold on a sec.* She had a fingerprint kit. Could she dust her upstairs window from the outside?

Neither one of them was in shape to climb a ladder. The dresser might be easier to lift a print from.

"Keep reading," she stated. Though the man had never previously left a fingerprint at a crime scene, you never knew when a slipup might happen. Then again, adding breaking-and-entering charges along with petty theft wouldn't exactly add much time to rape and murder charges.

The crime he'd committed today was peanuts compared to what he usually did.

Was she right about him biding his time? Targeting her?

Did he settle for stealing her undergarment when he realized she wasn't home alone? Had he intended to do much more to her? Or maybe the better question was, did he plan to rape and murder her?

*Over my dead body.*

Then again, he probably preferred it that way. She couldn't begin to think about Toby's sister's case. At eighteen, she'd been young and innocent. A baby in the grand scheme of life, despite feeling those first steps toward real independence.

Had Symes targeted her specifically because of her brother's job? It made sense when she thought about it as she retrieved her spare fingerprint kit from her garage, where she kept extra supplies. He would go after someone young and innocent. He would take pleasure in ripping her world apart, which made him one twisted individual.

No one had come forward to claim he was a brother, stepbrother, son or stepson in the articles she'd perused. Maybe Toby had found something when she'd left the room.

Then again, who would want to claim ties with a monster?

No former girlfriends gave interviews, as sometimes happened in high-profile cases.

Jules entered the house through the garage door leading into the kitchen.

"Hey," Toby said as he studied the screen. "I might have found a connection to Symes in Amarillo."

"That would give him easy access to Texas, New Mexico and Colorado," she said off the top of her head.

"Don't forget Kansas and Oklahoma," Toby quickly pointed out.

"Not to mention how easy it would be to cross the border to Mexico," she added.

"Someone, somewhere, has information about this bastard," Toby said. "My money is on figuring it out in Amarillo." He sized her up. "How soon before you'll be able to drive? Honestly."

"My personal vehicle is in the garage," she said, flexing the fingers on her free hand. "Seems like my hands work fine."

"Your knee, though," he said. "You're still in pain."

"There's not much I can do there," she responded.

"Except keep it elevated, which you wouldn't be doing while driving," he reasoned.

"Do you want to find this monster?" she asked, knowing full well Toby did. Would he do anything to catch him? Toby would draw the line if he thought an activity would hurt her. Other than that, she believed everything else might be on the table.

"You know that I do, Jules."

"So do I," she said. "He made this personal with me, Toby. This isn't just about you anymore."

"The investigators will say that we don't know for certain Symes was responsible for the break-in or missing underwear," he said, being reasonable. "They'll suggest we jumped to conclusions and might even ask how you can be certain your underwear is missing in the first place."

"You know how I operate," she said. "My drawers would pass the harshest military inspection. My underwear has been messed with and a pair is missing. I restocked after doing laundry before leaving for the trip." She felt her cheeks flame. "Plus, the sexier red silk pair is missing. It's my date pair." Not that she'd been on a whole lot of those recently.

Suddenly, the rim of Toby's coffee mug got real interesting. Was it the thought of her dating in general or specifically dating other men?

Their kiss, brief as it had been, had sizzled with the promise of the best kiss of her life if they hadn't stopped before the point of no return.

Toby had been clear about not wanting to go there and risk their friendship. She heard him loud and clear and was still embarrassed she'd actually considered asking him for more. Chalking her heightened emotions up to the heat of the moment, Jules needed to keep herself in check. Because it was a little too easy to imagine herself with Toby in the biblical sense. He didn't want that, and she didn't go where she wasn't welcome.

Getting a person to have sex with her had never really been a problem before, so she'd been mortified when Toby had pulled away.

It was good, though. This way, their friendship was still intact, and they would get to stay in each other's lives for the long haul.

And that was cool. Right?

"I can drive, Toby," she finally said. "Besides, we don't have another choice." She made a dramatic show of looking him up and down. "It's not like I'm letting you get behind the wheel."

"What about Mesa Point?" he asked after a chuckle that caused him to wince in pain. She felt bad about that part.

"I can't bring this monster home with me to Mesa Point," she said. "There's no telling who he will hurt to get to me. The hospital doesn't have enough security to ensure no one slips into my grandparents' room. How difficult would it be to pull a plug? Or tamper with a medicine drip? This needs to end with him being recaptured and then locked up for the rest of his life."

Toby sat there, contemplating.

There was no way she could do any of this without him. She would beg him to go with her, if that was what it took.

After what felt like an eternity, he said, "It's an eight-hour drive. Let's roll."

## Chapter Fifteen

After roughly four hours on the road, Toby insisted Jules stop to take a break. She'd yawned four times in the last five minutes, a sure sign she needed rest. Amarillo could wait until morning. Getting in at night wouldn't do any good anyway. It was the kind of place where the streets were rolled up after dark. Knocking on someone's door after sundown without being expected could get them shot.

Most folks didn't lock their doors and didn't need to. Not with a shotgun within arm's reach and, possibly, a couple of dogs bred for protection that ran loose on the property.

After stopping off near Abilene for food and a bed to sleep in, they were back on the road by five sharp the next morning.

"Do you think he followed us?" Jules asked as they entered Amarillo, also known as the gateway to Palo Duro Canyon State Park and for its location in the Texas Panhandle. The flatland had just sustained serious wildfires that were finally contained, but they could have impacted the person they came to speak to—Jodie Symes Benning.

If Toby's research was correct, he'd dug up Symes's cousin. If his hunch was right, someone had been hiding Symes. To be fair, Jules had had the same idea. Considering they both had the same feeling, it was worth investigating.

Besides, all they could do at either of their houses was sit and wait. Mack would probably say sit and heal, but even their supervisor seemed frustrated by the turn of events.

Since they were on medical leave, they could go anywhere they wanted and do anything that suited them. Their story was that a road trip would do them good.

Could Symes have beaten them to the punch?

Toby doubted it. Mainly because they'd slipped out of town not long after the break-in. He might circle back once he deemed the coast was clear, but he wouldn't risk sticking around when the area would be watched by law enforcement agencies. In part, the protection was for Toby and Jules. The other, larger factor was that every law enforcement officer wanted credit for taking Symes off the street.

"He sent me a piece of Lila's hair on the first anniversary," Toby said as they turned down the road leading to Jodie's home. She lived out in the boonies on five acres of land. According to Google Maps, she had a small barn on her property that most likely housed a horse or two. Her own home was a modest ranch-style. Jodie was widowed and had no children. Though, she was written up as school bus driver of the year two years in a row by the district where she worked.

"That's awful, Toby," Jules said, breaking into his thoughts. "I can't imagine how awful that must have been for you."

"It was in a Ziploc baggie with the label *LW* on it." The memory of standing on his front porch as he opened his mail to see a lock of dark hair with his sister's initials on it hit full force. Suddenly, no pain in his body could come close to the emotional damage on that day.

Jules shook her head.

"I dropped it," he continued. "It just fell out of my hands, and the winds were so strong that day they picked it up. It floated a little bit before landing on my concrete porch."

Jules pulled off the road, but he barely noticed. "What did you do?"

"Tried to hold it together," he shared. "Which was the most difficult thing I've ever done because I was supposed to protect her."

"It wasn't your fault, Toby."

"Really? Because it sure as hell felt that way at the time," he snapped. He didn't mean to snap at Jules, and she seemed to understand when she reached over and touched his hand.

"I think you've been holding on to that guilt and blame for too long." She kept the engine idling, but the vehicle was in Park. "When none of it was your fault."

Toby nodded, but he couldn't let himself off the hook so easily. "I was all she had, and I told her to fight."

"That gave her a chance," Jules said gently. "It might have even worked. Or at the very least given law enforcement something to work with, like his DNA underneath her fingernails. It's the same advice any of us would have given."

"Yeah, but you didn't," he pointed out. "It was me. I did. And she suffered for it."

"So have you," she reminded him. "Except that you have to live with this for the rest of your life."

"I need this bastard behind bars," he said, feeling the emotions push their way to the surface, begging for revenge.

"That's why we're here," she said. "To get information and put him away for the rest of his life where he can't hurt anyone else."

Toby nodded. The all-too-familiar anger rising to the surface and battling for control. It would be so easy to let it take the wheel, especially now that Symes had targeted Jules. Was he trying to take everyone Toby loved away from him?

The short answer was probably yes.

Then it dawned on him. This was personal. "It just oc-curred to me that I must have come into contact with Symes at some point in my life. Except I don't remember that name at all." He paused. "Shouldn't it ring a bell?"

"You think Lila was targeted because of you?" Jules asked. "Because I was under the impression that maybe this guy got extra pleasure out of finding out she was re-lated to a US marshal."

"I didn't recognize him," Toby said. "Wouldn't I?"

"Not necessarily," she said. "You didn't remember me from the coffee shop."

"I'm still questioning that one," Toby admitted.

"Exactly," she stated.

Toby searched his memories and came up blank. He would have remembered Jules if he'd seen her. But she knew who he'd been with, and he couldn't deny Dark Roast was one of his favorite Austin coffee shops. He'd most definitely been there with the brunette Jules had mentioned seeing. The proof was there. And yet it was still difficult for him to see it.

What else was he missing?

"Did Lila date anyone that you knew of?" Jules asked as she navigated back onto the dusty road. Most folks out-side of Texas thought major cities like Dallas, Houston and Austin still had tumbleweeds rolling around and that every-one rode horses to the grocery. Amarillo was the place that might actually happen. It was almost infamous in the state for its blistering wind and horrific ice storms.

"No," he said.

"No one she told you about or she didn't date at all?" she continued.

"Both," he said with confidence that was now shaky as they pulled in front of Jodie's property.

"The main thing I know from being a sister with two brothers is that I certainly didn't tell the boys everything," she said. "I'd be far more likely to tell my female cousins personal stuff like who I was interested in or hooking up with when I was younger."

Despite being friends, Toby wanted the subject of Jules's hookups to be off-limits. Was that wrong? He must have winced, because she popped him in the arm.

"What? You don't think guys were interested in me when I was eighteen?" she asked.

"Not the problem," he informed her. "I'm certain too many guys wanted to get to know you."

"I didn't, by the way," she said. "Hook up with strangers or guys on campus. I was too busy studying and trying to stay in school to date a whole lot."

He doubted it but appreciated the effort to spare him the details.

"What?" she asked, catching on. "You don't believe me?"

"Someone like you would have guys knocking on your door constantly," he said.

"I'm pretty sure that I didn't give off the vibe that any advances would be welcome," she countered. "Dating in college wasn't big on my list."

*Good.* Despite the fact it was none of his business, he was relieved she didn't date around. Part of him didn't want to share her with anyone else.

Jules pulled into the driveway of the redbrick ranch. The house looked smaller compared to the oversize lot. The gravel driveway contrasted against the yellow landscape where weeds choked out every sign of greenery.

*Survival of the fittest.*

JULES PARKED HER four-door sedan. "I've always wanted a convertible."

"Why not buy one?" Toby asked, clearly confused by the change in topic.

"Because I live in San Antonio, not Galveston," she stated, figuring she needed to get him out of his dark mood before they talked to Jodie. Prodding him back into investigation mode might help them better assess the person they were about to interview. Plus, his thoughts had taken him to a dark place. One she wasn't altogether certain she could drag him out of.

Toby needed to maintain sharp focus. He was one of the best marshals she'd ever worked with, and she didn't want him to lose sight of that fact, because he was clearly still beating himself up for his sister's death—a death he had no control over, no matter how much he believed that he could have somehow changed the outcome.

No one got to change the past. If Jules could, she would go back and drive her grandparents home the night they suffered a near-fatal crash. The people who'd taken her in and raised her didn't deserve to be fighting for their lives right now.

Life could be hella unfair.

Jerks seemed to live forever when lovely people suffered a horrific fate. No one knew which door they were going to get. She'd decided it was up to her to make the best of her life a long time ago.

But she hated realizing how much Toby blamed himself for his sister's murder. She hated how hard on himself he was. And that he couldn't let go of the guilt.

Could she?

The problem was that she blamed herself for her grandparents' crash. She blamed herself for not being there for them as they got older. She should have anticipated something like this happening and wasn't ready to let herself off the hook.

Except reality was dawning on her too. No one got to control what happened in life, least of all her or Toby.

Life had its own deal. It was their job to navigate it and somehow survive when a real awful hand was dealt to them.

Thankfully, they had each other to lean on. At least, when Toby let her in. Because more than anything, she wanted to take some of the burden from his shoulders. She wanted to ease some of his pain, but that meant he would have to open up.

Was that even possible?

She parked next to the redbrick home with green shutters. There were a couple of pots on the porch with dead branches sticking out of dry soil.

Toby exited the vehicle first and then came around to her door. Despite his dominant hand being in a sling, he opened the door for her. She didn't mind. It was ingrained in him to be polite, a gentleman, and she appreciated the gesture.

"Before we talk to Jodie, I just want you to know that you can talk to me about your sister anytime," she said. "I'd like to know more about her. What she liked to do in her free time and the kinds of books she liked to read." Mostly, Jules wanted to know more about the person instead of the statistic Lila became.

"I'd like that," Toby said, surprising her. He reached for her hand and squeezed. And then he locked gazes with her. For a few seconds, she could see all the bottled-up hurt that he'd locked away for the past five years since his sister's death. "What would I do without you, Jules?"

The way her name rolled off his tongue, that deep timbre that was so good at breaking down her walls, caused this moment between them to feel like one of the most intimate of her life.

But she couldn't keep walking down a path to nowhere. She pulled her hand back and gave his arm a light tap. "Let's hope you never have to find out, buddy." Her attempt at a smile was weak at best. *Buddy?*

*Wow, Jules, you're really bringing home the friendship point, aren't you? Great job!*

Toby's laugh was awkward at best. But, hey, there was no use tricking herself into believing that they could be more. She'd been tempted. He'd been clear about where he stood. Continuing to flirt with the idea they were perfect for each other would just be punishment at this point.

Jules exited the sedan. She'd changed into black slacks and a cotton pullover shirt. For a second, she debated grabbing her shoulder holster out of the trunk. Would it put Jodie on guard if they showed up looking official? Technically, they were on medical leave, and this was an informal visit. Curiosity about Theodore Symes brought them to the area.

This was dancing very close to a line that couldn't be crossed. As citizens, however, and as a victim of a breaking and entering along with burglary, Jules had a right to know more about Theodore the Terrible.

"Who should do the talking?" she asked, realizing they hadn't discussed strategy on the drive here.

"Do you want to take the lead?" he asked, clearing his throat.

Was he afraid his emotions would get the best of him? It wasn't like Toby to be unprofessional, but this situation was unique.

"Yes," she agreed.

Before they reached the first step on the concrete porch, the door swung open and smacked against the wall. A woman in curlers and a dress robe stepped out as she brought a shotgun up, aiming the business end directly at them.

"If I were the two of you, I'd turn around and get off my property before I shoot," the woman who had to be Jodie Symes Benning stated.

## Chapter Sixteen

Toby brought his good hand up in the surrender position, palm out. "Hold on there, ma'am. My friend and I want to ask a couple of questions. That's all. We aren't here to cause any trouble."

Jodie lowered the barrel and sized them up.

"Maybe we come inside?" Toby asked in the tone that was so good at getting him what he wanted from women in the office. "We just want to talk."

"Are you a reporter?" Jodie asked. She was average height with the body shape of an apple. Everything about her was practical and simple, from her brown house slippers to her rose-covered dress robe. At least, he thought that was what the zip-up covering was called. It fell well past her knees, revealing not much more than her ankles. She looked older than her forty-two years, which put her a decade older than both him and Jules.

Make no mistake about it. The woman seemed as tough as the landscape where she lived. On this early November morning, a cold front brewed. Crisp wind cut through his joggers.

He must look a mess when he really thought about it, showing up unannounced with his arm in a sling and bruises on his face and body. Jodie couldn't see the bandage where he'd taken a piece of metal underneath his ribs on the right side. Between the pair of them, they looked like they'd just come back from war.

"No, ma'am," he said, pulling on his Southern drawl. Most folks couldn't tell he was from Texas unless he needed to break out the accent to build rapport. In his experience, folks were comforted by someone they could relate to. Someone they felt like they could run into at the quickie mart or big-box store while running errands. "Rest assured, we aren't anything of the sort." He twisted his face in disgust to drive home the point.

"Then who are you and why are you on my property?" Jodie asked, suspicion keeping her eyebrow raised as she studied them.

"Two people looking for answers," he said before introducing himself. "This is my friend Julie."

Jules took a step forward and stuck out her hand. Jodie eyed the offering but didn't budge.

"What's your business with me?" Jodie pressed, unyielding. The fact she didn't immediately kick them off her property or shoot was reassuring. She'd also lowered the barrel and curled her arm around the shotgun in a relaxed position.

"We came to ask if you'd seen or heard from Theodore recently," he said. The ranch house could be a good hiding place. Jodie was a cousin, so there wouldn't be a whole lot of suspicion there unless it was revealed the two were close.

What motive would she have to hide Theodore? Putting her neck on the line to save her cousin without cause didn't ring true.

She tilted her head and shot a look that said Toby might be delusional. "No."

"When was the last time you spoke to him, if I may ask?" Toby continued.

"Four years next month," she stated without hesitation.

"The two of you were close at one time?" Toby asked, realizing there'd been a connection in the past at least. Had she figured out what a monster the man was? Banned him from visiting? From her life? Had she been hounded by reporters who figured out the connection between the two?

"Yes," she said, twisting her face.

Jules seemed to catch on to something Toby missed. She clasped her hands together, staving off the chill in the air. "Did you have some kind of disagreement or falling-out with Theodore?"

"Why would I?" Jodie asked, with more questions stamped in the creases in her forehead.

"So, you two were close at one time," Jules continued, unfazed.

"Two peas in a pod," Jodie said. "Right up until his death."

Whoa. Toby didn't see that one coming.

Jules must have pieced it together. She didn't hesitate in offering condolences. "I'm sorry for your loss, ma'am."

"Teddy was a good man," Jodie said.

"May I ask how he died?" Jules continued as Toby managed to pull out his phone. He'd never been all that great with his left hand. His current condition was giving him an opportunity to work on that.

He managed to pull up a picture of Theodore the Terrible.

"Black ice after a storm blew through," Jodie supplied with a face made of stone. "His truck sank into a pond when he went off the road, and he was pinned by his seat belt." She might see showing emotion as a weakness.

Had Toby done the same all these years? Or kept his feelings bottled up because he feared they might break him if released?

"That's awful," Jules said with so much compassion Jodie's chin quivered.

"Well, nothing can be done about it now," Jodie continued, straightening up broad shoulders.

"True," Jules agreed. "Still, it must be hard with the holidays coming up."

Jodie gave a slight nod.

"Would you mind if I showed you a picture of the man we're trying to locate?" Toby asked.

"Go ahead," Jodie said, taking a step forward as Toby did the same. He extended his arm out as far as possible so as not to make the woman feel threatened in any way. Not that he could do much damage in his current condition. Stretching out his arm hurt like hell.

Jodie shook her head. "Never seen that man before in my life."

"He has the same name as your cousin," Toby said.

"That must be what those reporters wanted to jabber about," Jodie said, shaking her head. Someone who lived out on a property alone didn't appreciate folks showing up unannounced. They also didn't trust the government in most cases.

"You didn't talk to them?" Jules asked.

Jodie's forehead creased again. "Why would I? Ain't done nothing wrong. My cousin's been gone four years. Figured there wasn't any good that could come out of those people being here." Her face twisted like she'd just sucked on a pickled prune.

"I can't stand reporters any more than you," Jules agreed.

In their job, news leaks could damage a case. In some instances, reporters could be useful. In his experience, they did more harm than good until a criminal was caught. Then they were good at getting information out quickly and accurately. The problem with news in recent years was speed turned out to be more important than accuracy in too many cases. Putting information on the internet from a law enforcement agency directly proved more useful.

Jodie's shoulders relaxed. "Never had much use for 'em."

"Is it possible your cousin knew the man in the picture?" Toby asked, shifting the conversation back to Symes.

"Anything is possible, I guess," Jodie said with a shrug. "My cousin was always taking in strays. He fixed up a shed on his property that he kept unlocked for folks heading through town that got caught by a storm or needed to bed down for the night."

"How did people find out they could stay there?" Jules asked.

"All anyone had to do was ask," Jodie supplied. "Everyone knew about Teddy's open-door policy."

"Everyone?" Jules echoed.

"That's right," Jodie confirmed. "Bernie at the gas station would send folks to Teddy all the time."

"Your cousin sounded like an amazing person," Jules said.

"He was," Jodie agreed. "Anyone who needed a meal just showed up at his back door at 6:00 a.m. sharp. He pinned a note next to the coffee machine for people who stayed over. The place out back was outfitted with a commode and shower but not much in the way of a kitchen."

What were the chances the two men randomly shared the same name? An idea was taking shape in Toby's mind. He needed to discuss it with Jules when they were alone.

"THANK YOU FOR taking the time to talk to us," Jules said as information swirled in the back of her mind.

"It was no trouble," Jodie said. "Stop by anytime."

The woman was being polite. She surely didn't want to be disturbed again.

"I have a couple more questions," Jules said. "If you don't mind."

Jodie nodded. "Go ahead."

"Did you ever stop by in the mornings and see any of the men who stayed over at Teddy's place?" Jules asked.

"Not really," she said. "No." There was no hesitation in any of her answers, which most likely meant she was telling the truth. That was one of many signs, including body language cues, that when put together helped an investigator determine the honesty of answers. "I'm sure I was there a couple of times over the years when someone showed up at the back door, though."

"Did you remember seeing anyone with tattoos?" Jules asked, digging for any hint the woman might have seen Symes—or whoever he really was—without realizing it.

"I've seen a few," she admitted. "In my cousin's house, cowboy hats could stay on, so most just hung their heads and ate, not wanting to disturb Teddy if he had company."

"Any of the grim reaper underneath a brunette?" Jules asked. It might be a long shot, but it was worth trying.

Jodie's gaze flew up and to the left, a sign of attempting to recall information. "Can't say that I did, but then, I don't remember anyone without sleeves on."

Of course, Symes would hide his tattoos from anyone who could identify him by those marks.

"We appreciate it," Toby said with his usual charm. He was probably the reason Jodie didn't come out shooting. One look at Toby disarmed women of all shapes and sizes. The whole square-jawed, model look broke down a lot of barriers.

He touched her elbow, causing a firestorm in her body on contact. The warmth helped deal with the cold air on the way back to the sedan. Temps were dropping by the minute.

"Have you checked the weather lately?" she asked after settling into the driver's seat.

Toby palmed his cell after clicking on his seat belt, then studied the screen. "Looks like a front is headed this way."

"Think we should get out of here before it hits?" she asked.

"We got what we came for," he confirmed. "What do you say we head back?"

"My house or yours?" she asked, not really wanting to go back to hers after the break-in. It had been too easy for Symes.

"What do you think about heading to Austin instead?" he asked, surprising her with the idea. "We could stay downtown. Use cash if we stop by an ATM."

"I know a good coffee shop," she stated with a smile as she started the engine and then backed down the driveway.

Once they were back on the road, Toby redirected the small talk. "Are you thinking what I'm thinking?"

"The reason Symes has been slipping through everyone's fingers is because he's stealing people's identities?"

"Yes," he said. "That way, he hides in plain sight."

"No one is looking for 'Teddy' Symes," she added. "But whoever he was last might be in question."

"I've been thinking we might be overlooking something important," he said.

"Like he has to have had some kind of training or experience that allows him to survive under all types of conditions and circumstances," she stated.

"Exactly," he agreed.

"Survivalist? Doomsday prepper?"

"Could be one of those," he said. "Or something more formal."

"Military training?" she asked. "Because I was afraid of that one."

Some doomsday preppers could be just as militant, living off the grid and placing themselves in extreme conditions to test their readiness for what they deemed the end of time. Others prepped out of fear and wanted to be ready to survive if the world as they knew it collapsed or there was another world war.

But former military who crossed a dark line could be the deadliest.

Still, something had to trigger a person to turn into a monster like Theodore the Terrible. Jodie would despise what the man had done to her cousin's name if their hunch turned out to be true. All signs pointed to it being the reality of what had happened.

Jules's first instinct was that Symes murdered Teddy in order to take his identity. Or he might have learned of the man's death and, much like a vulture, took advantage of the situation after it presented itself. Who knew how many other identities Symes had adopted over the past eleven years.

"Why Amarillo?" she finally asked, thinking they might need to turn around to find out Symes's connection to the location.

"He might have been passing through and needed a place to sleep for the night," Toby explained. "That could be how he originally found out about Teddy's place. Who knows how many years he's been using it. He could slip in and out without anyone ever knowing he was there."

"Makes sense," she said. "Wouldn't he have had to change his appearance enough to slip under the radar of wanted posters?"

"Folks mind their own business in places like Amarillo," he said. "Plus, the town rolls up the streets at dusk. He would have understood these kinds of details."

"True," she agreed. "And they would be so used to folks coming and going from Teddy's place they probably wouldn't even notice anymore."

"Symes is smart enough to figure out that he could slip through town under the radar with a network in place like Teddy's."

"He survived without being captured for eleven years for a reason," she agreed. "Which makes me think he had a reason to be in places like Amarillo before he started killing."

"Truck driver comes to mind," Toby said. "Is it too easy?"

"Not really," she said. "Not for this kind of criminal activity. Truck drivers moved through states with deliveries throughout the Southwest."

"There'd be records," he said.

"He might have worked under an assumed name then too," she said.

"If we're going to make any progress in this case, we're going to need his real identity," Toby reasoned.

"How do we go about that?" she asked, stumped. If they had a town or city name and approximate age, they could peruse school records. Yearbooks were a useful resource once some information was known about a person's identity.

"Good question," Toby said.

Jules glanced over and realized he had an idea. "Am I still driving toward Austin?"

He pulled up his phone.

"Give me a sec" was all he said as he studied the screen.

Why did Jules think she was about to bang a U-turn? Gray clouds filled the sky. She checked the thermometer gauge on the dashboard. The temperature had dropped ten degrees since she'd last checked.

"If we don't leave now, we could end up trapped in bad weather," she said to Toby a few seconds too late.

He had that look in his eyes.

Could they get what they needed and get out before the storm?

# Chapter Seventeen

"We need to stick around and ask more questions," Toby said. He had an idea, but he wasn't sure Jules would go for it.

"I don't like the sound of your voice right now, Toby."

"We need to try," he said. "We can ask at a gas station if the new owner of Teddy's home kept his tradition alive. At the very least, we need to poke around and see if Symes, or whoever the hell he really is, hid anything inside a mattress or floorboard." He heard his tempo rise alongside his excitement level. "Think about it. He's probably stashing evidence somewhere along his trail. It would be too risky to keep it on him."

"We don't know for certain he stayed at Teddy's," she countered, but there wasn't a whole lot of enthusiasm in her protest. In fact, based on the way she was tapping her thumb on the steering wheel, she was coming around.

"Have I ever told you what a great driver you are?" Toby hedged, attempting to use his charm on her.

"Compliments won't get you very far with me," she said, dryly. "You should know that by now." She tapped her thumb a little faster. "Plus, you know that I learned to drive in Texas."

"Meaning?"

"I have no idea how to drive on icy roads," she said with

a shiver. Did she recall black ice was the reason Teddy had died?

"I'd never ask you to," he said reassuringly. "You mean too much to me for that nonsense."

"Like I said, buttering me up will get you nowhere, Toby Ward."

"A guy can try," he shot back, thankful she still had a sense of humor, based on her tone.

Her stomach growled.

"How about we stop for food first," he said, realizing they hadn't eaten for hours. It was past lunchtime, and Jules wasn't the kind of person who could skip a meal.

"I can't remember the last time I've eaten at Whataburger," she said, motioning toward the orange-and-white sign past the next red light.

"Let's do it," he said, thinking he could go for one of their signature double meat burgers and fries about now.

Jules turned into the parking lot and then entered the drive-through line. "Okay if we eat inside the car? I'm not in the mood to be stared at."

"I'm good with it," he said. "We can watch traffic if you park toward the street."

"Sounds like a plan to me," she said, pulling around to the menu board.

Ordering took all of two seconds. There wasn't much of a line, so they were parked out front and eating in a matter of minutes.

Jules leaned her head back on the headrest, a small moan of pleasure escaping from her lips—lips that were none of his business. "I was hungry."

"I know."

"I feel much better," she said.

"I know."

"I should keep a protein bar in my purse at all times to avoid times like these," she said.

"I know."

The problem was that he did know her a little too well.

Ten minutes later, they were headed toward Teddy's small ranch that was off County Road 21, where there was a whole lot of dry ground. Tinder?

At least the weather front would douse what was left of the wildfires, especially if sleet came through like the weather app on his phone predicted.

"How much time do we have before it hits?" Jules asked. "The temperature dropped another twelve degrees since we stopped for lunch."

He studied the weather app. "You know how predictable Texas weather can be."

"You're avoiding the answer," she said. "Give it to me straight."

"I'd plan on staying the night here in Amarillo," he stated.

"Hell's bells," she said under her breath. The words she wanted to use were probably a whole lot stronger. "Then let's get some answers while we're here."

The biggest downside to being trapped in a town was the obvious fact they couldn't leave. Then there was the reality they might be here for a few days, depending on this front. Neither had packed an overnight bag. "We should probably swing by the store and pick up supplies for the night."

"As in camping?" she asked with a whole lot of concern in her voice.

"I was thinking more along the lines of clothes and food," he said.

"It's probably better to prepare for the worst-case scenario," she reasoned. "This isn't the kind of place you want to be caught off guard in during a storm."

She was right except for the goodwill of ranch owners. He suspected there were others who kept an open door for folks moving through. Seasonal workers, ranch hands and the like would need a place to bed down for the night while heading to their next job. Growing up outside of San Antonio, he was familiar with stories like these despite never having used one himself.

Jules pulled into the nearest big-box store. The convenience couldn't be beat. Being able to buy pretty much everything they might need in one stop made life easier.

"How many days are we shopping for?" Jules asked after parking.

"Let's go with three, just to be safe," he said.

Taking in a sharp breath and then releasing it slowly, she said, "Okay, then. Let's get to it."

"Let's roll."

JULES AND TOBY must look like quite a pair, considering how many folks performed double takes as they gathered supplies. Did they look as battle weary as she felt? She couldn't imagine the amount of pain Toby was in, considering he'd had a small piece of metal removed from his right side. His pain tolerance must be out of this world, because he refused to take medication on schedule, stating that his injury amounted to a scratch and he'd be fine. She suspected he wanted a clear mind.

Watching as he walked, she realized just how much pain he must be in.

"Should you take something stronger than ibuprofen?" she whispered as they neared the checkout with their cart full of clothing and easy-to-eat food. The chip and water aisles had been ransacked ahead of the storm, which made her smile. Some things stayed the same no matter where she was. Apparently, folks could do without a lot of things, but potato chips wasn't one of them.

"I need to stay sharp," he reasoned.

"What if you need to run?"

"Then I'm going to have to hope adrenaline kicks in," he admitted as he stacked items onto the conveyor belt while the cashier rang up the person in front of them.

"That's a risky move," she said.

"You have 'supplies' in your trunk?" he asked, referring to weapons.

"Yes, I do," she said.

"That should help." He grabbed more items, wincing as he moved. Both of them needed rest in order to heal.

The thought of Symes out there, able to continue his twisted activities, was the only fuel keeping her going at this point. Plus, he'd made this personal when he stole from her. The item he'd taken was surely meant to send a message to both Jules and Toby that he could take what he wanted right under their noses.

Jules involuntarily shivered.

As disturbing as it was, Toby was right. They needed to think like Symes in order to anticipate his next move. Recapture him or lead law enforcement to him—either way, the result would be the same.

Tapping her credit card on the payment terminal, she then helped place the bags inside the cart. Toby was stubborn enough to want to pull his weight, so she wouldn't argue. By the time they made it back to the sedan and placed the bags on the back seat, his skin was pale.

They would have to take a break once they got to Teddy's old place.

Toby leaned his head back on the headrest.

"Why don't you close your eyes on the ride to the ranch?" Jules urged.

"I tried on the drive here this morning," he said. His voice took the quiet tone it normally did before he shut down on her. "All I could think about was the memento the sicko sent the second year."

Jules navigated onto the roadway, her grip tightening on the steering wheel as she listened.

"A sterling silver *L*," he reminisced. "It was tarnished, cheap. One of those prizes you win at the state fair. I'd thrown a football and let her pick the prize when she turned thirteen." He issued a sharp sigh. "She didn't go anywhere without it from that day on. Said it was her good-luck charm."

"I'm so sorry, Toby."

"I know." His voice was the kind of quiet calm that came before a massive storm.

"It wasn't your fault," she said.

He didn't respond. When he did, he finally said, "Year three was a piece of her shirt."

"The man, if he can be called that, is twisted," she said.

"Year four was fibers from the rope he strangled her with when he was done, except he didn't kill her," he continued. "He didn't realize she didn't die right then."

Jules took in a deep breath and slowly released it. "What about year five? What did he send?"

"This year?" Toby began. "A piece of cotton from the underpants she had on while he took her life."

"There are no words," she said to him. Offering quiet re-assurances fell short but was the best she could do. Nothing could bring his sister back or take away the pain of losing her. Not to mention the fact he'd blamed himself all these years. Breathing must hurt under the weight of his guilt.

"There's nothing I can say to take away your pain. Just know that I'm here for you." Had Symes taken Jules's underwear as a reminder to Toby the man thought he could take whatever he wanted right out from underneath Toby's nose? "Was the last item he sent the reason you blame yourself for the break-in at my house?" Toby had taken it hard. Rightfully so, considering they were downstairs the whole time.

"Would you see it any other way if the tables were turned?"

"I guess not," she admitted with a better understanding of Toby's reactions to everything that had been happening.

"He's coming after me," he said. "Using anyone close to me to torment me."

"Once again, I have to wonder why," she said. "Why you? You're a good person. You wouldn't hurt anyone on purpose. This more than likely has to do with your line of work more than anything else."

Law enforcement workers were targeted at times for locking away a loved one or someone who was connected to a crime organization. It might be rare, but that didn't mean it never happened. There was a reason penalties went up for a perp harming a law enforcement official. The harsher sentences deterred criminals in most cases.

"I'm sure you already searched for anyone who might have a bone to pick with you," she said. "Someone you arrested who seemed particularly bent on revenge."

"The felons we track down, transport and put away generally have nothing to lose," Toby pointed out. "The list of felons who threatened retribution is long."

"The FBI would have tracked down that angle," she surmised. "Unless, of course, they missed someone." Again, a rarity.

Wind kicked up, blowing against the sedan so hard it shook. She checked the temperature gauge in the console.

It read a chilly twenty-seven degrees as the first shimmer of drizzle coated the front of her car. She'd taken note of the barbed-wire fence surrounding the property, the open gate and the home with a light on in what was probably the kitchen area.

Changing the subject, she asked, "Do you think we should knock on the homeowner's door?"

Toby shook his head. "If they mind us taking shelter, I imagine they'll come tell us. It's best to look like we know what we're doing rather than let them know we don't. You saw the way Jodie and the others at the store looked at us."

"Guess we stick out like sore thumbs with all these injuries," she said with a half smile.

"I thought it was my good looks," he quipped. The joke was meant to lighten the mood, even though he couldn't rally a lighter tone.

"Obviously," she reassured him with an eye roll. It was true, though. There'd been plenty of women in the store with their tongues practically wagging as he walked past. The fact he was impervious to it made him even more charming. But she'd spent enough time focused on his good qualities.

No one was perfect. She should probably remind herself Toby wasn't either. Her traitorous heart would argue the fact.

She parked behind the oversize shed. Wind bit through her shirt the second she opened the car door.

The wood structure might be old, but it appeared solid. It looked to be ten feet by twelve feet with cedar wood and a metal roof. The door was unlocked, as expected. Jules bolted inside to stave off the cold.

"Is there electricity?" she asked as she took in the space. A set of bunk beds flanked each wall. Each had pillows and blankets, a luxury for a weary traveler. There was a kerosene stovetop on the back wall, along with a coffee maker attached to an electrical cord that ran down the back wall and out a small hole that had been sealed with caulk. She didn't want to think about the small critters it kept out.

"I don't think there's much more than what's plugged into the electrical strip on the back wall," Toby surmised after stepping into the middle of the room and turning a complete circle.

"Is that a space heater?" She didn't wait for a response. Instead, she walked to the back wall and pulled out something that looked like a radiator. Bending down to plug it in caused her to groan.

"Let me do that," Toby said.

"My knee is in better shape than most of your body parts right now," she quipped with a smile.

"Fair point," he conceded.

Turning on the heater gave instant satisfaction. "It works. Oh, bless."

Toby smiled at the Southern remark. "Kerosene lamps should help get us through the night."

"The storm is getting worse," she said, moving to the window. Cold seeped in through the small frame. At least they had a heater and were out of the wind. "It's already getting dark."

"I'll grab our supplies," he said. "We should probably be thinking about bedding down here for the night."

The idea of sleeping where a serial rapist and killer once laid his head gave her the creeps. But driving in the storm in search of shelter was the worst of bad ideas. They'd made it here. The place might be dusty, and it was clear men stayed here, based on the minimalism and half inch of dust no one seemed to bother cleaning.

"You need help," she said, following Toby to the car.

They brought in a few bags of supplies in two trips. She

checked the small bathroom complete with a shower she could barely turn around in. The toilet needed to be soaked in bleach. A plastic tub of wipes sat on the back of the commode, along with several rolls of toilet paper.

Surprisingly, there were clean towels folded on the small vanity. The sink was recently used. Someone had been here.

Was it Symes?

Another shudder rocked her at the thought. Because another possibility was that he could be on his way here right now.

## Chapter Eighteen

It took the last of Toby's strength to set up shop for the night in the makeshift bunkhouse. Jules managed to keep pace with him and wipe down the bathroom with the bleach wipes she'd found.

There was dust on the wood floors and pretty much everywhere else. But the place wasn't filthy. Someone cared about it, took care of it.

Teddy must have had a kind heart to make a place like this on his land for travelers. The black coffee and pot would be a godsend to most who needed to get up early and get on the road.

Scavengers like Symes turned Toby's stomach. He searched his memory to see if he could come up with any link between the two of them. His face didn't ring any bells, but they were older now. Years changed folks. Symes was supposedly forty-two, a solid decade older than Toby. At least, that was the lie. It was anyone's guess what the man's real age might be, which meant they could be similar in age.

Toby kept drawing a blank.

The other option was Symes had no idea who Toby was until after he'd killed Lila. Then the bastard, who kept mementos from every kill, decided to taunt a US marshal as a way to increase his high and possibly draw out the enjoyment. *Enjoyment* was a bitter word in conjunction with rape and murder.

"We should be set for the night," Jules said, breaking into his thoughts as he moved around on the floor, checking for loose boards. "Why not take a break and rest?"

He glanced at her, not ready to stop.

She put her hands up in the surrender position. "It's just a suggestion. This place isn't big. Any evidence hidden here shouldn't be too difficult to find considering we're trained professionals." She sat down in front of him. "You've lost coloring on me again. I'm worried about you."

Who could argue with her compassion?

Toby scooted until his back rested against the nearest bunk bed. "I can't help but think a sweet person like Teddy didn't deserve to have a monster taking advantage of his kindness."

"Do you want water?" she asked.

Toby nodded. Even he couldn't ignore the pain for much longer. And his body was weak. He'd been lightheaded after bringing in the supplies.

"Here you go," Jules said after reaching for a bag and grabbing a bottle.

"Thanks," he said, taking the offering. One too many times, he found his gaze wandering down to her lips.

Toby cleared his throat and then took a drink of water.

"Creepy to think he might have slept here, isn't it?" she asked, taking a bottle for herself and opening it.

He nodded.

"I doubt I'll be able to sleep," she said.

"If we can doze on and off, that'll be better than nothing," he agreed. This close, he couldn't stop thinking about taking the bastard down.

"Did we make a mistake in coming here?" She bit down on a plump lip.

"I don't regret our choices," he said. "What else would we be doing, anyway? The man is hunting us. Otherwise, he never would have risked tracking us to your place."

She shivered.

"Do you think he'll keep coming after us until he's re-captured or finishes the job he started at the chopper?" she asked.

Toby shrugged. "I wish I knew. It's probably good that I don't think like him. Right?"

"Guess I never thought about it like that," she admitted. "It's true, though." She issued a sharp sigh. "I keep thinking about Captain Crawford."

"Same here."

"It's awful," she said. "What if he is someone's husband?"

"I noticed a gold band," he said.

"I did too," she admitted. "And then I kept thinking he might be someone's father. Now a kid or kids will have to grow up without him."

A gust of wind shook the structure. Jules gasped before bringing a hand up to cover her mouth.

They were both jumpy and for good reason. Under normal circumstances, Toby wouldn't doubt the two of them going up against one person. But now they were injured, barely operating. They needed rest.

Another gust threatened to shatter the window. Jules's eyes widened.

"Hey, come sit next to me," he said, holding up his good arm.

She moved over to him and curled up in the crook. "I was afraid of my own shadow when I was little."

"How did you get over it?"

"There was this one day when I distinctly remember deciding nothing got to scare me again," she said. "I think my fears stemmed from being abandoned or something. I remember waking up in the middle of the night screaming until Grandma Lacy came running." She didn't lift her gaze to meet his when she spoke. Instead, she drew circles on the floor with her finger. "She would stay with me until 'the monsters' went away. I'm told I was little when I started having the nightmares. I'm not sure the exact age, but I was terrified of waking up and everyone just disappearing. Like in *The Wizard of Oz* when Dorothy is caught in the tornado. She had that little dog, Toto, and nothing else familiar. I was a hundred percent certain that I would wake up one day and everyone would be gone from my life."

"Must have been terrifying for a kid," he said, holding her a little tighter.

"It was," she admitted in a rare moment of vulnerability. In times like these, with her, all his protective instincts sprang to life. "And then, one day, I decided that I was never going to be scared of anything again."

"Were you?"

"Surprisingly, no," she said. "I mean, we all have our moments, right? But I've never experienced anything quite like those nightmares since." She paused. "Until now."

"Because of him?"

She shook her head, confusing him.

"Because I'm afraid of losing you," she admitted. Those words cut him to the core.

"You'll never lose me, Jules. I give you my word."

"It's not a promise either of us can make," she countered. "No matter how much we might care about each other and want to."

"There are never any guarantees in life," he said after

a thoughtful pause. She was right. "But as long as I have breath in my lungs, I'll be here for you."

"What about the future, Toby? What if we do survive this twisted individual? What then? We end up in relationships with other people? Our friendship slowly dies on the vine? I almost think that would be worse." She yawned. Jules always lost her filter when she was dead tired.

Toby regretted thinking of the word *dead* in conjunction with his best friend.

The point she made couldn't be argued. He had no plans to get married, but she was a beautiful, intelligent person who would end up married eventually. Her husband wouldn't want her best friend to be a guy. Toby could admit that he would be possessive over her too, selfishly wanting to be the only man in her life aside from her other family members.

Was it right of him? No. Probably not.

Emotions weren't rational. They took on a mind of their own. Wanted things they weren't supposed to have. Where was logic in times like these?

JULES HADN'T INTENDED to go down that road with Toby tonight. The day had taken on a life of its own. They were stuck inside a small shelter in what was predicted to be a once-in-a-decade storm, and a very twisted person wanted them both dead. *Dead* wasn't the right word. He wanted to torture Toby by—what?—raping and killing Jules. Meanwhile, the two other people she loved most in the world were in a hospital in Mesa Point, where she should probably be. Except she didn't want to bring a murderer to their doorstep.

After talking to her boss and putting a text in the family group chat, everyone was on high alert. Or, at least, they should be.

Her normal filter had taken a vacation, and she had no idea what was up from down any longer. She would, however, apprehend and contain Symes should he show his face here.

Would he get to them first?

That was the burning question. Toby was operating at probably 40 percent at best. She wasn't exactly as strong and rested as she could be. They'd survived a chopper crash.

It occurred to her that she was unsettled about something that might not even be reality. The creepy feeling she'd had since entering this space might not be warranted.

There was one way to find out. "Maybe we should investigate this space a little more. Figure out if Symes stashed anything here. It might help settle my nerves."

"Okay," Toby said. His deep timbre had a low, husky quality. The word *sexy* came to mind.

Shaking the thought loose from her head, she said, "It might be easier for you to take the floors, and I'll take counters and ceilings."

She half expected an argument, but Toby nodded instead. He seemed to realize that he needed to take it easy, which was good. Normally, he would keep pushing himself until he dropped.

Teddy never locked the door to the shelter, but maybe they could place a chair or some kind of barrier to let them know if someone tried to enter. If Symes tracked them to her house, how difficult would it be for him to locate them here?

Not very.

Would the storm slow him down? Or would it give him time to search them out? Find them? Finish the job?

A headache formed at the spot right between her eyes. At least the shelter was warm with the space heater. Otherwise, she was certain they would freeze to death. Nature would do the job Symes couldn't.

Shoving those thoughts to the back of her mind so she could focus, she ran her hand along the counters and then walls.

"I found something," Toby said.

She joined him in a heartbeat as he sat on the floor next to a bunk bed, a plank in his hand. Taking a seat next to him, she tried to ignore the thumping in her head. The plank had been two feet underneath the bed, so he had to reach into unknown territory to dig around.

"What can I use?" he asked, realizing he could put his own fingerprints all over evidence if they found something.

"We can use the flashlight app on my phone to see inside the hole," she offered. "Can you get on your stomach and slide under the bed?"

He shook his head with a look of defeat.

"I can do it," she said. Having the use of both of her arms made the difference in being able to pull herself underneath the bed. Icy fingers of fear gripped her spine at what she might find in the hole.

Jules braced herself as she handed Toby her phone. He locked gazes with her for a few seconds as though willing her to have the strength to keep going. Because who knew what other types of souvenirs Symes kept.

A blast of wind caused the electricity to stutter. Her heart rate jacked up several notches as she lay flat on her stomach and tucked her head down low to fit into the space. Was she about to be face-to-face with unimaginable horrors?

When Jules was a little kid, she hated eating turnips. When they were on the dinner menu, she closed her eyes tight, held her nose and went for it. The faster she got it over with, the quicker she could move on to the food on her plate she wanted to eat.

This was no different.

Toby stretched out his good arm, illuminating the space.

Jules couldn't close her eyes, so she took in a deep breath and then held it before scooting underneath the bed frame as fast as she could to get this over with.

The hole was at least a foot and a half deep. There was a banged-up metal box inside that was almost a perfect fit.

A cold shiver raced down Jules's spine.

"There's a box in here, Toby," she stated after releasing her breath. "But I need to find a way to get it out without putting my fingerprints all over it."

For a split second, the light went out and Toby disappeared. He returned a few seconds later to a clap of thunder that shook the floor.

"Here's a fork," he said, handing it over as he lit the area underneath the bed again. "Will that work?"

"Let's give it a try," she stated. Using the fork as leverage underneath the metal handle, she lifted the box. It was the size of a small tackle box. This felt a lot like that game called Operation, where you had to pluck a fake body part out of the man with the red Rudolph nose. Make a mistake and the buzzer would sound. In this case, make a mistake and she could erase key evidence.

"Steady," Toby said. His calm, smooth voice washed over her and through her, giving her the confidence she needed to successfully lift the box out of its tomb.

Something dawned on Jules. *Spiders.*

She was able to bring the box out from underneath the bed frame and set it on the floor without dropping it, which was a miracle in its own right.

"The owner of this box was here recently and probably visits often," she said.

Toby cocked his head to one side. His left eyebrow arched. "How do you know?"

"There are no spiderwebs in the hole."

# Chapter Nineteen

Toby sat up, staring at the metal box in front of him. The metal clasps reminded him of old school lunch boxes. His pulse raced. His heartbeat thundered in his ears, smothering out all else.

"How can we open this?" she asked, and he could barely hear her over the noise in his head, despite her being right next to him.

"Let me try," he said, glancing up at her and locking eyes for a split second. That was all it took to ground him again. Jules had that effect on him. No matter how far gone he was, she always brought him back. Funny thing about it was that she never even realized it had happened or that she was responsible for bringing him back to the light.

Jules handed over the fork. He finagled it until the metal clasp opened. Then it was a matter of sticking the utensil into the handle to lift the lid.

"Here we go," he said as it opened. Split down the middle, the box revealed its contents as the lid hit the wood floor with a clank.

Jules covered her mouth as a gasp escaped. "It's here. We have proof the monster has been here."

There was an assortment of items in Ziploc bags with initials on them.

Toby sat back before bringing his left hand up to rake through his hair. He wiped down his face, realizing his chin had a couple of days' worth of stubble. It was strange what the mind noticed when faced with something so horrific.

Normally, his job was to track down felons after a warrant had been issued. Presently, he was on prisoner rotation, which was glorified babysitting while felons were transported. Until it wasn't, which was how he'd found himself in this current predicament.

*Predicament* was too nice a word. He was living a nightmare fueled by one twisted individual.

"Maybe these items will tell us more about him," Jules offered. "Help us locate him."

*He's coming for us.* Toby held his tongue. Jules knew it too. It was the reason her words held no confidence. They both realized this perp had set his sights on them. Would Symes pull back?

Using the fork, Toby shoved baggies around like unwanted peas on a plate. "There has to be something here to help identify who Symes really is."

The corner of something that looked a whole lot like a photograph could be seen at the bottom of the box.

Toby managed to shove the Ziplocs around enough to get a good look at what it was. There were two boys in swimming suits. One looked to be a teenager, roughly fourteen or fifteen years old. He had his arm around a younger boy who looked to be around eight or nine. The younger boy smiled wide, revealing a few missing teeth.

"It's him," Jules said on another gasp. "It's Symes."

Toby managed to flip the picture over with some finesse. The back read: *Reed and me.*

"The older boy looks familiar too," Toby said. It was then he noticed the folded-up newspaper article.

"What?" Jules immediately asked. "Toby? What is it?"

"I know Symes's real identity," he stated, feeling the blood drain from his face. Because he was guilty. No excuses. This was his fault. And that was how he knew this man wouldn't stop until Toby paid the ultimate price. But first, he intended to torment Toby and show him loss. "His brother drowned on my shift as a lifeguard years ago."

"How did it happen?" Jules asked.

"I saw him pick a fight with a smaller kid, pushing him under the surface of the water in the deep end, laughing," Toby explained. "I blew my whistle, thinking I was high and mighty, but the teen blew me off."

"Understandable," she said. "I'm sure you followed your training."

"I did," he agreed. "However, by the time I got in the water, the smaller kid was in serious trouble, so I went to him first without realizing the teen was being run over by a rowdy bunch on a blow-up canoe." He shook his head. "There was something in the air that day. It seemed like all the kids were restless, looking for trouble. We had a group of older teens. I'm guessing this guy thought he would look cool by picking on someone."

"Teens do weird things sometimes to fit in," Jules pointed out.

"All I could think about was protecting the smaller guy," he said. "I didn't even look back to see if the tormentor was all right."

"You couldn't have known what was happening," she said. "And there had to have been other lifeguards there that day."

"Jackson called in," Toby recalled. "Said he was sick,

but we all knew his girlfriend was throwing a party at her parents' lake house. We were short-staffed."

"And a teenager yourself," she was quick to remind him. But he didn't think that acquitted him. He'd been hired to do a job, which was keep swimmers safe in the water. No matter how much of a jerk the teen was being, it was Toby's responsibility to look out for him.

"My ego got in the way, and I turned my back on him," Toby said.

"And you've been carrying around the guilt ever since," Jules said quietly, almost reverently.

What else should he do? Saving lives was his responsibility.

"You do realize that you couldn't have known what was happening behind your back or that the teen would drown," she reminded him, reaching out to touch his arm. There was something special about the way she touched him. Like she always reached his soul with her lightest contact.

"Doesn't release me from my responsibility," he countered.

"I understand," she said. "Do you blame me for…what's his real name?"

"Axel Holmes," he supplied. "His brother Reed went by the nickname Champ."

"That's unusual," she said.

"According to the article—" he motioned toward the worn, yellowed piece of folded paper at the bottom of the box "—his father had named him based on what he wanted people to shout from the stands."

"A sports fanatic?"

"To the nth degree," Toby said. "The article said Champ had a promising football career. To me, he was just a bully in the pool."

"Someone who is athletic can usually take care of themselves," she added, trying her best to give him an out he had no intention of taking.

Jules caught his gaze and locked on. Determination caused her to bite down hard before she spoke. "Do you think I'm responsible for Axel's escape?"

"No."

"Do you blame me for the man breaking into my home and stealing my underwear?" she pressed like a defense attorney in court on a roll.

"Of course not, Jules," he quickly countered. The last person she should blame was herself. It took a second, but it dawned on him what she was trying to do. Rather than put up an argument, he shook his head and cracked a small smile. "I hear you."

"Then you have to let yourself off the hook too," she said. Before he could respond, she added, "And if you can't do that today, promise me that you'll go easier on yourself moving forward."

"Have you ever considered going to law school?" he asked.

His question clearly caught her off guard. Her face wrinkled.

"What does that have to do with—"

It was her turn to catch on.

She tapped his arm. "I'll look into it if you'll consider forgiving yourself."

He could add negotiator to her long list of good traits. Jules was one of a kind. But she was right earlier. They wouldn't be able to stay this close forever. Someone, at some point, would get in between them.

The thought nearly knocked his breath out. Could he do anything about it, though?

JULES WOULDN'T PRESS the issue. Not when Toby was seriously considering her point of view. He didn't put up a counterargument, which was a good sign. New ideas worked in the back of Toby's mind until he made a decision whether or not to accept them. More often than not, he came to see reason.

She would let her comments marinate and hope he could find some leeway in his heart for past mistakes—mistakes anyone could have made. Most would move on without a second thought. That was what made Toby so special. He cared. Deeply. Even when he didn't want to admit it.

He was also too hard on himself, demanding things he would never expect from another human being.

Toby's gaze fixed on a certain Ziploc with the initials *LW* on it. He managed to scoot it against the metal wall and then out of the container. Her heart hurt for him as he studied the contents: a ring, a piece of cotton from what looked like her pajamas, an ankle bracelet and eyelashes.

Those were the only remnants left in the baggie of his sister. The evidence storage system suggested the crimes were well thought out. The lack of DNA evidence left behind that could be traced to him meant Axel was thorough. That was to be expected from someone who'd evaded capture for eleven years.

Now they knew that he slipped in and out of other people's identities too. In the mix were Social Security cards and copies of driver's licenses, along with birth certificates. She had no idea on sight how many were legal copies or doctored. Axel held a genuine hatred in his heart for women. Rape suggested he felt inferior. What trauma in his life caused him to want to take out his rage on innocent women? His victims ranged in age from late teens to early thirties. None looked the same, so it was women in general the man hated. Blamed?

"I can't believe he would blame you for his brother's drowning after all this time," she said, mainly thinking out loud.

"He was eight or nine years old when it happened," he recalled. "Look at the way he's looking up at his big brother like he's some kind of hero."

"One person's bully can be another person's saint, I guess," she considered.

"Depending on the circumstances, yes," he stated. "There was a case that ended with me talking to a mother whose son had committed horrific crimes. She covered for him. Hid him. Refused to admit she'd even seen him around until the FBI threatened to arrest her nineteen-year-old daughter for prostitution if the woman didn't reveal where she was hiding her son."

Jules had had similar cases.

"Rather than give up her only daughter, she gave us the location of her son," Toby continued. "I was on the arrest team. We had to bring the mother in a van to point out her son's identity because he'd gotten one of his friends to box him, hitting his face until it was almost unrecognizable. The man could sit at a table next to law enforcement at a restaurant and not be identified."

She nodded.

"The mother ran out of the van, wrapped her arms around her son's knees while he was handcuffed and begged his for-giveness," Toby revealed. "Her son had killed the woman's new husband because he said the man looked at him wrong. Still, the mother believed the son was a saint."

"Hard to believe," she said, shaking her head.

"He'd been paying her rent for two years, ever since his

father's death, had bought her a Mercedes to drive around in and fancy clothes," he explained. "She believed he was the best son that a mother could have."

"Even evil lives in shades of gray," she admitted.

"I could have been a real twerp, but my sister would have thought I hung the moon," he said. "Would she ever be able to forgive a person who was responsible for my death?"

"You didn't hold the boy's head underwater," she felt the need to point out, even though she understood his point.

"To Axel, that's exactly what I did," Toby said.

"It doesn't excuse what he's doing," Jules stated. Talking about family made her realize she should touch base with hers. She palmed her cell phone and checked the screen. "Off topic, but do you have any bars?"

Toby checked, then shook his head. "Sure don't."

"I guess I should have expected as much out here in the middle of a sleet storm." Sleet pinging the metal roof sounded like they were taking live rounds.

An apology crossed Toby's features.

"It was my idea to come out here, remember?" She felt the need to point it out so he didn't add this to his list of reasons to blame himself.

"I know," he said. "But I should have done a better job of protecting you."

"You already are, Toby," she said. "I just wish you could see it too." Then she added, "Plus, we protect each other. It's what partners do. You have my back, and I have yours. Remember?"

Toby didn't answer. His slight nod said she'd gotten through what could be a thick skull when he wanted it to be.

Figuring it was best to let Toby sit in his thoughts, she got her own fork and then went back to the Ziplocs. There were twenty-three. Twenty-three lives cut short. Twenty-three families left devastated. Twenty-three women who would never grow old.

Moments like this put life into perspective.

As much as she didn't want her grandparents to leave this earth, they'd lived long, full lives filled with everything people were meant to experience. There'd been hardships, good times, surprises and setbacks. But most of all, their lives had been filled with love. They were quick to forgive and first to encourage.

They lived beautiful lives filled with work they wanted to do and people who loved them with their whole hearts.

Maybe they had it all figured out after all.

Still, as long as there was fight left in them, she would beg them to stay, wishing for at least one more hug, family dinner and holiday season with them.

Looking down at these Ziplocs brought home the fact that even the longest of lives was still short.

Why waste a second of it?

A gust of wind cut into her thoughts, causing her to jump practically out of her skin as debris slammed into the exterior wall.

"Toby," she said, reaching for him as she tried to breathe.

"I'm here," came the reassurance, quick as lightning to a dark room.

She hoped her sedan would be okay out there without being parked in a garage. It was their only mode of transportation. The second the storm let up and the roads were safe, she wanted to get out of here.

They were in Axel's territory now.

# Chapter Twenty

Jules shivered, even though it was warm in the shelter thanks to the heater.

"Wish we could figure out how bad this thing is predicted to get," she said, rubbing her arms as though to warm them.

Toby regretted her being involved. He wished one thing in his life could remain untouched, free from his curse. "We could always go to the main house and ask. The new owner is most likely stocked with better equipment, possibly a satellite for emergencies. The person would also likely have a generator in case power goes out, which I imagine happens a little too often around here."

Winds howled at this point. The noisy metal roof that sounded like bullets striking did little to calm his raging headache. His side ached. And he was long overdue to take a pain pill.

The problem with medicine was that it dulled his senses too much.

"With the phones out of range, we can't call any of this evidence in," Jules pointed out. Her forehead creased like it did when she was in serious contemplation. "We can't ask if there's been any progress in the investigation."

"I doubt we'd get an honest answer there," he stated. Not when they were considered suspects. Now that he understood his connection to Axel, Toby's thoughts circled back to Captain Crawford. "Do you think the captain was involved?"

Jules shrugged. "I've been wondering the same thing lately. At first, I didn't want to consider the possibility, to be completely honest. I'd never flown with him before, but he came across as a good guy."

"I had the same impression," Toby stated.

The heater flickered on and off. Jules cursed under her breath.

"There's enough kerosene in the lamps to get us through the night if the heat holds," he reassured her.

As frustrating as it was to get this far and have Mother Nature stop them cold, he wouldn't risk going back out. Not even to find a spot where he was in range to use his cell phone.

Could they trouble the homeowner to use an emergency satellite phone? If they were certain the new owner had one, it would be a no-brainer.

Toby pushed up to standing and moved to the window. There were no lights on at the main house. Was anyone home?

There was nothing more than a small barn on the property. Toby hadn't seen horses in the fields or a structure large enough to run a full-on horse operation. Which could mean the owner wasn't even around with no livestock to tend to.

He wished he'd asked Jodie a few questions about who'd bought her cousin's home and whether she knew the person well enough to see if he could ask them a few questions.

Then again, they hadn't planned on sticking around town. The plan had been to get Jules safely away from the incoming storm. It had been Toby's idea to circle back and check the shed. This was on him. He sat back down, frustrated with himself.

"Hey." Jules's voice broke through his heavy thoughts. "What are you thinking?"

He shook his head.

"You look worried," she continued. "Is it the storm?"

"In part," he admitted. That was as far as he was willing to go.

"We can barricade the windows to keep debris from flying through them," she started. "And we can block the door with…" She glanced around the room. "The dining chair." There was a small square table pushed up against the corner of the back wall that had two wooden chairs tucked in. She hopped up and went to work, securing the door by wedging the back of one of the chairs under the knob. "There. That'll keep us from being surprised."

She stood in the center of the room, glancing around.

"We don't need all of the blankets, so we can use them to insulate the windows," she said. "Thankfully, there are only two to cover."

Before he could get to his feet, she'd fixed blankets to cover the windows. It was smart because it would also keep glass contained in the event a window was hit with debris hard enough to break it. There was a reason weather people advised against standing next to a window during a storm. Being hit and killed by debris or broken glass took more folks out than anything else in a storm. Texas's version of Mother Nature knew how to throw one serious temper tantrum too. She had no qualms about tossing cars around or upending fifty-year-old oak trees to send them flying through home windows.

"You're amazing, Jules. Do you know that?" He couldn't

help himself from saying those words out loud. They were words she deserved to hear.

Jules shot him a glare that shocked him.

"What?" he asked. "It's not a crime to tell your best friend what she should hear every day."

"That's not the problem, and you know it."

She studied him. Hard.

"Then what?" he asked. She needed to tell him because he honestly had no idea why she would be upset with him after he complimented her.

Jules brought her hand up to her hip, where she fisted it. "You better not be saying goodbye to me, Toby Ward."

Was he?

JULES KNEW TOBY well enough to realize he would do anything in his power to protect her, including draw Axel away from her. "You better not plan to slip out of here when I go to sleep."

"I would never do that to you," Toby stated with enough conviction for her to believe him.

"Let me decide what's best for me," she said. "Promise you won't make a decision on my behalf without letting me weigh in."

He cracked a smile.

"Promise," she urged.

"You have my word," he finally agreed. Toby's word was better than gold bars in the bank. Gold prices fluctuated based on the market. Toby was unchanging.

"Okay, then," she said, realizing just how drained she was. The dull ache in between her eyes felt like a tiny person with a jackhammer working the inside of her skull. "I'm tired and I want to know that if I take a nap, you'll be here when I wake up."

He gave himself a once-over. "Where am I going to go in this condition?"

This time, she smiled despite the hammering hell going on inside her brain. "You make a good point there."

"Besides, leaving you alone would put you at greater risk," he reasoned. "Because he'll go after you either way. If we're together, we have a better chance at fighting this bastard."

"You've thought this through," she said.

"I have to because you're too important to me to lose," he explained, like it was as plain as the nose on her face.

The sentiment went both ways.

"Let's freshen up and try to get some rest," she said. "Maybe by the time we wake up, the storm will have passed."

Toby nodded. "You go first."

Jules figured she might as well shower while she had the chance. She piled her hair on top of her head and made quick work of washing off. She changed into the fleece joggers they'd bought at the store and then brushed her teeth.

Rejoining Toby, she asked, "Do you need help with a shower?"

"Is that an invitation?" he quipped, clearly proud of his comeback.

"Funny," she said, shaking her head now that the pain had lightened up somewhat. Showers had a way of washing off the day and hitting the reset button. "Do you think we should put the evidence box in the trunk before we get too comfortable?" It dawned on her they should do their best to preserve it. They had a name now and evidence. Axel would have a much more difficult time hiding. "While I'm thinking about it, I might as well send a text to my family and Mack."

Toby cocked an eyebrow.

"When we get cell coverage, the messages will go through," she said. "That way, I won't have to keep checking my phone."

"We should definitely tell Mack our current location, what we found and the reason we're here in the first place," he said, catching on to her logic with a proud smile.

Toby being proud of her shouldn't warm her heart in the way that it did. What could she say? The man had an effect on her like no other, and she'd learned not to fight it a long time ago.

He attempted to stand up on his own, immediately landed on his backside—a backside that wasn't awful on the eyes. "About that offer of help with a shower. Does it happen to start with helping me up?"

"I might be able to arrange a little assistance," she said, needing a few lighter moments to recharge her battery after the heaviness of finding and opening the metal box.

"And, yes, we should put the evidence in a safer place just in case," he said, a little more solemn now. "For safekeeping."

"I can do that," she offered after helping him to his feet. "Why don't you strip as much as possible while I run it out to the trunk?"

"I'd rather keep watch behind you if you don't mind," he said, reminding her of the ever-present threat.

Jules nodded. "Let's see. How should I carry the box?"

Fingerprints were a tricky beast. Whether or not a good print could be lifted was affected by multiple conditions. For one, they had to remain intact to be worth anything. Evaporation could impact the quality of the print. Other things, like sunlight, temperature and humidity, could change what could be lifted and speed up the evaporation process. As a material evaporated, it lost volume, and if it shrank too much, fingerprint dust lost the ability to detect a print at all. Rough surfaces were notorious for making dust unreliable. Dried paint was the opposite. The smooth surface would make the print easier to lift. There were other ways to lift prints—using light, for example—but that was above Jules's pay grade. There was a reason agencies employed forensic specialists; DNA evidence wasn't as cut-and-dried as TV shows would have the public believe.

This box could be tricky considering it was tucked into a floorboard in a room that was cold, humid, hot and every other condition the weather concocted on a given day. This part of Texas experienced all seasons. Sometimes in the same day.

"Closing the lid is easier than clasping the lock shut," he reasoned as he studied the box.

"I can wrap it in a dish towel," she offered. "We might lose some prints externally, but this surface and these conditions might have already done that job."

"I agree," he said. "Let's close the lid first." He did so using one of the forks. That part was easy enough. Closing the clasp was going to be harder. Was it necessary?

"Let me see if I can find a paper bag in the kitchen," she said, moving in the direction of the small space. There were a couple of cabinets with minimal supplies in them. She located a carton of Ziploc bags, decided not to touch those. There was a hot plate, so maybe she could find something better to use than her hands.

She opened a drawer by the hot plate and, voilà, located a pair of tongs. "We should have checked the drawer sooner." She turned around with the tongs in hand.

"Yes, we should have," he agreed with a smile. "But what a find."

"I think we should take the carton of Ziploc bags from the cabinet," she said.

"Definitely," Toby stated. "Are they the same as the kind we found in the box?"

"I believe so," she said. As far as evidence went, they'd hit the jackpot here. Amarillo was a centralized location, which would make it easier for Axel to move through neighboring states as well as Texas. So much clicked into place with this find. Everything but the one lingering issue of Captain Crawford. If he was guilty of working with Axel, the pilot had paid the ultimate price. Among the artifacts found here so far, money wasn't one of them. It was the only thing she could think of in terms of swaying Crawford to mess up comms. "We need a list of names of anyone who had access to the chopper before we took off."

"I'm sure investigators will chase names down," he said. "And I'm also certain we're the last people they'd share them with."

"You have a good point there," she said. "Now that we're under scrutiny and on medical leave, all of our access will be cut off."

"True," he said. "But we wouldn't be naive enough to tap into work computers. If Mack gets the list, we have a shot at him sharing the names. Or at the very least, giving us a heads-up that it was confirmed foul play with regards to the chopper."

"Not sure how much good any of the information will do when I really think about it," she reasoned. "What we have here is so much more powerful. Crawford didn't survive the crash, so it isn't like we can go to him for information or squeeze him if he's dirty."

"It would be good to know what we're dealing with," he said. "And if anyone higher up is involved in aiding Axel."

"You make any enemies lately that I should know about, Toby?" she half teased. She removed the Ziploc carton with tongs, using a small plastic trash bag to collect more items with a smooth surface and a better chance at providing a good print. The more ammunition she had to connect Axel to the crime, the better. If he actually used the Ziplocs here, they were a good find. They'd prove he came to this place in case no fingerprints could be lifted from the metal box or evidence inside. In fact, it linked him to the evidence box. He'd been meticulous with his crime scenes. No prints had ever been lifted, and he'd never left behind DNA.

Then again, he'd been caught once. He'd led investigators to several crime scenes, proud of his work.

And now he was coming for her best friend.

## Chapter Twenty-One

After gathering evidence, Toby moved to the bathroom and managed to shimmy out of his pants. Those dropped to the floor with ease compared to trying to take off his shirt.

"All right," he said into the crack. The door was ajar in case he needed help. He hadn't been ready to admit defeat until now. "I give. I'm tapping out. I need you."

"Thought you'd be calling me," Jules said as she opened the door.

"You must have been standing right outside," he said.

"Figured it would save time when you needed me," she supplied. "Why don't you sit down on the toilet lid, so I can help you off with your shirt."

He'd managed to get out of the sling okay. Taking off a sweatshirt was a whole other ball game. That had to come over his head. He struggled to pull his bad arm inside, figuring it was a good first step to pulling the sweatshirt over his head.

"Here, let me help with that," Jules said.

He ignored the way her beautiful eyes glittered every time they were this close, focusing instead on something that wouldn't cause all blood to fly south and him to tent his boxers. An oil change. The pickup he used to tool around on his property needed an oil change.

Yep, that did it. Blocking out all thoughts of Jules and focusing on something mundane did the trick as she helped him remove his arm from the sleeve and then tugged on the left sleeve to make it easier for him to repeat that on his working side.

After that, it was her job to slide the sweatshirt over his head.

"Remind me to wear button-ups or zip-ups from now on," he said as he raked a hand through his wild hair.

"We might have only bought pullovers," she said with that characteristic sneaky smile that had ways of burrowing deep inside his chest.

"Sounds about right," he said with a chuckle that was worth the pain. "I might need a little more help than I realized."

"Okay," she said, the nervous edge to her voice threatening to unravel his resolve. "What can I do?"

"Stay close, just in case," he said.

"Will do," she said. "I can hold up a towel if you'd like to finish getting undressed."

"Sounds good," he said, holding off on standing up and stepping out of his boxers until she gave the green light. It came a couple of seconds later.

Then his boxers were on the floor. He would have to be careful not to get wet the bandage underneath his ribs where the doc had removed a small piece of metal. His body didn't seem to realize how small the piece had been, because it hurt like hell. The last thing he wanted to do was rip out twelve stitches, so he was careful not to raise his arm too high as he stepped into the shower stall and turned on the water.

The cold hit him fast and hard, but it also reminded him that he was alive.

The water took a second to warm up. By the time it did, his entire body was like ice.

But when warm water sluiced over him, he felt halfway decent for the first time today.

He kept the shower short and sweet. As he turned the spigot off, Jules stuck a towel inside the stall.

"Here you go," she said. "Do you need help drying off?"

"I should be good from here on out," he reassured her. "Thanks for being here, though. And for everything else you've done for me over the last few days. Hell, years, if we're being honest. I'm still trying to figure out why you chose to sit down next to me on your first day."

"Because you were the smartest person in the room," she said.

"You couldn't have known that," he countered.

"True," she said, "so I had to go with the best-looking guy in the room instead. I just told you that you were smart to pump up your ego."

He could hear the smile in her voice—that same damn smile that burrowed a little deeper this time.

"Jules, you never told me that you had a crush on me," he quipped.

Another crack of thunder boomed, shaking the structure that was protecting them from the elements.

It reminded Toby to hurry and get dressed.

Working faster meant more pain. To hell with it. No choice.

With heroic effort, Toby managed boxers, joggers and socks. Next came a T-shirt.

"Found a zipper hoodie," Jules said with a hint of pride in her voice. "Turns out we weren't completely oblivious to how difficult getting clothes on and off would be for you."

He accepted help in shrugging into the hoodie and then

moved out of the small space that felt a little too intimate. They'd moved the evidence to a safer location. Jules had texted their supervisor with the latest information. She'd updated her family so they wouldn't worry. They'd gone over the shed a couple of times to make sure there was no other evidence hiding in the walls, cabinets or flooring.

"Think you can get a little rest?" he asked. There wasn't much left to do while they waited out the storm.

"I can try," she said.

Toby already realized closing his eyes would be a bad idea. Seeing the Ziploc with his sister's initials had sent him into an emotional tailspin. One that had been working in the back of his mind no matter how much he was trying to force it out.

Close his eyes and those horrific images from the crime scene would haunt him.

"Keep me warm?" Jules asked, a catch in her voice as she motioned toward the bottom bunk farthest away from a window.

"Of course," he said, hearing the low, gravelly quality to his own. What could he say? Jules had an effect on him. She would always have an effect on him. He'd learned to live with it because they weren't always this together. Distance kept him from going for something that he could regret later.

Would he, though? Because he was beginning to think it was far worse not to step up to the plate than to bat and miss.

Toby shook off the sentiment as an effect of him being bone-tired. His thoughts took on a life of their own when he was exhausted. And *exhaustion* wasn't nearly big enough a word for what he felt.

Jules took his left hand in hers and led him to the bed. "You want in first?"

"No, you" was all he managed to say.

She climbed into the den-like space and then scooted all the way back to the wall. The twin-size bed wasn't nearly large enough for him to spread out. Before joining her, he retrieved both of their weapons.

After tucking their guns under the mattress, he maneuvered himself underneath the covers. Her warm body pressed firmly against his as she curled herself around his left side. On his back, Toby positioned himself so that she could settle into the crook of his arm.

Being like this with Jules made the world right itself in Toby's eyes.

Within a matter of minutes, her steady, even breathing indicated she'd fallen asleep. A growing piece of him liked how safe she must feel in his arms in order to surrender to sleep. He closed his eyes and, surprisingly, drifted off too.

JULES WOKE WITH a start. She immediately sat up and banged her head on the top bunk. Toby reacted to her movement. Gun in hand, he was up and out of bed in a heartbeat.

"What is it?" he asked. "What did you hear?"

She looked around, trying to orient herself. "Wind?"

Toby sat on the edge of the bed and then rested his elbows on his thighs as he leaned forward. "What time is it?"

There was no clock in the shed, nothing that would require electricity beyond what the strip was capable of producing and nothing that required babysitting with battery replacement. Folks passing through here brought their own time with them.

She checked her phone. At least the clock function still worked. "Three."

Toby rocked his head, still on high alert.

"Did you sleep at all?" she asked, scooting beside him after stretching out her arms.

"A little," he said.

"You woke me up twice, snoring," she teased. It was true, though, and she hadn't wanted to wake him.

"Guess I got more than a little, then," he said with a laugh that caused him to wince.

Seeing him in this level of pain made her question their decision to be so far away from home. "How do you feel?"

"I've been better," he quipped with a devastating little half smile. The show of clean, white, straight teeth was enough to cause the ladies in the office to talk at a higher pitch. She'd be lying if she said he had no effect on her.

"Same here," she admitted. "Coffee? I think I can figure out how to make some."

"Might as well go for it," he said. "Who knows how much longer we'll have electricity."

He barely got out the words when the power went out.

"I think you just jinxed us, Toby."

"Sorry about that," he said with too serious a tone for her offhanded comment. It reminded her just how much he blamed himself for everything that went wrong.

She wanted to point out that he should give himself more credit. Focus more on everything he did right, which was a lot. Since her words would likely fall on deaf ears, she held her tongue. For now. When the right moment struck, he was going to get an earful. He should know just how wonderful he was, how many lives he'd saved and how important he was to everyone around him, including her.

"We should check on the main house," he said, cutting into her thoughts. "Living out here, the owner should have a generator."

"Let's go," she said after checking out the window. "I saw a chimney in the front of their house when we drove in. Worst-case scenario, we beg to stay inside their living room to keep warm. At these temperatures and with sleet, we'll freeze by morning if we don't regroup."

Jules grabbed their shoes and placed Toby's down in front of him. She worried about the evidence being damaged by the cold while in her trunk. It was still the safest place to store the metal box and Ziploc carton. They couldn't risk those items returning to Axel's hands. He would destroy evidence. Every single young woman represented in those Ziplocs deserved to be acknowledged. Their families deserved to be notified. It was the only way they would find any peace, considering Axel hadn't admitted to all his crimes. Some families might still be waiting up at night, waiting for news of a loved one.

After sliding into her runners, Jules laced them up and stood. Hands on her hips, she asked, "Ready?"

They had no idea who owned the home now or what kind of reception they would receive. Someone who'd kept Teddy's tradition alive with the shed couldn't be all bad. Or so she hoped.

"Let's roll," he said after pushing to standing.

"We should probably take the backpack with us," she wondered out loud.

"I can get it," he said.

Jules stopped him with a hand up. "I'll take this one, big guy."

Toby's mouth opened to protest, then clamped shut just as quickly. She wasn't being stubborn. She was being realistic. He needed to conserve energy. He offered a quick nod of concession.

She shouldered the backpack after removing the chair wedged underneath the door handle. But first, she collected their weapons and placed them inside.

Toby led the way to the main house, where a light was on in the back room. Kitchen?

He must be right about the generator. Could they throw themselves on the homeowner's mercy? Ask to spend the rest of the night inside the home?

They could circle back to Jodie's house. She might let them stay there if push came to shove. Hopefully, it wouldn't come to driving on icy roads.

"You should do the knocking," Toby said, stepping aside as they reached the back porch.

Sleet that felt like needles against her skin came down in sheets. Ice had already built up on the concrete porch, causing Jules to slip and nearly bite it. She grabbed Toby's arm to steady herself and more of those rockets shot through her. That was one way to keep warm, she mused, trying to keep her mood light instead of panicking.

Mother Nature was the great equalizer. She didn't discriminate. Frostbite affected everyone equally. So did hypothermia. Cold was cold.

She shivered against the biting wind as she raised a fist to knock on the screen door. The wood door swung open before she had a chance to bring her knuckles down on the glass.

An older woman stood on the other side of the door. She had to be in her late sixties if she was a day. Her full head of gray hair was piled on top of her head in a bun. She had a kind but worn look, like she'd spent too many hours in the sun. She wore a thick flannel nightgown that fell past her ankles, revealing sheep-colored bootee slippers and a peek of wool socks. "I've been concerned about you two."

How did she know there were two of them? Did she watch the shed to see who came and went?

A glimmer of fear passed behind her eyes as she opened

the screen door. "Please, come inside before you freeze to death standing out there."

Jules was already shivering from the frigid temps and needlelike sleet. Her body wanted to step inside the warmth despite warning bells going off in the back of her mind. She glanced to Toby, who hesitated.

Was he getting the same weird feeling that something was off?

Then the door opened wider, revealing a man standing next to the older woman with a gun pointed at her back.

*Axel.*

## Chapter Twenty-Two

Jules's thoughts immediately snapped to the guns inside her backpack. Was there any way she could get to one of them without alerting Axel?

Coming face-to-face with the monster brought a cold chill down her spine that even an Amarillo ice storm couldn't beat.

Deciding against making a move that could cause Axel's trigger finger to twitch, killing an innocent person before he turned the weapon on them, Jules shifted her weight to hide the backpack behind her.

"Ms. Haven asked the two of you to come inside nicely," Axel said. "Now do as the kind lady said."

Toby stepped inside first as the pair backed away, keeping enough distance that he couldn't make a move for the gun. Axel had to realize they would never jeopardize an innocent civilian. Thus the hostage.

After her friend, Jules entered the kitchen. Toby intentionally placed his body in front of hers.

"Close the door," Axel demanded, shutting off their means of easy escape. He studied Jules for a long moment. "And set the backpack on the floor where I can see it."

Jules did as instructed, muttering a curse that only Toby

was close enough to hear. Setting Axel off while he had a gun in his hand would end in disaster.

"Kick it over to me," Axel commanded, clearly feeling in charge of the situation.

She did, biting her tongue. Staying calm and assessing the situation might just keep them alive. Without being obvious, Jules studied the room in search of anything that could be used as a makeshift weapon. She'd once used a glass flower vase on a restaurant table.

"I knew it was you the minute the story broke after I killed that bitch of a sister of yours," Axel said to Toby.

Toby's hands clenched into fists. Anger rolled off her friend in palpable waves.

Ms. Haven stood there as her five-foot-four-inch frame shook with fear. She mouthed an apology.

Jules gave a slight head shake. It broke her heart that the elderly woman blamed herself in any way for this nightmare. Ms. Haven didn't need to apologize for a monster's actions. None of what was happening was her fault. She was caught in the middle of something that had nothing to do with her. If anything, Jules should be the one to apologize. If she hadn't insisted they go searching for answers, Ms. Haven would be safe in her bed right now.

If there was a hell, there had to be a special place there for bottom-feeders who took advantage of the kindness of strangers. For jerks who used them and then tossed them in the trash like garbage. For monsters who wrecked so many lives by feeding their own twisted desires.

"You did this to me," Axel said, his gaze intent on Toby. "This is all your fault. All those women you made me kill. Their blood is on your hands."

It was taking all Toby's willpower not to make a move toward Axel. Jules could read her friend's intent in his tense body language and the way he clenched his jaw, the way his muscles corded and in the way he leaned forward ever so slightly, like a runner about to jump-start as soon as a whistle was blown.

"You're off base," Toby finally ground out.

"Really?" Axel's voice was higher pitched now, like he was working into a frenzy. "Are you trying to tell me that you weren't the one who turned your back on my brother at the pool? You aren't the one who let him drown? Because I stood there on the edge of the pool and watched every second of it."

Toby didn't immediately speak.

"You took him away from me," he said, his voice almost to hysterics. "He was the only one who ever cared, who took a beating so I wouldn't have to because I was bad."

"You weren't bad," Jules said as calmly as possible. "You were a kid."

"Bed wetters get a beating, my stepdad used to say," Axel continued.

There was something almost sympathetic about the man standing in front of them now. Like he'd transformed back to that little kid taking beatings right before their eyes. Jules had never met a criminal who didn't have a horrific story behind them. But not everyone who'd been beaten or abandoned took their pain out on innocent people. There was no excuse for the monster Axel had become.

"But my brother stood up for me," Axel continued, like he'd been wanting—no, *needing*—to unburden himself for years.

"This is your chance, Axel," she said. Using his name was a calculated move. He would either ramp up his hate or be calmed by it. She needed to figure out which way he would go since calming him down might save their lives. "Tell us what your stepdad did to you."

His eyes filled with fire and rage. For a split second, Jules thought her instincts were off and she'd just made a fatal mistake.

"He punished me just like I punish others," Axel bit out, spitting out the words.

"You're still alive," she pointed out. "Why did you kill your victims?"

He became indignant now. "I showed them mercy."

"How? By killing them?" she pressed. If Axel ended up with the upper hand, she deserved to know why he killed her.

"I ended it for them," he raged. "I'm merciful, not like that son of a bitch who hurt me. They don't have to wake up every day afraid I'll come back and hurt them all over again."

"Rape," she corrected. "Not hurt. You raped them. And then you took their lives in the most horrific way, watching them die by your hands. That's not mercy, Axel." Jules's brain was working overtime to figure out how to get Ms. Haven away from the monster and give them a fighting chance to take him down. He'd come out better after the chopper *accident*, if that story still held water, than all three of the other occupants. Had he known it would go down? Somehow anticipated the crash?

How was that possible?

"It ended for them right there," he argued. "They didn't have to deal with the pain that came after. The nightmares that haunt you."

"You were a child, Axel," she said. "You didn't deserve what happened to you."

He took in a sharp breath, expanding his chest until he

looked like the six-foot-two-inch man he'd become. His eyes glazed over like he was in some kind of trance. Bad signs.

"Bed wetters get a beating," he began chanting.

Ms. Haven slowly moved her hand behind her toward a drawer as she caught Jules's gaze.

*No. Please. Don't do anything that could get you killed.*

They needed time to figure out their next move.

"Bed wetters get a beating," the chant continued. Axel was working himself up. Was this his routine? How he worked himself up to rape and murder?

The man had decided he was freeing those he tortured by killing them. He built himself up to be a saint inside his own mind.

Between Ms. Haven taking matters into her own hands and the energy building inside Axel, any little misstep could cause his finger to twitch. One shot was all it would take to send a bullet through the older woman's heart.

She needed to figure out a way to stop this runaway train from accelerating.

Before Jules could think of a next move or a way to warn Ms. Haven to stop, the drawer slowly opened. Axel was so focused on chanting and staring the two of them down, he didn't seem to notice Ms. Haven's slow movements as she slipped her hand inside the drawer.

A moment later, she came out with a chopping knife.

Tension caused the muscles in Jules's shoulders to pull taut. At this rate, she feared they might snap. Not that it would matter. If Axel had his way, she'd be dead first.

She needed to think up a distraction.

"We found your metal box," she shouted at him, causing his gaze to refocus onto her. There was so much rage in his eyes she was almost knocked a step back when his gaze landed hard on her. "I sent it off to be analyzed. Soon enough, the whole world will know what you did and who you really are."

"That's not… It was… You did—"

"Yes, we did," she countered, trying to take control of the situation.

Toby reached back and squeezed her hand. Panic sent her pulse racing. He wanted her to keep going because he was about to make a move.

"THAT'S RIGHT," Jules continued, just like Toby hoped she would. He'd given her a signal, hoping she'd picked up on it.

So far, Toby had had to fight every instinct inside him that caused him to want to launch himself across the kitchen and dive into the bastard who had squeezed out too many innocent lives, including his sister's.

For five years, this man had taunted Toby. Axel had haunted Toby's dreams and caused him to relive the horrific details of his sister's rape and murder.

Staring the man down, Toby realized he'd allowed this bastard free rent in his head far too long. Lila was gone, and there was nothing Toby could do to bring his baby sister back, no matter how much it pained him to admit that he hadn't been there to protect her when she'd needed him most. He would take that knowledge to the grave.

The fact she fought back wasn't what killed her. In Axel's twisted world, he was releasing her from the pain he'd caused her—pain that would follow her the rest of her days. That bastard was going to kill her either way. He considered it mercy. It had nothing to do with the advice Toby had given her. Lila had lived long enough to tell law enforcement who'd killed her in her own way. And now the man stood in front of Toby.

The rage he'd felt in those first moments in the kitchen

was dissipating. Anger had kept him in his own mental prison far too long. It was time to let go, accept the fact his sister wasn't coming back and realize she would never have wanted him to live this way.

Lila would have asked Toby to forgive the bastard who'd murdered her. Not for Axel's sake but for Toby's. He could see that so clearly now.

The monster standing on the opposite side of the room had his own mental prison to live in. But he was going to jail for the rest of his life so he couldn't hurt another innocent soul. It was the best way to honor Lila.

Toby noted the knife Ms. Haven was currently trying to conceal. The long, sharp blade glinted from the side of her bony wrist. He practically willed her not to make a move.

"Your brother was a bully," Jules sounded off, causing Axel to shift the barrel of the gun to point at her.

Ms. Haven used the opportunity to spin around and then stab Axel. She'd reached for his chest, but he sidestepped in time to take the blade into his shoulder instead. For a split second, he stared at the blade that she jabbed farther inside him.

"Run!" Jules said to the elderly woman, drawing Axel's fury.

He fired the gun at the exact moment Toby pushed Jules out of the bullet's path. Instead of hitting her, it clipped him. He'd add it to the long list of injuries sustained in recent days and move the hell on.

Because Axel still had a weapon in his hand.

Toby dived toward the big guy, focusing on all the rage he'd had inside him over the last five years to cover the pain. He'd pay the piper later for that move. Right now, though, it worked.

He slammed into Axel's knees and heard a crack. A groan

followed as Jules managed to knock the gun out of Axel's hand. It went flying across the floor as Axel gripped the counter to brace himself.

Axel went down anyway, fighting as he slammed into the tile floor.

Toby rolled over, attempting to free his good hand, but Axel stopped him cold. The monster's knee came up, slamming into Toby's inner thigh. He released a grunt and tried to rally.

And then the snick of a bullet engaging in a chamber stopped them both.

Feet squared in an athletic stance, Jules stood just out of range with her weapon trained on Axel.

The monster froze, caught off guard by the turn of events.

Toby seized the moment, rolling out of grasp despite the pain to his right wrist.

"Hands where I can see 'em," Jules demanded as Toby caught his breath.

He managed to sit up, half expecting Axel to do the same.

Instead, the man looked dead straight at Jules.

"You're going to have to shoot," he said with a steady, even tone. Resigned? Ready to meet his maker?

Or was this a trick? A distraction from a monster who'd mastered the art?

Jules's hand was steady on her weapon.

"I'll shoot," she said, calm as you please. "But I'm not going to kill you. You don't deserve it." She rocked on her heels while maintaining sharp aim. "I'll shoot your right leg first and then your left, so you won't be able to run." There was a steadiness to her voice that said she meant business.

"You won't do it," Axel warned. "And if you tried, I'd move so you hit my heart."

"You won't be fast enough," Jules stated as Toby panted, trying to bring his breathing back to a reasonable pace.

As it was, he'd been nicked by a bullet and was bleeding.

It had taken all his energy to dive into the bastard. Toby had nothing left to give.

"You might as well do it now," Axel said, almost begging despite trying to cover it up.

"Or what?" Jules asked.

"I'll do it myself," Axel warned.

"No, you won't," Jules countered. "Do you know how I know?"

He didn't respond, just shot knives at her with his glare.

"Because you would have done it by now," she continued. "You're a coward who hurts innocent, unsuspecting people." She bit those last words out in a harsh tone. "You're not merciful. You're a monster."

He started toward her. The man was going to force her to shoot. Their training taught them to shoot to kill.

And then from behind, Ms. Haven sneaked back into the room without Axel realizing the older woman was coming toward him. She grabbed a cast-iron pan from on top of her stove and delivered a knockout blow.

Axel's gaze widened in surprise as his head snapped forward. He didn't have time to put his hands out before his head smacked the tile and he slumped over.

Ms. Haven stood over him. "Bastard made me miss my beauty sleep."

The snappy comment shouldn't have made Toby and Jules laugh as hard as it did. But it was over. Axel was going back to jail, where he belonged.

Toby had no energy left to get up as Jules went to work tying Axel's hands and feet behind his back and Ms. Haven tended to Toby's newest wound.

"Thank you," Jules said to the elderly woman, wrapping her in a hug as the sounds of vehicles pulling up outside caught their attention. As far as they knew, Axel worked alone.

## Chapter Twenty-Three

Jules raced to the front window two steps behind Ms. Haven, needing to be prepared for whatever they were about to face.

"It's the cavalry," Ms. Haven said, sounding as confused as Jules felt.

"What the hell?" Jules asked before relaying the message loud enough for Toby to hear. "We have a deputy, an ambulance and a fire truck."

Ms. Haven opened the front door, ushering everyone inside as she rattled off her statement to the deputy.

"Officer down in the kitchen," Jules immediately said to an EMT. She did an about-face and bolted down the hall as he followed, hot on her heels.

By the time she got to Toby with help, he was unconscious.

She immediately dropped down beside him, cupping his face. "Don't leave me like this, Toby." Tears welled in her eyes, blurring her vision. "Please. You're my best friend, my love, the person I want to spend the rest of my life with. Stay with me." Tears streamed down her face.

"Ma'am" was all she heard as the EMT urged her to take a step back as he placed an oxygen mask over Toby's nose and mouth.

This was real. This was happening. Toby was in danger of slipping away.

"Please don't go," she whispered when she could get close enough to his ear again as another EMT started working on him. "I don't want to do this life without you. You're my world. You're everything to me. I love you, Toby. Do you hear that? I can finally admit it to myself, to you. I've been in love with you since I saw you at the coffee shop that day. You didn't belong to me then, but everything inside my heart says you belong to me now. Don't leave me alone now that I've finally realized how much I love you."

"I'm sorry," the EMT said, interrupting the moment to lift Toby onto a gurney.

"Can I come with you?" she asked.

"No, ma'am," the EMT said. "But you can follow us to the hospital in your own vehicle." He paused for a second. "I wouldn't recommend it on these roads, though."

All Jules could do was helplessly stand there in the kitchen as the man she loved was wheeled away from her, fighting for his life.

A second later, Ms. Haven was at her side, wrapping her in a hug. "You shouldn't drive right now."

"I have to," Jules said, doing her level best to stem the flood of tears staining her cheeks. "I have to know that Toby is going to live. He's my partner."

"That's it—you're coming with me," Ms. Haven said. The woman might be tiny, but she was tough as nails.

Jules must have looked at her like she had three foreheads.

"I have two coats and a snowmobile in the garage for when my grandson comes to visit," Ms. Haven said. "Let's go."

Jules wasted no time in following the elderly woman. Though, the word *elderly* didn't apply to this spunky senior.

Before they left the kitchen, she stopped long enough to ask the deputy, "How did you know to come here?"

"My boss got a call from yours," the deputy said. "Said he got a series of texts from you."

"Keys to my trunk are in the backpack," Jules stated. "You'll find more evidence inside." She hesitated for a moment, dropping her gaze to a still-unconscious Axel. "He's slippery."

"I've been warned," the deputy said, pulling out the kind of restraints that reminded her of the ones used on Hannibal Lecter in *The Silence of the Lambs.* "Don't worry." He lifted one of the metal restraints. "I got this."

Axel would be locked up in similar fashion to the animal he turned out to be.

That was all Jules needed to know as Ms. Haven reached for her hand, clasped it in hers like a schoolgirl and led her to a closet where she kept snowsuits and helmets.

Once suited up, Ms. Haven brought the snowmobile around to pick Jules up on the front porch.

They got to the hospital less than a minute behind the ambulance.

"Go on," Ms. Haven urged. "I've got a lot to clean up back home."

Jules hugged the woman before bolting inside the glass double doors of the hospital. She immediately spotted an information desk, headed straight to it.

"I'm afraid you'll have to wait in the waiting room," a worker wearing a *Jeannie* name tag said from the visitor's desk.

"Not an option," Jules said. "I need to be in his room when he wakes up."

"It's policy, ma'am," Jeannie continued with a frown.

"Send your supervisor if you need to, but I'll check every room in this ER until I find my partner's," Jules stated, leaving no room for doubt. She might get into trouble for being insistent, but she refused to leave Toby alone.

Jeannie seemed to know when she'd lost a battle. "Go ahead, but don't say I told you that he's behind curtain seven in the ER." The middle-aged woman winked.

"Thank you," Jules said with as much gratitude in her voice as she could muster before racing to find Toby. The thought of him opening his eyes to find an empty room pushed her feet to move faster.

Curtain seven was easy enough to slip inside. Beeps and whoosh sounds filled the air, along with the low hum of voices. There was no real privacy in a place like this. The curtain being closed only gave the illusion they were alone. Feet scampered around, visible at the gap between the curtain and the sterile tile flooring.

Jules pulled the roller stool next to Toby. It had to be a good sign he'd been left in a room alone so quickly. Right?

Or was she grasping at straws, willing him to be okay?

She took his hand in hers, linking their fingers. He reacted to her touch with a twitch of his hand.

His eyes blinked open. "Hey."

"Toby," she managed to say through tears that were so ready to well up and fall. "Hey."

"He's…"

"Under arrest and not going anywhere but a lifetime of prison," she reassured him.

Toby nodded, exhaled. Really exhaled. It was almost like he released all his anger and hurt with the air from his lungs. "Good."

"Yes," she confirmed.

He turned his head toward her and studied her. "You're crying."

"I thought I lost you," she said.

He brought her hand up to his lips and feathered a kiss. "You couldn't."

She wasn't sure how deeply that comment ran, but she finally got her courage up and had to tell him the truth about how she felt about him. Because life was too short not to tell someone how special they were.

"I hope you mean that, Toby Ward," she started, finding the courage to keep going as she spoke. "Because I have something to say to you."

His forehead wrinkled, concerned.

Telling him exactly how she felt meant risking his friendship, but she couldn't hold back or lie to herself any longer.

"I never believed in love at first sight until I met you," she started. "Standing there in that coffee shop, I was hit with something so fast and hard that I could barely breathe." She paused as he studied her. *Keep going.* It was her turn to take in a fortifying breath. "And then I looked up, and you were gone. Just like that. I'd missed you. Which was strange, because from the moment I laid eyes on you, something told me that you were going to be special in my life."

He didn't speak, which she took as a bad sign.

But she was going all in, no matter what. Once he had all the information, he could decide how he wanted to move forward.

"I made a deal with myself right then and there that if I ever felt that way again about another soul, I wouldn't let him get away," she continued, feeling her heartbeat thunder inside her chest. She'd never felt so shaky before in her life. "Fast-forward to when I walked in the conference room and saw you sitting there." She compressed her lips at the sweet memory. "I forced myself to take the seat next to you so you'd have to talk to me. And then I chickened out because we were coworkers, and I had no idea if you felt the same way. I settled for friendship, and we became best friends." She drummed up a little more courage. Enough to keep going. "But recent events have forced me to reevaluate what I'm willing to accept. I should have told you from day one that I was crazy about you, Toby. But I didn't." She didn't dare meet his gaze while feeling so vulnerable. "And I'll regret that for the rest of my life because I've been in love with you from that first day." She paused as more tears filled her eyes. "It's okay if you don't feel the same way. I decided it's better to know one way or the other. This way, I know that I took the chance and risked it all because I finally found my person. I found the love of my life. I found home."

Tears spilled out of her eyes as she exhaled, steeling herself for the rejection she was certain would come.

"I'm not sure what you see in me, Jules," Toby started, letting go of her hand to bring his to her chin, forcing her to lift her gaze to meet his. "But I'm the luckiest damn man on earth. I've loved you from day one, and I agree on one thing." He hesitated. "We've spent way too long fighting our feelings for each other. You're the best thing that's ever happened to me. I'm so in love with you that it's hard to breathe when I first see your face every day. I love you and, more than anything, want to make a life together."

Jules couldn't hold back her smile at hearing those words.

"I never want to leave your side again," he said. "And when I'm strong enough to get out of this bed and down on one knee, I intend to ask you to do me the great honor of marrying me."

Jules climbed in bed with Toby, curling up against his body as he feathered kisses on her face before finding her lips.

"Yes," she said when they finally pulled back. "In case you were wondering, my answer will be yes."

"Then let's not waste any more time," he said. "Marry me."

Jules couldn't hold back her smile. "Wild horses couldn't stop me from marrying you, Toby Ward."

She'd found the man she wanted to spend the rest of her life with, and as soon as he was cleared to leave the hospital, it was time to take him home to Mesa Point to meet the rest of her family—a family that would welcome him with open arms.

And she couldn't wait to bring him home.

\* \* \* \* \*

# HUNTING THE CROSSBOW KILLER

## LENA DIAZ

Sending thanks to my sister, Laura Brown, for telling me about the mysterious Lake Lanier that gave me the idea for this series. The inspiration for this particular book in the series was the emotional, heart-tugging song 'Bobby' by Reba McEntire.

# Chapter One

Grace paused on the brick-paved sidewalk, subtly smoothing her hand down her light jacket to make sure her pistol was still secure in her shoulder holster and out of sight. Just steps away was a narrow c-obblestoned street. The street was deserted at the moment, likely because most of the people were attending the fall festival on the other side of the lake that split the town in two.

The sun had risen over the Smoky Mountains hours ago, but its rays were only just now beginning to penetrate the thick woods surrounding the town and burn off the mist rising from the water, partially obscuring the clusters of boats bobbing up and down.

The locals had dubbed this isolated Tennessee mountain town Mystic Lake, both for the lake of the same name and for its mysterious origins. Over seventy years ago, a series of unprecedented superstorms had dumped so much water on the mountains that mudslides had diverted a nearby river permanently. The resulting flash flood submerged a tiny logging town whose name had long since been forgotten, tragically drowning most of the residents. Those who'd survived never got the chance to retrieve their dead or rebuild what they'd once had. With the river now feeding the new lake, the water never receded.

This new town had gradually emerged. But as time went by, an alarming number of mysterious deaths and disappearances began to occur in the area. Speculation was that the original people who were killed when the lake covered the logging town were now haunting the area, reaching up from the lake's murky depths to punish those who dared to claim the land or drive boats over their watery graves. The lake was eerie, oppressive, dangerous. Or, at least, that was what Grace had read on the internet. Reality was proving to be something else entirely. Mystic Lake, both the water and the town, was beautiful, enchanting and compelling.

The festival appeared to be in full swing now with people milling around colorful tents set up in front of the town's only bed-and-breakfast and a couple of homegrown restaurants. Some of those tents no doubt held musicians, because Grace could hear the faint notes of a haunting melody drifting across the water.

Children laughed and played on slides and swings in a park at the end of the street. But a petting zoo just past the park appeared to be the largest attraction for families. A menagerie of farm animals bleated, mooed or clucked as they mingled with the townspeople behind a temporary rope fence that had been set up. And just to the left of that was a sloping hill where the lake and town both ended and thick woods began.

Towering oak, ash and hemlock trees in varying shades of green covered the mountains. Giant swaths of maples created a gorgeous sweep of oranges and yellows across the lower elevations, their leaves just starting to turn. It was as if an artist had purposely planted them so their leaves would flicker like brilliant flames as autumn descended. A few weeks from now, maybe even a month, this place would be bustling with tourists. Leaf peepers would brave the town's ominous reputation and take the hour-long drive down the winding two-lane road that was the only way in or out so they could witness nature's fiery display. But Grace was no tourist. And she wasn't here to soak in the sights or even partake in the festival.

Turning around, she studied the long row of fanciful-looking shops and businesses that bordered the sidewalk on her side of the lake, searching for one in particular. Would it be covered in stone and ivy like some of these buildings? Or was it one of the wooden structures with whitewashed cedar shakes and colorful wood trim gleaming brightly in the sunlight? The only thing for certain was that it would have flowers in front. All of the buildings did. Pink and white spilled over the sides of window boxes or filled large terra-cotta pots, whimsical like the cover of a book of fairy tales. But that fairy tale exterior could very well be hiding something dark and twisted, an evil that no one suspected was living here among them.

No one, that is, except Grace.

She continued down the sidewalk, noting the names of each shop or business as she passed. When she found the one she was looking for, she pulled on the door, nearly running into it when it didn't open as she'd expected. Frowning, she pushed, in case the door swung in instead of out. It didn't budge. It was locked.

Cupping her hands against the dark tinted window, she peered inside. Sure enough, there wasn't anyone sitting at the small cluster of desks. There was a glass-enclosed conference room on the back wall that was obviously empty. And the other areas she noted were empty, as well. But there were two doors on the left wall that were closed. Maybe someone was behind them. She knocked. When nothing happened, she knocked louder. Still nothing. She sighed and shook her head. They must have closed for the festival. Unbelievable. What kind of police department locked up the building and didn't leave at least one officer to handle emergencies? She'd have to go find them.

She whirled around and stepped onto the sidewalk.

"Ooof," she muttered as a man slammed into her.

He grabbed her around her waist, saving her from what would have been a nasty fall on the brick sidewalk. As soon as she was steady on her feet, he dropped his hands and hastily moved back.

"Sorry, ma'am. You okay?"

The slight Irish brogue in his deep voice had her looking up at him, her face heating with embarrassment over her clumsiness. Good grief, he was tall, and buff from the looks of his broad shoulders and the way his denim jacket tapered at his narrow waist cupped by faded jeans. But it was his face that had her cheeks heating even more. There was no other word to describe it except beautiful, like an angel's might be. His angular, sculpted cheeks were kissed by the sun, his skin a golden color that gave way to a barely-there beard and mustache. Wavy brown hair was just long enough to look in need of a cut and to save him from total perfection.

Then she met his gaze.

Grace had to suppress a shiver. His eyes were so dark they were almost black, with shadows seeming to swirl in their depths, giving him a sad, tortured look that hinted at mysterious secrets that took him from angel to fallen angel.

Her face heated even more as she realized she was staring. She cleared her throat and held out her hand to shake. "Sorry about that. I didn't look before I stepped onto the sidewalk. I'm Grace—"

Ignoring her hand, he circled around her and strode away at a brisk pace.

She blinked, her embarrassment giving way to annoyance. "Nice to meet you, too," she muttered as she straightened her jacket, automatically checking her weapon again and smoothing her hands down her slacks.

After giving one last frowning glance at the darkened building behind her, she headed in the same direction as the fallen angel, who was already heading around the end of the lake toward the other side. But something, or someone, must have caught his attention, because he abruptly changed direction and started up the hill toward the woods.

Near the tree line he stopped and sat in the shade of a maple tree, knees drawn up, his hands clasped across them. He was too far away for Grace to see his expression, but his posture seemed tense, like a bird of prey ready to swoop down or maybe fly away. The question was which would he do? And why were the few other townspeople on the same hill giving him wary looks and moving away?

Grace added him to the top of her list of people to speak to while she was here. Well, not the very top, but second for sure. The first person she had to speak to was no doubt somewhere in the crowd by the tents.

As she rounded the end of the lake and started across the bottom of the sloping hill, she spotted the man she was looking for, as evidenced by the flash of sun on the old-fashioned gold star on his uniform. She supposed he could be one of the regular police officers instead of the chief. But she doubted it. Confidence and authority seemed to surround him like an aura. The townspeople gave him the deference and respect that one would expect of someone in his position, politely smiling and greeting him as they passed.

Before approaching him, she couldn't resist one quick

glance up at the morose stranger she'd run into earlier. He was still in the same spot, but this time she was close enough to make out his expression. His mouth was drawn into a tight line of displeasure. And as she followed the direction of his gaze, she realized it was focused on the same group of people she was approaching, the one that included the police chief.

She started to make her way through the small crowd to introduce herself to the chief when something whizzed through the air just past her toward the lake. Someone screamed. Grace blinked in shock when she saw a large white feather on the haft of an arrow sticking out of the side of one of the small boats docked near the shore.

Chaos erupted as some people fled and others swarmed the boat, checking on the two people inside. The police chief shouted orders. Two officers emerged from the crowd and began moving people back. The chief sprinted toward the hill, charging past her. She whirled around just in time to see the fallen angel disappearing into the woods with the chief in pursuit.

Grace wanted to rush after him to provide backup, but she was more worried about the safety of the people on the hill. There didn't seem to be enough police officers for crowd control, so she sprinted up the hill herself, directing the few families and children there to move away from the woods and down toward the cover of the tents and playground area.

Once everyone was safe, she headed toward the dock, ready to offer medical assistance if needed. But it didn't seem that anyone had been injured. Another officer appeared from around a group of people and motioned to one of the two by the boat. Together, he and that officer headed up the hill where the stranger and the chief had disappeared.

With everything under control now with the townspeople,

Grace decided it was time to join the police. There was no such thing as too much backup.

She jogged up the hill but stopped when one of the officers stepped out from the trees carrying a crossbow and a quiver of arrows, each one bearing a long white feather on the end.

Grace's breath caught when she noted the bloodred line painted down the center of each feather. She swallowed, hard, as the police chief emerged from the woods a few feet away leading a man in handcuffs. The fallen angel.

His tortured, angry gaze met hers and she couldn't help but wonder if she was looking into the eyes of the man she'd come here to find.

The serial killer known as the *Crossbow Killer*.

## Chapter Two

Grace tugged on the door to the police station, relieved when it opened this time. A quick glance to her right reassured her that the suspect was sitting in the holding cell that she'd seen earlier when peeking through the window. He glanced at her, then quickly looked away.

"May I help you, ma'am?" The smiling young officer who'd been carrying the bow and arrows earlier had been sitting at one of the desks when she'd stepped inside. Now he was walking toward her, stopping a few feet away. "You were on the hill when we brought out Mr. O'Brien, right?"

"O'Brien? That's the man who was handcuffed?"

His smile dimmed, as if he realized he'd shared information that he probably shouldn't have. "I'm Officer Danny Ortiz. You don't appear to be from around here. I know pretty much everyone in town by sight, if not by name. And the tourists haven't invaded quite yet this fall."

"You're right. I'm not from around here." She hesitated, preferring to introduce herself to his boss first. "I was hoping to speak to the chief. On the front door it says his name is Beau Dawson."

He nodded, his dark eyes showing curiosity. "He's busy at the moment. Is there something I can help you with?" He motioned to the two other empty desks near his. "There are only three police officers, aside from the chief. We pretty much all do whatever's needed, from investigations to throwing drunks in the tank. I'm sure I can help."

She tightened her hand around the handle of the leather satchel she'd just retrieved from her car in the parking lot at the end of the street before returning to the station. "I really need to speak to your boss first." When he continued to hesitate, she added, "It's really important. My name is Grace Malone, but he won't recognize that name."

He motioned toward a folding chair beside his desk. "Have a seat. I'll let him know you're here, Ms. Malone."

"Thank you."

He headed to the right door of two closed ones on the other side of the room. Gold lettering similar to outside listed the chief's name. A second door bore the traditional male/female restroom symbols. And past that were snack and drink machines and a little table with a coffee maker and supplies. This was definitely a no-frills police station.

After Ortiz headed into the chief's office, another officer came in through the front door carrying a large brown paper bag. The haft of an arrow stuck out from the top with a familiar-looking white feather with a red streak down the middle. He smiled at Grace and glanced around, noting the prisoner in the holding cell who was sitting on a cot watching them. Then he set the bag on top of one of the desks and offered his hand and a friendly smile to Grace.

"Hey, stranger. I'm Officer Chris Collier. May I help you?"

Grace shook his hand. "Grace Malone. Officer Ortiz is letting the chief know that I need to speak to him." She motioned toward the bag. "Is that the arrow that was embedded in the boat at the festival?"

"Sure is. I had to cut a hole in the boat to get it out intact. Bobby was cursing a blue streak the whole time."

"Bobby? The boat owner I presume?"

"Bobby Thompson, owner of the boat and the marina outside of town. He didn't care that it's evidence. Can't say as I blame him for being angry, but there was already a hole from the arrow. He'd have had to make a repair either way. He'll get over his mad once he figures that out. You want something to drink or a snack? We have vending machines, nothing fancy. Everything's free, no charge."

"No, thanks. I'm good for now. I don't mean to take up your time. Go ahead and do whatever you need to do while I wait."

"Not a lot to do around here right now aside from a few petty theft investigations we're working. The festival is prematurely over and everyone's either gone home or to the main restaurant and bar to drown their disappointment." He frowned toward the holding cell. "Thanks to you, O'Brien. What were you thinking letting loose with that arrow so close to people? You could have hurt someone."

In answer, the prisoner crossed his arms. He might not be talking, but he was clearly paying attention to their conversation.

Collier shook his head. "Dang hermit. No telling what was going through his head."

"Hermit?" The word evoked an image of an old man with a long beard and torn, dirty clothes in Grace's mind. The gorgeous well-groomed man behind bars was nothing like that. His neatly trimmed barely-there beard and mustache were complemented by the slightly shaggy hair. If she were to describe him she'd label him a sexy rebel. Not that it mattered. If he was the one responsible for the shooting today, or turned out to be a serial killer, she'd do everything in her power to bring him to justice.

Collier continued. "He keeps to himself up on the mountain and—"

"Officer Collier, don't you have a report to type and evidence to log?" The police chief stepped out of his office with Ortiz following behind him.

Collier seemed unfazed by his boss's criticism. "Yes, sir. I'll take care of it right away." He picked up the brown bag and carried it toward a line of metal cabinets along the back wall, to the left of the glass-enclosed conference room.

The chief stopped in front of Grace as Ortiz took a seat at his desk. "Ms. Malone, I'm Police Chief Beau Dawson. How can I help you?"

She stood and shook his hand. "Special Agent Grace Malone."

His eyes widened in surprise. "FBI? Homeland Security? ATF?"

"FBI." She showed him her badge, then hefted her satchel. "I need to speak to you. In private."

"We can use my office."

"Actually, unless your office is really large, the table in that conference room might work better. I have a lot of papers and photographs to spread out."

"All right. Ortiz, Mr. O'Brien's parole officer is on her way. When Mrs. Whang arrives, let her speak to her client about what happened at the festival before I interview him."

"Will do, Chief."

As soon as the conference room door closed behind them, Grace set the satchel on the table and faced Dawson. "Your prisoner is on parole? What did he do that landed him in prison?"

Instead of answering her, he asked a question. "Why did

the FBI send an agent to Mystic Lake? And why is this the first I'm hearing about it?"

The displeasure in his voice was nothing she hadn't heard dozens of times before from other police or sheriffs. Jurisdiction or just a general distrust of Feds who might try to take over or take the glory for some operation was a real obstacle in her line of work. And as always, she did her best to tamp down her own irritation at once again having to soothe someone's ruffled feathers.

"I'm from the FBI field office in Knoxville. An anonymous tip sent me here to see whether the man I'm looking for might be in Mystic Lake. I did come to the police station first to introduce myself and bring you up to speed. But the station was locked."

His mouth tightened. "Sorry about that. Small town, small police force. When there's a festival, like today, we're spread pretty thin. This anonymous tip you got, what did they tell you?"

"That the killer I'm investigating might be here, that someone who lives in the mountains above town has a bow and arrow and keeps to themselves."

"That's the tip that sent you all the way here from Knoxville?"

"Pretty much. We can't risk ignoring a tip, however weak. You never know which one will pan out. Or which unexplored lead a defense attorney will use to try to drive holes through a future case."

He let out a deep sigh. "I wouldn't put much credence in what they said. You might have noticed the stores up and down the street outside, Main Street, are small boutique shops offering clothes, jewelry, local-made items that are more for the tourists than the town residents. We do have one convenience store of a sort, a locally run place with essentials, perishable goods, medical supplies. But for anything more than that you have to drive at least an hour out of town. That's why most of the people here own rifles or handguns. And for bow hunting season, a surprising number have bows and arrows. Hunting isn't just for sport in Mystic Lake, it's a way to feed our families. Someone telling you to check out a person with a bow and arrow around here is wasting your time." He cocked his head, studying her. "But you don't seem surprised by anything I just said. You knew all of that, didn't you?"

She smiled. "I know what I researched on the internet about this town. I don't pretend to be an expert and I'm sure what I read is likely half the truth, if that. But, yes, I knew most of the inhabitants hunted and likely quite a lot have bows and arrows. But I'm searching for someone who uses something a bit more sophisticated, the kind of bow not allowed for hunting in many places. A crossbow. I'm searching for the Crossbow Killer."

He swore and slowly sat in one of the chairs, a look of dread on his face. "The serial killer I've heard about on the news. He's killed, what, six people so far?"

"That we know of. Yes, sir."

"You think he's here?"

She sat across from him and pulled her satchel toward her. "That anonymous tip was light on details. There's no proof he's operating here or fled here when the heat got bad in Knoxville. But, as I said, we have to follow up on every lead. If it's accurate, and we don't perform our due diligence, people could die."

"And the Feds would be eviscerated in the press, giving the FBI a black eye."

"True. But we're people, too. While we don't want our reputation smeared, it's more important to us that we save lives."

He smiled for the first time since she'd met him. "Touché. All right, I'll answer your original question. The reason that Aidan O'Brien is on parole is because he was convicted of murder. He served ten years in prison and was paroled a little over a year ago. He's not from around here. He's from the Nashville area. From what his parole officer has told me, he petitioned the parole board to allow him to move here. He wanted a fresh start, somewhere that the people might not have heard about his case."

She glanced past him at the man they were discussing. He was still sitting on the cot in his cell. When his dark gaze met hers, he didn't turn away or try to pretend he wasn't watching the chief and her. She vaguely wondered whether or not he could read lips.

"Mr. O'Brien seems keenly interested in our discussion."

Dawson didn't bother to turn around to look. "No doubt. Strangers make him nervous. When the tourists arrive to see the leaves turning or to enjoy our lake in the summer, O'Brien disappears. He's not exactly the outgoing type."

"Understandable. It's hard for a convicted felon to get past people's expectations and fears that he might reoffend. I noted he made a point of avoiding you in particular at the festival."

"Can't blame him. When he first arrived in town and his parole officer briefed me, I put a notice on our internal town website to alert people that a convicted murderer was now among us. It wasn't fair to him to do that. But my priority is to keep my citizens safe. Keeping them informed of potential danger is part of that."

"It's not my place to judge you."

He smiled again. "But you are. I can see it in your eyes. You're young, what, mid-thirties?" He held up a hand to stop her from responding. "Forget I asked. My point is I have a few more years on you and I'm probably a whole lot more jaded. I've learned that people don't typically change. Offenders usually reoffend. Period. So I keep my guard up."

"You expect him to murder again?"

"If you're asking whether he's done anything alarming before today, or showed a propensity toward violence, the answer is no. But I'm open to the possibility and vigilant. I can well imagine you're interested in looking into him, too, given his past, and this morning's incident. You think he could be the killer you're after?"

"I guess I'm like you, open to possibilities. Particularly after I got a quick look at the bow and arrows your people found, and the one that was cut out of the boat. While we don't have any eyewitnesses about the crossbow that our killer uses and what it looks like, we do have confirmation that the kinds of arrows used are made specifically for a crossbow. And the feather with paint down it attached to each arrow is well documented from our crime scenes."

She emptied the contents of the satchel onto the table and fanned through them until she found one particular picture, one that showed the feather that was this particular killer's signature.

He stared down at it a long moment, then turned to glance at his prisoner before meeting her gaze again. "You have my attention, Special Agent Malone. Show me everything you have and tell me exactly what that anonymous tipster told you."

## Chapter Three

Aidan paced the length of the holding cell, which took him all of three strides. He occasionally glanced at the glass-walled room where the chief and the FBI agent had been talking for the past half hour.

He had no clue what they were discussing, but it must be important since the chief was delaying interviewing him. Dawson had flat out told him he believed he was behind that stupid stunt at the festival. Refusing to listen to Aidan's protests, the chief had promised to get the truth out of him after he made a few phone calls to try to calm the town leaders about the ruined festival.

It shouldn't bother Aidan at this point that he was the first person the police picked up whenever something bad happened around here. After all, he was the only parolee in Mystic Lake and this wasn't the first, second or even dozenth time they'd brought him in for questioning. But it *did* bother him. It bothered him more than any of those other times, because this wasn't for something juvenile like knocking over someone's mailbox. This was shooting an arrow into a crowd, something Aidan would never do, especially with innocent children running around. But Chief Dawson couldn't look beyond Aidan's past. To Dawson, a killer was a killer, regardless of the circumstances.

Aidan stopped pacing and plopped down onto the cot. As always, when he was at the police station he couldn't help thinking about the past. He'd had a family once—a young son he adored, a wife he'd loved so much it hurt. They'd planned to grow old together, to spend their golden years with a score of grandchildren running around their front yard. But that was never going to happen. Not anymore.

He shoved to his feet again to continue pacing.

The front door opened. When Aidan saw who was coming into the station, he groaned. His parole officer was here. His shoulders slumped as he stepped to the bars to greet Mrs. Whang. But instead of taking her to see her client, Collier ushered her into the conference room.

His parole officer was speaking to an FBI agent, presumably about him. This couldn't be good. Visions of having his parole rescinded and being sent back to prison had him sweating. He fisted his hands at his sides and waited at the cell door to be taken to the chief's office, where he and his parole officer always met in private.

She wasn't in the conference room for long. But whatever they'd told her had a notable impact. Her face was pale and drawn as she headed toward him. But rather than one of the officers letting him out to speak with her, Whang stood outside the locked door to his cell.

"Mr. O'Brien. We need to talk."

A few minutes later, Whang left and it was Aidan's turn to be led to the conference room. For the first time since leaving prison, in addition to handcuffs he was wearing leg shackles. He clenched his jaw against the added humiliation of two officers, Collier and Ortiz, escorting him into the conference room. Even more humiliating was what his parole officer had told him.

That he was under suspicion of being a serial killer.

Maybe it was a good thing that he was cuffed and shackled. Because right now a burning rage was flowing through his veins like molten lava. If his hands had been free he'd have likely punched a hole through a wall, or slammed a chair against one of the glass walls of the conference room.

Ortiz motioned Aidan to sit at the far end of the table. Once Aidan was seated, the officer secured the length of chain between his handcuffs to the steel ring bolted into the top of the table. Collier did the same with the leg shackle chain underneath the table, attaching it to a steel ring on the floor that Aidan had never even noticed before. No doubt he had the FBI agent to thank for being trussed up and for blackening his reputation even more than it already had been.

As the door closed, the agent smiled and nodded, since hand-shaking was obviously out of the question. Aidan wouldn't have shaken her hand anyway. Right now he considered her enemy number one, ruining what little progress he'd made over the past year. Gossip blew through this town like the winds coming down off the mountains. By the time he was released—if he was released—everyone in Mystic Lake would be talking about his past again, and speculating about whether he was this so-called Crossbow Killer.

"Mr. O'Brien, I'm Special Agent Grace Malone. I work out of the FBI field office in Knoxville. If you don't mind, I'd like to ask you a few questions."

He sat back, grateful that the handcuff chain was long enough to allow him that small comfort.

"I do mind. I'm already under arrest for allegedly shooting an arrow through a crowd of people, an arrow that could have killed children, let alone the two adults on that boat. If you're here to arrest me for something I haven't done, get in line." He rattled the chains hanging from his handcuffs.

Her eyes widened.

Dawson swore. "We caught you with your bow and arrows after you ran into the woods to get away."

Aidan leaned forward in his chair, desperately trying to tamp down his anger. But it was impossible to completely hide that he was mad as hell.

"Let's deal in facts instead of conjecture, Chief. Fact— you found a bow and a quiver of arrows lying in the woods about ten yards behind where I'd been sitting on the hill, watching the festival. Fact—you don't know yet whose they are. We both agree that they likely belong to whoever shot that arrow. Officer Collier's your resident fingerprint expert, isn't he? Have him compare any prints on the weapon to my prints that you have on file. I guarantee they won't match."

Malone held up her hands. "Hold it. Let's step back a minute. First of all, Chief Dawson, I'd very much like to have your permission to send the evidence from the festival to the FBI lab for forensic examination. They can test for DNA on some parts and fingerprints on others. If that's done in the wrong order it can ruin our chances to get a profile or viable prints."

"How quickly can the FBI get that done?"

"The Crossbow Killer case is one of our highest priorities right now. I can have a courier pick it up this afternoon and have results in a few days."

"That's far better than me sending it to our state lab, which can take months. Keep me informed on the results. We'll get everything ready for transport. It'll be ready for your courier."

"Thank you."

Aidan wanted to shout his frustration about any kind of delay in proving his innocence. But he knew that wouldn't do any good, so he remained silent.

"Mr. O'Brien," the agent said. "The second thing I wanted to do was ask you, if you really aren't the shooter, why did you run away when Chief Dawson took off after you?"

"Lady, I didn't even know Dawson was there until he tackled me from behind. I wasn't running *from* anyone. I was running *after* someone, the idiot who sent an arrow whizzing past my ear."

Dawson's jaw tightened with anger. "You expect us to believe that the only person in town who's an admitted, confessed killer—you—just happened to be sitting where another killer, or would-be killer, takes a potshot from the woods? And then that phantom guy happens to drop his weapon as he runs away, making it look as if you're the shooter? Is that the cockamamie story you're trying to feed us?"

Aidan's voice was hoarse from suppressing the urge to shout as he responded. "What I want you to believe is the truth. I don't have all the answers. Conducting an investigation isn't my job. It's yours. But if you want to pin this on me, I'm warning you right now. I won't go down without a fight. I'm not pleading guilty to make your job easier."

Malone held her hands up again in a placating gesture. "I don't believe anyone here is trying to pin anything on you. Chief Dawson and I are both after the same thing as you—the truth. Let's try to set aside hurt feelings or even theories and focus on the facts, just as you suggested. You said someone behind you shot over your shoulder. When you turned around, were you able to get a look at them? Do you think you can give us a description?"

Dawson crossed his arms. "*I* can. The shooter is male, white, six-foot-two, late thirties with brown eyes, shaggy brown hair and light facial hair wearing a dark T-shirt, jean jacket, jeans and brown hiking boots."

The exact description of Aidan had him trying to jump to his feet but the shackles forced him down into the chair without being able to stand upright. He glared his outrage. But before he could respond, Malone rapped her knuckles on the table to get their attention.

Her blue eyes flashed with anger of her own as she looked at Dawson. "That didn't help things one bit, Chief. Unless you actually saw the shooter and he was Mr. O'Brien's twin."

Dawson's face reddened slightly. "I couldn't swear in court who shot the arrow. But it's obvious who did."

Malone rolled her eyes. "We'll have fingerprint and DNA analysis in a few days. That should help all of us."

Dawson stood. "I'll get my team working on readying the evidence for your lab."

As soon as the door closed behind the chief, Malone blew out a deep breath. "Okay. Let's try this again. Mr. O'Brien, if you're truly innocent, I well understand your frustration and anger. But I assure you that making assumptions and going down the wrong path in my investigation is the absolute last thing I want. If I pursue the wrong person, the real killer is free to continue his sick games. More people will die. That's not something I want on my conscience. You may not believe me, but we both want the same thing. The truth."

He'd only just met her. He didn't know anything about her other than her name and occupation. And yet her blue eyes were unflinching, clear, looking at him the way an honest person might, with seemingly nothing to hide. Her petite frame was relaxed. Her pink lips weren't tightened with indignation or disgust as some people's were when around him, knowing he was a convicted felon. The tailored navy blue blazer she wore, the perfect straight brown hair pulled back into a ponytail, screamed integrity to him. She was the quintessential federal agent. But she was still young enough to be somewhat inexperienced, idealistic, and naively believe that truth and justice were the same thing.

He knew better.

The truth could ruin lives, destroy people, annihilate families. Sometimes a lie was the only way to save someone. But that was a lesson he hoped this bright young woman never had to learn. He hoped she could cling to her idealism and view of justice forever and never experience the bitterness he tasted every single day.

"You want the truth?" he asked.

"Yes. Please."

He relaxed back in his chair. "All right. The truth. As a convicted felon, I'm not allowed to own a gun or even a hunting knife. The knives in my kitchen are dull butter knives. If I want to cut a steak, I have to use a pair of meat scissors like they use in Korea to cut their meat. When I take down a deer, a rabbit, a turkey, I can't clean and carve it for my own use even though I know how. I have to take them all the way to Chattanooga to have a chop house process them and package them for my freezer. That's a price I pay for the crime to which I pleaded guilty, and I accept that. I only bring it up because in spite of those restrictions, I *am* allowed a bow and arrows. I had to petition the court for special permission so I could use them to hunt, only on my own property, and for self-defense in case a bear ever comes after me. It took months, but my request was approved. I've become an expert with a bow, which is one of the reasons the chief is so willing to believe that I'm guilty of what happened today."

"But you're not?"

"No, Special Agent Malone. I'm not. Can I prove I didn't shoot today? No. But the question that really matters is can you, or Dawson, prove that I did? Unless one of you falsifies evidence, the answer is no. I've killed once in my life, over twelve years ago now. I went to prison, served my time, paid the price that society placed on my crime. It's over, done, in my past, and that's where I'd like it to stay. I'm not the serial killer you came here searching for. Now it's your turn. Truth. Why are you even looking at me for the murders you're trying to solve? Why did you come to Mystic Lake?"

She gave him a lopsided smile. "Fate maybe. If what you've said is accurate, if you have nothing to do with the murders I'm investigating, then maybe you can end up helping me instead of being a suspect. I could use an expert on bows and arrows. It sounds like you might be one."

"Somehow I can't quite see the FBI not having some obscure expert on staff who can answer any questions you have about that type of weapon."

"Humor me."

He hesitated. "What do you want to know?"

"The arrows that were found today, couldn't they be shot with a regular bow, not just with a crossbow?"

"Not likely. Arrows for a crossbow are shorter. Some call them bolts, rather than arrows. They're not interchangeable with the kind I use, for a regular bow. They're not even interchangeable with a compound bow."

"Compound bow?"

"It's something barely resembling a traditional bow. It has gears and pulleys and a lot of plastic. Not to my taste. If the arrows you've found at crime scenes are less than, say, twenty-two inches, they come from a crossbow. The kind I use are around thirty inches. But I'm guessing you knew that already. That's basic information to have researched when looking for a killer using a bow."

"You're right, to an extent. I knew the experts concluded the killer's using a crossbow because of the size of the arrow. But I wanted to make sure there wasn't some kind of exception, that their conclusions are correct. Like maybe a particular bow is supposed to use a different length arrow, but the killer is using another kind to throw us off."

"Not likely. Using the wrong length or even weight of arrow can not only destroy accuracy, it can be dangerous. Think of it the way you do guns. Different ammunition is designed for different types of guns. They're not interchangeable. I don't think you're dealing with a bow-and-arrow expert here, though. Even if he did want to throw investigators off in some way, he's not smart enough or experienced enough to know how to do it without hurting himself."

"Why do you say that?"

"The fletching on the arrows that were found today is all wrong."

"Fletching. You're talking about the fins on the end of the arrow."

"You did your homework."

She smiled. "I've read the files. We'll leave it at that. I know the fletching is for aerodynamics. Sometimes it's feathers, sometimes plastic. Our guy uses both."

"Technically, no. He doesn't. The arrows I saw today had—"

The door to the conference room opened and Chief Dawson stepped inside, holding a thick manila folder. Behind him was Officer Ortiz.

Ortiz headed to the end of the table where Aidan was sitting and knelt on the floor beneath it. The sound of chains falling had Aidan blinking in surprise. A moment later his handcuffs were removed and Ortiz left the room.

Aidan remained seated, rubbing his wrists and testing out the new freedom of movement of his legs, all while suspiciously watching Dawson.

"What's going on?" he asked. "Is this some kind of game?"

"No game. The interview is over. Mr. O'Brien, you're free to go. There will be no charges pressed against you for today's…incident."

Aidan eagerly stood, but his pathway to the door was suddenly blocked by Malone.

"Just a minute," she said. "Chief, even if you're dropping charges, I'd like to speak to Mr. O'Brien about my case. We were just discussing—"

"You can speak to him later," Dawson said. "Mr. O'Brien, I didn't see your truck in the parking lot down the street or anywhere out front. Do you need a ride home?"

"My motorbike's parked a few blocks down."

"Chief Dawson," Grace said. "I really wish you'd wait and—"

"Excuse me." Aidan brushed past her and quickly left. Once he reached his motorcycle, he hesitated. The man he'd been so long ago seemed to be stirring to life inside him, trying to guilt him into going back to finish answering the questions Malone had. But he viciously tamped down those softer feelings. She didn't need him, not really. She was with the FBI, after all. There were plenty of resources she could use to find out what he'd already figured out.

That this so-called Crossbow Killer wasn't targeting his victims.

They were all random. If law enforcement was focusing their investigation on learning about the victims and looking for links between them, they were wasting their time.

The aerodynamics of that arrow would have been thrown off so much by that long dangling feather that hitting that boat this morning was completely by chance. The shooter was more than likely just letting the arrow fly and didn't care who it hit. Did Special Agent Malone know that? How could she not? Someone in the FBI would have studied those arrows and come to the same conclusions he had and put it in that large file of hers she'd had sitting on the table. Which meant that Malone didn't actually need him.

More than likely, her questions had all been a pretense. She just wanted to keep him talking, hoping he'd get comfortable, slip up and confess to a crime he didn't commit.

His conscience quietened, if not fully assuaged, he put on his helmet and sent his bike roaring down the street.

## Chapter Four

Grace caught a brief glimpse of her only potential suspect zipping past the front windows of the police station on his motorcycle. If it was up to her, he'd still be sitting at the end of the conference table answering her questions. Instead, she was reorganizing her documentation and stowing it back in her satchel as the police chief stood on the other side of the table, still holding the folder he'd brought with him when he'd come back into the conference room.

"I'd like an explanation," she said. "You let my suspect go and didn't even have the courtesy to speak to me about it first."

He arched a brow. "You're right. I should have spoken to you first. However, I felt I owed it to Mr. O'Brien to release him immediately." He pulled out his phone and swiped his thumb across the screen before handing it to her.

She stared at the picture, stunned. "Where did you get this?"

"I had another one of my officers, Fletcher, canvassing the people at the festival who were near the hill when the arrow was shot. When I was telling Collier to package up the evidence for the FBI lab, I called Fletcher to see how her canvassing was going. She told me that one of the families she'd spoken to had been taking pictures on that hill not too far from where O'Brien was sitting. They texted her that picture you're looking at."

"They caught the arrow in flight, going right past O'Brien's shoulder."

Dawson nodded. "Unfortunately, the person who shot that arrow is in the shadows of the trees and can't be seen. But this is proof positive that O'Brien isn't the shooter at the festival."

She handed him back the phone. "Agreed. He's not to-day's shooter. But that doesn't mean he's not the Crossbow Killer. He uses bows and arrows to hunt. And he's a convicted murderer in a town where an anonymous tipster said I'd find my killer. I wouldn't be doing my job if I didn't look deeper to either rule him out in my investigation, or keep him on my list."

"You have a list of suspects?"

"Officially, no. But we have a handful of persons of interest other agents are checking out in other locations. For now, I'm only looking at Mystic Lake. And O'Brien's my only suspect at this point. But after that festival incident, and seeing those white feathers with a red line painted down the center, it sure looks like either my killer is here, or there's a copycat. He's either just as deadly, or someone having fun, playing with the police."

Dawson groaned. "I sure hope we don't have a copycat. Someone toying with us though, that wouldn't really surprise me. Some of the teenagers around here like to have fun adding to the town's reputation for unusual or unexplained events. I can just see one of them doing this, not really trying to hurt anyone, but trying to cause a stir around town. I'll start looking into the usual culprits, see what I can find out."

"Tourism is the main industry here, isn't it?" she asked.

"During summer and fall, yes. Leaf peepers and those

wanting to boat or kayak or even camp near the larger part of the lake outside of town. But most of the people around here either commute to a job in Chattanooga every day or work remotely online. Why?"

"I'm wondering about your local economy. A lot of places that rely heavily on tourism have suffered from things like the pandemic and ups and downs in the economy since then. Could someone other than the teens you mentioned be trying to put the town more on the map, generate media and tourist interest by making it look like the Crossbow Killer is operating here?"

He grimaced. "I prefer the juvenile delinquent angle than to think an adult would be that reckless. But, point taken. We'll explore every possibility, not just focusing on our problem kids around here. As for you talking more to O'Brien, I can place another call to his parole officer to have her arrange another chat. He doesn't really have a choice, given the conditions of his parole. However, I've found that the more background I have on a suspect, the more prepared I am to get something worthwhile out of an interrogation. That's another reason I let him go earlier. I wanted you to be able to read through this first."

He finally set down the folder he'd been holding.

"What is it?" she asked as she slid her last stack of pictures into her satchel.

"Aidan O'Brien's arrest record and background on the crime for which he was convicted. It's a copy of the folder his parole officer gave me when O'Brien relocated here. I'm sure you can get the full investigative file if you want it. I never had a reason to dig deeper and request more information."

After quickly flipping through the contents, she frowned. "I don't see a trial transcript."

"There wasn't a trial. He pled guilty."

"What about his sentencing hearing?"

"Like I said, I didn't dig deeper. You'll have to make a records request if you want a transcript of that. Collier made that folder for you. You can keep it."

"Thanks. I appreciate it." She slid it into her satchel and strapped it over her shoulder. "I'll call my office from my car, arrange for a courier to pick up your evidence. Shouldn't take more than a few hours to get someone here."

"We'll be ready." He held the conference room door open for her.

At the front door, she stopped. "One more thing. If the evidence is authenticated, if the Bureau confirms it's consistent with the evidence we already have, be prepared for a few more agents heading this way to help with my investigation."

"Trust me," he said, "if there's a serial killer in my town, I'm grateful for any help you can provide. There won't be any jurisdictional fights or egos getting in the way. We'll take this guy down, together, whoever he is."

She smiled. "That's wonderful to hear. It will make everything easier, and faster."

He handed her a business card. "My office and mobile are on there. When you're ready to set up another meeting with O'Brien, just shout." He pointed toward a two-story whitewashed cottage on the other side of the lake. "That's Stella's Bed and Breakfast. Locals use it to house family and friends that come to visit. And once tourists start bombarding us in a few weeks, the place fills up fast. But there are probably a few vacancies right now. Stella's main source of income is actually the restaurant downstairs. It's open seven days a week and is the best place in town for a hot meal. I highly recommend it."

She smiled her thanks. "I'll head there now and see if you're right about vacancies. I'd assumed I'd have to stay in Chattanooga and drive in each day that I'm here. Stella's would be much more convenient."

After shaking his hand, she headed down the brick sidewalk toward the parking lot at the end of Main Street. Although the only parking she saw on the other side of the lake was parallel street parking, she couldn't imagine the B and B and its large, attached restaurant not having parking for the customers. There must be a lot behind it or maybe farther down the street on that side of the lake. She figured she'd head over there and find out. If she was wrong, she'd just park back at the large lot at the end of Main Street and walk around the lake to Stella's.

As she'd hoped, there was indeed a good-sized lot behind the B and B. She just had to go a block down and loop back behind the row of shops to get to it. The bumpy gravel and incline that led up to Stella's lot had her grateful she'd insisted on a four-wheel drive vehicle when she'd rented the SUV. It would be handy when she checked out the marina and campground she'd researched, too. Both were about a mile out of town where the lake widened and deepened and attracted boaters and fisherman. There were even some class two and three rapids where the river flowed down from the mountains and fed the lake.

Having learned to pack light over the years, all she had to bring inside the B and B was a small rolling suitcase and her satchel that contained her laptop, her investigative files and notes. The check-in desk downstairs doubled both for the inn and the surprisingly busy restaurant. It seemed that half the town must be either at the bar or sitting at the tables and booths drinking or eating. No doubt with the festival canceled, they were finding another way to have the fun they'd been denied.

The owner herself, Stella Holman, checked Grace in, reserving a room for her plus two more at Grace's request in case more agents were needed in the next few days. After Stella took Grace upstairs to her room and was about to head downstairs again, Grace stopped her.

"Ms. Holman?"

The petite, white-haired lady smiled. "It's Mrs., but we don't stand on formality around here. Call me Stella. How can I help you, dear?"

"I need to go see someone up in the mountains a little later. I have the address, but it's not showing up on my GPS."

Stella laughed. "If you go by those fancy GPS things around here you'll get lost every time, or drive off a cliff. Half the time phones don't even work in these mountains. What's the address?"

"It's on Niall's Circle."

The other woman's smile faltered. "I see. Well, that won't be on your GPS because it's not the official name of any road. It's basically a driveway. A very long one, but technically a driveway. Head out of town and take the first right up Harper Road. You'll find the turnoff to Niall's Circle at the top of the mountain, where Harper ends. I can draw it out if you need me to."

"No, no. Those directions sound easy to follow. Thanks so much."

Stella patted Grace's shoulder. "I hope you enjoy our little town, maybe take a boat out on the lake. It's gorgeous this time of year. If you're hungry, come downstairs for lunch before you go sightseeing. With the festival canceled, there's a party going on. There's a game room, too, with tables set up for cards, some pool tables and even a dartboard. I'm sure you'd have fun. And the food's not bad either. I hear that Mr. Holman is an excellent chef." She winked and headed downstairs.

Grace briefly debated going downstairs right now. Not to party or eat, but to mingle with the townspeople to try to get information that might help her investigation. But as loud as it had been when she'd passed the opening to the restaurant before coming upstairs, it was doubtful that conversations would be easy or fruitful. She'd have to make the rounds another time.

Talking to O'Brien was her number one priority anyway. And she had no intention of notifying his parole officer or having him return to the station at this point. Instead, she wanted to surprise him, catch him off guard at his own home, on Niall's Circle. If he was comfortable, in his own element, it would be easier to build that rapport she'd need to get him to speak freely.

She put her things away, then sat down on the king-size bed she'd splurged the FBI's money on and made a call to the office. Her favorite admin took down the information that Grace gave her, promising to email her the full investigative file on O'Brien, including a transcript of the sentencing hearing along with one from the parole hearing if she could get that released. Sometimes those weren't shared. Well, most of the time they weren't. But when the FBI asked for something, they usually got it. And this particular admin was a bulldog when it came to getting what the agents needed. If anyone could get it, she could.

Her next call was to her boss, Supervisory Special Agent Levi Perry. He wasn't happy that she'd driven the three hours here and spent several more hours in town before checking in without calling. He was a stickler for knowing where his agents were at all times. Not because he was controlling or a micromanager, but because safety was his number one concern. Grace suffered through the usual lecture about being careful and checking in daily. Then she gave him an update on everything that had happened since her arrival, as well as her plan to interview O'Brien as soon as she read up on his background.

"Just follow all protocols and be on your guard the whole time," he warned. "It doesn't sound like this is our guy, given that someone else shot that arrow. But with his background, he could still be dangerous. And while I agree you're more likely to get him to let his guard down and speak freely at his place, if any red flags go up while you're there, end the interview immediately and have his parole officer order him to the police station for further questioning."

"Of course. Absolutely. I'll be careful."

"I know you will or I wouldn't have sent you there on your own."

"You wouldn't have sent me here at all if you thought there was really a chance our killer was here. But I still appreciate you finally cutting the strings and letting me do some investigating without a supervisor watching my every move."

"Don't thank me too soon. If the lab determines the arrows you have on the way are consistent and the paint matches the arrows we already have in evidence, you won't be on your own anymore. That's not a statement about your readiness to be a full-fledged agent. It's a statement about how dangerous this killer is that we're after. I don't want to add one of my agents to his victim list."

"Understood. I'll keep you posted. And if the lab confirms our killer is here, I'll stand down immediately and wait for backup to continue the investigation."

"Regardless of what the lab determines, use all those

skills you've been practicing under Special Agent Kingsley's mentorship. Approach every assignment as if it's the most important, and potentially dangerous one you've ever worked and you'll always come out ahead. Got it?"

"Yes, sir."

"Keep me updated."

The call ended and Grace blew out a relieved breath. Someone on the outside looking in would think her boss was being extremely protective because she was a woman. But she knew better. He was this way with all his agents, particularly the ones like her who were finally out of training and no longer working under the guidance of another agent. While she appreciated that he wanted everyone working for him to be safe, it could be smothering at times.

Her final call was to the lab to make sure they had no questions about what needed to be done once the evidence arrived. They assured her they'd log it in and assign a technician to it immediately. Even so, unless the fingerprints were found to be a match to someone in the Bureau's Integrated Automated Fingerprint Identification System, IAFIS, then it would likely take several more days to get results on any DNA.

If the person who'd shot that arrow had been arrested for a felony in the past and the arresting agency had entered their DNA profile into the Combined DNA Index System, then CODIS would spit out the name of a potential suspect. A hit on either IAFIS or CODIS could make their investigation take off. But not if the arrows from Mystic Lake didn't match the arrows already known to have come from the Crossbow Killer.

The absence of viable prints or DNA on the evidence was another very real possibility. Which meant she needed to stop counting on the lab's potential results and start pounding the pavement to determine if the anonymous tip was right or not.

Her boss agreed with her decision to interview O'Brien even though he wasn't the one who'd shot that arrow today. Because yet another theory they'd discussed was that if O'Brien was the actual Crossbow Killer, he could have realized someone suspected him and that they may have called in a tip. The best way to throw law enforcement off his trail would be to hire someone else to shoot that arrow during the festival where there'd be lots of witnesses. And having someone take a picture just as the arrow was being shot over O'Brien's shoulder, well, that was either incredible luck or a well thought out plan. The person who took the picture could have been paid, too. She'd have to contact the police and get the name of the person who took the picture so she could interview them, as well.

But first, she needed to focus on O'Brien.

The biggest question in her mind right now was the identity of his victim all those years ago and the alleged motive behind the murder. Dawson hadn't volunteered that information. And she'd planned on asking O'Brien about it at the station after first building some rapport with him. With the interview ending so unexpectedly, she'd never gotten the chance.

Even knowing that the man was a murderer, it was hard to believe. He was well-spoken, sounded well-educated, and money didn't seem to be a problem for him to solve by killing someone for their assets. The motorcycle he'd ridden wasn't exactly cheap. The chief had mentioned that O'Brien owned a truck, too. And O'Brien himself had talked about hunting on his own land. It didn't sound as if he was hurting financially, so a financial motive seemed unlikely.

Other common motives for murder were love and revenge. Did one of those explain why he'd crossed that terrible line and taken the life of someone else years ago? Or was he a thrill killer, a sociopath who took the lives of people as a way of playing God and experiencing the high of total control over another person's life?

Three pages into O'Brien's folder, the identity of who he'd killed had her frozen in shock. The man she'd met couldn't have done that, could he? But there it was in black-and-white as she read it again. The woman he'd murdered all those years ago was Elly O'Brien. His wife.

## Chapter Five

Aidan crossed his arms and leaned against the railing of the front steps of his cabin, watching the black SUV coming down the long driveway through his property. It was straight, by design. It gave him plenty of time to see anyone coming. And to prepare to either welcome them, which was rare and reserved for only a few, or turn them away. Since none of his extremely small group of friends drove a vehicle like that, turning them away was exactly what he planned to do.

But when the driver's door opened and Special Agent Grace Malone emerged from the vehicle, he swore beneath his breath. If she had been a civilian, ordering her off his property was a given. He had every right, even as a felon, to make her leave. But an FBI agent? Since he was on parole, he was at her mercy. He couldn't make her do one damn thing. Unless she allowed it.

As she approached, he forced himself to ignore the way his breath hitched at seeing her curvy little body again, or the way he was instantly intrigued by the intelligence shining out of those incredibly blue eyes. It didn't matter that her smile made his gut tighten with desire. She wasn't his friend or a potential lover.

She was his enemy.

He needed to remember that. She was a Trojan horse, compelling and beautiful on the outside but deadly on the inside. The only reason he was this affected by her had to be because he wasn't used to being close to a beautiful woman these days. So few women dared to get anywhere near him. His unwelcome reaction to the agent certainly wasn't because there was something special about her. And it wouldn't matter if there was. She worked for the FBI. That alone was reason to avoid her.

Her smile broadened as she stopped in front of him and held out her hand. "Mr. O'Brien, it's good to see you again. Grace Malone, in case you've forgotten since this morning."

He glanced at her hand, but didn't take it. "I haven't forgotten, Special Agent Malone. You're trespassing. Leave."

She dropped her hand, her smile still firmly in place. "Irish, right? That slight brogue. It's barely noticeable, but it's there. Your family is from Ireland?"

"I'm busy, working. I've got nothing to say to you, so return to your vehicle and head back down the mountain."

She sighed as if arguing with a recalcitrant child. "We both know the conditions of your parole. We can either talk here or I can escort you to the police station. Your choice."

He stepped toward her until they were only a few feet apart, forcing her to crane her neck back to meet his gaze. To her credit, she didn't move or cower away. If she was intimidated by his size or his reputation, she was doing an admirable job of hiding it.

"Special Agent Malone—"

"Call me Grace. I'll call you Aidan."

"Special Agent Malone, I'm a convicted murderer. You're standing at the top of a mountain, alone, with me. The nearest neighbor is halfway down this mountain and likely not even home this time of day. You could scream as loud as you want and no one would hear it. You being here must mean that you still think I could be this serial killer you're looking for. Think very carefully. Are you really sure you want to play your law enforcement trump card to stick around and try to force me to answer your questions? Without backup?"

She flipped back her jacket, revealing a shoulder holster and the butt of a pistol sticking out of it. "This is my backup."

He snorted with reluctant amusement. "You're gutsy. I'll give you that. I'll also give you a tip. Standing this close to me, it doesn't matter that you have a gun. I could wrestle you to the ground or snap your neck before you'd have a chance to draw."

Her smile disappeared and she quickly moved out of his reach. "Is that what you want to do, Aidan? Snap my neck?"

"It's Mr. O'Brien to you. And if I wanted to snap your neck, you'd already be dead. I'm giving free advice I learned the hard way, after spending a decade in prison. I've seen the horrible things that human beings can do to each other, things I never thought I'd see. And I pray to God you never do, even if you are in law enforcement."

"What do you have against law enforcement? No one framed you. You didn't even go to trial because you confessed, pled guilty. You weren't mistreated by the justice system."

"If you consider the time before I went to prison, I agree with you. I got a fair shake. It's once they lock you up that everything changes. Ever wonder why recidivism is so high, why convicted felons reoffend at such a phenomenal rate after getting out of prison? It's because the guards, law enforcement, everyone in the justice system treats them like animals while they're locked up. Security for those in prison is a joke. There isn't any. You have to be vigilant all the time, learn to be a light sleeper, watch your back constantly. I despise everything about the system from beginning to end because there's no humanity or mercy in it. I'm wary of police, of people like you, because one wrong step and I can be snatched from my home and thrown back behind bars. I may look as if I'm free, but it's in name only. I have to watch my back all the time or my life can change in a blink. Good people can go to prison, Malone, because they make some kind of terrible mistake. But whether you were good or not going in, you're a completely changed person coming out."

She stared at him, eyes wide. "Is that what you think? That you were a good person going in? Does a good person murder their wife?"

He could feel his face flushing with heat as anger rode him hard.

She subtly moved her jacket, giving her better access to her weapon if she needed it.

He swore and turned around, heading toward his workshop building on the far side of the cabin. At first, he thought maybe she'd changed her mind about risking being around him, that she was heading to her car. Unfortunately, a moment later he heard her footsteps behind him. From the sound of it, she was keeping well back, not so close he could turn around and grab her. At least his safety lecture had gotten through to her. Who knows? Maybe his advice would save her life in the future when dealing with some other criminal.

Not that he should care—about her, about anyone these days. He tried not to, especially when people treated him like the man they believed him to be. The townspeople often went out of their way to avoid him, making it painfully obvious they were afraid of him or that they despised him for his past. Perhaps because he understood how they felt, and knew he'd likely feel the same in their position, he couldn't hate them for it or even hold it against them.

But he wished it didn't bother him so much.

And he wished he could ignore when he saw someone in trouble. Like at the festival when that arrow flew past him and into the boat. He was so angry that someone had shot close to children that he'd whirled around and run after the shooter without once thinking about what might happen to him.

And it hadn't done one whit of good.

The police had thrown him into a cell and immediately branded him the villain while the real villain got away. Even now he wasn't sure why the chief had dropped the charges. Maybe because Dawson was stepping back to let the FBI agent have first dibs at him, convinced he was the serial killer she was after.

Rounding the end of the cabin, he stepped through the enormous double doors that were standing open on his workshop. Stopping beside the table in the middle of the building, he picked up the sander he'd been about to use before he heard an engine coming down his driveway.

"Whoa, are you making that?" she asked.

He was careful to set the sander on the table before turning, not wanting to do anything that might seem threatening and could end with a bullet in his chest. But Malone wasn't even looking at him. She was staring at the table, her eyes wide.

She stepped forward almost reverently and gently smoothed her hand across the wood, over the rounded edge. "This is incredible. Your work?"

He nodded, mesmerized by the gentle movement of her hand.

Her fingers continued to slide across the wood as if she

couldn't help herself. The pleasure in her expression was such a joy to behold, all he could do was stare.

"Purpleheart wood, right?" She glanced up in question.

He blinked in surprise. "You're familiar with it?"

"I know of it, but have never seen it in person." Her cheeks flushed a dull pink. "I'm pretty sure I saw it on an episode of a house renovation show on TV. But it's so beautiful I didn't forget about it. Is this for your cabin?"

"It's a custom order for a man in Montana, for his deck. He wanted something beautiful for outdoor dining that could withstand the harsh weather without being ruined. Purpleheart wood is extremely hard, resistant to insects, rot, decay."

She sighed and stepped back. "It's gorgeous. Will the color stay that brilliant purple?"

"Not forever, no. But I'll put a UV protectant finish on it that should help it keep its color for several decades." He noted the wistful look on her face as she admired the table again. "Have you ever done carpentry?"

"Only if you count using a block of sandpaper to help my dad in his shop behind our house. Woodworking was one of his many hobbies. He didn't make furniture, certainly nothing grand like you're making. But my mom and I got new handmade jewelry boxes every birthday and he put custom molding all over our house. The shelving in the garage was his pride and joy. I wouldn't say he was an expert or even really good at carpentry, but he enjoyed it."

"Sounds like you enjoyed it, too, or would have, if he'd let you do more than sand."

She smiled. "I didn't want to do anything more difficult than sanding. I didn't crave the experience of hammering or sawing, nothing like that. What I did crave was my father's attention. He always wanted a son and got a daughter instead. Helping him out, even if it was just to fetch tools or sweep sawdust, made him happy. And that made me happy."

"Daddy's little girl."

"Daddy's little tomboy to be more precise. Did you have your little boy with you watching you do woodwork? His name is Niall, right?"

His heart seemed to clench in his chest at her callous reminder about his son. It took him several moments to gather his composure as best he could. "It's getting late. I'll finish this up tomorrow." He began putting his tools up.

Once again she surprised him. She helped him gather his hand saws and chisels and expertly figured out where they went, putting them up on the pegboard wall exactly where they belonged. When she finally faced him, he motioned toward the broom in the corner.

"Are you going to sweep, too?"

"You wish."

He laughed. "I'll do it tomorrow, or later tonight. Come on. The cabin's more comfortable for an interrogation. It's starting to get chilly out here."

"I'm not going to interrogate you."

"Regardless of how you try to soften it, you're here to ask questions. You've brought up my past twice now. And I know darn well it wasn't my sparkling personality that got you to drive all the way up here."

"Fair enough. I do want to talk. I need to ask some tough questions, too. I hope you'll answer them."

"So you can arrest me?"

"So I can rule you all the way in, or totally out as a suspect if you truly have no bearing on my case."

"At least you're honest." They both stepped outside and he slid the doors shut and settled the wooden bar through the handles to keep wild animals out. He motioned toward the cabin. "Are you okay going inside my cabin? Or do you prefer the porch? Unlike this workshop, there are chairs up there but it will be cold."

She snugged her jacket closer. "I don't want to inconvenience you any more than necessary—"

"Too late for that."

"Are you always this ornery or am I special?"

He cocked his head. "This is me being nice."

She let out a bark of laughter, then cupped her hands over her mouth, obviously mortified that she'd done so.

"Don't worry," he said. "I won't tell your boss that you dared to laugh at a killer."

Her jaw tightened and she dropped her hands. "I wish you wouldn't talk like that. I'm trying to give you the benefit of the doubt. There are things I read in your file that, well, I'd like a better understanding of what happened to put you in prison."

"Why? What's my past got to do with anything you're investigating?"

"Maybe nothing. Maybe everything. You never know what piece of information will be helpful and what won't until you put the whole puzzle together."

"That only makes sense if I'm the one you're calling the Crossbow Killer."

She arched a brow.

He swore. "Fine. We'll talk. But you'll have to brave my lair to do so. I'm no longer willing to be cold on the porch for you."

Without waiting for her, he jogged up the steps to the wraparound porch and headed around to the front door.

# Chapter Six

Aidan left the front door open and headed into the kitchen area, having no doubt that Malone would follow him inside the cabin. She was tenacious and wasn't about to leave without getting what she came for. He just hoped that wasn't him, in handcuffs.

"Holy moly," she breathed as she came inside.

He grabbed a bottle of beer and a bottle of water from the refrigerator and carried them to the round table in the front right corner of the cabin. He set the water on the table, opposite him, and twisted open the beer for himself. As Malone toured her way around the great room of the cabin, mouth slightly open in wonder, he sipped his beer and watched her. Part of him couldn't help feeling pride at her wide-eyed surprise as she ran her soft-looking hands over the rocking chairs, end tables, even the wooden animals he'd painstakingly carved over the past year for the grandchildren he'd likely never have.

She headed into the kitchen area just past him and stood in the middle, turning in a slow circle. "The cabinets," she said. "Maple?"

He nodded. "Locally sourced."

"Beautiful. You made those, along with most everything

in the cabin? They have the same look, the same…expert craftsmanship as that table in your workshop."

"They're my work, yes." He took another sip, telling himself not to let his ego get the best of him. Maybe she was impressed with his work, or maybe this was all part of a facade to make him like her, to feel comfortable enough to tell her whatever it was that she wanted to know. She wasn't his friend, wasn't on his side. He needed to remember that, no matter how much a part of him wished it could be different. The one consistent thing about his life ever since his wife's death was an aching loneliness that no amount of hard work could fill, no matter how desperately he tried.

She finally joined him at the table, ignoring the chair across from him and instead sitting beside him. Maybe she hadn't learned that lesson he'd tried to teach her after all, about getting too close to a potentially dangerous person.

"It's incredible, gorgeous," she said. "Everything you've built here. The cabin is amazing, too. These two-story-high ceilings are stunning. The carved banister on the staircase is amazing. And the picture windows frame the mountains like a master painter. Did you build this home, too?"

"Didn't need to. I was lucky enough to find this place already here when I moved to Mystic Lake. The previous owner was retiring to Montana to be with his kids. He's the one who commissioned the purpleheart patio table and chairs. The only thing I did was add the workshop and renovate the kitchen and bathrooms."

She pulled the water bottle to her and twisted it open. "Thanks. Didn't realize I was thirsty until I saw this."

He nodded as she took a sip, then grudgingly said, "If you're hungry, there's some venison stew in the refrigerator, plenty enough to share. I've got fresh fruit, things for salad, too, if you want."

She set the bottle down and crossed her arms on the tabletop. "It's crystal clear that you don't want me here, and yet you offer me food and drinks and welcome me into your cozy, warm cabin. Which man is the real Aidan O'Brien? The one who can't help but act the host even when he doesn't want any visitors, and offers safety tips, or the one who committed murder and went to prison for ten years?"

He winced and set his beer down. "No beating around the bush with you. You go right for the jugular."

"I don't know any easy way to ease into asking you about your wife's death."

He briefly closed his eyes, then sat back in his chair and crossed his arms. "You obviously read my record. Everything is in my files. Why do you want me to talk about it?"

"Because I want your perspective, your side of it, not what police officers and lawyers summarized in their reports. You've lived most of your life in Nashville, right? That's where you met Elly?"

He sighed deeply, then cleared his throat. "Her name was Elly Larsen back then." He cleared his throat again. "My parents came here from Dublin when I was a teenager. That's the Irish brogue you mentioned. They moved several times until they settled in Nashville, bought a house two doors down from the Larsens. Our parents became best friends. Elly and I naturally became friends, too. That lasted through high school, then college where we began dating. A few years after graduation, once I had my furniture-making venture up and running, we got married."

"Furniture-making. You started your own business right out of college?"

"Pretty much. My grandparents on both sides were woodworkers all their lives. Although my father wasn't into that, I was fascinated by the stories my grandparents told and loved the carpentry and carving projects they involved me in whenever they visited. The only reason I went to college was to learn about running a business so I could start mine as soon as possible."

"Judging by this cabin, the sixty-plus acres that you bought with it, your business must have done really well."

"It's eighty-plus now that I bought out the only other neighbor on top of this mountain. You really did read up on me."

"That's part of my job."

He shrugged and took another sip of beer.

"How long was it before you and Elly had your son, Niall?"

He stared at her a long moment before answering. "He was born seven months after we got married. Elly lied during the entire pregnancy to her parents, telling them she wasn't as far along as she was. When he was born she swore to them that he was a preemie. She didn't want them to know we'd slept together before marriage. Considering that Niall was eight pounds at birth, and her parents weren't stupid, they obviously only pretended to believe her to help her save face."

"They sound like loving parents, not wanting their daughter to be embarrassed that she didn't follow tradition, or perhaps her religious beliefs."

"Both, and yes, they were loving, good people. Still are."

"Where's your son now?"

He glanced sharply at her. "With Elly's parents, my former in-laws."

"Did your parents try for custody?"

His throat tightened. "No. They had me late in life and weren't in the best of health when…all of this began. They didn't want to start over with a young child. They left the raising of Niall to the Larsens and moved back to Ireland when I went to prison."

Her eyes widened. "I'm so sorry. For your son, and for you."

"Don't be. My parents are...different. I know they care... about both of us. It's been difficult on them and they needed help I was no longer around to provide. They're with extended family and do what they can to keep in touch long-distance."

"So then Niall is with the Larsens full-time."

"Yes. The court terminated my parental rights and Elly's parents adopted him. My lawyer sends my child support payments to their lawyer and provides basic updates on Niall's health. But that's it."

"Child support. He's not an adult yet?"

"Almost. He turned seventeen back in the spring."

"So when your wife died, he was—"

"Five years old. I doubt he even remembers me. I hope to hell his grandparents are keeping his mother's memory alive for him. She deserves that." He took another swig of his beer and eyed the whiskey on the bar in the great room, longing for something stronger.

"Elly's parents didn't bring your son to visit you while you were incarcerated?"

"Why would they after what...what I did? I wouldn't have wanted them to even if they'd offered. Prison is no place for a child."

"So you've never seen him, not even after you got out a year ago?"

"Twelve months and ten days ago. Aside from an annual picture the Larsens' lawyer sends my lawyer, I haven't seen Niall since the day the Larsens took him away. My lawyer has made an open invitation that if Niall ever wants to meet me, the lawyer will arrange a supervised visit on neutral grounds. But I doubt his grandparents have ever even passed the invitation along. I can't blame them. He's better off without me in his life. Dredging up old memories, a painful past, wouldn't do him any good." He crossed his arms again.

"I'm sorry. About your son."

"It is what it is. But…thanks."

She leaned forward, her gaze searching his. "I know this is difficult, but could you tell me about the night of the fire?"

He winced and shoved back from the table. "Give me a minute." He strode into the main part of the great room and stood in front of the large picture window that framed the incredible beauty of the Smoky Mountains in the distance.

When Malone joined him, quietly standing beside him as he looked out the window, he couldn't help putting off the discussion about the fire just a little longer. Instead, he told her, "Elly loved the mountains. She wanted to spend our honeymoon in a cabin in Gatlinburg. I wanted to take a cruise, soak up the sun on a beach. We went to Gatlinburg. How could I not? It made her happy. And she was pregnant with our first…" He swallowed. "With our only child. It's the least I could do. She was already experiencing morning sickness. It was easier on her to be pampered on the back deck of a mountain cabin than to sit out in the hot sun by the ocean."

He could feel her staring at him and he shifted uncomfortably.

"Your voice changes when you talk about her," she said. "You loved her, didn't you?"

He frowned. "Of course I did. That's why I…why I let her go."

"Because of the fire."

He nodded.

"Tell me what happened. Please."

He drew a shaky breath, then motioned toward one of the couches. "I need to sit down for this."

Once they were seated, to his surprise, she helped him ease into the conversation about that awful night by talking about more mundane things that really didn't matter. She asked about his business, things he and Elly did, the first few years of life as young parents with a rambunctious son running them ragged.

"Earlier you mentioned your parents try to keep in touch, even from Ireland. What about your grandparents? Or are they all gone now?"

"If by gone you mean have they passed away, no. They're all remarkably healthy for their ages, doing really well. But after I...confessed...they cut me out of their lives. I'm an only child, no siblings. The only family who speaks to me these days is my parents, and then, only rarely. As I said, they aren't in the best of health."

"I'm sorry."

He glanced at her, surprised to hear the empathy in her voice, see the sorrow in her eyes. He gave her a curt nod of thanks and looked away again, staring toward the mountains, which were beginning to mist over, giving them the smoky look for which they'd been named.

"We'd only been in the house for a few weeks," he finally began. "The business had taken off. I was making millions, investing the profits and making millions on top of that. I never expected the high-end custom furniture market to be that lucrative and successful. But it was. I took it international and it really exploded. I had over a hundred people working for me at the time, far more now in several locations around the world. In spite of that, all Elly wanted was a slightly bigger house than our starter home so we'd have room for more children. But I wanted a statement home, something grand that reinforced the image of success."

He shook his head in disgust. "My ego and pride had me overrule her desires that one time and insist on getting a mansion in the foothills outside of Nashville in one of the upper-crust neighborhoods. It was huge, beautiful, but old. The inspection pointed out dozens of things that needed to be upgraded. One of those was the electrical system. It was original to the house and the inspector warned it wasn't capable of handling all the modern smart appliances and technological toys that people have these days. We could have waited, had the electrical completely redone before we moved in. But I didn't take the inspector's warnings seriously enough. I thought we had time, that we could do the renovations after we were settled."

He shook his head in self-disgust. "Obviously, I was wrong. I was working late one night at my company, meeting with my more senior craftsmen about new equipment and tools they felt we needed. Once all of that was wrapped up, it was past the dinner hour and dark outside. I could see the flames lighting up the night sky before I even turned down our street. Firefighters and police officers were everywhere, lights flashing, hoses pouring water onto the second story of our home. I jumped out of my car and tried to run inside, but they held me back. I screamed at them that my wife and son were in there. One of the policemen told me they'd been rescued, that my son was fine and with a neighbor, but that my wife was at the hospital."

He squeezed his hands into fists. "*Rescued*. That word scared the hell out of me. What did it mean? I was afraid to ask. I checked on Niall, then sped to the hospital. Once there

I…" He closed his eyes, reliving the nightmare yet again as the horrible images bombarded his mind.

"Elly," he whispered, his eyes still closed. "My God. Elly."

She was in the burn unit, soot and burns over large swaths of her body. But it was her silence that was more terrifying than screams of pain would have been.

"Aidan?"

He opened his eyes, glad that the agent had brought him back from the darkness. Not that he'd thank her for it. "I told you to call me Mr. O'Brien."

"And I told you to call me Grace."

He couldn't help but smile at that. Then he blew out a shaky breath and gave her a sanitized version of what Elly had suffered.

"The fire started upstairs. An electrical short. Elly was downstairs and heard Niall screaming. She ran and didn't realize there was a fire until she reached the landing. Flames were between her and our son's room. She ran right through them to get him. She…she grabbed the comforter off his bed and soaked it in the shower, then covered both of them as she ran through the flames again to the stairs. They'd just reached the bottom when a beam fell on her. Niall was able to scramble out from under her and run outside. The firefighters had to pull the beam off her and take her out."

Malone gave him another one of those empathetic smiles he didn't begin to deserve. "She was paralyzed, correct?"

"From the chest down. She had to be on a ventilator to breathe. After months of treatment in the burn center, she was well enough to go home. But the vent was permanent. She'd die without it. She had partial use of her right arm, and she could turn her head, blink her eyes. Little else. In some ways the paralysis was a blessing because she didn't suffer as much as she would have during burn treatments. But she'd have traded the pain to be able to walk again, to breathe on her own, to hold her son."

"How do you know that?"

"She told me."

"I thought she had a ventilator. Doesn't that prevent you from speaking?"

"Her ventilator was connected to her trachea. Her mouth wasn't covered. And it had this…valve, a… Passy Muir Valve. That's what it was called. It helped her speak. She could write a little, too, with her right hand. But it was really difficult. She preferred the valve."

"I didn't read about that in the reports in your file."

He shrugged. "I don't know that it matters either way. Why do you keep asking these—"

"Let's skip to the last day of her life, seven months after the accident."

"Surely those details are in the police reports."

"Not as much as I'd expect. The investigative file is surprisingly sparse. Even though it was several months after her death before you were brought to court, there doesn't seem to have been much of an investigation."

"Why would there be? I told the police what happened. When the day nurse who watched over Elly whenever I was at work left, I unplugged my wife's ventilator. I let her go." He swallowed, his throat tight as he struggled to keep his composure.

Rather than accept his confession, Malone frowned as if she was weighing it for the truth. "From what I've read, there are alarms on the machine that was keeping your wife alive. If you unplugged it, the backup battery—as long as it was charged and working correctly—would have kicked in to keep the machine going until it was plugged in again or the battery died. The particular model your wife used has ten minutes of battery life. Alarms would have been going off that whole time."

He hesitated. "Right. They were. I knew all about the alarms. I was trained to use her equipment, to suction, clean, keep it going if any alarms went off during the night while there weren't any nurses there watching over her. Again, why do you feel you need to—"

"Aidan. You ran into the woods this morning with no way to defend yourself against a man with a lethal weapon. You risked your life because you didn't want him to shoot an arrow near strangers, people who weren't your loved ones. Do you honestly expect me to believe that you unplugged your wife's machine, your son's mother, and sat there for the ten minutes for the battery to run down with all those alarms going off, then several more minutes watching her struggle until she died, before finally calling 911?"

His face flushed with heat. His pulse raced and he could feel a bead of sweat running down his back.

"Aidan?"

"I don't expect you to believe anything. And I don't care whether you do or not. I confessed to my crime, went to prison. Why does it even matter at this point?"

"Your son was in the house at the time?"

Good grief, she was tenacious. And getting far too close to the truth. He needed her to stop digging. That was the only reason he hung on, continued answering her questions as he desperately tried to assuage her curiosity and convince her, somehow, to let it go. To move on to something else, to someone else, in her investigation.

"Yes," he finally said. "He was in his room, playing."

"Did he come into his mother's room when he heard the alarms?"

Another bead of sweat raced down his back. "He... No, he stayed in his room." At her look of disbelief, he quickly added, "He'd gone on a field trip that day with his kinder-garten class, to the zoo. He was worn-out, fell asleep as soon as I got him home. His door was shut, and... Elly's door was shut."

"I see. How far away was your son's room from Elly's?"

His throat ached with the urge to shout at her. *Stop. Please. Just, stop.*

"Far enough that he didn't hear anything. And I... Right, I silenced the machine. I forgot about that. I turned off the alarms."

"You just said the alarms were going off. Now you're saying you turned them off."

He stood. "I've answered your questions, far more than I should have to, given that none of this even remotely touches on your investigation into the serial killer you're looking for. It's time for you to go."

She stood and looked up at him. "I know this has been difficult. But I appreciate your cooperation. There is one more thing, though. It's not about your wife. Earlier today, you told me that you use a bow and arrows to hunt. Can you show them to me?"

He swore beneath his breath. "I always keep a bow and quiver of arrows in my truck. You can look at those on your way out. It's parked beside the cabin. My other equipment is in here." He headed to the first bedroom under the stairs. He flung open the door and headed into the closet to grab his bow and one of the quivers of arrows to give her. But when he turned around, she was standing in the closet doorway.

"I need to verify for myself," she said unapologetically.

He tossed the bow and arrows down and left the room.

A few minutes later, she joined him by the front door. "I

don't see anything remotely resembling a crossbow anywhere. And as you said earlier, your arrows are longer,
without any white feathers for fletching. Oh, wait, that was
another question I had, about the fletching."

He opened the door and leaned against the frame. "Make
it quick. My patience is at an end."

"It's what you were saying at the station during our earlier interview, before Dawson cut it short. I was talking
about the arrows from the incident at this morning's festival. I said the fletching was both plastic and feathers. You
corrected me, said that the arrows you saw... What? What
were you going to add to that?"

He frowned, trying to remember, then nodded. "Right.
I think I was making the point that the plastic on the arrows was the fletching, for the aerodynamics. That's a cru-
cial part of the arrow to make it fly straight and true. The
feather isn't fletching, not the one dangling from the arrow.
That wouldn't help stabilize the shot. It would wreak havoc
on the aerodynamics. Anyone shooting a bow and arrow
using a large feather off the end like that isn't concerned
with accuracy."

Her eyes widened. "Meaning whoever he shoots just happens to be in the way of the arrow. He's not really aiming."

"Exactly."

She swore. "We've been focusing too much on victimology, trying to dig into the backgrounds of our victims and
figure out what links them together. The answer to that
is—"

"Nothing," he said. "Wrong time. Wrong place. The victims are random. Unless he attaches the feathers after he
shoots someone. I suppose that's possible, too. Then you're
back to looking at victimology."

Some of her excitement drained out of her. "True. Well,

it's another angle to look into, regardless. Thank you, Aidan. You've been extremely helpful." She held out her hand.

He sighed heavily. Her use of his first name was a technique to build a connection with him so he'd answer questions. He knew it. But dang if it wasn't working to some extent. Feeling spiteful at this point if he again refused to shake her hand, he shook it. And immediately felt his anger draining away. Her soft, warm touch was like a soothing balm over the wounds in his soul that had been reopened during the interrogation. That simple human contact that he normally avoided sparked a stirring in his heart that he'd thought had died years ago. He quickly broke the contact out of desperation and self-preservation. He didn't want the man he used to be to wake up, to feel everything so deeply and painfully again. He needed to lock away that part of himself just to survive.

She gave him a sad smile as if she understood what he was thinking. And that scared the hell out of him.

"Aidan, I know there's more to what happened the night your wife died than you've ever admitted. Whatever it is that you're holding back, remember that the law can't punish you a second time for the same crime. You've served your time. Have you considered that telling the truth will unburden your conscience, lift a terrible weight off your shoulders and allow you to finally begin the healing process?"

He motioned toward the open door. "Goodbye, Special Agent Malone."

She sighed and headed outside.

The sound of another car engine and wheels crunching on gravel had him stepping onto the porch to see what was going on. As Malone was walking toward her car, one of the police station's Jeeps was heading toward her.

"How did I get so lucky today?" Aidan muttered.

The unmistakable sound of an arrow whistling through the air had him shouting a warning.

"Hit the deck!"

Malone dived to the ground a split second *after* the arrow embedded itself in the back of her SUV, with a large white feather dangling from the end. If the arrow had been a little to the left, it would have driven deep into her back.

Aidan whirled around just in time to see someone disappearing into the woods on the far side of the cabin. He immediately took off after them.

"Freeze, or I'll shoot!" Dawson's voice rang out.

Aidan slid to a halt and slowly raised his hands.

# Chapter Seven

"I'm fine, I'm fine," Grace yelled as Dawson stopped to check on her. "Go! Get him!"

Dawson ran past her, past the front of the cabin and into the woods. Grace climbed painfully to her feet, flicking off the worst of the gravel that had dug into her legs through the tears they'd made in her pants. But she didn't have time to feel sorry for herself. Ignoring the stinging in her skinned knees, she yanked her pistol out of her holster and jogged up the porch steps to check on Aidan.

"Are you okay? No arrows hit you, did they?" she asked.

He slowly turned and lowered his hands, a look of confusion on his face. "You're not arresting me?"

She frowned. "Arrest you? Why would I do that?"

"I figured you both thought I was the…" He shook his head, seemingly stunned. "You saw the shooter?"

"Dawson did. He's on his trail right now. And I need to back him up. Lock yourself in your cabin and—"

"Hell, no. I'm not hiding while some fool runs around on my property playing cowboys and Indians, not caring whether he hurts someone, or worse." He took off across the porch.

"Wait. That's an order!"

"I'm not one of your agents to boss around." He took the stairs two at a time, then sprinted toward the woods where Dawson had gone.

Grace said a few unsavory words and took off after both of them. As she ran, she called the station and updated Fletcher about what was happening. Fletcher promised she'd rally the troops. Grace ended the call and slowed, realizing she'd already lost the trail. She searched the ground, trying her best to track where the suspect, Dawson, and Aidan had gone.

She loved mountain views and outdoors as much as most living in the beautiful state of Tennessee. But that didn't mean she was Danielle Boone. She'd never gone hunting or camping, and her version of roughing it was a three-star motel. Trying to figure out which way someone had gone, by looking for shoe prints or bent grass or whatever, was proving to be beyond her skills.

She finally gave up and tried calling Dawson, but he didn't answer his phone. Another call to Officer Fletcher got Aidan's cell phone number from his police folder. Grace punched it in, but like the police chief, he didn't pick up.

Worried they might be in trouble, she kept going, desperately hoping she was headed the right way. A few minutes later, the sound of male voices had her stopping again. There, up ahead through a break in the trees, she saw Dawson and Aidan. Side by side, shoulder to shoulder, they were jogging in her direction. They weren't smiling or laughing. But they weren't arguing or exchanging blows either. They almost seemed…friendly. She was so surprised that she forgot for a second why the three of them had gone into the woods to begin with.

She never saw the second arrow coming.

"I'M FINE. Stop fussing over me," Grace assured Aidan and the chief for the dozenth time as she sat beside them on one of Aidan's couches. Kneeling in front of her was Officer Collier. Apparently, he served as one of the town's part-time EMTs in addition to his police duties. "The arrow barely touched me, just a scratch. Doesn't even need stitches."

Collier shook his head. "Actually, I'm having trouble getting the bleeding to stop. I may have to stitch it closed."

Her face flushed. "Seriously? Isn't there a doctor around here who can do it?"

"Nope. But if you're squeamish, I can put a pressure bandage on it for now and take you to the hospital."

"The hospital? Where is that?"

"The other side of Chattanooga. About an hour and a half away."

"Good grief. What do you people do around here for something really serious?"

"Helicopter," Dawson told her. "The town purchased a used medevac chopper last year after a little girl nearly died because it took so long to get her to the hospital. An anonymous donation put us over the top on our fundraiser and we had enough money left over to stock it with medical supplies and train several key people in town as EMTs, including Collier."

Remembering how worried Aidan had been this morning about children being in harm's way, and knowing he had money to spare, she glanced at him beside her, wondering if he could be that anonymous donor. But he didn't react, gave no indication either way.

Dawson leaned around Aidan to get a better look at Grace's injured arm.

Aidan shoved him back. "Give your guy room to work. He needs to get that bleeding under control."

Dawson narrowed his eyes, but didn't retaliate over the shove. That was amazing since if Aidan had shoved him this morning he'd have likely been thrown in jail. They must have come to some kind of agreement in the woods earlier to set aside their mutual differences and suspicions. Maybe it was because they'd agreed to work together toward the common goal of finding whoever was terrorizing this town.

"Chief Dawson," Grace asked, "in all the chaos that's happened, I never got a chance to ask why you came up here in the first place."

"Yet another anonymous tip. A man called to say that a woman was here visiting O'Brien and that she might be in trouble. And before you say it, yes, I know how thin that is. Considering that's the first anonymous tip I've gotten—"

"Mine, too," Grace said. "Although the tip was to the FBI, not me specifically. I listened to the recording, of course."

"Was the FBI tipster male?"

"He was," she said. "But his voice was tinny, like he was using a device to alter the sound of his real voice. We put a trace on the call, but it led to a burner phone, a throwaway. We've still got people on it, but so far no luck in identifying who made the call."

"I'll see what kind of trace we can do, too, after we're done here."

Aidan glanced back and forth between them. "Hold it. You're saying an anonymous caller sent the FBI here looking for this Crossbow Killer, and another caller sent the police here to my place. Then, both times someone shot an arrow from over my shoulder, making it appear that I was the one who'd shot it. Does that smell like a setup to you?"

"Yes," they both said.

"And it was a good one," the chief added. "Because if

one of the townspeople hadn't taken a picture of their family at the festival and it captured you in the background, with that arrow zinging past you, I'd likely still have you locked up. Likewise, when I drove up here, if I hadn't seen a shadow behind you shooting that first arrow at Malone, I'd have locked you up then, too. The game this guy's playing isn't turning out the way he hoped. Instead of convincing us of your guilt, he's done the opposite. You're the real victim here." He glanced at Grace. "One of them, anyway."

"It's just a scratch," she repeated.

He rolled his eyes again.

"O'Brien," Grace said, purposely using his last name in front of the others. "Do you have any idea who would hate you enough to try to frame you as a serial killer?"

His jaw tightened. "I would think my in-laws despise me. How could they not? We never got a chance to speak after I was arrested. They were grieving, too upset and shocked to seek me out. I sent an apology, again, through my lawyer. But how do you apologize for something like that? Regardless, I can't see them coming after me, or even having someone else do it on their behalf. They're truly good, decent people. They just… No, it's not them."

"There has to be someone else, then. Help us make a list." This time it was Chief Dawson who spoke. "If not your former in-laws, then who? Who else could it be?"

Aidan thought for a moment, then shook his head. "No one. I mean, there are plenty of people who'd love to see me dead based on the hate mail I received in prison. But they were strangers, people who get fired up over news reports. I can't imagine any of them actually coming after me all these years later."

"Do you still have those letters?" Grace asked.

He hesitated, his gaze capturing hers. He was silent for several moments.

"Do you?"

He looked away. "I threw them out. They certainly weren't comforting or sentimental, something to take with me to reread after I was released. No. I don't have the letters."

Grace didn't believe him. That hesitation told her he was holding something back. Was there someone who'd written him that he'd just realized might be the one trying to frame him? If so, why not tell them?

Dawson leaned forward to get Aidan's attention. "What about people here in Mystic Lake? Other than the obvious—people being wary of you because of your past—has anyone gone out of their way to antagonize you? Have you made any enemies?"

This time, he didn't hesitate. "No. I can count on one hand the friends I've made here, with a couple of fingers left over. But I keep to myself for the most part and haven't made any enemies. I'm sure that, like other strangers who heard about my case, many of the townspeople wish I'd go live somewhere else. They likely have strong feelings against me. But again, to go this far, to frame me and risk the lives of innocent people over what they think I..." He cleared his throat. "For what I did, I can't think of anyone who would do that."

Grace stared at him, the words he'd stumbled over running through her mind. *For what they think I... For what I did.* Was he going to say for what they thought he did? Had he slipped up and almost admitted that he *didn't* kill his wife? She noted that Dawson and Collier were both studying Aidan, too, as if weighing the words he'd just said and realizing there might be more to his past, a truth no one else knew. Except Aidan.

Aidan cleared his throat and stood. "Anyone need a drink?" He headed into the kitchen side of the large, open room.

Hoping to break the tension that had fallen over everyone, Grace called out, "Yes, please. The coldest beer you have. None of that light stuff, either."

"No way," Collier said. "We're all on duty, including you. And you're my patient. I won't be able to give you any pain medicine if you drink."

"Meanie."

He laughed.

Still debating whether or not to allow a part-time, relatively new EMT to stick a needle in her arm to stitch her up, she asked Collier, "Who flies the helicopter?"

He pressed some fresh gauze against her arm, mumbling an apology when she winced. "Bobby Thompson. He's—"

"The owner of the marina. I remember you told me earlier."

"He's also retired military, flew a chopper for most of his career. He oversees the maintenance and flies when needed. Stella Holman, from the bed-and-breakfast, was a career nurse before vacationing here, then meeting Frank, getting married and staying for good. She's the one who rides with Bobby to take care of the patients until they reach the hospital."

A loud knock on the open door of the cabin had all of them looking over to see Officer Fletcher standing there. "Justin's arrived with his scent dog."

"About time," Dawson said. He stood and Aidan met him at the door.

Dawson arched a brow. "Don't even think about it. You might not be a suspect anymore, but you're still a civilian."

"Who saved you from tumbling over a cliff's edge earlier. Remember that?"

Dawson's face reddened. Now Grace understood why the chief was treating Aidan more like a friend than a foe. She could well imagine how much he loathed owing his life to an ex-con. Judging by the hard set of his jaw, he didn't like it one bit.

Aidan continued. "It's my land. I know the best ways to get through the brush, where the slopes have loose rocks and dangerous footing, where the cliffs—"

"Okay, okay. You made your point," Dawson grumbled. "You can go, but only as a guide. If we find this guy, don't make any attempts to intervene or take him down. That's for the police to do. Understood?"

Aidan crossed his arms.

Dawson swore but didn't waste more time arguing. "Let's go, while we still have daylight left." He strode onto the front porch where Fletcher, Ortiz, and the man with the scent dog were waiting.

Aidan grabbed the door to pull it closed behind him, then hesitated. "Collier, don't let Special Agent Malone out of your sight. I expect she'll want to head after us again after you patch her up. But if the shooter is still in the area, he might try to finish what he started. Under no circumstances allow her through this door."

"Yes, sir," Collier called out.

Aidan pulled the door shut.

Grace blinked in shock. "Did you just take orders from an ex-con?"

Collier snorted. "Emphasis on ex. He served his time. And I'm not convinced he was ever guilty to begin with."

"He confessed."

"With all due respect, Malone, I'm not one of those officers who thinks everyone in prison is guilty. Innocent people do get convicted sometimes, probably more than most people realize. They make false confessions. It's a proven fact. New evidence, like DNA, has exonerated plenty of them."

"You think his confession was false?"

"Let me put it this way. The chief has accused him of just about every petty crime that happens around here since the day O'Brien came to Mystic Lake. He hasn't exactly made it easy on the guy. Then we get proof he's being framed. And even though O'Brien has every reason to want payback against Dawson, when the chief's foot slips and he could have fallen to his death, O'Brien risked his own life to grab him and haul him back to safety."

"Dawson told you that? I mean, I heard Aidan say something about it but I didn't know any details."

"When I got here, he told me what happened, yeah."

"I get what you're saying," she said. "But what makes you so certain he wasn't a different person years ago, that he didn't kill his wife? Did he tell you he didn't?"

"Ever heard of a Freudian slip? That's what he did earlier, if you ask me. He basically admitted he didn't kill his wife. You heard that too, right?"

"Yes. I did."

"So did Dawson. We've all wondered about O'Brien, played devil's advocate about how he could kill his wife. If you read his case file you'll see interviews the prosecutor did with people who knew him. And pretty much every one of them said he and his wife were wild about each other and that if he did take her life it was out of mercy. You know about the fire, right? That she was paralyzed and in terrible pain."

"Yes, but that doesn't excuse killing her. That's not how our society and our laws work."

He gave her a hard look, then shrugged. "Whatever happened, he's not the bad guy people think he is. Not even close. He may be gruff, rude sometimes. Okay, rude a lot of times. But that's how he protects himself. If you don't let people in, they can't hurt you, you know? Anyway, my point is that he's never, not once, done anything to hurt anyone around here. Just the opposite. He doesn't advertise it or try to take credit, but he helps people all the time."

She was stunned to hear a police officer speaking about Aidan this way, particularly an officer who'd helped another lock him to a conference room table this morning. "How does he help people?"

He swore when he pulled the latest gauze off her arm and it came away bloody. He grabbed a fresh one and pressed hard.

She forced herself to hold still and not give any indication about how much he was hurting her. He was a gold mine of information and she didn't want him to stop talking.

"Collier, how does Aidan help people?"

"Oh, you know. Lots of ways. You've heard about the town's, the lake's, reputation, right? Unexplained things happen around here. Mysterious deaths, disappearances, strange accidents. I mean, we really do have a lot of wacky stuff that goes on. Did you know Mystic Lake has more drownings per year than any other lake in the country?"

"You're kidding. Why? What makes it so dangerous?"

"If you ask the townsfolk, most will tell you it's the spirits of the people who drowned in the lake when the superstorm came through decades ago and flooded this place."

"For real, Collier. What makes the lake so dangerous?"

"Because of the flood."

"Collier—"

"No, no, I'm not talking about ghosts. I'm serious. I'm talking about what's underneath the water. An entire town is at the bottom of the lake. Houses, cars, church spires, trees, lots and lots of dead trees. We do cleanups every year. Hundreds of volunteers pull out debris so boats and swimmers won't get hung up in all that stuff on the bottom. But some of it is too deep to reach. And the lake is huge. Not the part downtown, but the part outside of town by the marina. It's impossible to clean it all. We post warning signs in areas where drownings or boating accidents have occurred, and focus on those areas during our cleanups. Tourists are warned. Locals are reminded all the time about the dangers. But the lake is beautiful, and relatively safe if you stay within the markers. So people come here in droves in the summer to enjoy it. But things still happen."

"Okay. But what does any of this have to do with Aidan?"

"Since when did you start referring to him by his first name?"

Her stomach tightened as she rushed to cover her mistake. "Since I started trying to build rapport in search of the truth. You were saying?"

He gave her a suspicious look, as if he didn't believe her. But he continued. "He's one of the main sponsors on cleanup days, pays to have salvage boats come in and take out debris in the more dangerous areas. And, last summer, on one of those rare days when he showed up around the crowds, he ended up saving some swimmers. They got hung up in some sunken tree branches. He dived in before anyone even realized the swimmers were in trouble, got them free. One of them wasn't breathing when O'Brien pulled her out. He performed CPR until she was breathing again. But it was touch and go for quite a while."

"The little girl who almost died, before the chopper was here?"

He nodded. "And that's not all. There are other things. Like, if someone can't pay their rent, suddenly an envelope of money appears in their mailbox. And the anonymous donor of the chopper money like you said. Nothing like that ever happened around here until he showed up. I can't be sure what exactly occurred in his past with his wife. But I am sure of one thing. The man he is today is a good man. And I trust him more than I'd trust half the people here in town who make themselves out to be way better than they actually are."

The silence stretched out between them.

His face reddened as if everything he'd said was already coming back to haunt him. "It must be because you're an FBI agent that my mouth got the better of me. You tell the chief I said any of that and I'll deny it. He wouldn't take kindly to one of his officers, as you said earlier, talking that way about an ex-con."

She shifted slightly forward on the couch. "I won't tell if you don't tell him about me."

He frowned. "What do you mean?"

"I have the same doubts about Aidan as you." She winced and motioned toward his hand on her arm. "Unless you're trying to completely cut off all circulation, you think you could ease up there?"

"What? Oh, sorry." His face reddened again as he reduced the pressure. "That bleeding isn't going to stop on its own."

"Stitches?"

"Stitches. I'll get that pressure bandage in place and drive you to the hospital."

"Heck, no. I'm not riding in a car for over an hour for two stitches."

"More like three. Maybe even four."

She blinked. "Four?" She craned her neck to try to see the underside of her arm.

He pushed her back against the couch. "Stop worrying. I'll give you a shot of painkiller first. You won't feel a thing."

"Except the shot," she grumbled.

He laughed and, a little too eagerly for her peace of mind, reached for a hypodermic needle in his medical bag.

## Chapter Eight

Grace stood at the largest picture window in Aidan's cabin, staring out at the rapidly darkening sky. "They've been gone too long. And once again no one's answering their cell phones."

"Standard operating procedure," Collier called out from the kitchen. "Radio silence while hunting a suspect. Or, in this case, phone silence. Hey, looks like some venison stew's in here. You think O'Brien would mind if we had some? I'm starving."

"Accepting drinks from a civilian is one thing. Eating up their food is another."

"I skipped dinner."

"So did I." She headed for the door. "I'm going to check on them and see if they—"

He was suddenly in front of her, his back to the door. "If you want to find out whether I'm more afraid of you or my boss, trust me. Dawson trumps you any time."

She flipped her jacket back, revealing her holster. "I have a gun."

He snorted. "Mine's bigger."

"Oh, good grief. I know karate, Collier. Don't make me hurt you."

"You've got four stitches in your arm and it has to be

sore. Besides, your black belt doesn't scare me. I weigh twice what you do, at least. All I have to do is sit on you and—oof!"

Grace stood over him where she'd flipped him onto his back. "Can't say I didn't warn you."

"Nope," he groaned. "Can't say you didn't. If you ripped your stitches out don't ask me to patch you up again. You hurt my feelings." He grimaced. "And my back."

"I'll buy you a day at the spa." She headed to the door again and threw it open.

Aidan stood in the opening, arching a brow. "Going somewhere?"

She groaned. "Great timing."

He looked past her. "Seriously, Collier? You're twice her size. And she's injured. Did she put you on the floor?"

"Afraid so." He groaned again. "I might need help getting up."

Aidan stepped inside, forcing Grace to back up. He stopped beside Collier, shaking his head. "Pathetic." He grabbed Collier's hand and hauled him upright.

"Ouch, sheesh. Some warning would have been nice, man."

"Twice her size, Collier," Aidan reminded him. "Unbelievable." He headed into the kitchen and opened the door to what must have been his pantry.

"Trust me," Collier said. "I won't underestimate her again." He gave Grace a hurt look and limped to the couch. "Not that I should be nice to you after that, but I meant to tell you earlier to keep your bandage dry when you shower. I'll need to change it tomorrow and make sure an infection isn't setting in. Just promise you won't flip me over your shoulder again."

"That depends on whether you deserve it or not," she teased.

He rolled his eyes. "Oh, hey, O'Brien. I saw some venison stew in your refrigerator earlier—"

"Collier," Grace warned.

He gave her a sullen look and settled deeper against the cushions.

"Where's everyone else, Aidan?" She moved toward the door again as he spread a checkered tablecloth over the table.

"Right here," a voice said.

She had to step back for Dawson and Fletcher to come inside. Dawson was carrying a quiver of arrows. Fletcher followed, wearing latex gloves and holding a quart-sized can and a brush with dried red paint on it. She set her bounty on the tabletop and gave Aidan an odd look when he sat at the table.

"Should you be here with the evidence?" she asked.

"Officer Fletcher," Dawson said. "Is there a reason the owner of this property, the victim in an attempted framing scheme who helped us find this evidence and is allowing us to temporarily use his home, shouldn't sit with us and discuss what we've found?"

Her face reddened. "No, sir."

"I didn't think so."

Aidan gave him a subtle nod of thanks.

Fletcher's face turned even redder. Obviously, she wasn't in the same camp as Collier, or even Dawson now, about Aidan's character.

Dawson set the quiver on the table and then made a detour to the couch, looking down at Collier. "Do I even want to know?"

Collier grimaced. "No, sir."

Dawson shook his head and returned to the table, sitting beside Fletcher. Grace sat to Aidan's left. Collier made an amazing recovery and jogged over to take the chair between Aidan and Fletcher.

"What happened?" Grace asked. "Is Ortiz taking the suspect to jail?"

"No," Dawson said. "Ortiz is at the station. A 911 call came in while we were out so he had to rush back and take care of it. False alarm. Everyone's fine. But he'll hang there for now."

"So you didn't find the suspect, but you found his things in the woods?"

Aidan motioned toward the pile in the middle of the table. "The dog led us to a creek at the outer edge of my property. He lost the trail after that, likely because the suspect crossed the creek or maybe walked in it to help dilute his scent. We'd have split up and kept going, figuring we could catch up to him even without the dog's help. But it was getting dark, too dangerous. Most of my land has been left in its natural state."

"Meaning," Dawson added, "it's full of thick brush, downed trees and steep drop-offs. Far too dangerous in bad lighting. We'll search again tomorrow in case he comes back, or has hunkered down somewhere and never left. Speaking of which, O'Brien, you might want to stay at the B and B for a few days, at least until we catch this fool. Him shooting Malone when you were with me means he knows the game is up, that trying to frame you any longer isn't going to work. I think he took that first shot by the SUV to get us into the woods and give him time to get away. I'd rather you not be here alone without a gun to defend yourself if he comes back tonight."

"I can stay and guard him," Grace offered.

Aidan's jaw tightened. "I'm not going to cower behind—"

"A woman?" Grace snapped. "I'm perfectly capable of defending you, myself or anyone else."

Collier raised his hand. "I can attest to that."

"I was going to say that I'm not going to cower behind anyone else putting their lives on the line for me. I'll call Stella, see if there's a room available. If there is, I'll stay downtown for a few days. That should free up my cabin as a base of operations for the search tomorrow. I can give you a key, Dawson."

"I appreciate that. I'd also appreciate it if you help with the search. But only if we can keep you safe in the process. We'll discuss it in the morning."

"I'd definitely like to help," Aidan said.

"You don't have to call the B and B," Grace told him. "I reserved three rooms for the next three days. One is for me and the others are for more agents if I prove the real Crossbow Killer is operating here. We won't likely have that answer until the lab comparisons between the original arrows and the ones you found today come back. They're also running prints and DNA. I'll go online tomorrow and see if any results are ready. But I doubt it."

He nodded his thanks. "I'll pack a bag." He pushed up from the table and headed up the stairs.

Dawson motioned toward the arrows and the paintbrush. "I'm no expert, but these look the same to me as the ones from earlier. What's your take on these, Malone?"

"I didn't bring any gloves. Does anyone have a…" She laughed as all three of them offered her some latex gloves. "You run a tight ship, Dawson. Always be prepared, right?"

"Always."

She took the pair that Fletcher offered, thanking her as she pulled them on. Careful not to touch anything more than she had to, she picked the items up in the least likely places where the suspect might have touched them so that she could try to avoid destroying any viable latent prints.

After a careful examination, she set the evidence down and took a picture of the paint can to send to the lab, as well as the arrows.

"I can have this all couriered to the FBI lab tomorrow morning if you're okay with that."

"I was hoping you'd offer," Dawson said. "But I'd like to dust one of these arrows for prints locally to see if we get anything and put it into IAFIS. We've collected several arrows, so destroying any DNA on just one of them should be an acceptable trade-off to try to get a leg up and speed this along."

"I agree," she said. "For now, since we can't prove or disprove that the suspect is or isn't the Crossbow Killer, we can work on this as a team if, again Chief, you're okay with that."

"Absolutely. We've already set our other investigations aside to focus on this. The more resources we have the more likely we'll be to wrap this up sooner rather than later." He checked the time on his phone. "Speaking of later, it's been a long day for all of us. I recommend we head down the mountain and get a good night's sleep. We'll meet up early to continue the investigation."

"What about the search?" she asked. "You can't run an investigation and a full-blown search at the same time. You need more people."

"Which is why I told Ortiz to contact the sheriff's office to get some bodies up here. Ortiz will be the liaison for our department and manage the search along with whoever Sheriff Galloway puts in charge from his side. He'll also make some casts of the shoe prints we found tonight. Justin will be here with his scent dog again, too. He already agreed to that. We have search-and-rescue volunteers we can call in a pinch. But this guy is dangerous and I don't want civilians out here as more innocent targets for him."

"Sounds like a well-thought-out plan. With Ortiz up here tomorrow, that leaves a desk free at your station. Mind if I operate out of there? I've got my own laptop and can show you the results as soon as the lab uploads them to our portal."

"Of course. Use anything you need. If you want the conference room, consider it yours, as well."

Fletcher grinned. "You might prefer the conference room, honestly. Ortiz is a bit of a slob. You'd be wiping crumbs off your nice blouse and slacks."

Grace looked down, making a face at her clothes. "They used to be nice. That tumble on the gravel driveway earlier pretty much ruined them. But I brought several more changes of clothes with me."

Fletcher gave her a commiserating look and stood. "Since Ortiz was my ride up here, boss, I'm going to have to bum a ride back with you."

"What about me?" Collier asked. "I can give you a ride."

"I'll ride with the boss." Fletcher made a face at Collier as she gathered up the paint can and brush again.

He rolled his eyes.

Aidan jogged down the stairs and joined them, a black leather overnight bag slung over his shoulder. "Special Agent Malone, I'll follow you to the B and B if that's all right, so you can let Stella know I'm taking one of those rooms you reserved."

"Since we're going to the same place, why not leave your truck here and ride with me?" she asked.

He glanced at Dawson. "I think it would be better if I take my truck. I'll need it in the morning. But thanks."

Grace realized all three of the police officers were looking at her. Fletcher was obviously no fan of Aidan. Dawson was grudgingly coming around, but his expression clearly said he didn't think it was appropriate for her to ride with a felon convicted of murder. Even Collier seemed surprised that a federal agent, no doubt especially a woman in this situation, would be so lax.

"Right," she said, her face heating. "That makes more sense. I'll meet you at the front desk." She couldn't seem to get out of the cabin and to her car fast enough.

Good grief, what was she doing? It was one thing to believe that a man was innocent and feel comfortable around him. But she was an FBI agent. She knew better than to allow emotions to override good judgment. Something about Aidan called out to her on a primal level, and it wasn't just that he was, well, hot. Really hot. That shouldn't matter, not right now. What mattered was maintaining her professionalism and following her training. This was her first time out solo. She couldn't screw it up.

## Chapter Nine

Grace stood at the front desk, watching Aidan enter the lobby of the B and B. She'd already notified the young man at the front desk that Aidan would be taking one of the rooms that she'd reserved. Aidan signed the register. Then she and Aidan headed upstairs.

At the top landing, she pointed to the room across the hall from hers. "That one's yours. But before you go inside, I'd like to ask you something."

His expression turned wary. "Go ahead."

"At your cabin, when I asked about the hate mail you received in prison and whether you kept it, you hesitated. Is that because you threw away most of it, but kept some? Are you protecting someone by not telling the whole truth?"

He leaned against the wall beside her door, his overnight bag still slung over his shoulder. "What are your plans in the morning?" he asked.

"You're changing the subject."

"Yes. I am. I already answered your question earlier. Now answer mine. What are your plans in the morning?"

"My plans. Are we talking...breakfast? Together?" Her stomach tightened with a mixture of pleasure and dread. Was he asking her out? If so, she'd have to put the kibosh on it. She'd already screwed up royally tonight in front of other law enforcement officers. She had to be careful or something would get back to her boss. He'd order her back to Knoxville and it would be months before she'd be allowed to fly solo again.

He smiled. "The restaurant downstairs is the main one for the town. It's a large open room with tables fairly close together to accommodate the crowds. I certainly wouldn't mind sitting with you, but given the circumstances, that's not a good idea."

"Aidan, I—"

"You need to start calling me O'Brien again. Even if you think you can trust me, most people, like Officer Fletcher, don't. It can't be good for your reputation to be seen on friendly terms with an ex-con."

"You're actually worried about my reputation? Just this morning I was trying to nail you as the Crossbow Killer."

"Which only reinforces my point. It was this morning, a little over twelve hours ago. Regardless of your instincts or whatever it is that makes you so…comfortable around me, you need to stop. It could kill your career."

She stared at him in wonder. "Aidan, I can't believe after everything you've been through that you're worried about my career. I'm astonished, actually."

"O'Brien."

"What?"

"Don't call me Aidan."

Her fact heated again. "Of course not," she snapped. "Thank you for the reminder."

"Don't look at me like that."

"Like what?"

"Like you're a puppy and I just kicked you. You're not the only one around here feeling a little too comfortable."

Her eyes widened. "Oh. Well, um, then...all I can say is that you sure hide it well."

He stared at her. "Do I?" Ever so slowly, he lifted his hand and gently traced the contour of her cheek.

His touch sent a shock wave through her senses, making her long for so much more. She leaned into his touch—

He jerked his hand back and swore. "I'm trying to warn you and here I am doing the same thing." He shoved both his hands through his hair, leaving it rumpled and disheveled.

Grace's fingers curled with the desire to feather her hands where his had been, to smooth the waves in his hair, to draw him close.

"Stop it," he bit out. "Don't look at me like that, either."

"Like a wounded puppy?"

"Like a damn temptress. You're dangerous. We're dangerous. This has to stop, this...whatever's happening between us. I don't understand it and I sure as hell don't welcome it. Stop being nice and touching me and calling me Aidan with that sexy voice of yours. Nothing good can come of it so just...stop."

He scrubbed the light stubble on his chin. "For the love of... How did we go off on this tangent? That's not what I... The reason I asked about your plans is that I'm worried about your safety, your physical safety. Don't assume that because you were able to put Collier in his place tonight that you'll have the same success against another man who's larger and stronger than you, especially if he catches you off guard."

"Are you trying to scare me into thinking you might hurt me if I'm not careful?"

"Oh, I'd hurt you. No question. By getting you fired as an FBI agent if we aren't careful. But physically? No way.

I'd never be violent toward you or any other woman. Under no circumstances could I ever do that."

She stared at him, searching for the truth in his eyes. "You'd never hurt a woman physically. Are you saying that you didn't hurt Elly?"

"What? That's not what I…" He swore again. "This isn't going the way I… Hell. Malone, just be careful, all right? Don't go around stirring up trouble, trying to find the shooter on your own. Take one of the police officers with you."

She started to cross her arms, but the soreness in her bandaged left arm had her straightening instead. "As you've repeatedly pointed out, I'm a federal agent. Before that, I was a police officer. Notice that I'm in town without a partner. My boss trusts me to take care of myself. You should, too."

"Does your boss know that your first day in Mystic Lake has ended with two attempts on your life? And an injury from one of them?"

Her face heated. "That's none of your business."

His jaw worked. "You're right. It's not. But for some reason, when it comes to you, I can't just look the other way. Don't risk your life by heading out alone anywhere. Please. You've been lucky the first two times this guy shot at you, lucky that you're still alive and only have a sore arm and a few stitches out of it. Don't assume he won't make another attempt, and that this time he won't hit something vital."

His impassioned plea, the concern in his expression, had her more confused than ever. Even though she knew he was right that she needed to be careful how she acted around him in front of others, how was she supposed to act in private? She was so convinced he was innocent. Was this sizzling attraction between them completely clouding her judgment?

Could he really be guilty of killing the woman he'd claimed to love? The mother of his child?

"Be careful," he repeated, his voice gruff. "Please." He crossed to his room and went inside.

She stood outside her own room, her mind a whirlwind as she considered everything that he'd done or said today. He was hiding something, had to be. Was it about the letters? Had their earlier discussion about them made him think of a possible suspect as their shooter? If so, why not tell her? Because he wanted to handle the situation on his own?

She was just about to go into her room when the rich brogue of Aidan's voice sounded from the other side of his door. He must be on the phone. Who would he call this late at night? Did it have something to do with the case?

Looking around to make sure no one else was in the hallway and that the stairs were empty, she quietly crossed to his door and put her ear against it. Either he was being careful not to be very loud, or the walls in the B and B were insulated really well. She could only make out a few words and phrases.

*"Yeah, I know it's late but—"*

*"Tomorrow. Can't wait for—"*

*"—what I pay you for."*

And finally a name. *"Barnes."*

After that, there was only silence. Fearing she'd made a sound and he was coming to the door to check on it, she hurried across the hall and eased her door shut behind her. Then she crossed to the bed and took her laptop out of her satchel.

When it was fired up she put two names into the internet search bar. Aidan O'Brien, and Barnes. She tapped Enter, then gasped at the huge amount of search results on her screen. They were mostly news reports about Elly's death,

Aidan's arrest, his pleading guilty without a trial. The name Barnes showed up over and over, Nathanial Barnes.

Aidan's defense attorney.

## Chapter Ten

Grace adjusted her leather satchel on her shoulder, careful not to hit her sore arm as she headed downstairs the next morning. Her steps were slow both because of her arm and because she was dreading running into Aidan again.

She'd barely slept last night going over everything that had happened and all she'd learned since coming to Mystic Lake. She'd read and reread his folder, searching for inconsistencies, proof about his guilt. Or innocence. But no sooner would she find the answer to one question than she came up with another one. She was more confused than ever.

As soon as she passed the main desk and entered the restaurant, she stopped in surprise. A large group of men and women stood around two long tables that had been pulled end-to-end on the far side of the room. The wording across the backs of their jackets read Polk County Sheriff's Office. They must have arranged for the search party to meet at the restaurant, rather than the station. Seeing how many people were here, it made sense. They'd never have fit in the conference room.

As she headed their way, she saw Chief Dawson bending over the tables, running his fingers across a large map. Beside him were Ortiz and Fletcher. Collier must have been left at the station to run things and take any emergency calls.

"Morning," a familiar brogue said behind her.

She slowly turned around. "Aid—I mean, O'Brien. Morning. Looks like they decided to use this place as their base of operations today."

He nodded in silent approval at her use of his last name. "This is where the town meets for most large gatherings. They say it's for the space. I think it's more about the good food they serve."

"Thanks, Aidan." A smiling Stella had just stepped out of the kitchen with a huge tray of piping-hot blueberry muffins. Grace realized that Stella was the first person she'd heard in this town, other than herself, who'd referred to him by his first name. Did that mean they were friends?

"I won't tell Frank you complimented his cooking," Stella continued. "His ego is too inflated as it is. Morning, Special Agent Malone. Grab a muffin before those deputies pounce on this second batch. You'd think they were starving the way they inhale their food."

"Thank you, ma'am. Looks delicious." Grace took one of the napkins on the tray and picked up a muffin. Her mouth was watering at the aroma. "They smell incredible."

"That's because they are, dear." She winked and offered Aidan a muffin. Instead, he took the tray from her.

"I'll carry it for you," he said.

She put a hand on his shoulder. "That's not necessary. Everyone over there is in law enforcement. I know you're not comfortable around them." She winked at Grace. "Present FBI agent company excluded, of course. You two are obviously friendly. I heard you're both staying together."

Grace almost choked on the bite of muffin she'd just taken. She hurriedly swallowed and cleared her throat. "Um, no, ma'am. I gave up one of the rooms I…" She stopped when she saw the laughter sparkling in Stella's eyes.

Aidan looked mildly alarmed. "Are you teasing us, ma'am?"

Stella only laughed and reached for the tray of muffins.

Aidan shook his head. "I've got it. I have to work with the deputies and police today anyway. I'm helping them search for the guy who shot the boat yesterday with an arrow."

"Oh my. Well, do be careful. And don't let those outsiders push you around." With that, she headed back into the kitchen.

Grace followed Aidan to the other side of the large room. Conversation died as soon as he slid the tray onto the table. Not because everyone was reaching for food, but because Aidan's reputation obviously preceded him. Just as Stella apparently feared, the deputies moved away from him, acting as if he wasn't worthy to breathe their air.

Anger had her face heating. She started to say something, but Aidan bumped her shoulder. When she looked up, he subtly shook his head.

She realized that Dawson was watching her, too. She nodded in greeting and kept her silence.

Dawson returned his attention to the map. "Let's assign out the grids we just reviewed. You'll work in teams of two. Check in with your team leader every half hour. And don't assume your Kevlar vests will completely stop an arrow. Sometimes they don't. It all depends on the speed of the arrow, the distance it travels, the angle of the hit, any number of factors. I'm no expert on bows and arrows. But I know about Kevlar and spent over an hour last night researching the kinds of vests Polk County uses and my team uses. So trust me when I tell you not to take your safety for granted today. The guy we're dealing with is extremely dangerous and has already proven that he's willing to target law enforcement."

Grace took that as her cue to step away from the group. She didn't want Dawson to point to her as his warning to the others to be more careful. She still needed to report to her boss about her injury and wasn't looking forward to it. Having him hear through the law enforcement grapevine that an FBI officer was shot with an arrow in Mystic Lake wouldn't do her any favors. She needed to call him first thing when she got to the police station.

Fletcher, who'd been standing near Dawson a moment ago, caught up to Grace near the front desk. "Hey, Malone. The chief assigned me to work with you today, if you need me. Did you want to do knock-and-talks?"

"I'd like to. The first people I want to speak to are the ones who were at the festival, especially any witnesses to the shooting. That includes the family who took that picture of…of O'Brien. And the men on the boat, of course."

"I took statements from them yesterday, so I can give you those. If you want to talk to them again, I'll set it up."

"Perfect. I want a tour of the town, as well. In particular, I'm interested in places where a stranger may hide in plain sight without causing suspicion. On the internet I saw there's a large campground near the marina. Or, at least, there used to be. Is that still there? And open this time of year?"

"Colby opened it for the leaf peepers just this week. Colby Wainright, the owner. The first official picture-taking tourists are scheduled to stay at the campground this weekend." She grinned. "I was up early and already called over there."

"Well, there's nothing for me to do, then."

Fletcher laughed. "There's plenty. But I'd like to think I can be helpful in your investigation."

"*Our* investigation. The guy we're after is either a serial killer or a copycat. Either way, we need to stop him to
keep everyone safe. I not only appreciate your help, I need
it. And I have to add that I've never had such a welcome
reception by a non-federal law enforcement agency before.
Or even just the locals. Everyone I've met so far, like Stella,
the front desk clerk, the few customers who were in the restaurant late last night when I came down for a quick snack,
they've all been so friendly. I don't know how Mystic Lake
got a reputation for being so, well—"

"Wacky? Weird? Mysterious?"

She laughed. "All of the above, I suppose."

Fletcher rapped her knuckles on the front desk. "That's
me knocking on wood, hoping none of our mysterious stuff
happens while you're here to ruin your current impression
of our town. I kind of like the idea of us being known for
being nice instead of our usual rep. Are you ready to head
over now? My Jeep's parked out front. I got a prime parking
space. Didn't have to drive around back or double-park."
She frowned at Grace. "Actually, you might need a heavier
jacket today if you plan on canvassing the town, interviewing people. It's chillier this morning than it was yesterday.
And it'll be at least ten degrees colder up in the higher elevations."

"Noted. I'll hurry upstairs and be right back."

"I'll get the heater going in the Jeep. Meet you outside."

Once Grace entered her room, she grabbed some napkins from the coffee area to wrap up her barely eaten blueberry muffin to finish at the station. The one bite she'd had
was amazing and she was looking forward to finishing it.

Once she had her heavier jacket on, she couldn't resist
peeking into the restaurant one more time to see how things
were going. To her surprise, Aidan was the one speaking to

the group now. He was pointing at the map and she could just hear enough to realize he was warning them about specific areas on his property that had dangerous drop-offs or were perfect locations for an ambush.

Dawson spoke up then, telling them that he'd slipped and started to fall over one of those cliffs yesterday and that Aidan had quite literally risked his own life to save him. Grace could have hugged the chief for admitting that. He clearly knew something needed to be done to change the atmosphere of the team if the search was going to be successful. Sure enough, some of the deputies were looking at Aidan with far less suspicion now, even respect.

As Dawson answered a question from one of the men, Aidan glanced up and met Grace's gaze. He quickly looked away. She sighed and hurried outside to meet Fletcher.

DISAPPOINTMENT SETTLED OVER Aidan as Grace left the restaurant. While he was glad that she was being more careful about how she acted around him, he'd hoped to at least have a couple of minutes to speak to her. He wanted to know where she was going and remind her to have someone with her for safety. And if he could somehow *accidentally* show up where she was later today and check on her, he could at least reassure himself that she was okay. Instead, he'd probably be worrying about her all day not knowing her plans.

He sighed in frustration. What an idiot he was to have his thoughts so consumed with her. He needed to take his own advice and be careful. The man trying to frame him was likely on the hunt for him. And if that meant he was waiting up on Aidan's property, there was likely an arrow with his name written on it. The only way Aidan was going to survive was to stay alert and focused. Somehow he had to stop thinking about the beautiful, smart, delightfully sassy woman who'd somehow managed to crack the wall around his heart that he'd spent the past twelve years erecting.

"O'Brien." Ortiz motioned to him. "Let's get you fitted in a vest since you're going up with us. It's not a hundred percent protection but it could save your life if you do get hit."

"What about Malone and your officers who aren't participating in the search? If this guy has left the mountain and ends up somewhere they go today, they could be in danger, too.

"Good point. I'll talk to the chief."

## Chapter Eleven

Grace followed Fletcher into the police station and was met by Collier wearing a Kevlar vest and holding up two more. "Chief's orders, ladies."

Fletcher settled her hands on her hips. "You're making that up. I've been here two years and have never had to dust one of those off."

"We've never had someone running around town shooting at people with a bow and arrow before, either. Until he's caught, we've been ordered to wear these while on duty."

"Even if we're in the office?" Fletcher complained.

"Even if." He held one out to her.

She grumbled and took it.

"Malone?" He offered her the other one. "Obviously the chief can't force you to wear this. But he highly recommends it. There are a few more in the supply closet if this one doesn't fit."

"Does O'Brien have one? He's with that search party heading up to his place. If anyone should have one it's him since the shooter obviously has a vendetta against him. He might as well have a target on his back."

He grinned. "Funny you should say that. He's the one who asked the chief to make sure you have a vest. And the rest of us, of course." He cocked his head as if considering. "Should we read anything into that?"

Grace rolled her eyes, but her face flushed with heat.

"Leave her alone," Fletcher scolded. "You need any help with those straps, Malone?"

"I think I can manage." She slid it on and began adjusting the Velcro. "This vest is bulkier than the one I normally wear. I may exchange it for mine the next time I'm in my car."

Fletcher motioned toward the conference room. "Did you want to set up in there or use Ortiz's desk? It's not as bad as usual. No crumbs this morning." She chuckled.

Grace smiled and glanced at the proximity of his desk to Fletcher's and Collier's. The angle meant they'd see everything she was doing on her computer, which wasn't necessarily a bad thing. But they'd also hear her on the phone—like when she called her boss to tell him about the fiasco yesterday.

"It *would* be easier to spread everything out in there," Grace said.

"Sounds good. Supplies are in that cabinet by the vending machines if you need anything. For lunch we often have a sandwich shop farther down Main Street deliver. Let me know when you're hungry."

"I appreciate it." Grace headed into the conference room and set her satchel on the table. No sooner had she unloaded her laptop and folders than Collier knocked on the glass door and headed inside. She groaned when she saw he was carrying his medical bag.

"Warned you yesterday that I'd need to check your stitches today and change that bandage. I'm still going to help you, even though you crushed my ego by flipping me over your shoulder. I still don't see how you did that with a hurt arm, especially as small as you are."

"Training. Want me to show you?"

"I'd rather not."

She laughed and sat beside him so he could work on her arm.

"Looks good," he said after he cut the bandage off. "No sign of infection. I'll put some antibiotic ointment on it again and wrap it back up." He set a bottle of pain pills on the table. "Take two of these and call me in the morning." He winked and smeared the ointment on her arm, then expertly re-bandaged it.

"Thanks. Seriously. It feels much better this morning. You did a great job."

"I'm a jack of all trades. Part-time doctor—"

"EMT."

"—full-time police officer who looks great in a uniform. Good-looking and single. Know anyone who might appreciate that?" He waggled his brows at her.

"Are you flirting with me, Officer Collier?"

"You can call me Chris."

"I'd rather not."

He dramatically pressed his hand against his chest. "My hopes are dashed."

The door opened and Fletcher stood in the opening. "Collier, leave the pretty FBI agent alone. I see what you're doing. The walls are glass. Plus, I know *you*."

"I was taking care of my patient."

"Asking her out on a date, more likely. Ignore whatever he said to you, Malone. He flirts with any woman who will talk to him. It's just what he does. He's actually harmless."

"Don't forget good-looking." He sighed at Malone. "Maybe next time."

Malone couldn't help laughing at his antics.

Fletcher grabbed his arm and pulled him out of the room, lecturing him on professionalism the whole time.

It was obvious that they were good friends in addition to being coworkers. Like a brother and sister, their good-natured teasing and nagging spoke of a strong bond beneath the surface. She'd sensed that same camaraderie from the whole team when they'd all been together. Grace couldn't help the tug of jealousy inside her.

She didn't have any close friends at work. The stress and high expectations and constant evaluations during her training hadn't allowed the time or casualness that would enable friendships to develop. Maybe once this investigation was over, if she did a good job, that would change. She'd love to experience the closeness the police here at Mystic Lake shared.

Grace started separating out her various reports and photographs, getting them organized so she could plan her next steps. Once everything was set, she logged on to the FBI portal to see whether the lab report was back on the first batch of evidence she'd had couriered yesterday. So far there was nothing. Unable to justify delaying any longer, she did the thing she'd been dreading most. She called her boss.

It didn't go well.

He was ticked about her being injured and wanted her to go home, immediately. He'd send another agent to look into what had happened to confirm or disprove her suspicions that the shooter they were dealing with wasn't the serial killer they were after.

She in turn appealed to his love of efficiency by arguing that the more experienced agents should use their skills to their best advantage by continuing to follow up on the leads from the Crossbow Killer's known crime scenes. It made far more sense to leave the junior agent following up on a lead they doubted would pan out. Besides, she had the entire police force of Mystic Lake backing her up, plus a dozen deputies from Polk County. The odds of anything else bad happening to her were almost zero.

What she'd said wasn't an outright lie. But she knew he'd assume the police force was more than four people. And he didn't realize the deputies were here only for today to assist with a search. Luckily, he didn't dive deeper into the logistics. But he didn't agree to let her stay, either. Instead, he gave her twenty-four hours to report back on her progress, and her health. Once she called tomorrow morning with an update, he'd make a final decision about her continuing role in Mystic Lake.

She blew out a shaky breath and ended the call. Assuming today's search didn't result in the arrest of a suspect, she needed to show solid progress and not get into trouble again. Those knock-and-talks had just become critical. But before she headed out to conduct interviews, she wanted to read the ones that Fletcher had already conducted.

Fletcher had been extremely thorough. Grace couldn't find any fault with her work. She'd asked all of the questions Grace would have, and then some. Her knowledge of both the town and its people was obviously a great asset. It gave her the background to know what types of things to ask about, specific to each person interviewed, things that wouldn't have occurred to Grace.

She secured her laptop to the metal ring in the tabletop using a cable lock. Then she grabbed a small notepad and pen and slid them into her jacket pocket as she exited the conference room.

Collier was on the phone, taking notes, and nodded at her, preoccupied with whatever he was working on.

Fletcher looked up from her desktop computer, her glance falling to Grace's jacket. "Are we going somewhere?"

"If your offer to help me with interviews is still open, yes. I was impressed with the ones you did yesterday. I'd appreciate your assistance today."

The officer's face lit up with pleasure. "Lo and behold, I impressed a Fed. I'll bet Collier can't say the same." When he didn't even look her way, she rolled her eyes. "It's no fun teasing him if he isn't paying attention." She grabbed her jacket and shrugged it on over her vest, frowning and readjusting the straps before zipping her jacket. "Did you have any specific place in mind where you want to start?"

"The campground."

## Chapter Twelve

Aidan dropped to his knees on the ground and peered over the edge of the cliff. Relief swept through him when he saw Ortiz standing on the rock overhang below, clinging to a sapling growing out of the side of the mountain. Another foot and he'd have tumbled down to the ravine.

"Did I or did I not tell you to stop?" Aidan laughed when Ortiz made a rude gesture.

"I tried to, but the dang rocks were like ice, sliding out from under me. Whatever you paid for this piece of property, you paid too much," Ortiz complained. "It's a nightmare of cliffs and rock and vegetation so thick you can hardly see twenty feet in front of you."

"The cabin and flat land around it are nice enough to make up for that. And it's the views I paid for, and great hunting. Those rocks and cliffs you're complaining about are a bonus. They make it secure and hard for people to trespass. Well, usually, anyway."

"Maybe the shooter decided the same thing and went somewhere else. Or better yet, maybe he's at the bottom of one of these ravines and we'll find his skeleton after the buzzards pick it clean. You gonna haul me up, or talk me to death?"

"I was thinking of taking a picture first to show Dawson when we rendezvous with the rest of the search party."

Ortiz swore and tried to climb up the cliff wall on his own.

"Stop, stop," Aidan said, laughing. "Give me a minute. I need leverage." He looked around, then chose two trees close to the edge to brace his legs. After taking off his belt, he made a loop, then held it down toward Ortiz. "Loop your belt through mine and around your wrists. Then use your legs to push against the rock and climb up while I pull."

Ortiz did as he'd said, then warned, "If you drop me, I'm going to come back and haunt you."

"Would you rather I call your boss and have him pull you up?"

"Hell, no. If you even hint that I needed rescuing, I'll swear you're lying."

Aidan snorted and pulled the belt tight. "Let's do this."

A minute later, they were both lying on their backs above the drop-off, trying to catch their breath.

"That was fun," Ortiz said between taking gulps of air. "Particularly the part where you said uh-oh as if you were going to drop me."

Aidan sat up. "Consider it karma, payback for handcuffing me to the conference room table. It's nice having law enforcement at my mercy for a change instead of the other way around."

Ortiz grunted and sat up, too, taking his belt from Aidan. Once they were both standing and well away from the edge, Aidan motioned toward a slight incline on their right. "That's the last part of our grid to search. This time, stay beside or behind me. Don't get impatient and speed ahead. Slow and steady means staying safe."

"I get it. Trust me, I get it." A moment later he called out, "O'Brien? Aidan? Wait."

Aidan turned in question.

Ortiz seemed uncomfortable, looking off in the distance before finally dragging in a deep breath. "I, uh, I don't pretend to know much about what happened in your past, the reasons behind what you did and exactly what took place." He held up his hands. "And I'm not asking you to explain. It's just, I may have misjudged you this past year. I lumped you in with all the other, well, criminals I've known through the years and assumed you were as bad as, or worse than, them. But none of those others would have done what you've done. I—"

"Forget it," Aidan said. "You probably could have climbed up that drop-off without my help. It just would have taken longer."

"That's not what I'm talking about. I mean, yeah, maybe I could have. But then again, maybe I would have fallen." He grimaced. "I appreciate your help, and that you helped the chief when he had a close call. And a lot of other things, like you running into the woods at the festival to try to get the shooter, with no thought for your own safety."

"Ortiz, we need to finish searching our grid and—"

"Just give me a second, man. I'm eating crow here. Let me finish."

Aidan sighed. "The sun will set soon. Let's search while you eat crow."

Ortiz followed him up the incline. "I'm just saying there's more to you than your past. Not that what you did was okay or anything. But I honestly believe people can change. And the man I've seen these past couple of days isn't the man I always thought you were."

Aidan stopped and pushed some small branches aside to peer underneath a bush.

"I'll try to give you the benefit of the doubt from now on," Ortiz said, stopping beside him. "And I'll make an effort to not always assume you're behind every little bad thing that happens around here. That's what I'm trying to say."

Aidan pointed beneath the bush. "Is that what I think it is?"

Ortiz leaned down to look at the plastic bag Aidan had found. "Well, I'll be. Look at all these feathers. At least now we know where they came from. It isn't his hunting prowess, unless you call going to a costume store hunting. I wonder if that shopping bag has a receipt in it. Or fingerprints." He pulled some latex gloves out of his pocket and pulled them on. "No receipt, but I recognize the bag. Comes from a party store in town. Not Mystic Lake—Chattanooga. I take my daughter there to shop for Halloween every year."

"The paint on the feathers looks fresh." Aidan bent down to check for a discarded paint can or brush, but didn't find any.

"Why would he leave the feathers behind after going to all that trouble?" Ortiz asked.

Aidan glanced back in the direction of the cliff that Ortiz had slid down. It wasn't far, maybe twenty yards. He located shoe prints near the bush, then backtracked, following them to see where else the shooter had been.

When he and Ortiz reached the cliff's edge, the officer's face went pale.

"He was here," Ortiz said. "He was standing right here, maybe trying to see where all the searchers were."

Aidan nodded. "He must have heard us coming and ran and hid in those bushes. That bag crinkles, makes noise. Most likely he ditched it because he was worried we'd hear him. He must not have had his bow and arrows with him or he'd have shot at us."

"Lord have mercy," Ortiz said, his face still pale.

"He's on the run. I doubt he's gotten very far. This is the most treacherous terrain on my property. It's slow going. There are only two ways out: the way we came, or off to the left over there, northeast."

Ortiz pulled out his cell phone. "I'll warn the others."

# Chapter Thirteen

The sun was beginning to set before Fletcher and Grace completed most of the interviews that Grace felt were necessary for her investigation. There were a few more they'd do tomorrow. She just hoped the work she'd done today was sufficient for her boss to allow her to continue. Investigations took time and at least she was making progress. And, bonus, there hadn't been another attempt on her life. So far.

The campground had been a bust: no new leads. But it covered several acres and it took a long time to thoroughly search the surrounding woods for signs that someone may have been staying there, hiding out. They didn't even find a cigarette butt or a beer can to indicate anyone had been there. Then again, since the owner, Colby, was in the process of getting it ready for his first reservations of the season, he'd been cleaning daily. So there was no real way to know if he'd thrown away what could have been evidence.

He didn't remember seeing anyone suspicious but admitted there were always a few hikers or walkers in the area and he didn't pay them much attention. He maintained a network of trails for his campers. The locals used them as well, which he appreciated because it kept the vegetation from taking over. But, no, he hadn't seen any strangers, or at least, he didn't remember any.

Although Grace and Fletcher had spoken to just about everyone Fletcher could think of who'd attended the festival, which was actually easy since so many of them were regulars at Stella's restaurant, none of the people they'd spoken to remembered seeing any strangers.

As Fletcher's Jeep bumped around the back roads on their return to the police station, she apologized that they hadn't accomplished anything.

"Sure we did," Grace said. "We spoke to almost everyone we needed to talk to. That's progress."

"I don't see how. We didn't learn anything."

"We learned quite a bit. Think about it. Everyone we spoke to said the same thing, that they didn't notice any strangers around. What does that tell you?"

Fletcher steered around a tree that was blocking half the gravel road they were heading down. "I'll have to call that in, get someone up here to clear it. Um, let's see. What does that tell me. I guess just that no one saw our guy. Maybe he's a ghost, one of those poltergeists who can move things. It would fit in with other alleged spiritual sightings in the area."

"Fletcher—"

"I know, I know. No one saw him even though we know he exists, poltergeists excluded. Like I said, we made no progress."

"We know he's around, has been for a few days at least. If no one saw a *stranger*, then our shooter is…"

"I don't know, he's…wait. A local. That's what you're saying?"

"It's a possibility."

"No way. Can't be. There's no one in this town that I can picture shooting at people with a bow and arrow. Not even the rottenest of the teenage menaces who like to have bonfires in the woods without caring that they could set the whole forest on fire would go around shooting arrows at people. It can't be a local."

"Let's add those teenage menaces to the list for additional interviews. I'm not ready to discount that our suspect could be a local. But let's say you're right and he isn't. What does that leave us with, remembering that no one has noticed anyone unfamiliar to them in town?"

Fletcher thought for a moment, then shrugged. "No idea. What's your theory?"

"It's more like a building block than a theory, something to start giving us a more clear idea, or profile, of the person we're after. If he's a stranger, not a local, then to not have been seen around town means he's not going to the restaurants or shops. He's not staying at the campground and not stealing a boat or canoe from the marina since they didn't report any missing. He's likely not broken into anyone's homes or vacation cabins looking for food or shelter or you'd have had someone reporting that."

"Oh, I get what you're saying. He's comfortable with the outdoors. He's self-reliant, used to camping in the wilderness, on his own, away from everyone else. He's avoiding the town and the people in it, except for when he wants to strike, like at the festival or at O'Brien's place. Most likely he has a tent, a sleeping bag, provisions. When he came here he came prepared with all the supplies he'd need to survive until he accomplished whatever he came here to do."

Grace grimaced. "To get revenge against O'Brien for something. Framing him didn't work, so his next step may well be to try to kill him. But go back to what you just said. You mentioned when he came here. How did he get here? There's only one road in and out. I suppose the river is an option."

"No, it's not. It feeds our lake, but if you trace it up the mountain you'll see a giant waterfall, Mystic Falls. It's one of our tourist attractions around here, especially in the spring when it swells from the winter thaw. It's pretty incredible, but it's in no way navigable. Even a boat or canoe would be busted up on the rocks if someone tried to navigate the river over the falls. The only way to get a boat here is on a trailer behind your vehicle. Most people just rent a boat already at the marina rather than go to that kind of trouble."

Grace considered what she'd said and looked up at the steep, treacherous mountain Fletcher was carefully descending to get them back to town. "I suppose, in theory, someone determined enough could hike in over the mountains, couldn't they?"

"Ha. Not likely. You've seen how unforgiving the land is around O'Brien's place. We've got spots like that all around here. Makes it darn near impossible to approach our town that way. It's one of the reasons our town stays small, even with the attractions for tourists. To move here, you have to either buy someone out or have the money to dynamite and excavate a part of the mountain to make it possible to build on in the first place. We're truly landlocked. One way in, one way out."

"The road through the mountains and forest to reach Mystic Lake is an hour by car," Grace said. "How long would it take to walk that distance?"

"Me? About a week." She laughed. "Okay, maybe not that long. But you drove here, you saw how the road winds around the mountains, constantly going up and down. It would be a challenge to anyone to do that without a vehicle. Even one of those iron man athletes would struggle. No, I think he drove here."

"All right, then how hard would it be to hide a vehicle once you arrive so that no one reports seeing it?"

"I like where you're going with that," Fletcher said. "Collier, to his credit, is an explorer at heart. His idea of a vacation is to hike the mountains around our town. I think that's crazy. I'd rather go to some nice warm beach and work on a tan. But my point is that he knows the land that surrounds our town better than most. We can put him on that, have him map out the area and figure out the places where someone might likely hide their vehicle so we can check them out. Who knows, maybe we'll get lucky and catch our suspect napping in his back seat or the bed of his pickup."

"There's something else we could do," Grace added. "With only three officers, I know you can't spare someone to keep an eye on the road out of town 24/7. But maybe a camera could be set up to record the license plates of anyone leaving the area. We can check those out in case our suspect leaves. That would be like a gift from heaven, having a plate to track. Unless of course his vehicle is stolen. But even that would give us another clue. Maybe he stole it in an area where he's most comfortable. You never know what that might lead to."

Fletcher stopped at the very road they were discussing, checked for cars, then turned in the direction of Mystic Lake. "I think a camera on this road is a perfect idea. We can borrow a trail camera from one of our local hunters, the kind that's activated by motion so the battery doesn't run out right away. One of us can change out the video card every day and bring the used one back to the station to check out on our computer."

"About how many vehicles head out of town every day?"

"More than I'd like when it comes to figuring out which cars belong to people who live here and which ones don't.

Since the pandemic changed how people do business, a lot more of our town telecommutes, works from home. But there are still quite a few who have to drive to Chattanooga every day. Don't worry, though. We'll track everything down, see if there's a lone, unexplained vehicle coming in or out of town."

Grace was happy to have a plan, even if just one to try to get a license plate and vehicle description that may or may not help them find the killer. That was the thing about investigative leads. You could never predict which one would pan out, so you had to follow up on all of them.

"You haven't heard any updates about today's search, right?" she asked.

"Not a peep. But I'm sure everyone's okay or we definitely would have been called. Most likely the deputies are either on their way back to Chattanooga or are there already. No one's going to search up here at night, especially on O'Brien's property. That's some of the roughest terrain I've seen anyone living on around here. It's downright dangerous."

"Which means our suspect is even more comfortable and knowledgeable about the outdoors than your typical hunter or even camper would be. He was able to get away from your boss and O'Brien when he shot at me." She grimaced. "*Both times* he shot at me. A novice outdoorsman wouldn't have been able to get away, not without getting hurt or cornered. He's highly skilled."

Fletcher snorted. "Except for that stupid feather thing on the end of his arrows. He'd have way better aim if he didn't use that. He must not know much about using a bow and arrow or he'd ditch the feathers."

Grace stared at her a moment. "You may be right. O'Brien theorized that the shooter doesn't care who he hits. The victim is random. They just happen to be in the way of wherever the arrow lands. Honestly, that makes the most sense for our profile since our other evidence points to this guy being an experienced outdoorsman. He knows the feather throws off his aim and he doesn't care. It's because he's bragging. He wants everyone to know that he's the one hurting or killing people. The feather is his signature."

"You're talking about this Crossbow Killer again. I thought you were thinking our shooter probably wasn't him, that he was someone specifically after O'Brien."

"I can't discount the possibility that the real serial killer could also be after O'Brien for some reason. It seems unlikely. Doesn't fit in with typical serial killer behavior, if you can call any of their behavior typical. But we don't have enough information to arrive at a conclusion about that. As for the picture of our shooter that we're trying to draw, I think we *can* conclude that he's in good physical condition or he wouldn't be able to run through the woods in rough terrain to escape the police. That means he's young, but old enough that he's likely had years of experience in the wilderness. I'd say mid-to late twenties, maybe even early thirties."

"Honestly, I'm leaning more toward those teenage locals again," Fletcher said. "Kids around here start hunting and hiking and practically living outdoors from a really young age. They can be experts outdoors before they even graduate. I'll draw up a list of our frequent offenders. And I can ask the school principal if there's anyone else he thinks we should consider, maybe someone who's a loner or even a bully, something like that."

"I wouldn't have thought Mystic Lake was large enough to have any schools. Or do the kids commute to Chattanooga?"

Fletcher laughed. "Believe it or not, we have enough residents to support a K-through-twelve school and a one-truck fire station in addition to our little police force. You don't see everyone because the town's population is spread out over a vast area, all up and down the mountains. There's even a subdivision past the marina. We ran out of time today to go that far. But we really have a lot to offer for just about anyone, whether you want to live in the mountains or the burbs." She rolled her eyes. "Listen to me. I should be on the town council heading up the tourism task force."

"You do make Mystic Lake sound pretty nice."

"Except for our resident serial killer or copycat?"

Grace laughed. "Except for that."

They were close to where the woods ended and the town began. Grace tapped her hand impatiently on her thigh. "I hope the lab gets back to me soon. I really need to know what they've found, whether the evidence we sent matches the evidence from our previous crime scenes. It will help us cull all these theories and ideas of ours if we know whether we're looking for the Crossbow Killer or someone else entirely."

Fletcher turned onto Main Street, then slowed to a stop. "What the ever loving...the dang media's here. Look at that news truck parked a few spots down from the station. They wouldn't have driven all this way for a story about a random arrow shot during our festival, especially since no one was hurt. And, honestly, that's not exactly unusual around here compared to other things that go on. I'm betting one of those Polk County deputies sprang a leak. He probably has a friend at the news desk and told them we were searching for a potential serial killer out here."

She glanced at Grace. "Seeing an FBI agent, or even knowing you're here if the deputies shared that information, too, is going to make the reporter rabid. It could spread like a disease and we'll have even more of them here tomorrow. Let's enter the station through the back door. There's a service alley behind all the shops we can use."

She parked on the far side of the main parking lot. As soon as the two of them sneaked into the station, Collier looked up with a relieved expression on his face. "I was just about to call you two and warn you that—"

"The news media's outside," Fletcher interrupted. "We saw the van."

"A cameraman and reporter got here about fifteen minutes ago demanding to see the chief about the search being done for a serial killer. I did what I could to laugh that off and said we were actually after some kid playing pranks. They asked me if that was the case why was there an FBI agent in town. I told them we take the security of our citizens very seriously and when the kid almost hurt someone at the festival we called in the FBI to help us nip this thing as quickly as possible. But as you can see, they're still here. I don't think they believed anything I told them."

Grace groaned. "My boss will love this. He wanted to keep everything quiet until I determined if our killer is really here or not. Does Dawson know the media is waiting to pounce on him?"

"I warned him right before you came in. He should be here soon. They called the search off half an hour ago and the deputies are on their way back home."

"Good riddance," Fletcher said as she hung her jacket on the back of her chair.

"Agreed. They did find signs of our suspect and that he was there recently. But he's a slippery devil. No one actually saw him in spite of all those searchers. Justin's scent dog pulled up lame, so he wasn't any help today or they might have had better luck."

"What kinds of signs did they find?" Grace asked. "Is there more evidence for our lab to process?"

The squeak of the back door followed by footsteps had all of them turning. Chief Dawson entered, followed by Ortiz and Aidan.

"Lock the front door," Dawson told Collier. "Quickly, before that reporter notices I'm here. I'm not in the mood to be civil at the moment. The search was a bust."

Collier hurried to lock the door while Ortiz set a large paper evidence bag on his desk.

"Not a total bust," Ortiz said. "We have a plastic bag from a costume store in Chattanooga and half a dozen white feathers, painted with the same red stripe as the earlier ones, ready to be attached to more arrows."

Grace hurried over and looked in the bag while Ortiz held it open. "This is great. I'll arrange for another courier in the morning to get this to the lab. But I'd like to follow up with the store you mentioned. I don't see a name on the bag."

"I'll give you the info," Ortiz said. "That sparkly bag is unique. Even without a store name on it, I recognized it immediately."

Grace glanced at Aidan. "O'Brien, did everything go well? Any close calls?"

Ortiz shot Aidan a look as if in warning and answered for him. "No close calls. Nothing happened except that we got lucky and found that evidence. Like the chief said, it was a waste of time. I don't know how this guy keeps managing to give us the slip. At this point it's embarrassing."

"Dang right it is," Dawson said. "Which is why I have no interest in speaking to the media. We can deal with them tomorrow. Everyone head home—the back way, of course. If you do get cornered by a reporter the answer is no comment. Understood?"

"Yes, sir," all three officers chimed in at the same time.

Dawson crossed the room toward his office.

"I'll let dispatch know we're transferring the phones to them now," Collier said.

At Grace's questioning look, he explained, "As long as one of us is at the station, we take any emergency calls. When no one is here we transfer emergency calls to a call center, basically the same 911 operators who support the sheriff's office. If there is an emergency call at night, which is rare for us, the operators do what they can to talk the caller through whatever emergency is going on. And, of course, they contact whichever one of us is on point."

Fletcher bumped his shoulder. "Lucky you. You're on call tonight."

He made a face at her.

Dawson came out of his office carrying a small satchel, perhaps paperwork he wanted to take home, and motioned to Grace. "Make sure you keep your jacket covering your vest. You, too, O'Brien, unless you want the reporter to hit you up with questions thinking you're a cop. If everyone's ready to go, we'll head out the back together. As soon as we hit the lights, that reporter is going to realize they've been tricked and I'm not giving them an interview. They'll figure out pretty quickly that there must be a back door. We'll have to hustle if we're going to get in our cars before they find us. O'Brien and Malone, I'll give you a ride to the B and B to run interference, just in case. Hopefully you can get upstairs before being ambushed."

No sooner did the chief drop off Grace and Aidan than the news van pulled up behind his Jeep. Luckily for them, the reporter ran up to the driver's door to talk to Dawson. Grace and Aidan ducked down and hurried into the B and B and upstairs without having to deal with the media.

When they reached the landing at the top of the stairs, Aidan nodded goodbye and turned toward his room.

"Wait," Grace said. "Please."

He hesitated, then faced her with a questioning look.

The sound of voices in the lobby had her glancing toward the stairs. She lowered her voice so no one downstairs would hear. "I really need to talk to you."

"That's not a good idea—"

"It's work-related. I want to brainstorm with you about the shooter."

His jaw tightened. "You mean you want to interrogate me again."

"You're not a suspect. You're the suspect's target. So far, that's the best lead I have to figure out who this guy may be. I'd like to ask you some questions and see if we can come up with any ideas, a new direction for me to take my investigation. Otherwise, I'm stuck waiting on lab results and a search for a vehicle that may or may not exist."

"Vehicle?"

"I'll explain, once we sit down to talk. We could go in one of our rooms and—"

"No."

She put her hands on her hips. "Are you afraid of me, Aidan? Afraid I'm going to jump your bones or something? I'm not that desperate."

He choked on a laugh, then cleared his throat. "My ego just got crushed knowing you'd have to be desperate to want me. But at least I'm safe knowing you won't try to jump my bones."

"As much as you complain, I think you're the one who's worried you can't keep your hands off me if we're in a bedroom together."

Instead of the immediate denial she'd expected in response to her teasing, he simply stared at her. The amber brown of his eyes seemed to get even darker, more intense. There was no sign of amusement or an impending snappy comeback. Instead, he reminded her of a sleek panther, ready to pounce.

An answering hunger flared inside her. When he quickly turned back to his room and unlocked the door, she was there right behind him. He whirled around, his hands clasping her wrists with a solid yet remarkably gentle grip, stopping her.

"Grace, don't. I'm trying to do right by you. But you're not making it easy."

The sound of voices again froze both of them in place.

"Can't say I've ever met a TV reporter before." The sound of Stella's voice in the lobby seemed louder than usual. Her next words had Grace in a panic. "Two nights then. I don't have any more vacancies after that. We're all booked up for the fall season. It's number three, top of the stairs then take a right and it's at the end of the hall."

Footsteps sounded on the stairs, quick and light, heading up.

"Ah, hell." Aidan yanked Grace into his room and shut the door.

## Chapter Fourteen

Aidan leaned past Grace and flipped the dead bolt. Then he froze. Without meaning to, he'd pressed her back against the door. There wasn't an inch of space between them. Even with their jackets and vests on he could feel her heat and the pressure of her generous curves crushed against his chest. He should back up, put as much distance as possible between them. But he couldn't have moved away right now if the fires of hell were licking at his heels. She felt so… dang…good.

His body responded against his will, hardening against her. The soft intake of her breath had his pulse rushing in his ears. And then, the impossible happened. This smart, beautiful woman who was too good for him for so many reasons slid her hands up his coat, their heat practically burning him when she stroked the sides of his neck. Standing on tiptoes, she thrust her fingers into his hair where it touched the back of his collar, stroking, kneading, fanning the flames.

He shuddered against her and suddenly they were both stripping each other's jackets off, then their vests, tossing them onto the floor. She plastered her body against his, her mouthwatering curves fitting perfectly against his hard planes.

"Kiss me," she whispered. "Kiss me, Aidan."

His good intentions, his self-control, melted away in the inferno they'd created. He spanned her tiny waist with his hands and lifted her. She wrapped her legs around him and he pressed her against the door, shoving one hand through her hair, the other supporting her bottom as he claimed her mouth with his.

It was as if dynamite had exploded between them, burning away all logic, all reason, every thought in his mind except loving her. He couldn't get enough, stroking, caressing, kissing her the way he'd wanted to from the moment she'd impressed him by knowing what type of wood he was using to make that dang table in his workshop. She was a confusing mix of intelligence and wonder, aggravating him one moment and enthralling him the next. And just when he was about to end their kiss, his lungs starving for air, she deepened it and thrust her delicate tongue inside his mouth.

His legs nearly buckled. He groaned and matched her wild hunger with his own, no longer even trying to hold back. He wanted this, needed this. And he could sense the answering need in her. They were ravenous for each other. Turning with her in his arms, he rushed to the bed, careful not to crush her as he followed her down to the mattress.

He forced himself to slow down, to savor, to be gentle to this beautiful, delicate woman who was so much smaller than him. But as much as he wanted her, he wanted to make this good for her, to show her with his actions how obsessed he was with her even if he couldn't put it into words or had tried to pretend indifference.

"I'm not going to break," she whispered against his neck. "Love me. Just love me. Let yourself go."

Her sexy plea had him groaning again, shaking with need. It had been so long, so dang long.

*Twelve years.*

He stilled.

It had been twelve years since he'd made love to a woman, the only woman he'd ever been with.

*Elly.*

Shame washed over him like a bucket of ice water. Not because he was betraying Elly, but because he was thinking of his wife while loving Grace. It was wrong. This was wrong. If he made love to Grace it needed to be in the right setting, the right frame of mind, without a ghost between them. She deserved better. *Grace* deserved better.

"Aidan? What's wrong?"

He swore softly and pressed a kiss against her forehead, before shoving himself to his feet. Leaning down, he gently grasped her hands and pulled her to stand in front of him.

"I'm so sorry, Grace. I just… I can't do this."

Her brow crinkled in confusion and she looked down. "Um, yes, you can. Trust me. You're standing at glorious, rather impressive attention."

He laughed, then groaned. "I *won't* do this. Believe me, I want to. I can't tell you how badly I ache to…but it's not… I can't… Elly—"

She gasped and scrambled away, her cheeks flushing a bright pink. "My name is Grace. Oh my gosh, I can't believe this happened, or almost happened. Were you thinking about her all along, from the moment we touched?"

"What? No, no. You don't understand. It's been a long time and I—"

"I get it, okay?" She grabbed her vest and jacket off the floor. "I really do understand. And I'm not mad or even hurt. It just…startled me. You're still in love with her." She hesitated, then stepped to him and cupped the side of his face, her gaze searching his. "And there's nothing wrong with that. She was your wife, the mother of your child. You lost her in a horrific way and you're not ready to move on." She grimaced. "I admit I'm mildly mortified for throwing myself at you. But I'll survive. I'm a big girl. I'll be okay. We're okay, all right? Just…forget this ever happened."

She hurried to the door and looked through the peephole, then glanced back at him. "Maybe you'll be able to heal and move on once I prove your innocence and exonerate you. I promise I won't give up until I find a way to clear your name."

He stared at her in shock. "What? Grace, no. You don't need to—"

"Don't worry. I've got this." She hurried out of his room and quietly closed the door behind her.

Prove his innocence? Exonerate him? This was a nightmare. He adjusted his clothes with a grimace, then strode to the door and flung it open.

Grace had opened her door, but instead of going inside, she stood in the doorway, both hands covering her mouth, her vest and jacket forgotten on the floor where she must have dropped them.

"What is it?" he asked. "Did someone break into your room?" He jogged across the landing, then stopped behind her, his mouth going dry. Framed in the large picture window on the other side of her room was the highest mountain in Mystic Lake. And the very top of it was consumed in flickering reds and yellows lighting up the night sky. Flames.

"Aidan," she breathed, "do you know what's up there?"

Dread settled deep in his gut. "There's only one thing at the top of that mountain. My home."

## Chapter Fifteen

The anguish Grace felt as she helplessly watched the volunteer firefighters pump water from one of the creeks on Aidan's property onto the inferno that was his cabin was nothing compared to watching Aidan.

He stood a good twenty feet away from Grace and the police, his face stoic as his personal belongings were consumed by the flames, everything except the eight-by-ten picture frame he cradled against his chest. He'd risked his life running inside the cabin when he and Grace arrived and he'd had to be forced outside by firefighters—all to save a picture of his wife and son. It broke Grace's heart seeing him clutch that photograph, knowing he could have died trying to save it.

Everything he owned outside of his business was burning to the ground. Even the workshop on the far side of the cabin had been torched. The smell of some kind of accelerant was heavy in the air. This wasn't an accident. Someone had purposely set Aidan's home on fire. The only question was, did they know he wasn't there? Or had they hoped to trap him inside as they'd doused the logs and lit them up?

Grace coughed, the air smoky and hot. But in spite of that, she longed to get even closer to the fire, because that was where Aidan was standing. She wanted him to know she was there for him, her career be damned. But other than telling the firefighters that no one else lived here and that he didn't have any pets inside, he hadn't even looked her way. But she didn't have to see his eyes to know what she'd see: the same haunted look they'd had when she'd bumped into him on the sidewalk on her first day in Mystic Lake.

This land, this cabin and workshop, had been his fresh start, his chance to rebuild his life after a decade spent in prison. Now it was crumbling to the ground in front of him.

The firefighters shouted a warning. They hurriedly backed away from the structure moments before the upper floor crashed down onto the first floor. Seconds later, the rest of the building caved in. Nothing about the mass of broken, burning logs resembled the majestic cabin that had once stood in their place. All of Aidan's hopes and dreams had just disintegrated.

Did he feel as if nothing he'd done in the past year mattered? Once again he was the felon, the ex-con with no home, nowhere to go. The road ahead must look bleak, an endless stretch of loneliness and emptiness. It broke her heart seeing him this way. There was no magical fix for his pain, nothing she could do but wait and be here if he should turn to her for solace.

"Malone." Dawson moved close to be heard over the crackling roar of the flames. "We're heading down the mountain to wash off this smoke and get a few hours' sleep. We can't work with the fire marshal on the investigation until the fire's out and cold anyway. I recommend you do the same. You'll be as busy as us in the morning trying to see if this is linked to our as-yet-unnamed bow and arrow suspect."

She glanced at Aidan, still staring at the flames that were finally beginning to die down.

"Go ahead without me."

"Malone." He leaned even closer, his voice low, for her ears only. "It won't look good if you stay here with O'Brien. The firefighters will notice. People talk. Don't forget that reporter's in town. She'll be up here as soon as she can sneak around the roadblock our volunteers set up farther down this mountain."

"I'm staying."

He sighed heavily, then motioned to the others.

IF IT HAD been anything but fire, Aidan didn't think it would have bothered him all that much to lose the cabin. It was insured. He was financially sound, easily able to bear the costs of living somewhere else during the process of rebuilding. But seeing his home engulfed in flames had hit him like a runaway freight train, catapulting him back to that awful night when he'd turned onto his street and had seen the fire engines, the police, his home burning to the ground. The pain of not knowing if his wife and son were alive or dead had ripped him apart. He'd been so relieved and overjoyed to discover that his son was unharmed and being taken care of by a neighbor. But then he'd learned about his wife.

Burned.

Her spine crushed by a falling beam.

Paralyzed.

On a ventilator the rest of her life.

Many months later, a small miracle had him overjoyed and full of hope. Elly had regained enough movement and control in her right hand to try writing. He'd hurried to position a pen between her fingers and set a pad of paper on her lap. For the first time since the fire, she'd finally be able to communicate with him. But his happiness had quickly

turned to horror when he'd managed to decipher the painstakingly scrawled words she'd written.

*Let me die.*

He squeezed his eyes shut, but it didn't erase the image
burned into his mind. His vibrant, beautiful young wife
wrote that same thing on the pad of paper every day. And
later, when he'd gotten her that special valve to allow her to
speak, she'd verbalized what she'd been writing.

*Let me die.*

"Mr. O'Brien? Sir?"

Aidan's eyes flew open. A fireman stood in front of him,
his tan-and-yellow jacket blackened with soot.

"Sir, an investigator will be up here later in the day when
the rubble is cool enough to allow an inspection. Please don't
try to search for any mementos yet. It's too dangerous."

Aidan glanced at the remnants of his life, shocked to see
that the fire truly was out. He was equally surprised to realize that he and the firefighters waiting in the truck were
the only ones who remained. Everyone else had gone. Just
how long had he stared off into space, focused on the past
and not even aware of what was going on around him?

"Mr. O'Brien? Did you hear me, sir?"

"Sorry, yes. Is everyone okay? None of your people got
hurt fighting the fire, I hope."

The fireman smiled. "Nothing that a hot shower and long
nap won't cure. I recommend you do the same. Standing
around here breathing in the smoky air isn't good for anyone. Do you have somewhere to stay?"

"I've got a room in town."

"What about food? Money for clothes? We have a victim's fund. It's not much, but it can get you through for a
few weeks until insurance kicks in."

Aidan stared at him, shocked at the kindness he was offering when most people crossed to the other side of the street when they saw him coming. "Do you know who I am?"

"If you're asking whether I've heard rumors about your past, yes. I have. I'm not here to judge. I'm here to help. All of us are." He pointed over his shoulder at the firefighters waiting in the truck. "It's why we do what we do. That victim's fund is open to anyone in need. I can give you the information and you can submit an application. Approval in a situation like this is a guarantee. You'll have some funds within a few hours of submitting the application and—"

"I don't need the money. But thank you. I appreciate it. And thank you for keeping the fire from spreading and endangering anyone else."

The other man clasped Aidan's shoulder in sympathy. "I'd ask if you need a ride down the mountain, but it looks like you've got transportation over there. The sooner you get some fresh air, the better. Don't stay up here much longer."

With the fire truck slowly picking its way down the treacherous mountain road, Aidan took one long last look at what remained of the life he'd tried to build here. He had no idea what he'd do next, whether he really would rebuild or just sell the land as is and move on, perhaps to another town, or maybe a big city where people had never heard his name. Maybe this was fate's way of telling him he'd made a mistake in coming here and that it was time to go.

As soon as that thought occurred to him, he rejected it. In the long run, he might leave Mystic Lake. But not yet, not until he discovered who had risked the lives of everyone living in this town by setting the fire. A few days ago, he'd have had no idea who that person might be. But when Grace had asked him about hate mail he'd received in prison, a name had popped into his head. He'd rejected it at first, but the more he'd thought about it the more it made sense. He'd called his lawyer the other night to ask him to hire an investigator to look into that possibility. If it panned out, Aidan didn't know what he was going to do about it. He just prayed to God that his suspicions were wrong.

He shoved his hand in his jeans pocket for his truck keys, then frowned. He didn't have them. But he'd driven up here by himself...no, with Grace. Did she take the keys and forget to give them to him before she left with the police?

He headed for the truck to see if maybe she'd left the keys in the ignition. But when he opened the driver's door, he stopped in surprise. In the passenger seat, Grace was curled up like a cat, asleep. And in her arms, snugged up against her chest, was the one picture of his family that he'd managed to save from the fire. He didn't even remember her taking it from him. And yet here she was, keeping it safe.

His throat tightened and he crossed to the passenger side of his truck. Careful to open the door as quietly as he could, he eased the picture out of her grasp and slid it under the seat. As he clicked her seat belt in place, she grumbled in her sleep and swatted at his hand, making him smile. Good grief, this woman had a hold on his heart. He didn't want to care about her. It made no sense in such an incredibly short amount of time. But he did care. Not that it mattered. There wasn't any way that he could be with her without ruining her life as she knew it.

Even if she was willing to give up her career, she shouldn't have to. And being with him would set her up for ridicule and strangers judging her and slighting her. She didn't deserve that. She deserved so much better.

She grumbled in her sleep again, hugging her arms against her chest. With the fire out, the chilly mountain air was moving in. Grace had likely retreated to the truck to keep warm, and here he was standing with the door open making her cold. He eased it shut until it clicked, then crossed to the driver's side. After one last look at what used to be his home, he started his truck and began the slow descent down the mountain.

It turned out that Grace was an incredibly deep sleeper. In spite of all the bumps and turns, she didn't wake up during the drive back to town. She didn't even awaken when Aidan parked his truck behind the B and B. If he didn't have to worry about her reputation and how people would judge her, he'd scoop her up into his arms and carry her to her room. But people *would* judge her. So he leaned into the passenger side of the truck and gently shook her.

She swatted at him again and said a few salty phrases, making him laugh. She might look like an angel, but there was a bit of a devil in her, too. In other words, she was pretty darn perfect.

"Grace," he whispered, not wanting to startle her. "Wake up, Grace. Come on. You can't sleep all night in the truck." He shook her again, harder this time, and her eyes finally fluttered open.

As soon as she saw him, she blinked, then looked around in confusion. "Aidan? What…where…" Her eyes widened. "We're at the B and B? I don't—"

"The fire was out. You were already in the truck so I buckled your seat belt and drove you home, or, well, to the B and B. Come on. Let's get inside. We both need a shower and some sleep. The sun will be up in a handful of hours. I'm sure it's going to be a long day for both of us."

She nodded, still not seemingly firing on all cylinders. But as she got down from his truck, she suddenly grabbed his arm. "Wait. The picture, it's—"

"Right here." He pulled it out from beneath the seat.

"Thanks to you it's safe and sound. I guess I was kind of out of it up on the mountain. You must have realized I was going to drop the frame and you took it to make sure it didn't get broken. Thank you for that. It means a lot. That's the only picture of Elly and Niall that I have. Most of the others burned up in the first fire, twelve years ago. And now, well, that's it unless I can find something in the ruins when I head up later today." He locked the truck. "Do you think you can walk inside on your own?"

She blinked again and shook herself. "Yes, yes. I'm fine. Sorry. Once I get in a deep sleep it's hard for me to wake up. My mom is the same way. I have to put my alarm clock on the other side of my room or I'll turn it off in my sleep. Once I'm on my feet, I'm okay."

"If you say so." He grinned as he followed her inside. She was wobbling like a drunk.

Luckily, there was no one around to see her as they went inside or rumors might have started about her being out late drinking with the town ex-con. But the danger was still very real to her reputation. The reporter was likely in her room. The two of them had to be very quiet as they headed upstairs.

Once Grace's door was open and she stepped inside, he nodded good-night. He was about to turn away when she pressed a hand to his chest, stopping him.

She glanced toward the reporter's room, then leaned in toward him. "Aidan, I'm so sorry for your loss tonight," she whispered. "I know a house can be rebuilt. But the personal items you had can't be replaced. I promise that I'll do everything I can to find out who did this and bring them to justice." She motioned toward the frame he was holding down at his side. "Remember that it's the pictures in your mind, the feelings in your heart, that no one can destroy.

The love you have for your family can never be taken away, no matter what anyone says or does."

She started to close the door, but this time he was the one who stopped her.

"Grace," he whispered, his throat tight with emotion. "Thank you for tonight. You were there for me at my darkest, with no concern for what it might cost you. I don't ever want to be the cause of anything bad happening to you. But it means more than you'll ever realize that you were there for me." Unable to resist the impulse, he leaned down and pressed a soft kiss against her lips.

When he pulled back, the melting look she gave him had his body instantly hardening. It was all he could do to leave before he did something they'd both regret.

## Chapter Sixteen

While Chief Dawson, Ortiz and Collier spent the morning at the top of the mountain with Aidan searching for anything salvageable from the fire—or evidence pointing to who may have set it—Fletcher stayed at the police station with Grace. They'd spread all of the reports, interviews and pictures from the physical files out on the conference room table as they brainstormed what they had, and didn't have, to prove who was responsible for the bad things happening in Mystic Lake. They also used their laptops to perform searches on law enforcement websites, trying to identify any similar types of recent crimes.

Fletcher sighed and sat back, shaking her head. "I literally have no leads. I mean, we have fingerprints but no match to any known person. Have you gotten any DNA results back from the FBI lab yet?"

"Not yet, but when I spoke to my boss earlier he said he'd call the lab and push them. They should have had enough time to process any DNA profiles by now. I have a feeling they moved other high-priority evidence ahead of mine."

"How can anything possibly be more important than getting DNA to match against your known Crossbow cases? That will tell you right there whether this killer is operating in our town."

Grace smiled. "That's pretty much what I told my boss. That's why he's calling to put the fear of the *special agent in charge* into the lab. I really do think we'll get something soon."

"I sure hope so. I'd like to know for myself whether we've got a deadly serial killer around here or just some dumb teenager doing stupid stuff. The first one is scary. The second one just makes me mad."

"What exactly do you have against teenagers? You seem to want to blame them for everything that happens around here."

Fletcher snorted. "That's because they generally are. I'm half convinced that most of the spooky, unexplainable things that happen in our town are the result of an evil group of teens on the loose."

"Remind me someday to sit down with you and discuss this prejudice you have against the town's youth and what exactly caused it. But for now, we need to get back to figuring out the case. My boss has granted me another twenty-four hours to try to wrap this up. After that, he's yanking me back to the Knoxville field office to work on something else."

"Ouch. Why is he being such a hard—um, so difficult?"

"I honestly can't fault him. We have a lot of agencies wanting our help on their cases and this one, if it's not related to the killer we're after, will easily be trumped by another more urgent case where people have actually been killed. If the DNA comes back and says your guy isn't my guy, there's no justification for us continuing to spend resources down here."

"Except that we need you."

Grace gave her a doubtful look. "I appreciate that. But you're doing a great job without me. All of the interviews you've conducted and leads you've followed up on are exactly what I'd do. I don't have any secret sauce to solve this thing or I promise I'd share." She pulled the stack of interview reports toward her that she'd been reviewing. "I've noted a few people I'd like to speak to again. But overall, our interviews have yielded pretty much the same answers—that no one has seen any strangers in the area. They don't have any ideas as to who might be terrorizing your town. The best lead right now still seems to be in finding out who is focusing their rage on O'Brien. If we can figure that out, we'll have an excellent suspect to match against our fingerprints and DNA."

Fletcher tapped her nails on the tabletop. "We've been focusing all morning on rehashing the interviews. I'm all for going with your O'Brien angle, that someone's after him. Bring me up to speed on that. I mean, if you think I can help as a sounding board. I don't want to waste your time if you'd rather work it by yourself."

Grace glanced at the glass wall behind Fletcher to make sure no one was around before answering. "If you really don't mind, I'm happy to bore you with my half-baked theories and how I'm looking at this. Maybe you can come up with something I haven't. But we need to keep this just between us to some extent. My thoughts on this aren't flattering to some of the police and I don't want that getting out and offending them."

Fletcher's eyes widened. "Sounds serious. Go ahead. I won't share anything you don't want shared. And you have me dying of curiosity now."

"It's not that big a secret or anything. It's just, well, I'm confused about how the Nashville police handled O'Brien's case."

"You're talking about the murder he committed? And confessed to?"

A surge of annoyance shot through Grace, but she tamped it down. If she hadn't met Aidan and considered herself an excellent judge of character, she'd no doubt feel the same way as Fletcher. She'd assume Aidan really was a murderer. But the case didn't make sense to her and she couldn't see him killing his wife. If she'd harbored even a shred of doubt about that, it had evaporated last night when she'd seen him hugging that picture of his wife and son after nearly getting killed in order to save it from the fire.

"I'm referring to his past, and yes, my research into the investigation of Elly O'Brien's death. My goal is to come up with a list of people who hate him enough to try to frame him at the festival, and for shooting an arrow at me."

"Speaking of which, are you doing okay? You don't seem to be favoring your hurt arm."

"Thanks to over-the-counter pain pills, I'm really good. It only hurt a lot the first night. As for my list of potential suspects, I looked into any issues he had in prison. Like if he had altercations with some of the other prisoners, made any enemies who are now out of prison and trying to pay him back for some real or imagined slight."

"I bet that's a long list," Fletcher said. "Ten years in prison for a convicted murderer no doubt means there are a lot of guys he didn't get along with. He's proven to be predisposed to violence. So I'm sure he didn't put up with anything from the other men while in there."

Once again, Grace felt a surge of annoyance at the policewoman. It was becoming harder and harder to hide her anger. But she did, or hoped she did.

"Actually, he was a model prisoner. There were zero

fights on his record. He seemed to get along with everyone as best as could be expected."

"Huh. Surprising. So no suspects from prison then? No one's name to add to a list?"

"Not fellow prisoners, no. Although I did have an admin dig into that a little more for me to see which prisoners he may have known at the time who were recently released, or at least released since O'Brien was paroled. There were a few, but they all came up clean. Actually, two of them re-offended almost immediately and are now back in prison, which clears them since they couldn't have been in Mystic Lake during the festival. But the others we researched have checked out so far as it being unlikely they could have been here to cause any trouble. That leaves visitors or people from O'Brien's past from before he went to prison. That list is a lot longer to go through. He owns his own business and knows a lot of people through that, in addition to those he called friends before his wife's death, and his former in-laws of course. I'm still going through that list. I've made some calls, but of course haven't been able to go to Nashville just yet to follow up in person."

"How many people are we talking?" Fletcher asked.

"His company in Nashville on average has about a hundred people on payroll, far more if you consider other locations. But I'm focusing on Nashville first since that's where he used to live and he would have met a lot, if not all of those workers. Most of them are long-term employees who were there back when O'Brien was convicted. Any one of them could hold a grudge for some reason or other. That's in addition to the twenty-plus friends and his in-laws."

She whistled. "That's a huge list. I'd probably focus on the friends and in-laws first."

"Agreed. I've already looked into the friends. Nothing came of it. I'm looking into the in-laws right now."

"So we need to whittle the other hundred or so down. I'd look for workers' comp claims in case they blame him for injuries. Maybe human resource complaints about unfair practices, things like that. I'd look into promotions and who might resent him for choosing someone else over them. Seems petty, but when it comes to people's salaries, that stuff gets pretty personal."

"All of those are great suggestions. I'd also like to see whether anyone has been fired who might blame him."

"If you want, I can work those angles," Fletcher offered. "I worked my only local investigation yesterday to get it out of the way, a petty theft at the grocery store."

"*The* grocery store? There's only one in town?"

Fletcher laughed. "Pretty much there's only one of anything in this town. Guess who the culprit ended up being?"

Grace sat back to think, but the grin on the other woman's face told her the answer. "One of those evil teenagers. Am I right?"

"A hundred percent. I wanted to arrest him and make him cool his jets in our holding cell for a day or two. But the chief made me check with the store manager first. The guy had no backbone. Didn't want to press charges once he heard it was a fifteen-year-old. So I did what I end up having to do most of the time around here. I went to the kid's home and spoke to him with his parents present, putting the fear of the almighty police into him. He swore he'd never do it again. But his parents were so quick to pony up the money to pay for what their kid had done that he likely didn't learn a thing. I'll probably have to scare him again in another month or two."

Fletcher held out her hand. "Give me what you have—

the prison visitor logs for O'Brien, the employee lists, all of it. I'm begging you. I'd love to speak to some adults and put the fear in them for a change. It'll be fun."

"Emailing it to you now."

"Awesome. Wait, you said there was something about the Nashville police that had you concerned. Did one of them hold a grudge against O'Brien, maybe beat him up or fabricate evidence? You think a police officer could be our suspect?"

"No, no. Nothing like that. It's more a question about the investigation that was performed after Elly O'Brien's death. The police reports are insufficient, really thin. And they didn't dig very deep. I'm just surprised, and disappointed, in the lack of depth of their research. Normally, they're a top-notch agency. But in this particular case, they didn't dig like I'd expect."

"O'Brien confessed. They didn't need to spend additional resources on the case. Makes sense to me."

Grace nodded, pretending to agree with her. Fletcher's obvious bias against O'Brien—which again she fully understood—made it difficult to expect any neutrality in looking at who might have it in for him. Rather than go into more detail about her concerns, she decided to keep those thoughts to herself.

"It's been bothering me," Grace said. "But I see your point. Are you sure you want to dig into that huge list I sent you?"

"Are you kidding? This is my catnip, something different to dig my teeth into. If one of these guys is our suspect, I'll find out. However, it's going to have to wait until after lunch. I'm meeting a friend at Stella's restaurant." She grinned. "It's a guy friend or I'd invite you to come along."

"No worries. I don't want to be a third wheel. I'll order

something from that sandwich shop. Is it okay for me to stay here by myself or do you need to lock up and switch the phone lines like you do at night?"

Fletcher's expression flattened with disappointment. "I didn't even think about that. You're becoming like one of our team. Normally, Collier or Ortiz would cover me for lunch. But I don't know how much longer they'll—"

The outer door opened and two men entered the police station, Collier and Aidan. A rush of pleasure shot through Grace at seeing Aidan, until she noticed the grim look in his eyes. The hunt for any personal items to have survived the fire must not have gone well.

"Looks like your lunch is salvaged," she said. "Collier's back."

Fletcher turned around in her chair, then shot to her feet. "For once, I'm actually happy to see him. Later, Grace." She rushed out of the conference room and after a brief chat with her fellow officer was out the door.

Grace locked her laptop, then left the conference room to greet Collier and Aidan. "How did it go? I'm guessing from your expressions, not very well?"

They both shook their heads. Collier said, "No evidence so far that might point to who set the fire. But it's early yet."

"What about you... O'Brien?" She'd just caught herself in time not to call him Aidan in front of Collier. "Any luck finding anything salvageable?"

"The fire department had to put out some hot spots that were smoking to make sure the fire didn't reignite. Because of that, I couldn't look for anything. I'll go back in a few hours and see if the fire marshal allows me to search then."

"Hopefully he will."

"She," Collier corrected. "Lieutenant Molly Graham. She was the marshal on call and drove in from Chattanooga. I'm thinking maybe I'll ask her to dinner later. You know, as a local courtesy from one agency to another."

Aidan smiled at that, apparently having heard about Collier's reputation as a ladies' man.

"Have you two had lunch?" Grace asked. "I'm about to head to that sandwich shop down the block. You're welcome to join me."

"You go ahead," Collier said. "I'm on duty. Can't leave the station unless another officer is here. Maybe bring O'Brien and me something back if you don't mind, after you finish your lunch. Hot ham and cheese sounds good. Tell them to put it on the station's tab. O'Brien, what do you want her to get for you?"

Aidan looked as disappointed as Grace felt. Perhaps he'd forgotten for a moment, like her, that the two of them going to a café together might not be the best idea.

"Ham and cheese works for me, too. Thanks, Special Agent Malone."

She nodded and hurried to the café. Eating there wasn't something she planned to do if Aidan wasn't with her. Instead, she grabbed their lunch to go and headed back to the station.

"Here you go, Collier. O'Brien, I'd like to reinterview you, ask some more questions to try to figure out who has it out for you. If you don't mind a working lunch, you and I can sit in the conference room. Sound good?"

"Sure. Happy to help."

Collier looked like he was about to offer to join them, but Grace led the way to the conference room and shut the door behind her and Aidan. When Collier didn't follow them inside, she figured he must have gotten the hint.

## Chapter Seventeen

They both took a few minutes to spread out their lunch on the table, her facing the glass wall so she could keep an eye on Collier and any eavesdropping or lipreading he might want to do, and Aidan sitting across from her.

Once Collier was diving into his food and surfing the web as an apparent lunchtime diversion, Grace quickly swallowed down the bite she'd just taken and took a sip from her water bottle before setting it aside.

"How are you holding up, Aidan?" She kept her voice low so it wouldn't carry through the glass.

He smiled. "I figured this wasn't about a reinterview. Don't worry about me. I've been through far worse."

"Well, of course I worry about you. You've been through so much hardship. It's not right that some nut has his sights set on making life even more difficult for you. My boss is threatening to pull me off this case if I can't prove a link to the Crossbow Killer soon. But that's not going to stop me from working on this investigation. I'll do it on my own time. I'm going to prove you had nothing to do with this, or anything else."

He stared at her in silence, his brows drawn down in a frown. Then he slowly shook his head, his expression a mix between confusion and something else. Anger? Fear? What?

"Malone—"

"You've had your tongue down my throat and vice versa. You can call me Grace."

He laughed, but quickly sobered. "Fair enough. I can understand why I'm attracted to you. You're smart, funny and beautiful for starters. But I can't even begin to understand why a special agent with the FBI would not only be attracted to me, but also seems to trust me. Why are you so determined to look into my case? Why do you insist on trying to prove that I didn't commit a crime to which I confessed and spent ten years in prison? I didn't appeal or try to have my sentence reduced. If I'm not trying to prove I'm innocent, why are you?"

"Well, first, thanks for saying I'm smart, funny and beautiful. You left out sexy, by the way, but I'll forgive you."

He choked on another laugh and shook his head.

"Second, the reason I'm so convinced you're innocent of any crime is precisely because I'm an FBI agent and a former cop. I'm experienced in reading people and facts. Your actions speak to your character. You've done nothing but help people from the moment we met, even the police who haven't exactly been nice to you since you came here. But it's what I've found and haven't found when looking into your past as part of trying to figure out who is trying to frame you for the crimes here in Mystic Lake that raise so many questions as to make it seem ludicrous that you could have killed your wife."

After another long silence, he crossed his arms. "All right. I'll bite. What makes it seem impossible to you that I'm actually guilty of murder?"

Excited that he was finally at least willing to listen to her about his case, and hopeful that she could get him to discuss it, she thumbed through a stack of manila folders and then pulled out the thinnest one from the middle. She slid it across the table toward him.

He picked it up, but hesitated without opening it. "What is this?"

"A printout of Nashville PD's complete investigation into the death of Elly O'Brien."

He dropped the folder onto the table as if it had burned his hand. "I don't need to read that. I know what happened."

"Care to share that knowledge with me?"

"Didn't we already have this conversation at my cabin, the day you were at my workshop admiring the table I was building? I told you about what happened the day...the day Elly passed."

"You told me what you told the police years ago. But I'm not convinced that's the truth, or at least not the whole truth." She picked up the folder and flipped it open. "There are a total of twenty-five pages in here. And that includes the eight-page autopsy report."

He winced, then cleared his throat. "Your point?"

"The police didn't even try to corroborate your so-called confession. I've never, not once, seen a file this incomplete for an investigation of any kind, let alone an alleged murder. Which led me to wonder whether you were threatened by the police and framed—"

"No to both."

"Okay. I'll accept that answer for now. Then the question becomes why would the police be so quick to take your confession and not look deeper, and of course the other glaring question of why would you confess to something you didn't do?"

"Grace—"

"The answer to the first is obvious once you look really closely at the file. There's an obscure handwritten note that

I didn't notice right away because it's on a printout of a copy to begin with. It's not very clear and part of it was chopped off in the margin." She flipped through the file and pulled out a single page and pointed to the right edge. "See that?"

He eyed the page as if it were a snake. "Not really, but I'm sure you're going to tell me."

Sighing, she pointed to some grainy handwriting. "I actually had to borrow a magnifying glass from Fletcher to read it myself. It says, 'Parents of deceased request speedy end to case so family can move on and heal. Prosecutor agrees.'"

He shrugged.

"Come on, Aidan. You know where I'm going with this. The odds of a DA agreeing to halt an investigation without corroborating your confession are about zero. They must have had pressure from both the parents *and the defense*. Your attorney had to have been consulted about this. If not, he could have argued to the court that the investigation was rushed and insufficient and requested that your case be dismissed. Heck, he could have easily argued that if you really did unplug your wife's ventilator that you weren't in your right mind, that you did it to show her mercy. Without a criminal record and this being your first offense, he could have brought forth witnesses to talk about your relationship with Elly and how madly in love you were. But he didn't, even though everyone I've called and spoken to says exactly that, how close you were. Your attorney could have said you were in despair seeing her in pain, paralyzed, unable to breathe on her own, and that it clouded your judgment. Even I could have probably gotten you a reduced sentence and I'm not an attorney. Yours didn't call one single witness at your sentencing, which happened just a few days after that report was written up with that note in the margin."

She waited, but when he didn't say anything, she continued. "As you pointed out earlier, you never submitted any appeals even though you had a strong case for one based on insufficient evidence. That all leads me to believe that you probably colluded with your wife's parents to bring the case to an end prematurely."

He crossed his arms on top of the table. "So what if I did? Dragging it out would only hurt them even more. Bringing the case to a quick close was the least I could do."

"And nothing a little bribery from a wealthy man couldn't handle, is that it?"

His jaw tightened.

"Right. No comment. Let's skip to the second part of my earlier question, the part about why you would confess to a crime you didn't do. That one has had me stumped, but I'm working it out. For one thing, I tried to get a transcript from your parole hearing to find out what was said and who spoke at the hearing."

His eyes widened and for the first time since coming into the conference room, he looked worried.

"In spite of repeated attempts by both me and an admin, we haven't gotten the transcripts. They've been sealed. That's pretty dang convenient for you if you're trying to hide the truth that may have come out during the hearing."

His brow smoothed out and he seemed to visibly relax after she'd said she couldn't get the transcript. Time to go for the jugular.

"The admin did, however, manage to get the prison's visitor log for the date of your appearance before the parole board."

His eyes widened.

"It's not a surprise that your wife's parents were at the hearing, until you consider one thing. Typically, if the family of a convicted murderer is at the first parole hearing and argues against parole, the board goes along with their wishes. But they didn't come to speak against you, did they? They spoke on your behalf—whether you wanted them to or not. That's why you were paroled. Which tells me that Elly's parents don't believe you killed their daughter any more than I do. Something changed their mind during the ten years that you were in prison. They found out the truth about what really happened, didn't they?"

His face paled. "Grace. Don't."

She swore. "I knew it. Your reaction just confirmed it. What's more, you lied to me about her parents when you said they hated you. They may have, at first, but definitely not toward the end of your incarceration. That's based not only on you being paroled and my conclusions around that, but hard facts I dug up about them. I didn't find one single thing that makes me believe they're the type of people who'd try to frame you as the Crossbow Killer, or even hire some- one else to do it. So where does that leave us?"

"Grace—"

"Fact. Elly's parents used to think you were the killer. Fact. They now are certain you're innocent. If that wasn't true, they wouldn't have testified for your early release be- fore the parole board. Fact. Everything I've read about them confirms they loved and doted on their daughter, so there's no question they'd want her killer to face justice. But they haven't gone to the police to request that the investigation be reopened to find her real killer. Why not?"

He let out a shuddering breath but remained silent.

"The only logical conclusion in light of all those facts is that Elly's parents know the identity of her killer and don't want him punished." She held up her hands. "Why in the world wouldn't they want him brought to justice? Why wouldn't you?"

He squeezed his eyes shut as if in pain.

She reached across the table and put her hand on his arm, no longer caring whether Collier noticed. When Aidan's eyes flew open, the anguish in them was almost enough to make her stop. Almost. But she couldn't, not when she was so close to finding out the truth.

"Aidan. Who are you and your dead wife's parents covering for? And why?"

He stared at her hand on his arm, his throat working. Finally, he looked up, his eyes clouded with despair. "I'm begging you. Let it go. The truth won't make anyone feel any better. It will only cause more pain. Please. Stop."

Her throat tightened with the urge to weep. But she held fast. "The last thing I want to do is hurt you. But this isn't just about you, or even justice for your wife at this point. Someone is trying to destroy you. And I'm betting it's the same person you're trying to protect. It's the only thing that makes sense when you look at everything that's happened."

"You don't know that," he whispered, his voice ragged and raw. "There's no proof."

"Do you expect me to believe that you've been protecting a killer all these years, and now that you're out of prison he's not the same killer who's trying to send you back? You see what he's doing, right? He's worried you're going to try to clear your name by finally telling the police what you've known all along. He tried to frame you first by almost killing two men in a boat. Then he shot at me, twice. When he burned down your house last night, do you think he went inside first to make sure you weren't there? Hell, no. He hoped you were there and would be trapped and killed. Why would you want to protect someone like that?"

She searched his gaze, then delivered her last volley. "He

already killed your wife. Who does he have to kill for you to finally do something about him?"

He made a strangled sound in his throat and pulled his hand free. "You think you have it figured out, Grace. But you don't. He didn't... He was too... Elly's death isn't his fault."

She stared at him in shock, his words bouncing around inside her brain like a Ping-Pong ball as things started to mesh together in her mind. She'd made one of the worst mistakes a law enforcement officer could make. Tunnel vision. She'd come up with a theory and had used the evidence to support her theory. Instead, she should have examined the evidence and let it reveal a theory.

Aidan stared at her, his handsome face drawn in lines of worry, frustration and a soul-deep sadness as he waited for the inevitability of her fitting all of the pieces together. She laid the evidence out in her mind's eye. In the end, it was so simple, so obvious, she was embarrassed that she hadn't realized it on day one of looking into Aidan's past. It was the fact that he'd confessed that had thrown her off. But even that should have been a glaring clue to the truth. So. Ridiculously. Obvious.

Aidan didn't kill Elly.

There was no evidence of an intruder.

Elly was paralyzed and couldn't have done anything.

Someone else pulled the plug on her ventilator.

The nurse had gone home for the day, leaving Elly's care to Aidan.

But Aidan wasn't the only person in the house after she left.

Aidan's words, just moments ago, flitted through her mind.

*"He didn't... He was too... Elly's death isn't his fault."*

She filled in the missing words that he hadn't said.

He didn't *understand what he was doing*. He was too *young*. Elly's death isn't his fault.

She stared at him, the last of it becoming clear. "The hate mail," she whispered. "Elly's parents found out about it, read the letters. And then they knew the truth. That's why they wanted to help you, but didn't want the police to reinvestigate."

He squeezed his hands into fists on top of the table and bowed his head.

"Niall," she said. "Your son. He pulled the plug. He killed Elly and now he wants to kill you to keep the truth from coming out."

He jerked his head up, frowning. "He was five years old, Grace. He doesn't even remember doing it. He remembers bits and pieces, just enough from that day to have made Elly's parents suspicious that something was off because what he said didn't match what I said. That's why they visited me years later, trying to understand what really happened."

"And that's why they supported your parole."

He nodded.

"Why not just tell the truth from the beginning? No one's going to prosecute a five-year-old child for pulling a cord out of a wall. He didn't realize what he was doing."

"It's more complicated than that."

"Then explain it to me. If your son isn't here to keep you from telling the truth, then he must be here for payback, revenge for killing his mom, right? After you were paroled, he must have gone on a hunt or maybe even hired a private investigator to find out where you were. Then he came after you. If that's the case, then why protect him?"

"Because he's my son." His voice broke, and he cleared his throat.

She stared at him as the truth came out, more shaken than she cared to admit. After a few calming breaths, she continued, determined to get the whole story, finally.

"Okay. I get that. I really do. I get that you want to protect him now, here as the copycat, to keep him from going to prison. I don't agree with it. But I understand it. What still confuses me is why you confessed to your wife's murder when it would have been so simple to tell the truth that your five-year-old son accidentally pulled the plug on her machine."

"Like I said," his voice was raw, strained. "It's more complicated than that. For one thing, I didn't want Niall to grow up knowing he'd helped to kill his own mother. It could have destroyed his life."

"Wait. Helped? I don't… Are you saying that you—"

"No." He shook his head. "No, Grace. You've been right all along about that. I never would have done anything to hurt Elly. I didn't go to prison just to protect my son. I went to prison because—"

The door to the conference room burst open, startling both of them. Fletcher entered the room, holding a piece of paper.

Grace swore. "Fletcher, we're in the middle of something here—"

"I know. Collier told me. My lunch date canceled and I came back to work on that list we talked about. You didn't even notice I was in the squad room because of whatever you two are talking so intently about in here." She gave Aidan the kind of look that someone would give a bug crawling across the floor right before they squashed it. Or a police officer would give to a man they believed had committed murder.

Fletcher pitched the piece of paper onto the table in front

of him. "That's a summary of visitor log entries from your time in prison, all ten years. Malone reviewed them, trying to figure out who has it out for you. But she didn't realize something that you and I know—that one of the people on that list visited you several times in the early years of your incarceration, and again the day of your parole hearing. Malone didn't realize the significance because she didn't recognize the name, probably hadn't had time to research it yet. But you and I know that your visitor got married after moving to Mystic Lake. So tell me, why did Stella Simmons, married name Stella Holman, visit you in prison?"

His eyes narrowed at her, his jaw tight.

Grace flattened her palms on top of the table. "Wait, Stella and Aidan were friends before he went to prison?"

Fletcher's brows shot up. "Since when did you start calling him by his first name?"

Grace's face heated. "You've heard of building rapport with someone you're interviewing, right?"

Fletcher's eye roll told Grace she didn't buy that excuse. "Whatever. I don't have all the answers yet, but something stinks to high heaven here. Stella and O'Brien have never mentioned to anyone in Mystic Lake that I'm aware of that they used to know each other, long before he moved here. So I put two and two together. Stella was a nurse, in Nashville, before she came to this town. Guess what type of nurse? The kind who works in people's homes to help them care for homebound patients."

Grace stared at Aidan. "Like Elly?"

He gave her a sharp look. "She was one of Elly's nurses. What's that got to do with anything?"

Fletcher snorted. "Your wife died because something happened to her life support machine, or whatever. Stella was one of her nurses. Then you just happen to move to Mystic Lake after you get out of prison, the same place where Stella moved. If I was a betting woman, I'd bet a year's salary you two are covering up something."

"And what would that be?" he demanded, his tone sarcastic. "I already went to prison for murder. There's nothing worse than that."

"Aidan?" Grace was barely able to force the next words out. "Is Stella the one who pulled the plug on the ventilator? Is that the complicated part you spoke about?"

His eyes darkened with anger. "No."

Fletcher held up her hands. "Whoa, whoa. Wait a minute. I thought we were trying to figure out who has a grudge against O'Brien. What are you doing, Malone? Trying to exonerate him or something?"

Aidan stood, towering over Fletcher. She immediately took several steps back, her hand going to her holster.

He gave her a disgusted look. "We're done here." He brushed past her and yanked open the door.

Grace jumped to her feet. "Aidan, wait. Please."

But he was already gone.

## Chapter Eighteen

Aidan paced back and forth in his room at the B and B. He'd worked so hard to hide the truth, had spent ten long, horrific years in prison to do so. And now everything was unraveling. He wanted to hate Grace for pulling at the threads, for refusing to stop in spite of him practically begging her to do so. But he could never hate her. As impossible as it seemed, he was half in love with her. She was the only person besides Stella who'd believed in his innocence almost from the very start. Grace believed him to be a decent man. And that felt too good to ignore.

Even though she was destroying everything he'd worked so hard to build.

He'd already spoken to Stella, to warn her that Grace knew the truth, or at least part of it. Now the question was what to do next. How could he protect the people he cared about without endangering anyone else? Was the person here in Mystic Lake the one he'd been protecting all along? Or was it this Crossbow Killer Grace had come here to find? And, oh God please no, were the two of them one and the same?

He slumped down onto the bed, his head in his hands. All these years he'd thought his decision that first day was the best way to salvage a disastrous situation. But what if it wasn't? Stella had certainly never agreed with the path he'd taken. She'd tried so hard to talk him out of it. Had she been right all along? Had his cover-up only made things worse? Would everything have turned out for the better if he'd faced the truth from the start? Embraced it and figured out another way to move forward? To atone for his own sins, as well?

Second-guessing the past wasn't doing anyone any good. He had to focus on now, to figure out how to stop whoever was stalking Mystic Lake, and him, whether it was his son or someone else. Grace had already been hurt. And others could have been hurt, or killed, when his home was burned. It was only a matter of time before someone was going to get killed.

Unless he did something to end this.

The lies were unraveling. The truth was coming out. It was time to accept that he couldn't cover it up anymore. Time to fix what he'd broken all those years ago. Somehow. Without making it even worse.

But to fix it, first, he needed to know if Grace was right. He had to know whether his perfect little boy, his son, had become the monster that Grace believed him to be.

He pulled his cell phone out of his pocket and speed-dialed his lawyer. "Hi, Nate. Yeah, it's me. Have you had a chance to look into what we spoke about?" He listened as his lawyer put the last nail in the coffin.

Niall had left the Larsens' Henderson, Kentucky, home a week ago.

His credit card purchases showed he'd driven to Tennessee and had spent several days in a Chattanooga hotel. He'd made purchases at a camping supply store, and bought a crossbow and several quivers of arrows. Another purchase was made at a party store, where he'd bought a large bag of white feathers and red craft paint. The last damning fact the lawyer shared was that Niall checked out of the hotel the morning of the festival. There had been no other charges on his card since then.

He was in Mystic Lake. Had to be. He was the one with his sights set on Aidan, with innocent people's lives at stake for just being in the same location.

"Nate." Aidan cleared his tight throat. "Could he be... do you think he's this Crossbow Killer they've been talking about on the news?"

His longtime lawyer, who'd also become a good friend over the years, told him what he'd feared and prayed wasn't true.

"Could he be? Logistically, it's possible, Aidan. It's a five-hour drive from his grandparents' home in Henderson to Knoxville where the murders have taken place. I looked into the dates of each of the six killings so far—"

"Six. My God."

"We don't know it's your son, Aidan. Have some hope."

"I've been trying, believe me. Go on. You looked into the killings and what?"

"All of them have happened on a weekend."

"Which works with Aidan's schedule since there wouldn't be any school absences to explain. Maybe the Larsens can prove he has an alibi for at least some of those dates. A family trip or something like that."

"Is that what you want, Aidan? You want me to contact them?"

Aidan thought about it, then straightened, his heart heavy. "I don't see how we can avoid it anymore. Niall's in a world of trouble for what he's done here in Mystic Lake. He'll need the only parents he's ever really known to help him through this. He'll need a lawyer."

"I can help his parents get one."

"I'm speaking to one of the best defense attorneys in the country."

Nate sighed. "I only wish you'd allowed me to be the best back when all this started, with you."

"You did what your client wanted. No one can hold that against you. Will you help Niall? If the Larsens agree?"

"Of course. I'd love a chance to keep an O'Brien out of prison instead of helping him into one. It would be my honor."

"Thanks."

"What are you going to do now, Aidan? What's your next step?"

His hand tightened around the phone. "I'm going to find my son."

GRACE SAT ALONE in the conference room. Fletcher had made no secret that she wasn't happy with her "friendliness" toward Aidan, as the policewoman had called it. Once Aidan had left, Fletcher had given Grace a look of censure, then returned to her desk. But, thankfully, she was still helping with the case. Fletcher had called Grace half a dozen times in the past twenty minutes to ask about entries on the list she was researching. That left Grace free to explore other leads.

Like finally viewing the lab results.

She'd just received an email that they were ready, so she excitedly pulled them up on her laptop.

The reports were detailed and full of geek-speak, so it took a while to cull through them. She made notes as she went, and then checked her list.

Shoe prints from the festival matched shoe prints taken up on the mountain at Aidan's place. Fingerprints on each of the arrows retrieved from the boat, the woods and the one that had struck Grace's arm all matched one another.

That was enough evidence to prove that the same person had struck both the festival and the mountain at Aidan's place. Although it really wasn't a surprise, it was a relief to have something solid, actual facts instead of conjecture. But what she really wanted to know was whether the Mystic Lake suspect was the Crossbow Killer.

She scrolled through page after page of measurements of arrows and feathers and paint chemicals as well as comparisons of types of shoes and sizes that could have left the print. Finally, she came to the part she most wanted to see.

The DNA results.

The FBI had already added the DNA profile of the Crossbow Killer into CODIS. The lab had submitted the profile from the Mystic Lake shooter to CODIS to search for a match.

They got one.

Grace read the lab report again, then reread it slowly to make sure she was interpreting everything correctly.

She was.

She locked her laptop, grabbed her jacket and rushed from the conference room.

Fletcher, who was on the phone, called for her to wait as she ran for the door. But Grace didn't stop. She had to talk to Aidan.

## Chapter Nineteen

The sound of a snapping twig had Aidan whirling around. He slowly straightened as Grace emerged from between two trees.

"What the— Grace, what are you doing here?" He scanned the woods surrounding them.

"They're not with me," she assured him. "I spoke to Dawson and Ortiz when I got here. They had just rendezvoused at the ruins of your cabin to confer about where to search next for our bow and arrow guy. They told me this section was where you were looking."

He scanned the woods again. "I'm not worried about where the police are. I'm worried about where the shooter might be. Please tell me you're wearing your Kevlar vest under your jacket."

She glanced down and grimaced. "Actually, no. I was hot earlier and hung it on my chair at the station. Didn't even think about it when I went looking for you."

He swore beneath his breath. "Then put mine on."

She stopped him from shrugging out of his coat to remove his vest by pressing her hand against his chest. "No. No way will I take your vest. If something happened to you, I couldn't live with that guilt."

"Then you're leaving. Now. Let's go." He grabbed her arm.

She pulled away from him and frowned. "I'll leave you to your searching in a minute. But I need to tell you something first."

What she didn't realize was that he was doing everything he could to make himself a target to lure the shooter out into the open. He was still clinging to a tiny shred of doubt that Niall was the shooter. But if he was, then Aidan had to do everything he could to make sure he was brought in safe and sound. He couldn't leave the capture of his son to the police who might be trigger-happy when confronted with a man with a deadly crossbow. The problem was, if Aiden standing on exposed cliffs and loudly stomping around the creeks and streams on his property in the areas where it made sense that someone might camp out or hide had attracted any attention, then his son was on his way right now to confront him.

And Grace could get caught in the cross fire.

"Talk to me while I escort you back to your vehicle," Aidan said, reaching for her again.

She jerked her arm away and frowned at him. "All right, all right. But stop grabbing me like you're about to throw me over your knee and spank me."

He coughed to hide a smile. "You don't like to be spanked. Good to know."

She rolled her eyes.

He scanned the path and trees again, then motioned for her to walk beside him.

"I got the results back from the FBI lab," she told him.

His stomach dropped. "Go on." His throat was tight as he waited to find out whether his theory about the shooter's identity was right.

"They confirm the man we're after is the one from the festival, and everything happening up here at your place."

"You knew that already."

"I suspected it. Now there's proof in the form of shoe-print analysis, fingerprint analysis and DNA."

He stopped. "DNA?"

"A full profile. The lab entered it into CODIS—that's the—"

"FBI DNA database. I know. When I confessed to Elly's murder they took my DNA sample and added my profile to that same database." He started forward again, his hand on the small of her back urging her to keep moving.

"The FBI has entered the Crossbow Killer's DNA into CODIS, too, from the crime scenes already attributed to him. The hope is that a suspect will eventually be identified to match against that profile at some point. But when the lab submitted the Mystic Lake shooter's profile it didn't come back as a match to the Crossbow Killer."

"Did *not* come back as a match?"

"Not even close. The anonymous call about the Crossbow Killer being in Mystic Lake was wrong. The suspect for these local events is someone else entirely. Which supports my theory that the Mystic Lake shooting suspect is probably the same person who submitted that anonymous tip in the first place, because he was trying to frame you and send you back to prison."

He held up a low-hanging branch to let her through, then joined her again on the path. "You came all the way up here and hiked a quarter mile through the woods to tell me the suspect all of us are chasing isn't the Crossbow Killer? That information could have waited."

"True. But *this* couldn't. I wanted to make sure you knew before you heard it from someone else. The DNA profile—"

"Malone? You out here?" Fletcher's voice rang through the woods somewhere ahead.

"Good grief. She's determined I shouldn't be around you," Grace said. "I'm here," she called out. "We're coming toward you."

"Okay," Fletcher called back.

"The DNA profile?" Aidan asked, stepping over a fallen log then lifting Grace over it.

She smiled her thanks, but put her hand on his chest, stopping him.

"Grace, we need to get going."

"Just one minute, okay?" She kept her voice low. "I want to tell you this before we reach Fletcher."

He sighed and looked around, actively watching the woods. "Hurry. Tell me what's so important."

"Our suspect's DNA wasn't a match to the Crossbow Killer. But it was a partial match, a familial match to another profile in the database. There were thirteen core DNA loci between the two, which is why CODIS spit it out."

He felt the blood drain from his face. "Familial?"

She looked at him with such sympathy that it nearly broke him.

"Just say it, Grace."

"The partial match was to you. The suspect, the one here in Mystic Lake, is related to you by blood. He shares 50 percent of your DNA. I'm so sorry. It's no longer just a theory. The shooter we're looking for is definitely Niall. Your son."

"I knew it," he whispered, barely able to get out the words. "But hearing it from you, knowing there's no room for doubt anymore, makes it so much worse."

She reached her hands up and cupped his face, her gaze searching his. "I'm so sorry, Aidan."

He gently tugged her arms down, even though he wanted nothing more right now than to find solace in the arms of this amazing woman. But he couldn't allow his selfish needs or desires put her at risk for another second. "We really have to go. I've done everything I can to draw out the—to draw out my son if he's hiding on my property. You can't be out here without your vest to at least offer some partial protection."

Her eyes widened. "What did you do to draw him out?"

He grabbed her hand and tugged her forward. "Everything but shout a dare from the top of the mountain. Maybe I'll do that next, after you're somewhere safe."

"Oh, Aidan. I wish you wouldn't be so careless about your own safety. You shouldn't—"

"Malone? Where are you?" Fletcher walked around some bushes and stopped when she saw Aidan. Her gaze flitted down to where Aidan was holding Grace's hand.

Aidan tugged his hand free, ignoring Grace's unhappy frown. He motioned toward Fletcher. "You brought Malone's vest?"

Grace blinked as if just now realizing that Fletcher was holding it.

"Of course," Fletcher said. "She ran out of the station without it, risking her life to come find you, I might add. I called Dawson and he told me where you were, so I figured that's where she'd go." She gave Grace a hard look. "Even though you aren't answering your phone."

"Sorry," Grace said. "When I saw you calling I turned off the ringer. I had something else on my mind and didn't want to lose my focus."

Fletcher snorted. "It's obvious what, or who, you had on your mind. You didn't want to hear me say anything bad about him. That's why you didn't answer."

Aidan stepped forward and took the vest from her. "Thank you for bringing this." He turned to Grace. "Over or under your jacket?"

She blew out a frustrated breath. "Under. Give me a second." She quickly worked at her buttons.

The barest whisper of sound had Aidan whirling toward the woods off to his left, searching for the source. A flash of white through the trees was his only warning. "Get down," he yelled, diving toward Fletcher and throwing her to the ground.

"He's here," Grace yelled into her phone as she scrambled behind a tree and yanked out her gun. "Dawson, the suspect just shot at Fletcher."

The policewoman was lying on the ground, looking stunned as she stared up at the arrow embedded in a thick oak tree just past where she'd been standing moments ago. "My God," she said. "That would have gone right through my head if you hadn't knocked me down."

Aidan grabbed her shoulders and yanked her behind the cover of a thick tree. "You'll have another chance to die if you don't pay attention and use your training. He's still out there."

Fletcher stared at him, then blew out a shaky breath. "Okay, okay. Right. Which way did he—"

A young man stepped out from behind a thick bush not far from Grace. The same young man Aidan only got to see in a new picture once a year through his lawyer.

Niall.

He was aiming his crossbow at Aidan.

Niall sneered. "Finally, after all these years." A single tear coursed down his cheek. "Killed anyone else's mom lately?"

"Drop it!" Grace yelled, aiming her gun at Niall.

"No," Aidan shouted. "Don't."

Niall whirled toward her, still holding his bow.

"Son, don't do it." Aidan jumped to his feet.

*Bam!*

A red wet spot appeared on Niall's shirt and quickly began to spread across his chest. His eyes widened in surprise as he fell to the ground, his bow landing harmlessly beside him.

Aidan froze, then looked at Grace in horror.

"No," she whispered. "I didn't shoot."

He turned and saw Fletcher still sitting on the ground, her pistol in her hands, pointed at his son.

"Dad?" A pitiful, confused rasp broke through Aidan's shock. "Daddy?"

"I'm here, son. Daddy's here." He dropped to his knees and desperately pressed his hands against Niall's wound to try to stop the bleeding. As if through a long, deep tunnel, he registered the sounds of Grace calling 911 for an ambulance and Fletcher calling Dawson, telling him they needed help. But all of that faded at the horror of feeling his son's lifeblood seeping through his fingers.

# Chapter Twenty

As Aidan sat beside Niall's hospital bed, watching his chest rise and fall, he couldn't help but wonder at the miracle that his anonymous donation to buy Mystic Lake a medevac chopper had saved his son's life. Two days after the shooting, Niall was still miraculously clinging to life in the intensive care unit at a Chattanooga hospital.

He was in a medically induced coma to help his body heal. But he was breathing on his own now. Seeing him on a ventilator that first day had nearly destroyed Aidan. He didn't think he could survive watching another loved one suffer the way Elly had. But Niall was young. And he was a fighter.

He'd need that fighting spirit not only to bounce back physically, but to live down the toxic lies the media was spreading. The reporter who'd been staying at the B and B had announced that the Crossbow Killer had been operating in Mystic Lake and that he was now clinging to life at the hospital after being shot by police. Aidan was grateful that his son's name had been suppressed in the news reports because he was a minor. But in today's world of social media, someone would leak his name eventually and it would spread across cyberspace.

A tap on the large glass window to the hallway had him

looking up to see Grace, looking nervous and somber beside her boss, Dawson, Aidan's lawyer and friend who was also now Niall's lawyer, and of course, Niall's legal guardians, the Larsens.

As if that odd mix of people wasn't enough to remind him that his son had yet another battle on his hands if he managed to recover, the uniformed police officer in the hallway guarding the door was more than enough to jog his memory.

Grace said something to Aidan's former in-laws. Judy Larsen hugged her and then she and her husband, Sam, entered the room. They headed directly toward Aidan, barely giving him time to rise from his chair before he was enveloped in yet another of their group hugs.

He was as astonished at their acceptance and support now as he had been at the parole hearing when they'd urged the board to grant him an early release. They'd told the board they were skeptical about his confession, always had been. But that even if he was guilty, they forgave him and were relieved that their daughter was no longer suffering. The fact that they were supporting him even now, and not blaming him for their grandson having almost died, humbled and shocked him.

It also shamed him that they still didn't know the full story, exactly what had happened the day their daughter died. But telling them now seemed cruel. What good would it serve?

He looked over the top of Judy Larsen's head and met Grace's worried gaze. He'd hidden the full truth from her, too. He hated lying, even by omission, especially to her. But he had to keep lying or hurt the Larsens even more.

After giving them a summary of what the doctor had said about Niall's condition while the two of them had taken a much-needed break at their hotel down the street, he headed into the hallway.

Grace gave him a smile of encouragement and the two of them followed the others down the long hall to the conference room that the hospital administrator had lent law enforcement for their interviews. Aidan had put off answering their questions as long as he could. But with the arrival of the supervisory special agent, Grace's boss at the FBI, they couldn't be put off any longer. Especially after Aidan's probation officer told him he had no choice but to speak to them or risk violating the terms of his parole. He was so tired of the threat of returning to prison hanging over his head. But he had several more years of parole to endure.

After following Grace into the room and shutting the door behind them, Aidan turned around and stilled, shocked to see so many people there, many of them strangers. But it was the only other person dressed in a casual shirt and jeans, like him, who had his stomach dropping.

Stella. She knew—and could prove—the full truth, that one detail he wanted to keep secret above all else.

"Aidan." Grace touched his shoulder. "Over here." She led the way to two empty seats in the middle of the long table and took the one on the left for herself, leaving him to sit beside her with his lawyer, now Niall's lawyer, on his other side.

"Aidan O'Brien," Grace said, "I'd like to introduce you to Levi Perry, FBI supervisory special agent of the Knoxville field office, my boss."

Perry leaned across the table and shook Aidan's hand. "Thank you for agreeing to speak with us, Mr. O'Brien."

"Did I have a choice?"

Nate subtly nudged Aidan's foot beneath the table.

Aidan sighed. "Sorry. This isn't the best time for an interrogation with my son in the ICU."

"Interview, not interrogation," Perry corrected. "Any suspicion that fell on you early on during the investigation has been proven to be wrong. What we'd like to do now is discuss a few remaining questions we have that only you can answer. First, let me introduce you to the other people in the meeting whom you haven't met yet."

There were several higher-ups in law enforcement for the county, as well as a man in an extremely expensive-looking business suit sitting beside Perry. He was introduced as Raul Garcia, a senior member of the Tennessee Board of Probation and Parole.

Aidan stiffened. His lawyer was already pushing his chair back to stand.

"As a reminder, I'm Nathaniel Barnes, attorney for both the suspect—Niall O'Brien Larsen—and his biological father, Aidan O'Brien. If the parole board is here to consider revoking Mr. O'Brien's parole, then I must advise my client to invoke his right to remain silent. This setting isn't the proper one for that kind of discussion."

Garcia held up a hand to stop him. "I assure you, Mr. Barnes, the parole board has absolutely no intention of revoking Mr. O'Brien's parole. Consider me merely an interested observer at this time."

"I appreciate that, Mr. Garcia. But I'm still advising my client not to speak." He motioned to Aidan. "Let's go."

Aidan remained seated. "What about my son? Niall? I was told the main reason for this meeting was to get my side of what happened and any information that might help explain why Niall did what he did."

"Mitigating factors." Perry nodded. "That's why we're here, yes."

"Then I'm staying," Aidan said.

Nate slowly sat. "This is completely irregular," he grumbled. "And for the official record, I'm still advising my client to remain silent."

Perry motioned around the room. "There's no court reporter here. Nothing is being recorded or written down. There will be no official record of this meeting. And if anyone asks after we leave here today, this meeting never happened."

Aidan frowned at Nate, then Grace. "What's going on?"

She cleared her throat. "The Mystic Lake police have already provided their statements. I've given mine, as well. We've been meeting since Niall was shot, exchanging information and reviewing the evidence. Before the district attorney decides what charges to press against Niall, a barely seventeen-year-old minor, they need to know if there are any mitigating factors that should influence their decision. That's why you're here, Aidan. To speak to those factors. To speak for your son. Do you understand?"

He stared into her deep blue eyes, her words replaying in his mind. Then he glanced down the table. "Stella? Is that why you're here, too? Mitigating factors?"

She nodded. "It has to end today, Aidan. No more lies. No more cover-up. Niall's life is on the line, his future. They need to understand *everything* that went into shaping who he is, and what may have triggered him to do what he's done."

*Everything.* That one word sent a surge of panic through him.

Grace squeezed his forearm, recapturing his attention. "It's time to tell us what really happened the day that Niall's biological mother died, the day that your wife, Elly O'Brien, passed away. Once everyone understands the full truth, only

then can they truly understand what Niall has gone through
and why he made the choices he's made."

"Mr. O'Brien," Perry began.

Aidan tuned him out and focused on Grace's beautiful
face. "Did you speak to Stella already?"

"I know that she has an audio recording that she brought
with her to play for us. But I haven't heard it yet."

He sighed deeply. "I can't do this."

Ignoring the potential repercussions to her career, she
took his hand in hers. "The truth has been a poison inside
you for years. It's been poison to Niall, too. We just didn't
know that until now. Let it out, Aidan. It's the only way
for everyone to truly heal. And the only way to ensure that
Niall gets every chance at going home after he leaves this
hospital, rather than going to a detention facility."

It was her last sentence that kept him in his chair.

"Just tell us what happened," she encouraged. "Start with
the fire, then go to the day Elly passed away."

He let out a shuddering breath, and began to tell the story
that had been stuck inside him for all these years. He spoke
haltingly at first, stumbling over the words. But Grace took
his hand again, this time beneath the table, and held on the
entire time he spoke. Without that anchor, he didn't think
he would have made it.

He told them about the fire at his home, finding out that
his wife had run through the flames to save their son. That
in spite of her burns, she'd carried him downstairs. Then
a burning beam had crashed through the ceiling, breaking
her spine and pinning her down, but miraculously not hitting Niall.

She'd suffered horribly, had been mostly paralyzed from
the neck down and would be on a ventilator for the rest of
her life, however long that was. Her parents had wanted him

to stop extraordinary life-saving measures at the hospital and let her go. But he couldn't. He still had hope that she would defy the odds, prove the doctors wrong.

Months after the accident she was receiving care at home, with two nurses who rotated day shifts when he was at work or running errands. One of those nurses was Stella Simmons, now Holman. At night, Aidan was the one who took care of Elly if any alarms went off on her ventilator.

It was difficult and frustrating trying to communicate with Elly. She eventually was able to barely control one hand. But she couldn't speak, not at first anyway. Through his research online he'd discovered that a special valve could be placed in her tracheostomy that might allow her to speak once again, even though she was paralyzed.

"And it worked," he said. "I was so excited to hear what her first words would be. She didn't say 'I love you' or ask to see our son. Instead, she said, 'Let me die.'"

Perry winced across from him.

"It's what she wrote on her pad of paper, too. That same phrase. Let me die. She wanted me to end her misery. I know that some people tolerate the vent, that even paralyzed they can live fulfilling lives and still experience joy. But Elly had been so active, athletic. No amount of counseling helped her accept her condition. She was truly miserable."

He shook his head in self-disgust. "I'm the reason she suffered so long. I could have withdrawn care, signed forms at the hospital to let her die a natural death. But I was too selfish. I'd failed her by not being able to save her from the fire. I wanted to be there for her afterward, convinced my money could buy some kind of miracle cure if she could only hold on a little longer. I was a foolish man."

"Skipping to the day that she did die," Perry said. "The version of events you told the police was that you wanted to end her suffering, that you unplugged the ventilator, then waited another ten minutes until the backup battery drained. After her heart stopped, you called 911."

"That's the story I've told all these years."

"But that's not the truth, is it, Mr. O'Brien? Special Agent Grace Malone has insisted to me that you're innocent. And even your in-laws seem to believe that. Did you kill your wife?"

"What the hell does this have to do with helping my son?"

"Understanding the trauma he may have witnessed or suffered himself can help explain the decisions he's recently made. It could make all the difference in the charges pressed against him."

"I'll tell them what happened." It was Stella from the other end of the table.

"Don't," Aidan said. "Please."

"Aidan was exhausted that day, as he often was," she said, ignoring his plea. "He worked long hours and had a five-year-old son to take to day care each morning, pick up after work, feed, bathe. He could have hired a nanny but he insisted on being there for Niall, to give him as normal a life as possible even though his mother couldn't hold him or help take care of him."

Aidan squeezed his eyes shut.

Grace whispered soothing words as she continued to hold his hand. He gripped it like a lifeline, both ashamed to be relying on her so heavily and desperate not to let go.

Stella explained that Aidan had come home, gotten the turnover report from Stella, checked on his wife, fed and bathed his son, then put him to bed. Then he'd gone out on the back deck to sit for a few minutes, to unwind, before he headed back upstairs to sit with Elly until bedtime.

"He fell asleep. It's probably the only time he ever did,

fell asleep on that back deck because he was so exhausted. When he jolted awake, he realized twenty minutes had passed. He ran inside the house and upstairs to make sure his wife was still okay. He didn't hear any alarms going off on her ventilator so he thought everything would be fine. But when he went into her room, he realized everything wasn't okay."

"Mr. O'Brien." This time it was the district attorney who spoke. "I know this is an unofficial inquest, but having your wife's former nurse tell the story is still hearsay. I'd like to hear the rest from you, especially since this is a whole new version of events that I'm having trouble believing after all this time."

"It's the truth," Stella snapped. "Not a version of events. He didn't kill Elly."

"It's okay," Aidan told her, a strange sort of acceptance finally settling over him. "I've lied for years. I don't expect everyone to believe me now. But if even one person does, and it somehow helps Niall, I'll tell the rest."

He explained that when he entered the room, the first thing he noticed was that his son, who was supposed to be in bed, was playing with toy police cars and trucks by the window. The next thing he noticed was that the cord to Elly's ventilator was unplugged and that Niall was currently using it to tie up one of his so-called bad guy action figures.

The DA leaned forward. "You're saying that you didn't pull the cord on your wife's machine. Your five-year-old son did?"

Aidan nodded. "But he didn't realize what he was doing. What he'd done. I told him to grab his toys and go back to bed. I didn't want him to see what I had to do to help his mother. I plugged in the machine, called 911 and put it on speaker so I could lay her on the floor and begin doing chest compressions, CPR. But it was too late. Her backup battery had died before I came in from the porch. There were no alarms beeping. She wasn't breathing. Her heart had stopped. Nothing I did made a difference."

"When the EMTs arrived and tried to resuscitate your wife," Perry said, "they said you went to check on your son."

"I had to get out of the way so they could try to help Elly. I went to check on Niall and asked him what had happened. He was still playing with his damn cars and trucks, making beeping sounds. He said...he said mommy played with him, told him she could beep like his cars. She told him... she told him to pull the plug to make the machine go beep."

There were several sharp intakes of breath around the room.

Grace placed her hand on his shoulder. "Oh, Aidan. I'm so sorry."

The DA scoffed. "Now you're not only blaming your wife's death on your five-year-old son, you're telling us his mother essentially ended her own life. You really expect us to believe this new story?"

"Well, of course I don't expect you to believe it," Aidan bit out. "I never expected, or wanted, anyone to believe it. It was horrific, awful. Can you imagine the pain, the absolute misery my wife felt, how desperate she was to end her suffering that she would actually convince her own child to pull the plug, knowing how that could mess him up later in life, knowing he was responsible for her death?"

He shoved his hand through his hair and tugged his other hand free from Grace to rest his forearms on top of the table. "Elly was miserable. All she asked me to do was let her go, let her die. And I was too selfish to grant her that end to her suffering. Instead, my five-year-old son did what I couldn't. He ended her pain."

The DA started to say something, but Perry stopped him. "Mr. O'Brien, if what you're saying is true, everyone in here, I'm sure, can agree that law enforcement wouldn't have done anything to punish your son. He certainly wouldn't have been prosecuted. So why did you confess to your wife's murder? What was the point?"

Aidan stared at him incredulously. "The point? Did you not hear what I said? He was a little boy. If the world heard that he'd unplugged that machine, that knowledge would have followed him the rest of his life. People can be cruel, horrible to each other. Parents would have talked. Their children would have heard. They'd have teased and bullied him at school. As it is, his grandparents had to move several hours away to raise him because of kids teasing him over his father killing his mother. I made a split-second decision to protect my son, choosing the lesser of evils. I believed it was far better for him to grow up thinking his father was an evil monster than to realize he'd inadvertently killed his own mother. That's why I confessed. To try to spare him that kind of pain. But even more than that, I was, in my own misguided way, trying to protect Elly, and the Larsens."

"Your wife and her parents?" Perry asked. "Please explain what you mean by that."

A single tear slid down Aidan's cheek. He angrily wiped it away. "Elly loved Niall more than anything. He was her world. If she'd been in her right frame of mind, not blinded by the agony of a life she couldn't accept, she never would have tricked him into doing what he did. She wouldn't want that guilt later in life to eat at his soul. And I didn't want her parents or friends to ever know that she'd done something that would have shamed her. So, as strange as it may seem to someone not in that situation, yes, I confessed to protect both my wife's reputation and my son. At the time, I felt my life was over anyway. And that because I refused to help her, I deserved my fate. Prison. But after seeing what's become of Niall, how tortured he was to discover his father confessed to his mother's murder, I wonder if he'd have been better off knowing the truth from the beginning."

"That brings us to those mitigating circumstances," Perry said. "If we take what you just said as fact—"

"There's no proof," the DA said, looking extremely skeptical.

"Assume it's a fact for now. What the Larsens told us earlier is that when five year-old Niall was told that his mother was dead, that he'd never see her again, he shut down. He was never able to answer questions about anything he saw that day because his mind blanked out his memories. But it must have simmered below the surface because he suffered night terrors for years. And he acted out, had all kinds of behavioral issues. His grandparents became desperate to help him. They'd kept in touch with one of his nurses, Stella Simmons, who is now Stella Holman, because they'd grown close in the months that Stella helped care for their daughter. When they asked for recommendations, Stella helped them find a child psychiatrist. And she took him to his sessions whenever the Larsens couldn't."

Perry looked around the table as if to make sure that everyone was paying attention. "Let's skip ahead to the year before Mr. O'Brien's parole hearing. The Larsens said that Niall as a fifteen-year-old at the time became curious to learn about his father. It didn't take much internet searching to find out everything that the media had reported. He believed his father killed his mother. And it ate at him. He sent Mr. O'Brien hate mail and in response, Mr. O'Brien had his lawyer contact them to let them know that Niall needed help."

Barnes spoke up to add a lawyer's viewpoint to the discussion. "Obviously, Niall O'Brien has been through trauma in his young life even if he's never had a clear memory of what happened. Finding out disturbing things about his father sent him over the edge. He came up with a plan to have his father sent back to prison where he felt he belonged. He'd heard about the Crossbow Killer on the news and decided to try to frame Aidan as the killer. An adult, especially those of us in law enforcement, would of course know that framing someone isn't nearly as easy as Niall thought it would be. When his actions didn't achieve the results he wanted, he became desperate, doing what he could to hurt his father. But I contend that he wasn't specifically trying to hurt anyone else. He only wanted to hurt Mr. O'Brien."

"Hold it, hold it," the DA said. "I'm one of the ones who didn't hear from Mrs. Holman in the meetings you've been having, or from the Larsens. What exactly did they testify to at the parole hearing that you mentioned earlier? If it's more of this unsubstantiated new story that O'Brien is putting forth, I don't see where any of that is relevant and will help the younger O'Brien avoid the charges I'm inclined to levy against him."

"They found out the truth," Aidan said, his voice gruff with anger. "They testified that they knew that Niall had pulled the plug, not me. I didn't ask them to speak on my behalf. I didn't want them to. But they did."

"Sounds convenient."

Aidan glared at him. "Convenient? Why the hell do you think my wife's parents would lie to a parole board? You think they'd want their daughter's killer out of prison? If you think that, you're an idiot."

The DA pointed at Aidan. "Now you listen here—"

"Don't you dare speak to him that way." Stella stood,

her expression one of loathing as she addressed the district attorney. "*You* listen. All of you. Aidan didn't come here today willingly to tell his story. He came because his parole officer ordered him to, and because all of you asked him. Enough people know bits and pieces about the truth to have pieced it together even though he has tried for years to keep it quiet. As to whether what he's saying is true or not, I've got proof that it is. I brought a recording I'd like to play for all of you that—"

"Stella," Aidan rasped. "Don't. Leave it alone."

"I'm sorry, Aidan. But Grace was right when she said this has been a poison in your soul, and that it's poison to Niall as well, whether he realizes it or not. The only antidote to that poison is the truth."

He shoved to his feet. "Then you'll do it without me." He strode out the door.

"Aiden, wait." Grace followed him into the hallway and shut the door behind her.

He turned and she wrapped her arms around his waist, hugging him tight. Unable to stop himself, even though he knew he should, he hugged her tighter and rested his cheek on the top of her head. Some of the pain and anger inside him melted away at the feel of her in his arms. She was the embodiment of kindness, of empathy, of caring. And he selfishly drew strength from her, even at the risk of someone seeing them.

The convict and the FBI agent.

A father with a murderous son and a woman dedicated to justice.

It could never work.

And even if, by some miracle, there was some way for them to be together, he'd made a mess of things with his son. Niall had to be his first priority now. Somehow he had to fix the damage he'd caused by trying to cover everything up in the first place.

Regret ate at him as he pulled away. "Go back inside. I'm sure they're waiting for you."

"Where are you going?" she asked.

"To see the Larsens. They deserve to know the truth before someone else tells them."

"Do you want me to go with you?"

He stared at her in wonder. "You're amazing, you know that?" Unable to resist the impulse, he feathered his hand down the side of her face, then pressed a soft kiss against her lips. "Thank you. But I need to do this myself." He quickly turned and strode away.

## Chapter Twenty-One

Grace remained in the hospital conference room long after everyone else had left. She was still reeling from listening to the recording that Stella had secretly made during one of Niall's visits to the child psychiatrist. It was both shocking and sickening to listen to the sweet, innocent voice of an eight-year-old child speaking under the influence of hypnosis. Without any true understanding about what he revealed, he'd walked the doctor and Stella as his guardian during that visit through everything that happened the day that his mother died.

And everything he said corroborated what Aidan had said.

Elly O'Brien had taken her own life with her son's help, using him to pull the plug while Aidan was out of the room.

Stella had explained that Elly likely heard the sound of the back door and knew that her husband had gone outside. Since he'd already checked on her and confirmed that her machine was functioning properly, there was no reason he shouldn't have felt secure stepping out for a few minutes. Even if he hadn't fallen asleep, at any other time on any other day the odds of anything bad happening to Elly while he was outside for only twenty minutes were very low. But the stars had aligned for Elly and she got her deepest, darkest wish—release from a life she considered to be unbearable.

At the expense of her five-year-old little boy and her husband.

It broke Grace's heart that Elly had been so miserable as to do that. And it broke her heart that Aidan knew and had taken on the guilt, and punishment, for not helping her and making her believe she had no other choice. Their beautiful little family had been irrevocably destroyed the day of the fire in their home, though none of them had realized it at the time.

But that wasn't the only thing on Grace's mind, or the only reason she was still sitting in the empty conference room trying to gather her thoughts and emotions. She was also reeling over the final conclusion presented by Mr. Garcia, the probation board member. He was going to meet with the rest of the board and recommend that they provide the governor with Aidan's name as someone who should be pardoned. Not just pardoned, but fully exonerated, his record expunged and all of his rights restored—including the cancellation of his parole.

It would take months, maybe longer, for all the red tape to be cut and the legal pieces set into place. But Aidan would have what he deserved: complete exoneration. The world would know he was innocent. It was what Grace had wanted all along. But now that it was being granted, she wasn't sure the cost was worth it.

Aidan had spent ten long years in prison to protect his son, Elly and the Larsens. Now the truth would all come out and they'd have to face the consequences. Everything he'd worked so hard for all this time was being nullified. And she couldn't help but worry what more that might cost him. She already knew what it had cost her.

Her career.

She looked down at the white envelope in her hands, given to her by her boss. It was official notice that she was being fired, effective immediately. It had been printed out before he'd even come to Chattanooga to meet with her. She was being let go because of unprofessional conduct and poor judgment in the execution of her duties. The team she'd worked with back in the Knoxville field office would go on to investigate and solve the Crossbow Killer case without her. That alone had her feeling empty inside. She'd so hoped that the anonymous tip that had sent her to Mystic Lake would have resulted in her leading the charge and solving the case. That would have been a major step up in her career. Instead, it had ended her career.

Opening the envelope, she pulled out the picture that her boss had included with the termination papers, a picture that had been snapped of her and Aidan kissing outside her room at the B and B after they'd returned from helplessly watching his cabin burn to the ground. The reporter they'd both thought was asleep in her room must have heard them and opened her door just enough to take that picture. And when she'd leaked the story about the Crossbow Killer supposedly in Mystic Lake, she'd included that picture of the FBI agent in town getting a little too friendly with the town's only parolee—a man who'd confessed to the murder of his wife. There was no coming back from that, even though Aidan had now been proven innocent, unofficially at least. At the time the picture was taken, he was still a convicted murderer with no hope of that ever changing.

Sighing heavily, she slid the picture back into the envelope and stood. As she grabbed her jacket off the back of her chair, she automatically felt for her holster to make sure it was in place. But she didn't have her holster or her gun anymore. She'd had to turn them over to her boss along with her FBI credentials and the Bureau's credit card. She'd even had to turn over her car keys so he could commandeer her FBI vest inside it and her laptop and files before he had the rental company retrieve the SUV.

She winced when she remembered the hole in the back of it from the arrow. But that was her former employer's problem now. As it was, they'd left her without any transportation. She'd have to arrange for another rental just to get back to her room at Mystic Lake to retrieve her personal belongings.

It had been nearly a decade since she'd first started her career as a beat cop before becoming a special agent. Without a gun, she felt naked, lost. She had absolutely no idea how to live life as a civilian.

Thankfully, she had a generous severance package that her boss had fought for due to her pristine service record prior to this fiasco at Mystic Lake. And she had her savings to fall back on. But neither of those would last forever. She needed to figure out what she was going to do with the rest of her life.

Before she left the hospital, she stopped in the ICU to check on Niall and his family. She hadn't expected Aidan to be there, and he wasn't. He was in another conference room of the hospital being briefed by his lawyer about everything that had happened after he'd walked out of the meeting.

The Larsens had red-rimmed eyes from crying, no doubt because they now knew just how horribly their daughter had suffered and the disastrous chain of events she'd unwittingly put into motion. But they were strong, relying on their faith to get them through. After she spoke to them for several minutes, they shared a prayer for Niall and Aidan. And it puts tears in Grace's eyes when they added her name in their prayer, as well.

She hugged them one last time and said her goodbyes. Then she headed downstairs to wait for her rental car to arrive.

Over an hour later, she emerged from the twisty, narrow road through the mountains into downtown Mystic Lake. She stopped at the Main Street parking lot, stunned to see thick black smoke rising from the trees off to her right, in the direction of the marina, and the sound of sirens as the fire department and police responded. She almost headed in that direction to offer help, but then she remembered she wasn't law enforcement anymore. She was a regular civilian and didn't even have the authority to direct traffic.

Instead, she drove around the end of the lake to the B and B and parked out back. Hopefully, Aidan would return soon. She really needed to talk to him, to see how he was doing, and maybe even feel around about where he saw his future heading. Right now her own future was both bleak and wide-open with possibilities.

She sincerely hoped one of those possibilities was Aidan.

As she stepped out of her car, another car pulled into the empty slot beside hers. She smiled a greeting at the man driving, then rounded the back of his car to head to the B and B.

He got out as she was passing him and smiled. "Heard you were looking for me."

She stopped in confusion. "I'm sorry, I don't—"

He pointed toward his car.

She glanced through the rear window. There on the back seat was a large crossbow and a quiver of arrows, with large white feathers attached to each of them. She whirled around to run. An explosion of white-hot pain slammed against the side of her head. Everything went dark.

# Chapter Twenty-Two

Aidan swerved to avoid a pothole as he navigated the long narrow road to Mystic Lake. When he'd set out a few days ago down this road, he'd been pushing his truck as fast as it could go on his way to the hospital. This time, he took the road at a more sane speed, and was actually, for the first time in a long time, enjoying the gorgeous views of the mountains and trees as he went. And he was smiling.

It was as if he'd come out of a long dark tunnel where he'd been living since the day of the fire that so horribly injured his wife. Today, everything had turned around. The truth, the full truth, was out. And what had happened once all the key people knew that truth had blown him away.

The Larsens had been sad, but not entirely surprised to hear that Elly had essentially orchestrated her own death. And they forgave him for keeping the truth from them. More importantly, they forgave him for not manning up and helping Elly when she needed him the most. They were thankful he'd never taken on that burden and hoped he could finally move on and be happy.

The DA, after listening to the recording of Niall as a little boy saying what he'd done, conferred with Chief Dawson and others and they agreed not to press charges against Niall as long as he received extensive counseling to help him overcome the trauma of his past. And that his record remained clean for the next two years.

Then Garcia, the parole board member, had stated he would work with the rest of the board and the governor to pursue having Aidan's record expunged and a full pardon and restoration of Aidan's rights.

An emergency meeting had been held just an hour ago. When Aidan's lawyer came out, he was grinning from ear to ear. He told Aidan that the governor and the parole board had heard enough today to immediately grant him an end to his parole. Everything else, expunging his record and spreading the news that he wasn't guilty, would take time. But Aidan didn't even care about all of that. What he cared about was that he was now free, truly free. He never had to face a probation officer again. And he could hunt with a gun in the future like anyone else, assuming he ever bought a gun. He was so used to hunting with a bow and arrow that he didn't know if he'd ever favor any other weapon.

But the best gift of all today was that his son had been weaned out of the medically induced coma and finally opened his eyes. Aidan had agreed with the Larsens that he shouldn't be there when it was done. Niall would need to be carefully updated on everything that had happened. It could take a while for him to let go of the hate and accept the truth. Until then, his adoptive parents and his court-appointed psychiatrist would help him. And one day, hopefully soon, a family reunion with Aidan would be in the cards.

He grinned and drove past Main Street, then slowed, frowning as he noted dark smoke in the sky far out of town, possibly near the marina. Whatever was happening, he hoped no one was hurt and that the fire was put out quickly.

Continuing on, he headed around back of the B and B, looking forward to talking to Grace and updating her about everything that had happened. Hell, he might even ask her on a date to celebrate. Wouldn't that be something? To be with her and not worry about anyone's opinions? After all, her boss had been in the meeting and agreed that Aidan was completely innocent. All of that time being so careful around her had been worth it. Her career was salvaged and now there was nothing standing in the way of expressing their intense attraction to each other. Heck, attraction was a paltry term and did nothing to describe the all-consuming need he had for her and vice versa. For the first time in years he was looking forward to his future. And more than anything, he wanted Grace Malone to be a part of that future.

If she would have him.

As he parked, he was disappointed that he didn't see her rental SUV in the lot. The Larsens had told him that Grace was going to the B and B when she left. She must have stopped off somewhere else, maybe a store back in Chattanooga. Or maybe she was helping with whatever was going on down at the marina.

He parked and pulled out his phone to call Chief Dawson as he exited his truck.

"Hey, Aidan," the chief said, sounding out of breath. "We're kind of busy out here. What do you need?"

"The marina? Is that where the smoke's coming from?"

"You guessed it. One of the boats blew up and is on fire. We're helping the fire department move other boats nearby to try to keep the fire from spreading."

"Injuries?"

"None, thank God. Sorry to be short, but why did you call?"

"Grace. I don't see her SUV in the B and B parking lot—"

"Didn't you hear? She doesn't have that SUV anymore. Her boss turned it back in when he fired her."

Aidan stopped by the last car in the lot. "What did you say? He fired her?"

"Oh, man. Sorry you heard it this way. She can explain when you see her."

He didn't need an explanation. The only reason Grace would have lost her job was him. He swore. "All right. Thanks. Do you happen to know what she's driving now?"

"No idea. Gotta go. It's all law enforcement hands on deck, all four of us." He laughed. "Your lawyer informed me about your parole being canceled. Congratulations on how things worked out. Enjoy your freedom, Aidan. You deserve it." The line clicked, ending the call.

Aidan's earlier euphoria was gone. In its place was a simmering anger at both Grace's boss and himself. He should have been more careful. Destroying her career was the last thing he'd wanted. He'd have to talk to his lawyer to see if there was something they could do to force the FBI to reinstate her. But right now he couldn't imagine what that might be.

He headed into the B and B. After a brief stop to make sure that Stella knew he harbored no ill feelings toward her and appreciated her good intentions, he hurried upstairs and knocked on Grace's door. After several knocks and several minutes of waiting, he jogged downstairs and sought out Stella again. But she hadn't seen Grace.

One of the customers in the restaurant overheard them and said he was walking into the restaurant when he noticed Grace pulling up in the parking lot. As far as he knew, she'd never come inside, but she could have and he just didn't notice.

"Do you remember which car was hers?" Aidan asked.

"Yeah, one of those smaller cars. A four-door, white.

Toyota I think. I was surprised because she normally drives a big SUV."

"Thanks." Aidan strode outside to the parking lot. He remembered passing a white Toyota and easily found it again amid the trucks and Jeeps in the lot. An uneasy feeling tingled down his spine as he peered into her car. Nothing looked out of place. The car was locked and all of the windows were rolled up. It simply looked as if she'd parked and gone inside.

But she hadn't.

So where was she?

He circled the car, looking for anything that might tell him what was going on. The small shoe prints outside the driver's door looked to be about her size. She must have gotten out of the car. The prints went around the back of another car and then...other prints converged on hers. They were large, the size of a man probably as big as Aidan. And the prints trampled over the top of Grace's. After that, the man's prints deepened in the dirt and gravel. But there were no more prints from Grace.

To anyone else, what had happened here might not be obvious. But to Aidan, who'd been tracking game almost daily for well over a year now, they were a glaring neon sign telling him something had happened to Grace. Something bad.

The car where her prints ended didn't appear to be the car that was parked here now. This car was a large SUV and was parked on some of those prints, which meant they were there before the SUV pulled in. So the man who'd scuffled with Grace had taken off in his own car. And Aidan didn't doubt for a minute that he'd taken Grace with him, against her will.

A bead of sweat rolled down his back in spite of the chill in the air as he whipped out his phone and called Dawson again. He walked back to Grace's car and slowly circled it, looking for other clues.

"Aidan," Dawson said, "I can't talk right now. I'm trying to dock a boat that—"

"It's Grace. She's been abducted."

"What the… Are you sure? Tell me what happened."

Aidan explained the situation, the clues as he continued to slowly inspect the ground around her car. When he reached the right front tire, he bellowed in fury. "He's got her, Dawson. That animal has her."

"Who? Calm down. Tell me what's going on."

Aidan bent down to inspect the arrow sticking out of Grace's tire, an arrow with a large white feather hanging from the end.

"The Crossbow Killer. The real one. He's here, in Mystic Lake. And he's got Grace."

Dawson swore viciously. "How much do you want to bet the fire at the marina was his doing, a diversion?" He yelled for Fletcher and Collier, shouting commands as he transferred responsibility for the marina scene to Ortiz to continue working with the firefighters.

Aidan followed the clues from the other car left in the gravel and noted the direction it had taken. Then he ran to his truck and jumped in.

"All right," Dawson said. "We're heading to our cars now. We'll meet you at the B and B and—"

"Forget the B and B." He raced his truck out of the parking lot, slowing to determine which way the other vehicle's distinctive tire tracks had gone. Then he made the turn and gunned the engine.

"Wait, why?" Dawson demanded. "Talk to me."

"He's in a Jeep, older model, four-wheel drive. I don't know the color. I'm judging by the tracks, the width of the wheel base. The tires are muddy. The tracks are fresh, so I've got something to follow. They're running parallel with the lake so far, heading out of town."

Dawson shouted orders over his radio to the others. "Older model Jeep heading northwest, parallel with the lake. Be on the lookout."

"Trace her phone, Dawson. See if you can get a bead on it. I don't want to call it in case the ringer is on and it alerts the guy, assuming she even has it at this point. He may have tossed it."

"Will do." He spoke into his radio to Fletcher, telling her to put a trace on Malone's phone. "And contact the FBI. Even if they don't give a damn about their own agent anymore, they should at least want to get their butts up here to help us find that killer they're all hot and bothered about."

Aidan suddenly slammed his brakes, fishtailing across the gravel road. He engaged the four-wheel drive on his truck and quickly backed up. Then he turned where the Jeep had turned and slowed to look for more signs of it passing this way.

"Give me an update, O'Brien. I'm four minutes out. Where am I going?"

"Old logging trail. He's heading up the mountain."

"By Jesper's hunting cabin, the one that's falling down?"

"That's the one. Wait. Ah, hell." He slammed his brakes again and slid to a halt, then leaped from his truck.

"What, O'Brien? Talk to me."

"The Jeep. I found it. Empty. He ditched it, a quarter mile up the road." Aidan ran back to his truck and flipped the seat forward. He pulled out his bow and an arrow and strapped the quiver of extra arrows over his neck and shoulder to let it hang out of the way. Squatting down, he searched the dirt until he picked up two sets of shoe prints leading deeper into the trees. "I've got their trail. Heading almost due west up the mountain through the woods. I'll mark an X in the dirt to help you find it, about ten feet off the right side of the road. I'm hanging up now, but you can do something fancy to track my cell to keep up with me."

"No, Aidan. Stay on the line. Wait for us. We'll be there in less than three minutes, coming in hot."

"To hell with that. Every minute she's alone with him is one minute too long."

"What are you going to do? You don't even have a gun."

He notched an arrow in his bow. "I'm hunting the Crossbow Killer."

## Chapter Twenty-Three

He shoved Grace in the back, making her stumble and almost fall on the leaf-strewn forest floor.

"Hurry up," he told her.

She glared at him over her shoulder.

He laughed.

"What do you want from me? If you're really the Crossbow Killer, you would have killed me in the parking lot. Abducting people isn't what he does."

"He, as in I, don't miss what I aim at either, like that idiot you cops arrested. I'm smart enough to attach the feathers to my bows after I take down my target instead of letting the arrow fly wherever it wants because of a feather dragging it down, like that kid you've been giving credit for my hard work. Oh, and I don't burn down cabins, either. Although now that I think of it, that could be fun, setting the woods on fire and watching an entire mountain burn." He shoved her again. "Keep moving. And show some respect or I'll end this right here."

"Where are we going? I can make better time if you tell me our destination."

He suddenly jerked her to a stop. "Oh, man. This is definitely new territory for me, taking a living victim. Your phone's on, isn't it? You've got an open mic, an open call and you're trying to get me to give up our location. Hand it over."

"I don't have it. I left it in my car."

He backhanded her, whirling her around. She fell against a tree, biting her lip to keep from giving him the satisfaction of crying out. The metallic taste of blood filled her mouth.

"Phone," he demanded. "Now."

She was about to lie again and say she didn't have it, anything to stall for time, to give someone a chance to trace her line. But suddenly the arrow was pointing directly at her head. He couldn't miss from three feet away, especially since he'd admitted he attached his feathers after shooting the arrows. He really did know what he was doing, which meant he was even more skilled and deadly than she thought. She pulled out her cell phone and handed it to him.

He dropped it to the ground and stomped on it until it crunched into little pieces. His lips curled in a sneer as he kept the arrow pointed at her. "Now move. Straight ahead. Hurry."

As much as possible, she tried to slow them down without being too obvious. She carefully stepped over fallen logs, skirted farther around bushes than necessary. And the entire time she scanned the woods around them, searching for something, anything or anyone to give her a chance to escape.

Had her former boss received the call she'd speed dialed in her pocket? Was he even still in the area where he could help her? She hoped he was, and that help was on the way. But she had to assume the worst, that she was on her own. She'd been trained in hand-to-hand combat, trained to try to outthink an opponent who was bigger than her or had her outgunned. There had to be a way out of this. All she had to do was find it.

The distant sound of gurgling water caught her attention. A waterfall? Or something man-made like an outdoor shower? How could she use it to her advantage?

He shoved her again, almost making her fall. "Quit stalling. I don't have time for this. I need to make my statement and get out of here before they figure out where I am."

She stopped and looked over her shoulder. "What kind of statement are you—"

This time he hit her with the bow, the arrow's razor-sharp edge slicing across her hand. She gasped at the fiery pain and grabbed the wound, pressing it hard to try to stop the bleeding.

"Move," he gritted out, holding up the bow again, the now bloody arrow less than a foot from her face.

She whirled around and hurried forward. His words kept running through her mind. He wanted to make a statement. And he'd complained about someone else taking credit for his work. Niall. He must have heard the media reports and come to Mystic Lake. He clearly didn't want someone else being labeled the Crossbow Killer. That distinction was entirely his. And he was here to prove it. To make a statement. How does a killer make a statement?

He kills.

Which meant he was definitely planning to kill her, but he apparently had a specific place in mind to do it. He was in a hurry to reach his destination and do what he'd planned. Knowing she'd had her phone on didn't change their direction. It only had him pressing her to hurry.

They were close, then. Had to be. Close to wherever his statement was going to take place. Which meant it was go time. She had to make a run for it. But she was bleeding, and wearing soft leather shoes that didn't grip the ground, not the kind of hard-soled hiking boots he had on. He was bigger, taller, with longer strides. And he was armed. How was she going to make a run for it with any real hope of getting away and not being shot?

*Think, Grace. Think.*

The sound of the water was getting closer, louder.

"Hurry."

She sped up. She was definitely hearing a waterfall. She'd studied the area on topographical maps before coming here, wanting to be sure she understood the main landmarks as well as the more dangerous areas to avoid. When she'd woken up in his Jeep, Mystic Lake had been on their right, barely visible through the trees. That meant they'd headed north. Then he'd turned left, west, up a dirt road, past a ramshackle cabin that had seen better days. A picture formed in her mind with the little Xs that marked areas for hikers on the local tourism map she'd gotten while in Chattanooga before going to Mystic Lake.

The old logging trail. That was where they'd gone. Which meant they were heading toward the marina. And toward Mystic Falls. Yes, that was what she heard. A waterfall. If only she could reach it before he did and find the path marked on the map, she might be able to take the upper loop above the falls. And maybe somehow she could fool him into thinking she'd taken the easier, downhill loop. It wasn't much of an escape plan, but it might give her a chance to put some distance between them.

It was better than nothing.

She sped up some more, searching the ground for what she'd need to try to fool him.

"Hey," he called out, "wait up."

She moved faster, then ducked down and grabbed a handful of small rocks from the trail and quickly tucked them into her jacket pocket.

A whistle of air sounded as something shot past her so fast and close she didn't have time to duck. She stumbled to a halt as she stared at the haft of an arrow buried in the tree a few feet in front of her. It had only missed her by a fraction of an inch. Her lungs seized in her chest and she started to shake.

He grabbed her shoulder and whirled her around, slamming her against a tree. His mouth curled back like a rabid animal, revealing his teeth. But it was his eyes that sent a burst of terror straight through her. They were so dark they were almost black. And there wasn't an ounce of humanity in them. All she saw was rage and bloodlust, a thirst to kill that was being kept in check by the barest thread.

"Do that again, try to run, and the next one goes in your brain." He shook her. "Got it?"

"Got…got it. No running."

"Move. It's almost over." He shoved her forward.

She drew a shaky breath, then another as she forced her feet to keep moving. He was going to kill her. No doubt about it. But if that was going to happen, it would be on her terms. No way would she meekly march to her death and let him choose just when he was going to shoot her. The upper loop above the falls was the only way, her only chance to at least try to put some distance between them. Maybe she'd get lucky and he'd fall over the waterfall to the rocky floor below.

Or maybe she'd end up with an arrow in her back.

She pictured the falls in her mind, the trails she'd studied on the map. The sound and smell of the water signaled they were almost there. Her possibly only chance at survival was coming, and she had to take it, no matter how terrified she was. Fighting him wasn't an option. She'd lose in that scenario. Flight was her only choice. She'd have to run as if her life depended on it.

Because it did.

A mist began to rise in the woods up ahead. No doubt it must be that time of day that had helped to give Mystic Lake its name, as well as the Smoky Mountains. It was a phenomenon of the climate, like little puffs of smoke moving in and making it harder to see.

"Just a little farther," he yelled behind her. "When we get to the falls, turn right, head down toward the lake."

"Okay," she called back, carefully pulling the rocks out of her pocket without making any sudden moves that would give her away.

Suddenly, the mist deepened, obscuring her view. She hesitated.

"Turn right," he called out.

She hurled the rocks off to the right, hoping he'd hear them and think that was her stumbling down the path. Then she took off to her left, as quietly as possible, up the trail toward the top of the falls. She was about to turn onto the loop that she'd seen on the map when he shouted from farther down the path. He must have already realized she'd gone the other way.

Pushing herself forward, she struggled against the incline. She could hear footsteps somewhere behind her as he struggled up the same incline, swearing at her and promising death.

"This way," a voice called out, a woman's voice. "Grace, over here."

A hand reached out of the mist and yanked her into the trees just before an arrow shot past her, so close she could feel its heat.

"Run," the woman told her, pointing to a break in the trees. "That way. Aidan's coming for you."

Grace didn't stop to ask who she was or why she was there. She grabbed for her hand as she ran past to pull the woman with her. But instead of grabbing flesh and blood her hand went through mist.

The sound of the killer's footsteps zipping past her up the loop galvanized her into action. She ran in the direction the woman had told her, back the way they'd come but on a slightly different path. Mist swirled around her as she ran and she would have sworn that somehow the rough terrain smoothed out, almost as if she were running so fast she was taking flight.

She was hallucinating. She had to be. And where was that woman who'd helped her? Grace slowed. She had to go back. She couldn't leave someone behind with a killer out here.

"Aidan, over here!"

Grace stumbled to a halt, startled to hear the woman calling out to Aidan in a voice that sounded like her own.

"Aidan!" the woman called again from the mist.

"Grace!"

It was Aidan's voice, somewhere up ahead.

"Aidan! Here! I'm here!" Grace ran forward, stumbled and fell, then leaped back up and ran again. "Aidan!"

"Grace! I'm coming!" His footsteps pounded on the earth up ahead.

Swearing sounded behind her along with the pounding of footsteps in pursuit. The killer was closing in. A bubble of hysteria rose in Grace's throat.

"Aidan, he's behind me! He's got a crossbow!" A sob caught in her chest, both from the terror of the man closing in from behind and the terror that the one she was running to was in the path of his arrow.

"Look out, Aidan!" she cried out.

"Grace, drop! Now!"

She dived to the forest floor.

The zing of arrows slicing through the air whipped overhead. A loud, gurgling scream sounded through the forest, sending a cloud of birds to flight above the trees. She lay there, afraid to move. Afraid she'd be shot if she did. And even more terrified to find out who had made that horrible gurgling sound.

Suddenly, Aidan was on his knees in front of her, scooping her onto his lap, his brow lined with worry as he ran his hands over her, apparently searching for injuries. "Grace, my God. Are you okay? Your hand—"

"The shooter, he's back there, in the mist." She looked behind her. "Where? Where is he?"

Aidan gently turned her head to look at him. "You don't need to see that. He won't hurt you, or anyone else, ever again."

"I don't… How did you see him? The mist is so—"

"What mist?" He ran his fingers through her hair, over her scalp. "Did you hit your head?"

"Did I…no… I mean, yes, he knocked me out but then—"

"We need to get you to the hospital." He stood with her cradled against his chest, his bow and arrows hanging from straps across his shoulders as he headed back in the direction he'd come from.

Grace clung to him and peered over his shoulder. "I don't understand. It was such a thick mist, a fog. If it hadn't rolled in I couldn't have gotten away. Where did it go?"

"We'll wrap that hand as soon as I get you to my truck. I've got a first-aid kit inside."

"Aidan, we have to go back. That woman…we have to find her. She showed me the path to take. She saved my life."

He stopped and looked down at her. "Grace, there's no one else out here."

"But there is!" she insisted. "She called your name. Didn't you hear her?"

He shook his head, looking even more concerned. "I only heard you. Come on. Let's get you to a doctor." He took off again, insisting on carrying her in spite of her insistence that she could walk.

The sound of more voices, familiar ones, came from up ahead. The Mystic Lake police.

"Over here," Aidan called out. "I've got her. She's hurt."

"I'm fine," she assured him. "It's just a scratch."

"And a huge knot on your head. I swear I'm going to have to wrap you in bubble wrap after this." He hurried toward the sounds of the others crashing through the woods toward them.

Grace gave up trying to explain to him that she really was okay. She looked over his shoulder. The mist was back again, in the distance. And as she watched, the outline of a woman formed, with a beautiful smiling face. A face that Grace recognized from the picture that Aidan had saved from the cabin fire.

Elly O'Brien.

## Chapter Twenty-Four

Grace stood at the end of the dock, looking out at the clear blue waters of Mystic Lake. It was beautiful here, and sometimes deadly. But it could be magical and miraculous, too. She was living proof of that.

The investigation into the Crossbow Killer had shown that when he'd abducted her six months ago, he'd first abducted someone else, a tourist passing through. He'd killed her in his usual way, with his crossbow and that showy white and red feather fluttering on the end of an arrow. And he'd laid her out on the ground at the bottom of the falls for the next tourist in the area to discover. His plan had apparently been to place Grace beside the other woman. Two kills in one day. He'd wanted to shock the world and turn all of the attention back to him instead of to Niall.

Thankfully, his plan hadn't worked. And now the world knew him for what he really was—a twisted sociopath with no excuses for any of the evil he'd done. Twenty-eight-year-old John Smith had a background as vanilla as his name. He was a single man working as a low-level manager in an office supply store. He'd had an average, uneventful childhood with supportive parents. There was no evidence that he was ever abused. He wasn't bullied in school. The most the FBI had been able to piece together was that he'd resented being so…average. And that he'd begun his reign of terror to get attention, to make himself appear as something more than he was—just an average forgettable man.

She shivered and shook her head. What a waste of life, both his and all of the people he'd hurt and killed. But it was over now. He'd never hurt anyone else again.

Warm, strong hands wrapped around her waist and pulled her back against an impressively muscled chest, making her sigh with pleasure. Aidan.

He nuzzled her ear and kissed the side of her neck before straightening. "Are you out here in the hopes that you'll see Elly again?"

"Do you finally believe me about what happened that day?"

"I believe you believe. Isn't that enough? You did have a concussion, you know."

"I like my version better, that Elly stuck around this world long enough to make sure that her little family was taken care of."

He hugged her tighter and leaned over to give her another kiss, this one along the side of her jaw. "You're the one who saved our family, Grace Malone O'Brien. If it wasn't for you, I'd still be living in that deep dark shell where I'd been merely existing for so many years. And there's no telling what would have happened to Niall. He's doing amazingly well now." Aidan slid his hand down her slightly rounding belly. "And he's looking forward to welcoming a new sister or brother in the summer, about the time our cabin is finally finished being rebuilt and we can move out of this rental."

She smiled and turned around.

He winced and adjusted her shoulder holster. "I like you better without a gun to dig into me when I hug you. Why do you have your uniform on? You don't start the new job until tomorrow."

"I wanted to make sure everything fit just right. And when I saw the sparkling water out the window, I couldn't resist a quick walk down to the dock before changing back into my regular clothes."

"Are you sure you really want to go back to work? You know you don't have to. We don't need the money."

"I've tried the 'staying at home while my husband is in his office working all day' routine. That's not my idea of fun."

"If you want your job back with the FBI, you know that Nate is confident he can force them to re-hire you."

"You're so sweet, always wanting to slay my dragons for me. But the FBI never felt like home, not like Mystic Lake does. Besides, why would I want a job that would take me away from you for large spans of time?"

He gently feathered her hair back from her face. "You shouldn't have to give up your dreams. Let me fix this for you, give you back your special agent career."

"Oh, Aidan. You've already given me everything I can possibly want. You." She pressed a soft kiss against his lips. "As for my career, it's going exactly where I needed it to go. I just didn't realize it when I started out. I can make a real difference here. Dawson and the team need me. So does Mystic Lake. Our population is growing little by little. The police force has to grow right along with it."

He grinned. "Our population is definitely growing." He pressed a hand against her belly again. "By one. For now."

She slid her arms up his chest. "For now? How many little O'Briens are you wanting, Mr. O'Brien?"

"What I really want right now is you. And since this is our last day of vacation together before you start your new job, I was hoping we could spend most of the day indoors."

She grinned up at him. "Oh really? And what do you plan to do if we're both closed up in the cabin all day?"

He gave her an answering smile and scooped her up in his arms, cradling her against his chest. "I plan to love you, Grace. Always. Today and every day for the rest of our lives."

She sighed happily and locked her arms behind his neck. "And I'll love you right back, Aidan. Forever and always."

He kissed her, a gentle touch of the lips that told her more than words ever could just how much he cherished her. But the kiss quickly changed, becoming hotter and more wild until they both broke apart, breathless and dazed.

"Aidan, if you don't get me inside, fast, I'm going to start shedding my clothes right here and completely shock the neighbors."

He grinned and took off running toward the house with her laughing the whole way there.

\* \* \* \* \*

# COMING SOON!

We really hope you enjoyed reading this book. If you're looking for more romance be sure to head to the shops when new books are available on

## Thursday 22nd May

MILLS & BOON

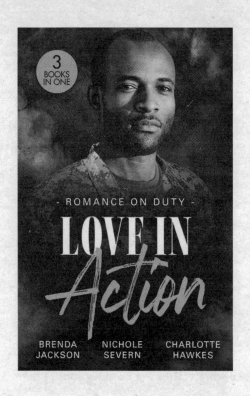

## LET'S TALK

# *Romance*

For exclusive extracts, competitions and special offers, find us online:

- **f** MillsandBoon
- **X** @MillsandBoon
- **⊙** @MillsandBoonUK
- **♪** @MillsandBoonUK

Get in touch on 01413 063 232